"Yuck," Cracey said while wiping the ball on her front. "You got doggy goobies on it." She tossed the ball into the air again with all the control she could muster with only two fingers holding the slimy thing.

This time the ball felt warm, hot, almost burning, and something about the smell of the dog wasn't right either. Its breath was stronger and worse smelling than before. Cracey felt funny inside her tummy and head.

"I don't think I wanna play anymore." Cracey stepped away from the cocker.

The cocker spaniel stepped toward her. The once appealing smile had disappeared from the animal's face. He looked serious. His tail had dropped and now stood still. His march matched Cracey's retreating steps and scared the five-year-old. His nose pressed against her hand.

"No!"

The dog stopped and a low growl burrowed from beneath his lips.

Cracey stepped back and got some room between her and the frightening dog. The dog stepped forward.

"Go away." Cracey threw the ball hard to make the spaniel leave her alone.

The dog sprung straight up, snapping its teeth into the ball's skin. Cracey felt the ground shake as the dog landed. The tennis ball fell from the canine's mouth, shorn open and no longer resembling a ball at all. Cracey took in a breath to scream for help.

Circle of Dogs
The New Paladin

Cover art by Brittany Grooms

Four Doors Publishing
Provo, UT 84601

First Four Doors Publishing edition 2010

Printed in the United States of America.

Circle of Dogs
The New Paladin

D.L. Fairchild

For all that is yellow
Dedicated to Miriam and Megan

With special thanks to:
Shannon and Ginger

Prologue

The night air was suddenly noxious. Thomas didn't recognize it and even the fresh scent of recently watered lawn couldn't mask the wafting presence of poison. The rancid stench crept in stronger and he knew the wind was trying to warn him. The moon had lied. It wasn't a peaceful night after all. He crouched close to the ground. His eyes flicked wildly about, searching for what might be hiding in the black world. Was it dog? Raccoon? Whatever it was, it was wrong. The smell grew stronger. It prickled the fuzz on Thomas's snout and raised his hair. An unwelcome torrent of heavy breath crept upon him. Thomas spun around, arching his back to its highest peak and met a gaze unlike any he knew.

The monster was large, two to three times larger than the most gigantic of dogs. Its eyes were a deep jade coated in a thin circle of black. Two shades of bloodshot swept through the empty parts of its eyes, swirling in and out of each other. The eyes were alive with their swirling and mixing, always moving as their hues mingled. They were set back in deep sockets under a fierce bushy brow. The fur was short on its face, but long over the head and neck. The snout was long and wide. It was easily the length of Thomas's body. Thomas dared not look away from this strange beast.

The beast growled, but it was unlike the growl known of any dog. The sound rumbled from inside its belly until the creature's mouth snarled open baring spindly, sharp and perfectly straight teeth. They were thinner and longer than the usual teeth, which Thomas had before encountered. At least a hundred sharp fangs lined the monster's gums as if they had been thin nails pounded through too shallow of a board. The bottom front row was sharp and shaped like needles. The top row had two pairs of hooked incisors. The rest of the top teeth were spaded and barbed. As more became visible, Thomas could see double rows of the straight pins, perfect for tearing flesh in ways he never hoped to know. Red stained them all and festered to brown and black. Thomas could taste the rotted meat hidden in the monster's breath. The gaping jaws closed in on Thomas.

Thomas struck fast, and he struck furious. Whatever this monster was, Thomas had to get away. He batted at the monster with every ounce of strength he could summon from the end of his tail to the points of his weathered claws. He felt one set of claws slice through the creature's nose

1

before he turned and scrambled down the hill. When he heard the shriek, which erupted from behind him, Thomas almost forgot how to run. His bones tried to freeze from the eerie sound, but somehow he continued to stumble down the plush hillside.

His instincts told him to pull himself into a ball a moment before he felt a shadowy touch careen over him. The dark silhouette landed before Thomas and spun around for a second stare down. The hair over its body was wavy and appeared soft, but the scarf of fur around the neck stuck out even longer now, resembling a mane. This creature moved faster than other dogs, but Thomas wasn't out of the game yet. He lashed out once more before the dog could finish fully turning toward him. His tensed nails scraped across the creature's left eye and down the side of its face. The beast reared back and cried in what should have been pain and Thomas took opportunity of his only chance to dart between its legs. The monster screamed a chilling curse.

The nights were beginning to get colder now and were beginning to take their toll on Thomas's poor, aged joints. He moved as best his body allowed and he yelled for help as he neared the school.

"Cat," called out a familiar voice. The shadow of a man appeared from the side of the building.

"What did you bring with you, Cat," Mr. Hawkes, the night janitor, called out as Thomas rushed for his dear friend.

Mr. Hawkes vanished around the corner of the junior high school building. Thomas was close enough to follow him. Somehow, Thomas had escaped the monster.

"Some dog givin ya trobble, Cat," the old janitor asked, appearing with a square-head shovel. He set down the shovel on the pavement and scooped Thomas into his arms. "We'll show some dog some of our own trobble."

Something in the way that Mr. Hawkes held Thomas helped him feel safer. Nevertheless, he felt the safe grip shudder when Hawkes finally saw the monster too. He knew Mr. Hawkes was frightened also. The monster crept into the haze of halogen bulbs overhead. Its eyes remained fixed on Thomas.

"Best get to runnin Cat." Hawkes practically tossed Thomas over his shoulder and snatched up the square shovel once again. He clenched it with both hands.

Thomas found a shadow to hide in and watched the Janitor.

"Chase muh cat wilya," Hawkes yelled. His eyes couldn't tear away from the menacing creature. The monster was close to the janitor now, taller than he was even, but kept its head at eye level with the old man. It curled its lips as it redirected its loathsome glare from the frightened Thomas to the wiry

2

white-haired man.

"Git," Hawkes yelled. The square, metal head of the shovel struck across the side of the freak-dog's head. The monster regained its posture and glared angrier than before at the elderly custodian. A stream of dark ooze trickled from an empty dark eye socket on the dog's face. A single green bloodshot eye looked to Thomas and back to the old man just in time for the shovel to dig out one of the creature's legs from under its giant body. As the dog stumbled, Hawkes smashed his shovel down on its head. The dog's chin slammed the ground and again the shovel clobbered the side of the creature's body followed by a kick, from Hawkes, to its stomach. Mr. Hawkes readied for another attack and thrust the shovel downward. The monster's barbaric jaws snapped into the steel head of the shovel and tore it like paper. The janitor bumbled backwards as he still held what used to be his shovel, its head now serrated and sharp.

Hawkes rebounded, thrust the new jagged points of the shovel into the monster's body and withdrew them for another stab. The creature fell away and struggled to stand. It limped out of range of anymore of Hawkes's devastating assaults. Hawkes clenched the ruined shovel tightly, probably realizing that without it, he stood no chance against the beast. The creature fled to the black walls beyond the halogen auras.

"That's right," said Hawkes shaking the shovel, at the beast, in celebration. "I survived one war and three divorces. Ain't no army of one agonna take me down."

The dog suddenly turned back to Hawkes. Thomas jumped, but not as much as his old man flinched. The dog's head cocked inquisitively to the side.

"What," Hawkes asked. "You want some more?"

"Ba-rooo," the monster suddenly screamed.

Its cry was deep, yet high-pitched. It ricocheted off the brick walls of the school, rattling the windows as if the school itself feared the monster's power. Mr. Hawkes covered his own ears.

"That's enough of this," Mr. Hawkes said twisting the shovel in both palms as if feeling for a better grip. He raised the shovel above his head and—

"Brooooo," cried a voice from the darkness.

Mr. Hawkes stopped. He stepped away from the assailant, unaware he had lowered his weapon. He stared out into the obsidian surroundings hidden even from the silent, blinking town lights, which were blocked by a dark grassy slope in the distance.

"Broooo," yelled a second voice, this time from behind Hawkes.

"Broooo," announced another voice from what sounded like the roof of the building.

Another voice from somewhere else in the black mimicked the call, followed by even more voices.

"How-roooo," howled the monster facing Hawkes.

A choir of voices cried out together. "Froo-ha-roo-roo-roooooooo!"

The song chilled Hawks' blood and seeped into the marrow of his bones. What was this dog's demonic strategy? He watched the slope surrounding the schoolyard come to life with glowing green dots, countless pairs of glowing green and red dots.

"There's more a ya," Hawkes asked. The broken shovel clanked against the ground as the old janitor turned and ran.

Thomas didn't understand what was happening, but he understood the need to flee. He ran a ways before realizing the sounds of Hawks' feet had stopped. Thomas turned back to the janitor. Hawkes punched at a shadow and recoiled, screaming. A second beast appeared and a third, both as dark and dangerous in appearance as the first. Hawkes stumbled aimlessly, but managed to kick at one of the monsters. Too many surrounded Hawkes now, snarling, circling and biting. In a moment, Hawkes disappeared into the mob of ungodly creatures screaming. Suddenly, the dog Thomas blinded broke from the others and gave Thomas chase once more.

The last thing Thomas heard, as he rounded a darkened corner of the building, was the sound of claws scratching pavement behind him. Thomas's joints were beyond tired and sore. The sound and smell of the dog's breath was upon Thomas once again. The fiend's jaws opened for him and snapped shut, but they missed. Thomas found the open window to the basement, which Hawkes left open just in case Thomas was ever late arriving at the school. He dove inside, where he ran over some oily shelves with dusty and worn cardboard boxes. Here, Thomas realized he could stop running.

The creature's long dark snout pressed through the open window. The black lips sneered and the needle teeth appeared even more menacing under the dim light given off by the two dirty yellow bulbs overhead. The window was too small to fit even the dog's head. Thomas would be safe here. The dog couldn't wait outside forever; he'd have to give up and seek easier prey. Thomas breathed the relieving, savory air of moldy school basement.

Massive black paws reached through the open windowpane, clawing feebly to dig through. The catlike claws were silver and long, not like a dog's at all. Thomas knew what would happen if those claws touched him. He shuddered at the thought of Hawkes and his mortal end in the schoolyard. The claws retracted into the intruding paw and its fingers began to move like no other dog's, feeling around the steel window frame and building brick. The paws gently fingered around the edges of the window. When the claws snapped into a view again, the rectangular glass pane shattered, filling the air with sharp shards. The claws sank into the steel frame of the window and tore it from its anchoring brick. The frame vanished through the small rectangular opening where the glass barrier once offered some level of safe comfort. When Thomas watched the first brick tear from its mortared hold, he knew it was time to run again. Brick fell, shattered and tore from the wall. The opening in the wall grew. The dog would be through soon.

An underground river ran beneath the school. When they were both younger, Mr. Hawkes used to let Thomas in to chase rats. Sewer systems and pipes poured into the river. He wasn't sure if he could remember his way out of it, but he knew the way in. He ran for the darkest corner of the room. He remembered the appearance of a hole, which had been chipped away through the foundation of the floor, most likely caused by adventuresome and truant students. He found the entrance and turned back to the window at the sound of the dog's feet striking the floor behind him. The monster was in the basement. How was this creature so fast?

Thomas leapt through the opening in the floor and landed in the river. He fought the mellow current to the muddy bank and climbed up the slippery river edge, pulling mud and silt into his fur. For a moment, he thought he would drown in filth before the creature ever could catch him. Finally, he pulled himself from the water and realized the sharp pain lingering in his rear leg. He reached back to clean his leg and tasted his own blood. The creature had struck Thomas. Again, the creature was stuck behind a small opening and again Thomas heard the shiny claws tearing apart the school floor and Thomas's ceiling. Thomas ran as best as the mud and his limp would allow.

The terrifying sound of falling concrete chunks plunging against the surface of the water pierced Thomas's ears and nerves, and the loudest splash of all set even Thomas's matted-down fur on end. Again, the monster was through the barrier between it and Thomas. Where would Thomas run next? But, where was the dog? Wasn't it through the ceiling? He heard nothing now, only silence. Had the dog drowned? Had the creature been overcome by the water? Reluctant, Thomas looked behind him. The dog wasn't there. The scratching had stopped. The splashing from falling concrete had stopped. The dog remained unseen. And the mold of the dark cavern seemed to overpower any other smell that might have given the creature away. Had it given up? The tired Thomas listened to the rippling water as it meandered past him and down the dark tunnel. He listened for the sound of something else breathing, a creature that wasn't him.

The river's surface erupted, spraying the ceiling. The water settled and Thomas saw the monster standing in the darkness with one glowing green eye still fixed on him. He believed the monster wanted its vengeance for its recent blindness. The shadow shrank. Thomas didn't know how, but the creature's size diminished before him. The creature took a step and water sloshed beneath its paw. The dog was flowing with the river. When he stepped again, water splashed beneath him and Thomas realized the monster was standing on the water, riding the current and ripples of the stream away from him. The black animal began to grow again. Little splish-splashes gave way beneath each step, but the water never buckled nor swallowed the creature.

Drip.

Where to go?

Drip.

This monster was unstoppable.

Thomas finally felt the water dripping on his head. He saw the mouth of the small pipe above him. He wondered if he could fit into it. The dog's splish-splashing steps were louder and suddenly quicker. Had the beast seen Thomas's chance at escape as well? He wasted no time, but leapt from a rock to a crevice, and clawed at the muddy wall. He heard the dog panting below him. He leapt, listening to the snapping of teeth behind him. He jumped again and bits of wall crumbled beneath his feet. He pulled himself into the pipe and the dog buried its muzzle, flicking its white sticky tongue around Thomas' tail. Thomas slashed and somehow pulled away from the thick stickiness.

The dog screamed and Thomas heard nothing but ringing in his head. His skull was breaking under the sound. He ran hard and fast into the pitch black in front of him. And just like that, he couldn't run anymore. His head hurt. His breath weakened and Thomas fell to his face and belly. His old limbs had no more to give him. His spirit wanted to flee, but his bones had all but died around him. He listened to the sound of steel pipe and dirt ripping under the creature's claws. The creature kept digging towards Thomas, who had no more fight in him. Thomas closed his eyes and waited for death to come.

*   *   *

The first thing Thomas noticed was the sweet scent of fresh air blowing in his face. His belly was wet and cold, but he didn't care. Light poured down the drain. He stood, stiff and wobbly, wishing he was in the warm bed of his master and mending his sore hindquarter. Behind him was the shredded pipe.

The monster had gotten so close. Where was it now? Thomas refused to go back the way he already came, for fear of the monster lurking there still. He hiked for the only other possible safe route out of the pipe.

At first, Thomas squinted from the blinding sensation of the rays of the morning sun. His eyes adjusted. He had found the exit, but a steel grate blocked his way through it and he couldn't push through the heavy bars. He saw a bench and in it sat a small man with his face and shoulders buried behind a newspaper. Thomas cried and hoped for the frail-framed man to notice him.

"What's this," The old man asked. He folded his paper and knelt closer to the cat. "Don't see many sewer cats around these parts." He chuckled a bit to himself and flagged down two passing teenagers to help him open the grating.

"It's got tags," said one of the teenagers.

"Well, we'll have to get you to your proper family. Won't we?" The old man cradled Thomas in his arms and shuffled along the roadside, assuring the fat old cat he was safe. Still, the man seemed like he might teeter off his bronze capped walking stick at any moment. The old man talked Thomas to sleep with stories of his life, old friends, and his dearly departed wife. He didn't seem to give notice to Thomas's bloody, muddy, and matted fur. When Thomas heard the click of the lock on the old man's house, he was relieved to have survived the night.

"Here we go." The old man scratched his new friend behind the ear. "Safe and sound."

The door opened and the old man escorted Thomas into his house, and the smell, that terrible, familiar smell.

The door slammed.

"Is this what you wanted so badly?" The old man tore Thomas by the tuft of his neck from his comforting cradle. The one-eyed dog cowered before him.

The house was dark and all the curtains were drawn.

"Beaten by this," The old man asked. "This squirming fur ball?"

The dog cowered more.

"Next time," scowled the old man. "You'll lose more than an eye."

Thomas felt the old man's release on his neck and he sailed toward the fiend.

Jaws opened wide.

Thomas's eyes opened wide and watched the nightmarish teeth close over his head.

1 — Playing Ball

Barbara stared across the kitchen counter to the small, round table near the picture window and wondered if she had seen him. She couldn't stop thinking about the face staring up from the local news page with the caption asking if she had. She knew Mr. Hawkes. Not only had he treated her son well when he was in junior high, but he was the Revlon's next door neighbor, a member of their church and a big bank of knowledge when it came to gardening. And suddenly he was gone? Where? Barbara was tired of hearing about missing people in Plattsville. She wondered how worried she should be for herself and her family. Was it safe from whomever or whatever could be causing such a stir in the community? She'd clip this missing article too and hide it in the box under her bed with the others.

For now, she returned to her cooking.

The stove was full. Four different-sized, copper-bottom pots sat on four burners with blue flames. One lid only partially covered its pot, allowing steam and the occasional froth of hot water and salt to boil out. Barbara pulled the lid from the midsized pot and breathed in the refreshing aroma of carefully stewed and smashed tomatoes. She disapproved of the scent and reached into a small cupboard with small crystal bottles filled with more scents and tastes. She took down two small jars filled with broken green and brown leaf crumbs, removed the caps and charged each one of a shake of their contents. She found a long-necked bottle and poured a small amount of its liquid into the red mixture. Next, she took up a long wooden spoon with a metal thermometer encased in a thick wooden handle, dipped the spoon into the churning sauce and stirred. After a few more gentle strokes, she removed the spoon and dared a taste from the thick coat over the spoon. She returned the lid to the pot.

"Whatchya cookin, Mom," Josh asked.

Barbara jerked and quickly turned. "Don't do that."

How did he get so good at sneaking up on her?

Josh breathed in the aromas loitering above the stove. "Do I smell meat?"

"You want meat? There's bacon in the fridge." Barbara smacked Josh's shirt with the fat end of the spoon and splattered spaghetti sauce over his chest. "Stop trying to convert me."

"Come on, mom."

"Meat is murder," Barbara said. "It's bad for you—lucky I let you keep it in my house."

Barbara was barely forty-five and often mistaken for ten years her junior. Her hair was sandy brown and semi-curly. If she ever had a gray hair, no one ever noticed it. At least, she wasn't the type of woman who ever looked old. This worked to her advantage when it came to selling her catering service. Employees mostly ran the business for her now, but she still found herself in the field selling her product. Her family joked about how her running around as much as she did was the only reason her figure stayed fit and trim. Josh, had even caught passersby steal glances at her. Barbara paid no attention. He would laugh to himself, but think it over and feel the urge to chase down the gawkers and bust someone's head.

"I just bought this shirt," Josh complained. He tried to wipe the red stain off the blue polo with his finger. "Sheesh." He gave up after watching the stain spread.

"Well, you shouldn't have frightened your mother," Barbara said. "You could have given me a heart attack."

"Hardly," Josh said licking the sauce off his fingers. His face puckered. "What did you do to it?"

"Oh knock it off." The spoon swatted Josh's chest again.

Josh stood barely less than six feet and had his mother's hair. In three months, he would turn twenty-two years old. A couple years ago he would have been bothered by his size, like when he tried out for the basketball team in high school, but he was a junior in college now and had more important things to occupy his mind. He wasn't a built person, but he ran the track righteously and was a fast runner. Sports, in general, didn't interest him. However, good grades had always interested him. Before he graduated high school, Harvard, Yale and Notre Dame offered him full-ride scholarships, yet he wanted to stay close to home. The rent was cheap, and he had a little someone special in his life named Cracey, whose life he didn't want to miss. He also had Natalie, and he wasn't leaving her for a second.

"I'm sorry mom," Josh said resuming his wiping and licking of sauce from his shirt and fingers. "It really is good. So what are we having tonight?" He reached for one of the pot lids.

"Don't you dare."

"Ow," Josh said pulling his hand away. "Chill mom."

"You know the rules." Barbara glared her son away from the stove. She was a beast at this practice. "You taste nothing till dinner."

DING-DONG!

"You knew that I had a date. That should account for a bend in the rules for tonight."

DING-DONG!

"Don't worry," Cracey yelled from the living room. "I'll get it."

"Thank you, honey," Barbara said and smacked Josh's creeping hand with her wooden spoon a second time.

"Don't worry that I'm playing a game or anything," Cracey continued to complain.

DING DONG-A-DONG-DONG-DONG!

"Ow, Mom, easy with the spoon."

The wooden spoon was the gavel in the home. The striking of the spoon was law. For as long as anyone in the house could remember, the spoon stood firm in upholding the rule that no one could have pre-meal tastes. Barbara could have fended ancient samurai guards back with it.

"I have spoken," Barbara said majestically.

"You leave me no choice," Josh said stepping to the sink.

"What are you talking about?"

"Drastic times call for drastic measures, Mom."

"Josh," Cracey announced from the living room. "Your stupid friend is here."

Water gushed from the sink faucet. Josh pulled the stainless steel sprayer hose from the back of the sink.

"Spray your mother and die." Barbara pointed her trusty wooden gavel at her son.

"Oh ye of little faith." Josh pulled the sprayer trigger.

Barbara screamed as the water stormed on her. She grabbed a lid from one of her pots and shielded her face. "My hair." The wooden spoon pulled from her hand.

"Aha." Josh dropped the sprayer. "I have the wooden spoon." He held it high above his head. "All shall bow to me now."

"You think you're some kind of comedian," Barbara asked cowering behind the pot lid.

"Silence ,old hag."

"Old hag? I'll show you old hag."

Josh clanged the underside of the pot with the wooden spoon. "I have spoken."

"What's with all the commotion in here, you guys," Dustin asked from the archway leading to the living room.

Cracey stood at Dustin's side and gasped, "You touched mommy's spoon."

"Dude," Dustin said. "Aren't you supposed to be dead now?"

Josh turned proudly. "I have conquered the spoon and now you shall all bow in my greatness for none have ever conquered the great wooden ow—"

"Give that back." Barbara ordered.

Barbara clanged Josh's head in between two pot lids as if they were cymbals. He fell and didn't move.

"Josh?" Barbara dropped the lids and they banged against the floor. She knelt next to his motionless body.

"You killed Josh," Cracey screamed. "You're a bad mommy."

"Oh baby." Barbara looked up. "Go into the living room."

"No," Cracey screamed back.

"Help me turn him over Dustin," Barbara asked.

Barbara pushed on Josh's side and Dustin pulled.

"What do we do," Barbara asked.

"Call nine-one-one," Cracey replied reaching for a phone just out of her grasp. "And then the police to tell them you killed Josh."

"I don't know what to do," Dustin said. His face grew pale.

Josh's eyes were wide open and rolled up into his head.

"But your dad's a doctor."

"My dad's a vet. Your husband's a doctor."

"That doesn't mean I know what to do," Barbara snapped. "You don't know, either?"

"You want me to spay your son?"

"Raise his legs up and down like in that cat and mouse cartoon daddy likes to watch," Cracey walked around and tried hefting one of Josh's feet. "He's heavy. Let him die."

"Cracey," Barbara barked.

"I was trying to play a game." Cracey marched out of the kitchen.

"OK I think I remember what to do." Barbara grabbed the dangling sprayer nozzle and shoved it in Josh's mouth. Water sprayed everywhere and Josh sat up coughing water.

"What'd you think? I was stupid? Give me my spoon back." Barbara snatched the spoon away from her son. "Think you're funny?"

"How did you know," Josh asked through his coughing.

"Call it a talent." Barbara stood up and glared as only a mother can do to her son. "Go change for your date."

"You're alive." Cracey's arms coiled around Josh's neck and choked him. She "hmphed" at her mother and stomped back out of the kitchen.

"Who are you taking tonight, Dustin," Barbara asked after contemplating her amusement with her daughter's attachment to Josh.

Some would say that Barbara had lost some of her health after she had given birth to Josh. Try as she and her husband, Stan, might, they simply couldn't conceive for many years.

Cracey was five. Growing up, Josh envied friends who had brothers and sisters. His little sister was blonde and loved to have her mother tie off pigtails with shiny ribbons. Today's ribbons were purple with pink edges. After hugging her brother, she stared her mother down as only an angry five-year-old girl can . She bounced back into the living room.

"Just Cadence," Dustin replied.

"Oh that's good," Barbara said. "I think you're cute together. Think there's anything there for future plans?"

"Not likely," Josh said.

"She's ok," Dustin said.

"Well, she is pretty."

Josh turned back for the living room.

"And you're taking Natalie," Barbara asked.

Josh had almost made it through the doorway. Here it came.

"Why her," Barbara asked.

"I'm going to change my shirt," Josh said turning to the stairs.

"I'm just saying that you deserve better than that Meade girl."

Josh stopped without turning back. "There is no one better than Natalie." Now, he did turn. "Except for you."

"Then, you should take my word for it. You can do better."

"I don't want any better." Josh's voice trailed off as he disappeared up the stairs.

"Honestly, I don't know what you boys see in girls these days," Barbara said to Dustin.

"I'm going to play games with Cracey." He also fled the kitchen before Barbara's talent for brutal one-on-one conversation trapped him.

Dustin's and Josh's friendship went back to elementary school when they saw each other, got in a fight, got suspended for three days, and found out each other had a load of He-man and Transformers. They played at each other's houses for the three days they were out of school. Ever since, they remained inseparable. Few friends held the respect and the loyalty for each other as these two had. Though they might deny it, they had come to depend upon each other for many little details, including avoiding divulging questions asked by nosy mothers.

Dustin was a little more athletic than Josh. Instead of books, he really liked

13

basketball, couldn't play it well, but he still liked it. He also liked hockey and rugby, which he did play well. That's not to say he wasn't smart. Actually, books and brains ran in his family. He continued the tradition of books, but somehow along the way lost the interest in using brain over matter. He wore small circular glasses. His hair was long and dark brown and he usually pulled it back into a ponytail that reached a little past his shoulders. He smiled a lot, loved to smile, even though his teeth were crooked. He had also watched Cracey grow up. Like Josh, he was an only child. Next to Josh, she was Dustin's favorite friend.

"What are we playing today, Tike?" Dustin asked as he fell back into a recliner.

"Captain Phlegm," Cracey replied. "It's new. Wanna play?"

"Yeah, hand me a paddle."

Dustin took the overwhelming game controller from Cracey. He never really had time for video games, what with homework, sports and girls and all. The paddle was bright pink and had about a dozen buttons and three different directional finger pads. None of which he understood how to use.

"OK," Cracey began to brief. "These buttons make you go. OK? This button makes you jump and this button makes you crouch. If you press both of them together, he does a special attack, but the special attack is stupid so don't use it. Okay? If you press up, here, and hit these two buttons, up here, and then this button, here, you can make your guy somersault and slap everything that's attacking him. It's really easy to do. Then, if you want to make him fart acid at— Oh it's your turn."

The large television screen flashed with a bright light. The sound of thunder flooded through the surround sound system speakers. Flickers of animated electricity flared on and off the screen and pulled into a little ball in the lower left-hand corner until it dissolved into a blue man with a green face and a purple cape. Large red letters announced that level one was about to begin.

"Let's kick some butt," The speakers ordered. The little green-faced man held a 'thumbs up' sign to show he was ready.

"You better go," Cracey yelled. "He's gonna get you."

Sure enough, Captain Phlegm stood in some kind of marshy area with floating logs and swinging dreary vines. From the right side of the screen charged a monster four times the size of the little hero.

"Okay, when I tell you run, you run." Cracey stood at the side of the big-screen television so that Dustin didn't miss a thing onscreen. "Ruuuuuun." She screamed and ran around in circles and started laughing. Finally, she

14

stopped running and took in a deep breath. "That was close. OK now jump up. Other button. Look out, he has a whip. Crouch. Good. Now jump up and kick him. Other button. Now, spit barf."

"Spit barf," Dustin asked as he tried to follow Cracey's alien instructions. At the same time, he discovered that his hands could wrap all the way around the room and his neck and it still wouldn't help move the character on the screen any better. "What is spit barf?"

"It's not that hard," Cracey grumbled. "Don't touch any buttons. There! See, he does it on his own."

"That's disgusting."

"Fun, huh? Look out. Kick. Kick. Crouch. Run. You're not very good at this, are you? Uh-oh! Do that somersault slap now. Now. Now. Not those buttons. *THOSE* buttons." Cracey handed the game controller back to the surprised Dustin after she had just ripped it from his hands.

Dustin took the demonic paddle and pressed all the buttons at the same time, hoping something would make Captain Phlegm punch out a bad guy.

Captain Phlegm did nothing.

But some deranged swamp monster touched the little blue hero and the Captain's head exploded. The swamp monster began dancing on Phlegm's green head. Dustin let the controller fall to the ground.

"You suck," Cracey said running in circles again and laughing.

"Where did you learn to talk like that," Dustin asked sharply.

"You suck. You suck."

Lightning flashed in red and blue down the front of the big screen and thunder echoed out through the speakers a second time. A deep bass voice filled the room with, "You suck."

"Time for a new game, I think," Dustin said.

Cracey stopped still. "What's wrong with this one?"

Dustin said nothing.

Cracey took up her controller and began clicking away at buttons as a new Captain Phlegm appeared in a yellow cape. Her entire body jerked up and down as she tried to get the new Captain Phlegm to move. A constant high-pitched scream became routine practice when playing games with her. "Phew. That was close."

Lightning flashed across the screen. "You suck."

"What? I totally got you!" Cracey reached down to the slender control deck and ejected the disc. "Stupid game."

"Where did you get this, young lady," Josh asked taking the round disk from her hand before she could throw it as she was preparing to do.

"From Daddy's game box."

"Does he know you have it?"

"Does he know *you* have it?"

Josh started to deny he had it, but the item *was* in his hands. "You little rascal." He laid the disk on top of the big screen and indulged in tickling his little sister. She laughed and screamed in one of the high pitches Josh thought made her cute.

"We're picking up our dates sometime tonight, right," Dustin asked.

"Dates," Cracey asked and she squirmed out from under her big brother's ticklish touch. "You have a date?"

"Yes I do."

"Mommy," Cracey said turning off the television. "I'm going with Josh and Dustin."

"You think so," Josh asked.

"Can I?"

"Next time,Tike."

"Promise?"

"I promise."

"Are you going with Natalie?"

"Yes."

Cracey pulled Josh's ear close to her mouth and whispered. "Mommy doesn't like her you know."

Josh sighed. "Yeah I know."

Josh realized that most mothers probably didn't like any girl her child was dating. Natalie was a good person, but try explaining that to his mom. All Barbara saw was some stranger taking her son out of her life. Josh didn't see things that way, though. Natalie was special to him. She looked at him from behind those deep crayon crystal blue eyes with only love and admiration. It was like magic. Josh could see it and he knew that his mother would ever refuse to acknowledge it.

On the other hand, Barbara had no problem with demonstrating her dislike towards Natalie. She constantly forgot to set the extra plate on the table when she knew Natalie was joining them for dinner. That's not to mention how Barbara martyred up her plate for Natalie. It was an attempt to make Natalie feel terrible for taking food from Barbara's mouth after the jealous mother conveniently forgot to make enough, which she never forgot to do except for when Natalie ate over. That behavior only went so far before Josh and Natalie started sharing food off his plate. Josh didn't plan to back down to his mother on this issue. He knew Natalie was worth fighting for. Natalie definitely

16

thought Josh was worth surviving Josh's mother for. Barbara just wanted her son to stay her son. Josh couldn't blame his mother, though. He wondered how he would handle Cracey's first boyfriend. He felt a little sorry for the poor sap already.

"But I like her," Cracey whispered even softer than before. "I think you should get married and have babies."

"Cracey!" Josh pulled back. He threw Dustin angry eyes. "Stop laughing, you'll only encourage her."

"I'm sorry man. But that was funny." Dustin ignored Josh's further glaring and kept on laughing.

"What's so funny in there," Barbara asked, unseen behind the doorway to the kitchen.

"Cracey just said the funniest thing to Josh," Dustin answered hysterically. "She just said that Josh and — OW!"

"Cracey," Josh cried. "Don't kick."

Dustin held his shin. "Oh my gosh. I should have never taught you how to kick."

"Oh, stop your whining you big baby," she said before smacking his arm.

"Cracey," Josh snapped again.

"But he was gonna tell mom 'bout what I said 'bout you and Natalie having a baby," Cracey defended.

"What?" A few stomping sounds accompanied by vibrations in the floor announced Barbara's appearance in the kitchen doorway. She glared coolly at Josh.

"Oops," Cracey said.

"Oops is right." Barbara scowled as she white knuckled her spoon. "You have something to tell me?"

"She was joking," Josh answered wringing his hands behind his back.

"She better be." Barbara turned to disappear back into the kitchen again and stopped. "I will neuter you first."

"What's neuter, mommy," Cracey asked.

Barbara looked down to her baby girl. "I don't know." She made a mental note to herself to filter her thoughts better. "Ask Dustin's father." She disappeared back into the kitchen.

"Sorry, Josh," Cracey said.

"It's OK," Josh replied. "But you should apologize to Dustin for kicking him."

"I'm not sorry to him though."

Josh gave his older brother look to Cracey, the look that attempted to tell

17

her that she should know better than to play innocent with him. He had tried mimicking his mother's evil glare, but he didn't even come close to capturing it. He developed his own look that seemed to work on his sister, sometimes. However, this was not one of those times. Cracey lowered her head and turned to Dustin's agony.

Dustin held his shin and rubbed it. "It's not polite to kick people Cracey."

"You big baby-head."

"Cracey," Josh snapped. "Apologize."

"I'm sorry you're a big baby-head, Dustin."

Dustin started laughing.

Josh felt his eyes roll at his sister, realized the futility of his battle and knelt in front of her. "Alright, Tike. Come give us a cheek."

Cracey's face brightened and turned into josh's arms. She planted a soft kiss on his left cheek.

Josh turned his face. "Cheek."

She kissed his right cheek. "Okay, don't forget to open her door for her."

"I won't."

"And don't forget to get her popcorn, the kind I like with lots of butter and no salt."

"But she likes salt."

"No salt." Cracey now gave big brother her little sister glare, the stare that told her brother to shut up or she'd bring mommy back into the room with an even louder temper tantrum. The little sister stare is always meaner than the big brother stare. "What did I say? You always don't listen to all the things I always tell you to do."

"I'm sorry," Josh said in amusement. "Anything else?"

"No tongues."

"Cracey." Josh stood up straight and tried to withstand the little sister glare. "Little ladies don't talk like that. Where did you learn that?"

"Him," Cracey said pointing a soft accusing finger at Dustin.

"You most certainly did not." Dustin scowled, now standing back up straight. "Ow!" He bent over to grab his other shin.

"Cracey," Josh snapped. "We don't kick. Go to your room."

"I'm sorry, Dustin." Cracey lowered her head.

Josh had done it. He beat the little sister. He knew this would come down to the battle of wits between himself and the five-year-old who had taken control of most sibling arguments since the day she was born. She was smarter than he was a thousand times over. It drove Josh crazy. This time, Cracey recognized that her days of lording it over Josh were over. A simple 'go to your room' was all it took. Josh couldn't help but feel proud. He felt the smile begin to form on the inside. He would have let it shed to his exterior was it not that he feared Cracey might think he was only joking and take advantage of the situation. This was a great victory for big brother. This was even better than overpowering the little sister grip on big brother's belongings that somehow suddenly became her toys. Josh was truly proud.

Cracey lowered her eyes and began sniffling. "I don't wanna go to my room."

She sat down where she stood and crossed her legs. Her face suddenly exploded with red. Her lips stretched out and quivered, gently at first, and soon rattled violently against each other. All of her pearly whites appeared from beneath beads and strings of saliva stretching from her upper lip to her bottom. Her eyes sealed tight and her eyebrows drooped over the edges of her sockets. Water began to seep from beneath the airtight lids and spill down her cheeks. The accompanying sound was horrid. It told Josh and Dustin that they were both in trouble now and they had missed their chance to flee the scene. The sound erupting from Cracey was louder and higher-pitched than her already normal high scream. It would be interrupted by a ghastly inhale and a strange unnerving sound created by Cracey's quivering lips as they rattled like a machine gun, shooting imaginary bullets straight at Josh's right to existence as a big brother. Shortly, she would suck snot back into her nose and make the sound again. No sound was ever louder than this. Anything louder or more demonic might shake the structure to pieces. More importantly, it would surely invite the evil eye to fall on Josh, Dustin and all they loved—and it did.

"What is going on in here?" Barbara stood back in the doorway and spit out each consonant precisely as if each were a dagger being thrown around Josh's aura, pinning him to some invisible wall.

Josh was no longer proud, nor brave. "Cracey kicked—

"Josh said I have to go to my room," Cracey exhausted every last bit of breath in her deceivingly small lungs to finish the last word until it didn't sound like a word any more. She took in another breath and continued to wail.

"Oh sweetie." Barbara got down on her hands and knees and scooped her little girl into her motherly grasp. "It's all right. I know. Why don't you go outside and play in the backyard until dinner is ready. And I'll kill the boys."

"Okay." As fast as they came, the tears left and Cracey skipped to the front door with a smile that clearly demonstrated she knew what the real score was between her and Josh. "She's probably gonna break your necks, you know." With a twist of the knob, the door was open. "Bye." She gave another conquering smile and pranced out of view. She listened to her mother's voice erupt from inside the walls as she skipped down the side of the house to the tall wooden gate of the backyard.

"Just what in high heavens were you thinking making your sister cry like that," Barbara started in. "Don't you realize how old I am?"

"I never learned to count that high," Josh returned.

What started as a mild scowl, turned into a deathly glare peering through slivers accompanied by tightly pursed lips. Her Shoulders raised under the strength of one powerful snorting breath. "Get out of here."

This time, Josh was sure he felt the walls of the house tremble.

Outside, Cracey heard it too as she approached the entryway into her backyard. The tall gate was made of hickory. Cracey's father wanted something that would be strong against the valley winds. Her father chose hickory because anything made out of hickory was assumed sturdy.

She pressed against the heavy gate made of four-inch wide slats. To a taller person, the resistance of the gate might not seem so great, but, to a three-foot-two-inch five-year-old girl, it was a monster. However, she had developed a system to help her open the gate. She would put her back against the gate and press against it. The traction of her shoes was usually strong enough to make it move. Her legs were short though and could only extend so far. At this point, she'd take a rock that she found in the yard and wedge it under the entry way to the backyard, long enough for her to reposition herself to push the gate a little more. She repeated this several times.

Cracey thought the challenge of opening the heavy door was fun. It reminded her of a show she saw once where a man from Egypt had to push a giant stone out of the way of a house, which went underground and held dead people in toilet paper. Every day she was able to conquer the gate, was a day that she was the champion of the entire yard. She could very well have used the back door of the house; it went right into the backyard after all, and it was much lighter than the hickory. But Cracey liked the friendship that she felt she had established with the magnificent portal.

A tall fence of the same wood separated the front from the back yard. It ensured privacy. The front yard was alive and attractive. A ceramic birdbath, fixed with cold concrete roses, invited robins to argue with blue jays about who got the next drink. A rock path meandered between the gray two-story rambler and the grassy knoll with the birdbath. The knoll tapered down toward a chain link fence, at the yard's front, and rose to the hickory barrier farther back. Pieces of decorative bark filled in around the base of a birch sapling. A cement driveway pressed carefully against one side of the house.

Behind the fence hid a land of even more beauty. Throughout the spring, summer and into the fall, a narrow bed of irises, daffodils and other regal blooms took turns walling in a flowery path down the center of the deep yard. Now, the irises were nothing, but recently trimmed green leaves. And the daffodils had all disappeared. Red and white roses with crusted brown and yellow edges still filled decorative white crosscut fences, and their numbers were growing sparse. They were dead, but no one bothered to let them in on that little secret.

On one side of the flower-lined path was the greenest of grass during the summer, but now it was yellowing. The lawn was level except around the trunk of an oak tree where the grass clung much thicker to its base and tried to climb up the bark. A pine tree, half the height of the oak stood nearby, but not so much as to contend with roots for water and nutrients. Bright-colored, miniature houses sprouted from various places around the yard and provided festive, little birds a place to sleep and poop. Beneath the oak's shade stood an antique-style picnic table accompanied by four aluminum folding chairs filled with brown pillows. Here, Barbara relaxed and got in touch with nature, or as close as she dared to get in touch with nature.

On the other side of the path, spices and vegetables dwindle away to the approaching cold. Barbara liked her veggies fresh, especially her many types of favorite peppers from sweet to hot. Any day her tomatoes would freeze. The farthest reaches of the garden held a variety of fruit trees from pear to peach and a male and female plum tree. Besides Barbara, no one really dared to venture into the garden, for fear of her wrath, except for the hired gardener from next door, Mr. Hawkes—and apparently no one had seen him lately.

Cracey continued to inch the hickory gate open until it finally allowed her enough room to enter her magnificent playground. Cracey saw her mother through the kitchen window, cooking at the stove, and waved to her as she always did before bouncing into the yard for fun. She heard the sound of her brother's wimpy car doors opening and shutting. The weak whispering engine started and a moment later her brother, his friend, and the car were out of earshot. Cracey knew they were gone for their night of excitement and the duty had fallen on her to make her own entertainment. One item remained before she could commence the festivities. Cracey couldn't open the gate as easily from this side. It would be the less adventuresome back door for her into the house when she or her mother decided playtime was over. She kicked the wedged rock from under the gate and applauded at the noise of the slamming lumber. She looked up at the kitchen window once again and waved a second time. Her mother waved back before nodding her head and disappearing from the view of the window, signifying that Cracey was fine to play within the confines of the protective fence.

Cracey ran farther into the yard where she took up an orange tennis ball from the shallow grass. Several other balls scattered across the lawn. She was supposed to put them away yesterday and forgot to, but her mother didn't say anything about it today. It didn't make sense that she should put her things away if it was more work to put them away only to get them out again. Mostly, she hated putting away her many balls. She liked the orange tennis ball the best of all. Three more of them laid around the yard. Dustin and Josh took her to the university on Saturdays to play the game with them. She really didn't like the rackets because they were kind of long for her to swing, but she liked to hold them and pretend she was strumming a guitar. She loved the way the tennis balls could bounce high when they hit the ground. Of course, they didn't bounce high in the grass, but they looked cool when Cracey threw them against the side of the house or the fence and they bounced back into her tiny hands, if she chose to catch them that is. Sometimes, she simply enjoyed throwing the ball and dodging it as it flew back at her. It was especially fun if she threw several balls at once and tried dodging them.

Cracey found her favorite section of fence to pitch against. The other hickory gate, which led to the driveway and the one car carport, was in this section. She threw the ball the way Dustin taught her. The ball bombed through the air and ricocheted off the fence. Cracey ran and tried to catch the ball before it hit the ground. It wasn't as much fun when she missed the ball when she was trying not to miss the ball. And it wasn't fun when she got hit in the face, when she was trying to not get hit in the face, like what happened yesterday. She caught the ball, turned back to the fence and threw again.

She caught it again.

The rule stood that she had to throw the ball from the spot she was in when she caught it. Sometimes, it landed too far away from the fence and it took her two or three tosses to get it back to the hickory slats. Other times, she would catch the ball really close to the fence and when she threw it again, she couldn't catch it fast enough and it would land really far away. That's what happened this time. She took up the ball and threw it hard. The ball bounced back and whizzed past her head. She felt the wind of it tussle her hair. Cracey ran after it, knowing that it was hopeless to catch this one. When she reached the ball, she dropped to her knees and picked it up. She stood with freshly green-stained overalls. She turned to launch her assault on the fence again, but something blocked her way.

"Mom," Cracey called out. "There's a doggie back here."

It was a cocker spaniel with soft golden brown hair, which curled and

22

tufted all over its sides and back, and was smooth around its head. Its tail wagged frantically from side to side, carving high in the air. The dog panted and Cracey thought he looked happy, even smiling. She'd never seen a dog smile before. Well, the dog in that one movie did, but she fell asleep through that. The cocker spaniel trotted up in front of Cracey and plopped right into a sitting position. It stared at her with its tongue bobbing up and down like a limp banner. It eyed the orange ball in Cracey's hand.

"You wanna play with my ball, doggy," Cracey asked.

The dog stood up and made the barking motions, but made no sound.

"Okay," Cracey said. "I'll throw it and you catch it and bring it back, Okay doggy?"

The cocker spaniel replied with another silent bark and an enthusiastic bounce.

Cracey launched the ball into the air. The dog turned and ran after it. The ball landed in the grass and the stray animal immediately picked it up in its jowls. The Spaniard ran back to Cracey, sat in front of her and spit the ball at her feet.

"Yuck," Cracey said while wiping the ball on her front. "You got doggy goobies on it." She tossed the ball into the air again with all the control she could muster with only two fingers holding the slimy thing.

This time the dog only had to run a little ways before catching the ball in its mouth in midair. Again, he returned with the ball to the little girl.

"You have to drop the ball if you want me to throw it again," Cracey complained. "Come on."

The dog returned an inquisitive look.

"Here, let me show you." Cracey took the ball in her hand and pulled it from the animal's mouth. "You smell funny."

Cracey stepped back and repeated her action of throwing the ball, this time with more disgust at the growing coat of dog saliva drenching her toy. She could never play with this ball after today. Again, the dog chased the ball and caught it, a little faster this time. The speed of the dog startled Cracey. She couldn't catch a ball that fast. The dog returned with the toy. Cracey had to pull the wet sphere from his mouth a second time. This time the ball felt warm, hot, almost burning, and something about the smell of the dog wasn't right either. Its breath was stronger and worse smelling than before. Cracey felt funny inside her tummy and head.

"I don't think I wanna play anymore." Cracey stepped away from the cocker.

The cocker stepped toward her. The once appealing smile had disappeared from the animal's face. He looked serious. His tail had dropped and now stood still. His march matched Cracey's retreating steps and scared the five-year-old. His nose pressed against her hand.

"No!"

The dog stopped and a low growl burrowed from beneath his lips.

Cracey stepped back and got some room between her and the frightening dog. The dog stepped forward.

"Go away." Cracey threw the ball hard to make the spaniel leave her alone.

The ball launched higher into the air than it ever had before from Cracey's small hand. The dog sprung straight up, snapping its teeth into the ball's skin. Cracey felt the ground shake as the dog landed in the very spot he leapt from. The tennis ball fell from the canine's mouth, shorn open and no longer resembling a ball at all. Cracey took in a breath to scream for help.

The cocker Spaniel was too fast for Cracey's cries.

*   *   *

Barbara waved to Cracey through the window. She lifted a lid and stirred again. Stan would be home at any moment and all she needed was to slice the celery and carrots for dipping. She stepped away from the stove and the window, found a long white plastic cutting board and placed it over one basin of the sink. She took celery, carrots, and a head of cauliflower from the refrigerator, turned on the sink faucet, sprayed the vegetables and placed them on the cutting board. She tended to her routine of stirring once more and turned the heat down on the gas stove. She looked out the window.

She couldn't fathom how something like this happened under her nose. In a moment, Barbara had her aluminum-handled broom in her hand and launched herself out the back door of the house. The hydraulic door spring broke apart. If Barbara had been concerned, she might have noticed the sound of falling broken door pieces from behind her.

"You leave my baby alone," Barbara wailed waving her broom.

The cocker spaniel's jaws clamped around Cracey's throat. Cracey couldn't make a whimper. The dog tightened his grip at the slightest sound attempting to escape Cracey's mouth. The canine began dragging the little girl away from Barbara. Barbara's child flailed her arms hopelessly at the dog. Barbara could see, she knew, the dog was in control of her baby, but this dog had made a mistake in crossing paths with this mother, in attacking her family, and she'd prove that mistake to him. Barbara charged the vile stray. The dog's eyes became sharp. Barbara stopped cold in her tracks.

24

"Leave her alone." She swung the broom.

The dog leapt and dodged the broom. Cracey moved with the creature, trapped tight within his jaws. The height of the cocker's jump was incredible, but did nothing to deter Barbara from attacking him. He jumped half the height of the tall oak, his front paws cradled the child so as if to protect her throat from tearing open in his jaws. He landed and immediately jumped again, higher this time. The dog and Cracey landed in the top of the oak. They stood on the yellowing leaves of the highest bough as if the leaves were made of steel and concrete, capable of holding the weight of a dog and a kidnapped child. A gush of wind streamed into the back yard and the branches of the trees began to sway back and forth. The dog peered down on Barbara and swayed with the wind on the tips of leaves. He appeared to be amused.

"I'll kill you," Barbara cried picking up the nearest toy she could find, a gold ball. "Give her back." She hurled the ball with strength that she hadn't used since she was younger and felt just how out of shape she had become since the days of her youth when she felt invincible.

The dog flew from the top of the oak and avoided the ball. The wind grew stronger as though it carried the canine, lengthening his jump farther than any dog should have been able to leap. He landed on the rose-covered garden arch just as the wind died. Barbara chucked a yellow croquet ball and the creature dodged it. Slats from the arch exploded into pieces. The dog jumped from the arch and landed on the narrow ridge of white decorative fence and ran along its top. Barbara ran at the animal, swinging her broom. The cocker eluded this attack too, leaping from the hickory fence to the steep roof of the rambler. As he jumped, Barbara cried and reached down to another croquet ball and hurled it at the dog.

The stray released his grip on Cracey, allowing it to duck the crashing blow. He leapt from the roof for Barbara. Cracey was now alone on top of the house.

Barbara thrust the handle of the broom up into the dog's gut and catapulted him over her head. The cocker landed on the grass on his side and recovered only in time to feel the blow of the broom handle across his back. It was a powerful blow echoed by a second and third before Barbara started stabbing the metal handle against the dog, but without leaving a single injury. How could this dog, this animal, so low on the pecking order, withstand her attacks?

Cracey screamed and began to sit up, sliding a little ways down the gray shingles.

"Lay down baby," Barbara screamed, knowing the danger her daughter faced of falling.

Cracey obeyed before she could slide any farther.

The dog used Barbara's distraction to his advantage and bit into Barbara's weapon. Barbara lost her grip on the broom and watched the creature snap the aluminum handle into two pieces.

Cracey's sobs made their way from the rooftop. Barbara would have leapt to her daughter if that were possible. She snatched up an orange tennis ball and threw it at the dog. She followed up with a croquet ball that she found rather quickly. The dog ignored the tennis ball but caught the croquet in his jaws and, just like the broom, snapped his jaws through the hard wood, letting it explode into a hundred splinters as if it were some sort of firework spectacular. Barbara was afraid. She had nothing to fight with anymore. She reached into her deep apron pocket and pulled out her wooden cooking spoon. If she could, she'd stab the spoon handle into the dog, break its thermometer off inside his body and let the bits of glass and mercury destroy him from the inside. It was her last resort and she hoped the dog was stupid enough to attack her, as he attacked her daughter, because she'd kill him fast and without mercy. And she'd do it far better than any mother protecting her young ever had. The dog launched into the air, back to the top of the oak.

Barbara used the moment to her advantage.

"Sit up baby," Barbara ordered.

"I'll fall," Cracey cried back.

"I'll catch you."

Cracey sat and began sliding down the roof, gaining speed as she neared the edge. Barbara positioned herself where she best thought she could catch her child, and watched Cracey's body topple over the edge towards her. Before she could catch her, the cocker spaniel leapt over Barbara's head and snapped his jaws once more around Cracey's throat. Again, it used one paw to cradle the child and the other gripped onto the eave of the roof. The dog pulled itself up onto the house and disappeared over the ridge with Cracey. Barbara ran through the heavy wooden gate to the front yard to search for any sign of the animal's retreat, but found nothing just as Stan's maroon station wagon pulled into the driveway.

2 — Into the Night

Bricktain Morris was a ding dong. He always wanted to be a field officer. He attended the academy, but he was too skilled with office procedures and annoying the wrong people. Following a ten-year marriage and a downhill divorce, he moved to Plattsville and was able to land his desired fieldwork position. One would think that he would have been more than ready for this line of work, but that wasn't the case.

He stood anticipating answers to his questions and jotted them down in his small notebook. He hadn't been invited into the house, so he remained under the shingled awning and wrote comments down he thought were important to his investigation. He dealt with a few speeding tickets on his first month of the job, even did good enough work that he was removed from his partner. Now he stood facing the most difficult task he ever dealt with. Earlier, Morris had asked for someone else to handle this case, but he was the only readily available officer at the time. Everything was so overwhelming.

"So, what were you doing when you first saw your daughter being attacked by the animal," Morris asked.

"Cooking dinner," Barbara replied. "Have you been listening?"

Her face had become tired. Her eyes were red and puffed. Stains from tears scarred her once appealing makeup. From time to time, she wiped her nose with a white handkerchief.

"What were you cooking," Morris continued to pry.

"Dog food," Barbara snapped.

"I'm just trying to figure out—

"Who is this idiot," Barbara asked Stan. "What was I cooking? Where's Richard?"

"Why don't you go lie down," Her husband suggested.

Stan was a doctor for the Plattsville Regional Hospital. He appeared to be a few years older than Barbara, but not enough to slow him down. He had a head full of dark brown hair free from any gray. His eyes, under different circumstances, would have looked young, even for his age, and unnoticeably wrinkled. However, at this point his eyes appeared tattered from trying to stay dry. Stan knew Barbara needed to see his strength if she was going to make it through this ordeal, although he really knew who was the stronger and wiser of the two. He knew that if he collapsed now, under the strain of the pressure of losing his daughter, that his wife wouldn't hold out much longer. Sure, Barbara was a strong person but she had her limits on what she could handle under her own mental strength. She was tempted to forget the police and hunt down the creature herself, but Stan convinced her to bring in his brother Richard. Before he knew it, the police department had the wrong man for the job at his door.

The married couple met when Barbara had made an unfortunate visit to the hospital during Stan's intern years. As a doctor, Stan was highly esteemed among his own peers for his unmatchable skill in trait and communication, and because of that was now the assistant hospital director. He had often found himself in situations where he had to tell people sad and brutal truths, but it was different for him to receive such news. It was uncomfortable for him to not have the control to know the exact status of his own daughter. If he were in control, he knew he would be able to repair his family because of his abilities. His voice, though sounding strong, quivered in ways only recognizable to Stan, or so he hoped. The way Barbara had squeezed his hand from time to time, conveyed that maybe she could see through his weakness. It wouldn't surprise him.

"I still have questions for her," The naive Morris said.

Stan let his wife disappear into the house, closing the front door behind her.

"Mr. Revlon, I know that this is difficult for you and your wife, but I really should—

"Perhaps you'd like to see the yard?" Stan pressed his way past the officer and led the way down the side of the house toward the hickory gate.

Morris followed.

The gate opened once again into the back yard. Stan stepped through first. He stopped for a moment to kick a triangular stone out of the way and continued to proceed through the gate, but stopped again when he recognized the significance of the rock he just removed from his path. Too many times he had moved the familiar stone out of his way, but only now did he appreciate how much it was there and how he missed having a little girl to get after for leaving it out to break his toe. It struck him that this might be the last time he got to kick it. He put the stone back where he found it and hoped it would leave a dead spot in the perfect grass. He couldn't help but wonder if he could have done something to help Cracey if he'd come home a minute sooner. The gate swung shut behind Morris.

The yard was a sight. How many times had Stan gotten after Cracey to pick up her playthings? Toys still strung out across the lawn. The once

28

beautiful garden archway, filled with roses, looked obliterated. A small pile of broken boards lay scattered on the ground around it. The signs of the day's earlier battle were everywhere. Upon seeing the two pieces of the snapped broom handle, Stan could only imagine the fight that had taken place.

"Is that the window that she saw the dog from," Morris asked. He knew it was a terrible question, but he had to ask something. All that Mr. Revlon would have to say was something sarcastic and Morris would know that he had truly established his lack of intelligence in this investigation.

"It is the only window on this side of the house," Stan replied, being careful to not seem snide, and did so to Morris's disdain.

"I'd like to take a look inside."

"Don't you think you should investigate the area out here first?"

"I think I would really like to see the kitchen," Morris replied. The process was clear to his mind. He wanted to look through the window and get the exact view that the mother had seen. It's just the way his brain worked and it was hard to explain that to other people. It might not be the best strategy, but it might at least narrow down a needless search of areas not in view of the window.

"I don't see how that's going to help," Stan said.

"I need to know—

"My daughter was taken from the yard, officer, not the kitchen. Why don't we start with the yard for now and then we can go look at the kitchen?"

"But I—

"Just take legible notes so someone else can read them."

Officer Morris fumbled through his thoughts trying to organize the polite way to tell Stan Revlon how to cooperate best with him. "Mr. Revlon, I understand this may be difficult for you."

"May be?"

"Is difficult."

"Not as difficult as it seems to be for you."

Morris fumbled with his notepad and pen. He reminded himself that Stanley Revlon had been through a terrible ordeal. Bricktain Morris, himself, didn't have any children, not that he didn't want children, but his wife had, in a way, made things clear that she didn't want to have children with him. She didn't think that he was father material, said he was too much of a klutz. In fact, he was so familiar with that particular complaint he actually believed it. Whenever he dwelt on this thought, which, for some reason, he was doing at this time when he should be investigating, he fumbled in all his other thoughts and words. Even when he was younger, he stuttered and fidgeted when he felt uncomfortable or cowardly.

He had many embarrassing moments in his life, and when they happened he couldn't help but feel his own stupidity setting him up for mockery. He felt set up for mockery now. He felt stupid now. Was he asking the right questions? He thought he was. Was he really investigating the right things? He believed he was. The more he thought about it, the more nervous he became. The heavy gate opened a second time, interrupting this horrible thought process.

A new man entered the yard. Morris turned, cued by Stan's glance towards the sound. He was a large man with brown, graying hair. His eyes were sunken, and dark. His brow was heavy, thick and whiting. His broad shoulders made his arms appear stiffer than they probably really were. As he walked, he limped. Perhaps one leg was a little shorter than the other, or perhaps it had been injured. It was hard to tell for sure. The way he walked, slightly rolled his body and winced, in what appeared to be pain, told Morris this man wasn't yet accustomed to whatever was causing his limp. He concluded the man was injured.

"Richard." Stan let out a cry of relief as the large man stepped closer.

"I would have been here sooner, but people don't think they can interrupt me when I have meetings with council members," Richard replied. "No one seems to think I need to know anything anymore."

Stan collapsed into Richard's arms and muffled sobs escaped him.

"Mister Revlon," Morris carefully interrupted "I know it's difficult, but we need to continue with this investigation if we're going to get your daughter back before something happens to her."

He caught it just as it rolled off his tongue. He wanted to lower his head and shake it in disbelief. How inconsiderate could he sound? To make matters worse, it finally hit him that the large man was Richard Revlon, Plattsville's chief of police. Morris couldn't be sure, but he believed this man to be the victim's family, like a brother or something. He had never met Police Chief Revlon and had hoped, when the day came to meet his boss, he would have been able to leave a positive strong impression. Officer Morris knew his comment just condemned him.

"Have you had any luck, officer?" The Sheriff's voice lingered with the final consonant.

Morris fed off the wallowing hint. "Morris, sir."

"And?"

"Well, I got a statement from the victim," Bricktain asked as he wondered how long he'd been standing silent.

"You did?" The chief cocked his brow at the rookie officer.

"Well, no, not the victim, the victim's mother."

"And?"

"I was about to go inspect the kitchen where the mother first witnessed the attack."

"The kitchen?" Richard seemed to be frowning.

"Of course sir." Bricktain's heart sank at his undoing and he knew only his precise notes could redeem him. "Would you like my notes?"

"Perhaps another time," Richard replied. "Why don't you return to work? We can discuss your notes later."

"Of course, sir." Bricktain Morris felt he could say nothing more. He showed himself through the heavy gate.

"Where's my niece, Stan," Richard asked.

"Barbara says a dog took Cracey."

Richard's face flushed. Those who knew him, knew he was angry. Cracey and Josh were the only children that he had known. He lived by himself ever since he lost his wife, swearing that he would never love again. He held true to that promise.

He filled the gap she used to fill with working out. He particularly liked running and lifting weights. He wasn't a bad fighter, either. He had studied boxing and kickboxing. He felt like martial arts were a little over the top, especially now that he was old and injured from twisting his ankle on the city building steps only twenty minutes earlier while running to his car. He'd admit that it was always impressive to see the little stereotype China man float in the air, spin, somersault, perform a side aerial and end with a single pointed foot before catching some unskilled moron just under the chin. However, Richard knew he could accomplish the same task with one maneuver, clench a fist and bust the opponent's jaw clean out of his head when the moment presented itself.

On top of being absolutely powerful, his strongest feature was his brilliance, and he was smart. He traveled the world and held correspondence and online Ph.D.s in anthropology, archaeology, literature and physics. At eighteen, while on a high school trip, he established himself in the police community after he helped British authorities track down a serial murderer. He loved to travel, but he still enjoyed the small town life. He enjoyed his hometown the best. He never thought he would break from his nomadic habits and settle down, but he had his reasons, and his niece was at the top of that list.

"What kind of dog," Richard asked taking a quick glance around the yard.

31

He noticed the broken pieces of fence lying on the ground. But something else caught his eye.

"I think she said a cocker spaniel," Stan replied.

"Is she sure?" Richard walked into the yard and knelt down in front of a small pile of what appeared to have once been a green croquet ball.

"You wanna go ask her about that." Stan watched his brother poke around the wood splinters. "What is that?"

"Shush," Richard ordered and he went to work.

Stanley stepped up behind his brother. Richard tore away grass from the ground. When he was finished desecrating the lawn he sat back.

"What does this look like to you," Richard finally asked.

Stanley stepped up. An imprint sank into the ground. The earth was still damp from an earlier watering. Stanley got onto his hands and knees to get a better look at what Richard saw. The imprint looked like that of a dog's paw. His attention remained locked on the deep print mixed with blades of flattened grass.

"There's another one to match here." Richard folded back a section of the lush lawn allowing a second print to show.

Stanley stared in disbelief. "Not a cocker spaniel is it?"

"It would have to be one heavy cocker spaniel," Richard explained. He stuck the pencil into the marking. "It's two inches deep."

The brothers remained silent, staring at the imprint. The imprint was different. It held the usual four pads characteristic of being found in a dog paw print. The claw marks at the top of each toe were narrower, sharper in shape and stuck out farther from the toe than normal. Most strange was that at the side was a fifth pad, which resembled what could be a larger than usual thumb. A shiver ran down Richard's spine.

"I have to go to work." Richard shot to his feet and trudged his way across the yard.

Stan acknowledged.

When Richard said that he had to go to work, he usually meant that he was already at work in his head. He was exceptionally skilled at piecing together his cases and once his mind got working, he no longer heard what anyone had to say. He especially didn't hear his own brother say that he was coming along to help. Nor did Richard remember telling Stan to stay with Barbara. Richard already knew the direction he needed to take his investigation and he didn't want to take his brother with him.

He pulled the door of the Lexus shut beside him as he took his seat behind the steering wheel. He pulled a cell phone from his belt. In a few beeps, his phone began to ring from his earpiece. He flipped a switch on a console surrounded by electronic devices and a laptop computer monitor flared on.

"Sheriff's office," Said the female voice on the other end.

"Monica, thanks again for coming in, have you heard anything on my niece yet," Richard asked. He tore a piece of paper from a pocket notebook and placed it on a small scanner.

"No luck yet," The voice replied. "Do we have that description on what she was wearing yet?"

"Didn't that officer, what's his name, call that in yet?"

"Not yet, and it's Morris."

"That's right. Bricktain Morris."

"Yeah."

"I'm sending some info to you now. I'll send the description of what she was wearing." Richard started tapping his finger against the dashboard, a habit he demonstrated often when he was upset. "Activate an Amber Alert."

"We're just waiting on that description," Monica said.

A long silence followed.

"Are you all right, Richard?"

Richard tried to speak a few times but couldn't find the words. He had dealt with some of the scariest cases and seen some of the most gruesome sights. He wasn't one who felt a sick stomach easily and he was known in some circles for being a mean cannon. However, right now he felt ill. He thought about the probability that he would find Cracey and was frightened. Yet, the dog scared him even more.

"I'm fine," He said. "Find out which precinct Morris works for and have him in my office tomorrow morning, his captain too. And get a termination package together in case I decide I want it."

"Of course. Anything else?"

Was there anything else? He wondered.

The county outskirts jumped to his mind. The only house around that part belonged to that fool Jasper Zheeghan. No one understood him and no one seemed to care about him. He just lived at that useless orchard, letting fruit grow and rot. Most people didn't even know he existed. Kids made up tales about the house being haunted. He just appeared one day and kept mostly to himself, disturbing no one. No one seemed to bother him either. His house sat near the bottom of a small hill. It was the highest hill in the county, but not much of a hill at that. In this mostly flat land, a gopher hole seemed to be a mountain. Some people argued the hill was a plateau, but others thought it was too small. Town settlers flattened its top. Half the community called it the hill and the other half called it the plateau. Regardless of what people call it, this small mound rose behind the old farmhouse leaving something that resembled a large outdoor amphitheater, filled with fruit trees. A dirt road ran in front of the house and it forked off to another, which led up the hill. This road overlooked the farmhouse and stretched for about six or seven miles to a steel fortress known as Reggie's Wrecking Yard.

Reggie Chambers was also an older man who bought the junkyard. In the past, he had called the police and animal control to annoying levels, complaining about packs of dogs on his property. Richard thoroughly, investigated the area many times himself. Eventually, he got fed up with chasing dogs that weren't there, and ten years passed without Reggie complaining. Ten years passed without any major kind of animal activity. Yet, tonight Richard felt because of the history of Reggie's reported animal activity in that area, it was worth checking out. He feared going up that mountain, or what he would find, but it was the most ideal area for wild dogs to hide out.

Wolves were different. They usually kept their distance from people. Usually they attacked other animals and drew their prey off for food. They wasted little.

Wild dogs attacked simply to attack. They ran rampant and rogue in large numbers. When they killed, they usually left their kill behind and often didn't eat it. Richard feared the wild dog he might find. He hoped he wouldn't find anything, and yet he hoped he'd find Cracey. He hoped he'd find her healthy and alive. Time was of the essence. What he wanted was to go home and get his four-wheel-drive Silverado, something more equipped for driving the rugged road and performing the type of search and rescue he wanted to do. However, his house was across town and those precious minutes it would take him to travel could cost Cracey her life, if she were still alive that is.

Was there anything else Richard needed of Monica? Yeah, but she had no way of getting it to him. He was running out of time. He'd have to do this old school, just him, a gun and his resourcefulness.

"Yeah," Richard replied. "I'm going to search mountain road."

"Do you want some help," Monica asked. "It's dark up there."

"Yeah have dispatch send some to meet me."

The two finished their friendly conversation. Next, Richard called the most experienced dog tracker he knew. He finally slipped the key into the steering column and forced the engine to turn over. The Lexus pulled away from Stan's house and made its way down the residential streets blanketed with flickering street lamps. The residential scenery turned into the commercial glib of billboards advertising sales, movie times and prices. Headlights of other cars multiplied as they cruised the strip of Plattsville City, leading drivers to some form of entertainment or another. One or two cars cut off Richard. He was tempted to pull one over that pulled into his lane. Its driver stepped on his brakes and gestured an unfriendly hand to the sheriff's unmarked sedan. But this was not the time for revenge traffic tickets.

The comfort of city lights turned into industrial darkness. The coal mine always seemed dark. He entered the historical dark residences of West Plattsville. The houses here were a little more rundown. Fewer lights appeared on these narrow streets. Alleyways frequented little shops and old saloons. A mile to the south was a junior high school. A wall of darkness gradually appeared out of nowhere and the lights of the historic avenues suddenly stopped sprouting up to illuminate the road as it became a little rougher. The city simply didn't have the money in the budget to upkeep these parts of the streets. It wasn't traveled enough to make it worthwhile, but it was a nuisance when drivers needed it. Every fifteen feet, either a pothole or a bump from old cheap, fill-in road repairs popped up and put the Lexus's springs to the test.

Richard flipped on the bright beams of his car as he ventured farther into the uncomfortable spell of enveloping darkness. Jasper's house appeared in the distance and gave the only light. It looked even more in need of a condemning than it did in the daylight. The Lexus passed Japer's house. Richard turned onto the fork leading to Reggie's and felt the slight incline begin to take his car up the nearly invisible hill. His headlights revealed several forms of tall grass, wild barley, local weeds and brush. In the distance, he could see two soft glowing light sources. One light belonged to Jasper's home now at the bottom of the hill. The other light, still farther into the hill, belonged to Reggie and his junkyard. Richard wished he had his truck, a Chevy Silverado, which he named Hickerbilly. That thing provided more illumination than most lurking creatures cared for.

He was now in unincorporated Plattsville and going deeper into the darkened night. The safe lights of the city diminished even from the sight of the rear view mirror. Darkness was thick on all sides of the vehicle. The gleam from the radiant headlights of the sedan saturated everything in its view. Dying grass, which was normally brown, appeared yellow, wild shrub skeletons turned white.

The outside darkness crept in more. It blanketed the Lexus save the powerful headlamps. The eerie black became an oily residue on the skin of the vehicle. Richard turned on a high-powered spotlight mounted on his door. Its rays burst through the blanket of night proclaiming its limited awesome power. Still, he found no sign of a little girl. Richard's eyes watched the terrain intently, filtering through the beam and all the little things that floated within it. The junkyard wasn't far; its spotlights opened in the distance. To the right, the hill rose a short ways. To the left, it dropped to a pool of black, which concealed countless apple trees. The stars above him weren't trying very hard to be bright tonight. And the not-so-full moon watched over it all.

Richard had seen bodies before, too many bodies. He felt nothing when he saw them now, but he might feel something if he saw a little one tonight. He hated to dwell upon it. The first image of him coming down by the river's edge was burned so profoundly into his brain that he could never forget the first body he had to face. Even still, no crime scene he had ever seen or collaborated on prepared him for what he felt now. It was as if the whole idea of death had become alien to him. This time it was a child, his innocent relation.

The hillside began to open and flatten. Once past the front of the hill, no one would ever believe it was the highest point in Plattsville. In the darkness, only flat land and gray shades of retiring vegetation existed. You could look in any direction and the land appeared to press on continuously, but try to walk it, especially in the dark, and your next step could tumble you down the hill into Jasper's apple orchard.

Out of nowhere, Richard saw Cracey.

The dirt road coughed from beneath Richard's tires as the Lexus maliciously tried to smash small stones deeper into its hard skin top. The Lexus halted. Richard pulled the emergency brake to help it. The driver's door flew open and, as Richard stepped out, he smelled the lingering dust slowly settle back towards the road's surface. He adjusted the spotlight and panned it over an area in the distance. Round drying shrubs smothered the area and made it difficult to see anything. Two of those shrubs concealed whomever's body was attached to the tiny hand protruding from beneath them.

Richard's stomach wrenched. Now, he faced the reality of finding a tiny body. He hoped it was Cracey, but he hoped it wasn't. He knew whoever was in the shrubs needed his help no matter who he meant to find. He had no other choice. He had to approach, even though the unsettling reality was that the tiny hand wasn't moving. Deep down he wished it would be the body of another person's child, but recognized the small silver bracelet around this little girl's wrist too well. It was just a small thin chain with small colored hearts dangling from it, and he gave it to her last Christmas.

Please let her be alive, he prayed.

He took a long black flashlight from the dashboard before exiting the

36

Lexus. Compared to the car's spotlight, the handheld gleam seemed futile. Gradually, its strength improved as he stepped into the darker reaches of the car's spotlight and uncomfortably closer to what he knew was the body of his niece. His own figure blocked the rays of the spotlight with his twisting and disturbing shadows. Were it not for the brightness of the insignificant flashlight, Richard might have lost sight of the hand several times to the darkness. Once again, he found himself entering the black of the night and recalled a familiarity he once held with it. What he wouldn't give for a helicopter right now to light the whole place up.

A sound filled the night, a whisper really, a crackling of dying brush nearby, perhaps a twig snapping, and Richard stopped in his tracks. For a moment, he thought he saw two green dots, but he wasn't sure and he didn't want his thoughts to get the better of him, not after all he'd accomplished. He listened for further clues to let him know what was hiding, what was watching, if anything at all. The harder he tried to keep his breath silent, the louder the noise became. For the first time, Richard realized he was indeed alone. He was used to having someone to back him up, but tonight he didn't. Fifteen feet behind him was his car. He could run back to it quick enough if he needed to, but first things first. He reached under his jacket and fit the familiar grip of his Venom .45 caliber semiautomatic into his palm. Something crackled in the brush to Richard's left. It wasn't loud, but was clear enough of a sound to let Richard know he wasn't as alone as he had previously hoped. He raised his gun to point where the flashlight shined. For the first time in a long time, Richard was afraid.

"I forgot how much I hate this," Richard mumbled to himself.

A light breeze lifted Richard's bangs and let them drop gently back against his forehead. Any sound from the darkness could be coming from anywhere. It would all sound the same to Richard. What he wouldn't give to have the ears of a wolf right now. That way he might have a better idea of where the danger lurked. He found himself looking to the land on his right wondering if he had heard the noises correctly, but realized he heard the echo. He turned away from the sound.

An idiot might have called out to ask someone hiding to show himself. Richard remained silent. Calling out would only let someone know he was afraid. Not to mention, Richard didn't want to call any wild dogs to him. He saw no reason to invite his prowler out of the darkness yet. In an instant, another cracking sound emerged, more boisterous, much closer. This time, it was loud enough for Richard to distinguish that the loathsome sound originated from behind his vehicle. Without thinking, the chief of police turned the beam of his flashlight and his gun upon his car. The spotlight blinded him, and he realized he had never made a more idiotic move. He knew something was watching him. He pulled back the hammer on his Venom. Behind him, he heard a rustle among the weeds and tall grass.

"Mommy."

Richard turned at the sound and ran as he had forgotten he was capable of, ignoring his twisted ankle. Cracey's hand clenched open and closed as though trying to grasp something that wasn't there. If an animal was hiding in the dark, it wasn't going to get the chance to get to the little girl before Richard did. He didn't hear anything over the echoing blasts of his footsteps. He turned around again, poised with his flashlight as though it were the scope to his gun. He was careful this time not to make the same mistake of looking directly into the car spotlight. Nothing seemed to be chasing him. Richard had been in this business a long time now, enough to know that the sound of nothing could actually be something extremely malice.

"Mommy," Cracey mumbled again.

Richard turned back, knelt down and tore apart three shrubs to uncover the five-year-old's tiny body.

Something had beaten her badly and scoured her face with dust and dirt. Lines of terrified wrinkles broke through her miner-like mask. Dried tear trails stretched from her eyes and off the sides of her usually darling face. A cake of grime bandaged a scratch mark over her cheek, and, clearly, the bandage had done its job in absorbing her blood. Her neck was not so bandaged. Hard, red, clotted trails embossed her throat. Her body shook, more so in her head than at any other point of her frame. Her eyes were sealed shut and she mumbled as though she were dreaming. She appeared as no child ever should. Upon closer inspection, he found another set of bite marks grooved into her shoulder like a circular tattoo.

"It's on," yelled Richard, and he didn't care who heard him. He holstered his gun and reached for his cell phone, but realized he had made another mistake by leaving it in the car.

Get with the game, Richard mentally screamed at himself.

Cracey jerked under his touch as he ran his hand under her matted hair. He found a once wet spot, now a clot, near the back of her skull. "Can you hear me, Tike?"

"Mommy," the little girl said as if talking in her sleep. Her body clenched into an almost fetal-like position and she turned to her side.

"Okay, we're going home." Richard scooped his arms under his niece and pulled her to his shoulder.

Without waking, she clenched her arms around her uncle's neck. "Mommy."

Richard stood and saw the reflective green eyes a short way off in the darkened field. Richard knew one thing. He wasn't ready.

"Come on,Tike," Richard said trying to reassure himself that he was comfortable with the green-eyed stranger. He needed to remain confident or if Cracey should wake up and see what Richard saw now, he knew she wouldn't understand.

Next, a sound, cold and paralyzing, trumped. When Richard heard it, his spine tingled with a fear he hadn't known in a long time. It ran from the very base of his skull and disappeared into the middle of his back. He began to step away as soon as his feet began responding to his frightened demands.

"Mommy," She cried, but this time, Richard noticed, with wide eyes. Her fingers clenched deep into her uncle's shoulder. She was frightened. So was Richard.

A low rumbling noise gravitated from the direction of the green eyes. The eyes blinked and reappeared a few feet to the left. The rustling continued. With Cracey in one of his arms, he held the flashlight with his only free hand. He caught the silhouette of the shadow, the large and monstrous shadow. Richard ran into the powerful spotlight hoping to blind any creature that might follow him into it.

Another sound emerged, moaning with a growl hidden in it.

"Ba-roo!"

Richard spun around and threw his flashlight at the green eyes poised behind him. The creature's massive prickly back arched away from the boundaries of the headlamps and it cried as the flashlight shattered into pieces against its skull. From the ground to the arch of its back, the creature must have been nearly five feet. Its head was square and hung down low in the light. It nuzzled its nose over the ground and took in an audible deep breath. The creature jerked its head up and glared at Richard. Richard felt himself trembling, or was it Cracey? He never trembled. He wasn't ready. The giant dark dog began to growl and a thick mane blossomed around its neck and shoulders.

"In my own backyard," Richard said. "All right, let's do this."

"Brooo!" The howling sound came from somewhere in the distance.

The visible but dark beast stepped up onto its hindquarters and cocked its head toward the sky. "How—

BANG!

Some things, Richard was still fast at. He had nearly forgotten the speed at which he was able to draw a weapon and shoot.

The creature crumpled and appeared to be clutching its chest. It snapped its head from side to side, scanning for Richard. Richard stood with his arm extended, holding his gun. In the gleam of the Lexus spotlight, a trail of thin smoke wrapped around the Venom's muzzle.

BANG! BANG! BANGBANG!

The stalker quickly disappeared from the view of the spotlight. Richard's first instinct was to chase the thing, but Cracey was clutching his neck and screaming in his ear. That and he didn't quite believe his bullets were capable of having wounded the creature. In fact, he was sure they did nothing and that the monster was laughing at him.

Richard felt cold. He had forgotten what true fear was. He held his gun high and dropped the clip into his hand. He examined the dent at the head of the next bullet in the cartridge. The dangerous hollowed tip would have gashed a hole in most animals. What he wouldn't give for that tip so much stronger than this one. He slammed the clip back into his gun. In the rush of things, he forgot that he changed out his usual bullets today at the shooting range, where his favorite ammo was considered illegal. His favorite bullets were in the gun case in the trunk of his vehicle. Richard ran to the driver's door and peeled Cracey's swollen grip from around his neck.

"Hold this, Tike," Richard said holding his cell phone to her. "Call Mommy." He laid her on the passenger seat. "You understand? Call Mommy. Talk to her now."

Cracey yanked the phone and held it tight to her chest.

"Now stay down."

A blood-curdling scream blasted from the little girl's lungs. The cell phone fell to the floorboard. Richard turned around in the front seat and squeezed out another shot. The shadow leapt to the right and was gone. Richard stood from the car and shot a quick glance to both of his sides. He spotted the creature standing outside the beams of the headlights. Its glowing eyes watching as if waiting for the right time to attack its prey. Richard didn't allow the creature the benefit and fired another shot. The animal disappeared from the headlights. Richard reached into his car and pressed a concave button near the steering wheel. A hollow click announced it had worked. The driver's side door slammed shut and Richard sprinted around to the now open trunk of his vehicle.

Where were the good bullets?

He was sure they were in here.

He dropped his Venom onto the nearly empty trunk bed and tore a sawed off twelve gauge from a small rack with rubber grips. Oh, how he wished he had his truck. As quickly as his fingers managed, they forced plastic sealed shells, which he took from a nearby trunk compartment, into the gun until the weapon couldn't hold anymore. The car jerked. Richard strafed from the trunk to the driver's side, pumping the shotgun as he stepped into view of the creature.

The trunk had blocked Richard's sight. The creature had nearly sneaked right upon him. It stood three or four feet away from the police chief. Several long slender flashes of silver appeared from within the monster's paws and sank into the driver's door. An eerie and haunting metallic sound shrieked as the creature began slicing the door metal open. The silver flashes disappeared and a burst of gunpowder flared from the end of the shotgun barrel.

The creature reeled, grabbed its side and retreated into the darkness. Silence followed. Richard could sure use his flashlight right now. The area around him grew brighter. Richard risked a glance backward and listened to the familiar sound of tires settling in the dirt. A new set of headlights had arrived on the scene. Blue, red and white lights stomped out their wicked judicial dance from atop the patrol car. The beam of a new spotlight erupted. Richard heard the sound of the door open, adjusting the view of the spotlight, and close. A bulky shadow of an officer with wide shoulders and a trim frame stepped into the blinding light.

"You alright, Chief," The shadow asked.

"Do what I tell you," Richard said. "Shoot anything outside that moves without question."

Something snapped in the surrounding brush

The officer's shadow twisted to its right bringing the flare of a flashlight with it. Richard held his breath as he watched the backup officer's narrow beam of light shine over the dry field.

"Broo!" The sound came from the distance once more.

"How-roo," came from the distance.

Richard fired off a shot in the direction of the much closer cry.

"That's how you know where to shoot," Richard said. "Don't let it call for help."

The monster snarled and its massive figure jetted past the dark shadow of the officer who had yet to draw his weapon.

The flashlight and the officer wrenched back and forth in confusion in the headlamps of the patrol car.

"I have the girl," Richard announced. "Call for a bird."

The shadow and the flashlight turned back to the frightened chief of police.

"Sir?"

Richard heard the fearful tone and hidden meaning of the officer's voice.

"Call now," Richard ordered. "And draw your weapon."

The officer drew and fired off a shot in Richard's direction. Richard turned with his shotgun and fired another shot into the creature, which now reflected the psychedelic police light colors only a few feet away from him. The creature left once more and the officer shot once again.

"Watch your shooting," Richard snapped. "I don't want you missing the creature and hitting me."

"I never miss," the officer replied.

The creature leapt out of the dark, fast enough to push past the shotgun-wielding police chief without retaliation. Richard felt sharp pains gash open over his left arm and side, all the way to his waist. Warmth oozed from his body. The creature was gone. Richard spun again; aware that his throbbing ankle, which he had done so well to ignore this night, suddenly didn't hurt so much as his side did now.

"Drop," Richard cried.

But the shadow of the monster was too fast. Both the outline of the officer, his flashlight and gun toppled into the air. The officer came down directly in front of the headlights of his patrol car. The flashlight disappeared after smacking the ground. The dark dog watched the officer straining to stand. The creature reared back. Another glint of silver gleamed, and another flash popped from the barrel of Richard's twelve-gauge. The creature staggered.

"Stay down," Richard ordered again before squeezing off another burst of shell and trying to push the evil presence from its fallen target. The chief felt the trickling of blood down his side continue to flow thick over his skin with each step he took toward the monster. He fired off another shot and another, hoping to reel the creature from his officer.

The wounded officer hugged the ground. Richard's finger continued cramping around the trigger of the sawed-off. The creature pulled straight up and onto its rear legs and, in an instant, kicked into the fallen officer. The officer's body flew towards Richard. The chief dropped to his knee to avoid getting clobbered by the hurling person. Anger, familiar with the night, swelled inside Richard and he couldn't repress it. He would kill this monster, tear it apart limb from limb with his bare hands if he had to. He could do it. He knew he could. He may be old, but no animal was going to get the best of him. The beast had attacked not only his niece, but an officer as well. For a moment, Richard thought about trying to catch the officer, but knew if he fell trying to help, that no one would be there to fend off the creature. The monster dropped back onto all fours. Glass cracked and shattered behind Richard as the officer smashed into the open Lexus trunk, hyper extending it over the rear window.

The chief plugged off another shot and another into the shadow's hind leg. He risked a glanced at his officer lying sprawled half in and half out of the Lexus trunk. The shadow officer had a face now to go with his blue uniform and bleeding head. Richard recognized the rookie cop from earlier that night at once, Morris something. Richard turned back to the creature. A longer moment of looking might have allowed him to notice if the rookie was breathing, but it could also allow the monster the small amount of time it needed to wipe out the chief. He returned his gaze to the hobbling, and yet somehow, charging monster only paces in front of him now.

Don't think, Richard thought. *Just kill it.*

Richard unleashed a barrage of shrapnel at the rushing beast. The creature's pace jerked slower with each shotgun blast. The final cartridge leapt from the side of the weapon. Richard watched the beastly shadow now hunker over as if catching its breath. Richard hoped the creature was dying, but wasn't going to wait around to make sure that the damage done was enough. He remembered the Venom.45 left lying on the floor of his trunk, too bad the wounded officer's body now blanketed it and the box of shotgun bullets. Probably wouldn't have done any good anyway, right now.

The dog stood once more on two legs and stamped down, kicking up dust and fogging the blinding lights of the patrol car, making them practically ineffective against the dark of the night. The red and green eyes still managed to appear from within the dark cloud of smoke. The creature grunted, opened its mouth and let loose sound once again.

"How—

The sleek steel barrel of the sawed-off struck under the jaw of the beast's massive head. Richard's adversary growled. The police chief struck again and again. Each blow threw the shadow's head. The long claws of silver appeared and slashed out at the chief. Richard blocked the blow with the barrel of the gun. Four metallic-appearing claws sank halfway through his shotgun barrel shield. The creature broke Richard's grip and tore the gun away. A moment later, Richard felt a blow to his stomach fierce enough to lift him off his feet. He landed face up by the driver side front tire of the Lexus. He forced himself to sit before his breath could return. He had to be strong. His niece had to get home. His officer had to survive. Richard had to survive. He was on a knee before he felt breath enter him fully and he ignored the new sharp pain in his chest and the cool seepage of blood seeping from his side into his dress

43

slacks. The shadow beast finished tearing the barrel of the gun apart and threw the pieces into the black oblivion.

Richard reached for the shredded car door; he had another gun in the glove compartment. Maybe the door handle would still work, despite the door's condition. Cracey had locked the doors. Smart niece. The only line of defense left was the black handled boot knife concealed beneath the cuff of his right pant leg. He drew it and vaulted himself over the hood of the car and listened to the tearing of metal from behind him, not realizing that he managed to dodge another of the creature's attacks. He turned back to the monster, which was now a blinding blur of black. The driver's side door tore from the car and the monster dropped it.

In the dim dome of the car's interior, Richard caught the terrifying view of the creature. Its eyes were horrifying and its teeth gleamed with stains of yellow and pink. It had black thick and thin fur with tips of silver and its mane stuck out as if static charged it. The creature leaned in the front seat towards the child cowering on the floor. Her scream pierced through the closed passenger window and into her uncle's heart. Somehow, she was able to elude the swipe of the beast's massive paw as she climbed her way into the back seat. Richard's elbow shattered the rear door's pane of glass. He cuffed Cracey around every bit of clothing he could grip and jerked her tiny body through the new opening.

A second eruption came as the creature punched through the front door glass in an attempt to swipe down Richard in his rescue attempt. Richard avoided the creature's claws and buried his boot knife through the monstrous wolf's wrist. As he turned with Cracey in his arms and ran for the patrol car a few feet off, he couldn't avoid the chill sent through his bones from the sound of destruction of glass and metal behind him. What if he hadn't gotten Cracey out before this destruction?

Richard dived behind the open driver's door of the patrol car and released the trunk. He sprinted to the back of the vehicle.

"Stay down,Tike," he said, setting Cracey inside the trunk.

He quickly located a fresh shotgun and a fire axe and took both. He dropped the axe to the ground and forced a shell into the chamber of the shotgun. He closed the trunk to hide Cracey from the beast. This monster wouldn't get her while Richard was still alive. Richard stepped around the side of the car with the shotgun in one hand and the red axe in the other. The perturbed creature was in the midst of charging for Richard and was halfway between the destroyed Lexus and the patrol car. Richard ran back at the creature, extended the shotgun and blew a shot from the end of the barrel. He let the kick from the weapon carry it over his shoulder and out of his hand. He began preparing the axe for its first assault. The devil dog stood tall again and clenched at its shoulder and, a moment later, grasped at its leg as Richard rushed by with a bash to the creature's right knee. Richard swung around, the axe over his head, and sank the pick deep into the back of the black dog's neck.

The creature fell forward and coughed.

The spike dug into the monster's shoulder next and when the wide silver blade swung again, lopping off the left hind foot. The beast fell forward, turning to Richard as it fell. It looked angrier than it did in pain. The spike found the monster's chest. Richard kept swinging: spike, blade, spike, blade—no mercy! Stabbing and hacking with each blow. He would destroy this menace.

Richard squared himself before the monster's head and raised the axe for the spike's next blow. "It's over."

Dark mucus spit from the creature's mouth. Richard jerked out of the pathway, but felt a burning sensation churning down the side of his neck and into his shoulder. The burning grew more violent. The monster lunged and Richard had time to react with the axe. This time, the creature caught the spike in his paw, but a moment too late. The monster's throat began gurgling. The black dog lunged once more and took hold of Richard's arm. He struggled as if to pin Richard in this new wrestling match. The strength of the beast seemed insignificant this time, but its weight was immense and Richard fought to keep the monster off him. The beast stared at the police chief, smoke rose from its fur over its throat. It was acidic with a stench burning at Richard's eyes. The creature's neck gaped open through smoldering fur. The dark mucus appeared to run down from inside the creature's neck. Smoke crept up from everywhere the mucus touched, melting hair, skin, and all on the dog. Richard noticed that his own dress jacket and shirt had burned from around his shoulder, revealing growing blisters on his skin. The monster rose on his hind legs, using the amputated stump to help maintain its balance.

"You're lucky I'm not wearing my good coat," Richard said glaring into the monster's expiring eyes.

The creature stumbled toward Richard.

The sensation on his skin grew hotter. Richard tried to step from the beast, but the weight of the monster was becoming awkward to hold away. The monster was limp, possibly dead. Richard began to turn the beast's mass carefully to keep more of the acid mucus from touching him further. He strained with every muscle in his body and felt success creeping in as the monster's weight seemed to be growing lighter. He beat this monster. In his old age and without his choice of weapon and ammunition, Richard beat this monster.

BANG! BANG! BANG! BANG!

Three bullets hit the monster and one tore through Richard's kneecap. He buckled backwards to the ground and the beast's dead body dropped onto him. The black and silver fur stabbed deep into his flesh. The police chief's chest began to burn.

"It's all right. I killed it, sir," Officer Bricktain Morris said, now standing over the fallen combatants with his handgun drawn. Blood ran down the side of his head and he held his ribs with one hand. "Are you okay?"

Richard felt his flesh burn away under the acidic secretion leaking from the monster's neck. Never had he imagined such pain. It overpowered the torment of his bullet-shattered kneecap.

"You idiot," Richard said. And a moment later, he felt his chest open and his ribs disintegrate.

Morris listened to a gurgle escape the chief's lungs. He pressed a button on the mouthpiece of his radio attached to the top of his shoulder. "Three-fourteen to base."

"Go ahead , Three-fourteen", answered the radio at Morris's belt.

"Requesting medical units to junkyard road." He had to turn away from the sight of the disintegrating police chief and brute dog. "Officer down."

"The chief is in your vicinity."

"It is the chief," Morris returned. "The chief's down."

Silence.

"And the girl," the radio asked.

Morris looked through the shadows cast from the high beams of his vehicle and the battered car in front of it. "I don't know where she is. The chief said he had her. She may have run into the field, scared." He remembered the chief's order from earlier. "Send a bird."

3 – Makin' Bacon

The fork tinked away at the plate through the half-eaten scrambled eggs, which were cold now after an hour of sitting. As Stan rolled his fork around, Barbara stood at the sink watching the backyard out the window, reliving the previous day in her mind. The ground grew brighter as the sun began to turn the world day. She held a cold plate of eggs mixed with Muenster cheese in her hand as well. She left the table to get a fork, began staring and forgot about the white decorative plate in her hands or the need for a fork.

The front door opened and shut, and footsteps crept towards the kitchen.

"We're back," Josh said.

"Where are the others," Stan asked.

"Dustin's taking Cadence home and Natalie's in the front room."

"She can come in," Stan said standing up and beginning to clear space at the table for two more people.

"I don't want her in my kitchen," Barbara said breaking her silence. "Tell her to go home."

"Mom," Josh refuted. "She's been out all night, like the rest of us, looking for Cracey."

"Get her out of my house," She snapped.

Her reaction stunned Josh. She'd been mean before, but this time, even Stan appeared shocked. The front door opened and closed again.

"Natalie." Josh turned and ran out of the kitchen.

Stan walked to his wife, wrapped his arms around her and watched out the window with her. "That was wrong, Barb."

"I know." Barbara set her plate and food in the sink and rubbed her fingers against Stan's hands. "I lost one of my babies already."

"You never could handle losing him."

"She's worthless."

"I like her."

"I don't."

"She'd give her last breath fighting for him, you know."

Barbara sighed. "Yeah."

When Josh returned, the sizzling sound of bacon frying in a pan and its sweet aroma greeted him.

47

Barbara didn't look up from the pan as Josh entered. "I'm sorry."

"She understands," Josh returned coldly. "Which is more than I can say for me."

"How do you want your eggs," Barbara asked, unaffected by Josh's comment.

"Cooked," Josh said slouching into a chair next to his dad's. He laid his head in his crossed arms. For a few minutes, he listened to the spatula scraping the fry pan and slowly the bacon stopped sizzling.

"Here you go hun."

Josh raised his head and watched a plate slide in front of him.

"It only takes a few minutes for the eggs to get cold so you better not think while you eat," Stan said. He had returned to stirring his own breakfast.

Barbara sat down with a fresh plate for herself. She held her fork to her mouth and prepared to bite down.

"Mom!"

Barbara jumped. "What?"

"Bacon."

Barbara stared, for what seemed to be minutes, at the strip of bacon stuck on her fork.

"Are you all right, Barb," Stan asked.

"I'm fine." Barbara faked a smile before pushing the bacon off her plate onto Josh's.

The phone rang. Its squeal scared everyone sitting at the table. Barbara ran to answer it. For a little while she could only say 'yes' or 'no' and ask simple questions.

She dropped the phone and cried as no mother should ever have to cry.

4 — The Reckoning

Two antique-stained coffins sat at the head of the quiet and dim chapel. One lay open while the other remained closed. The open one held Cracey. Her face, no longer blue from the lack of oxygen in the trunk of the patrol car, was instead plastered with thick, stinky makeup. While search and rescue teams patrolled miles of the tall grass throughout the night, she remained under everyone's noses ,sealed in the airtight trunk of Bricktain Moriss' patrol car. It wasn't until the next morning investigators finally discovered the child's suffocated and still body forever asleep. No one really knew how much of Richard's disintegrated remains lay in the closed casket.

Josh was the first to arrive, wanting to get to the chapel before his family and friends. He needed time for himself, to say goodbye, and he hadn't been able to take a moment to talk to his baby sister since he received the news about her abduction. His parents had gotten a little time to themselves after the viewing the previous night. Even Dustin had stolen a moment a few minutes before the viewing to wish his tiny friend a tearful goodbye. Now it was Josh's turn, here, within the cold walls of plaster and painted-glass scenery.

He was unable to get over the stillness of her once joyful countenance. Grim emptiness replaced a once frolicsome and trickster smile. Laughter seemed an impossible vision coming from this empty shell now. It was hard to believe. The sour ammonia and formaldehyde scent bestowed upon her by the mortician and makeup artist defiled Cracey's once free spirit further. Josh looked on his sister and wiped his nose on the sleeve of his black suit.

"I should have let you come along,Tike." He wiped his eyes. "All I had to do was say you could come along."

The velvet pink hair ribbon didn't look quite right. Josh adjusted it and set a pigtail straight.

"It's not going to be the same without you." He leaned close to her ear. "I had some news for you."

The room erupted with a thundering gale of squeaky hinges from one of two heavy decorated oak doors. The sound rattled off the walls and pews, disrupting Josh's calm.

"I'm sorry," a young woman said. The door screamed again as it sealed shut. The woman flinched at its calamity. "I was trying to be quiet." Her gentle voice bellowed almost as much as the hinge of the door. She moved silently along the narrow green path between rows of benches and her dress whispered with each step.

"It's all right," Josh mumbled before returning to his sister's ear. "We'll tell you the news later." He kissed Cracey's cheeks.

"Are you okay," the woman asked as she wiped at his swollen eyes with her black cotton-covered fingers. She let Josh pull her into his arms and lay his face on the top of her head. Tears seeped from his cheek through her short silky black hair. She reached under his arms and pressed her hands into his back, pulling him tighter against her, so she could find that familiar spot under Josh's jaw line that fit perfectly with the curves of her slender face. She breathed in his scent before he suddenly fell to his knees and buried his face against her waist. She cradled his head in her palms and ran her gloved fingers through his thick hair, letting him clench and twist the sides of her knee-length, leather jacket while he feebly attempted to silence his sobbing.

"I miss her, Nata," Josh sobbed.

Natalie continued stroking Josh's head.

"I didn't even get to tell her."

"I know," Natalie consoled him.

He looked up with red eyes. "Is anyone else here?"

"They're on their way." Natalie wiped more tears. "Do you want me to keep them out a few more minutes?"

"No." Josh stood up and hugged Natalie once more. "I'll be okay by the time they get here."

The hinges shrieked open again and both doors slammed shut. The entire room quaked.

"Forgive me," spoke the old man.

The old man repositioned the thin round glasses on his face and pulled his fur-collared jacket tight around his chest. "Cold in here. It's always cold in a church." He thrust the tip of his cane into the carpet and began pulling himself toward the open casket. "Some people might say it's the windows and the high walls. I say it's the benches." With a flick of his wrist, the old man rapped the side of a pew with his cedar stick. The chapel echoed with disgust as the old man continued to press towards the coffins and the towering pulpit. He laughed as if he were the only one who understood his disrespectful joke. "Blasted pews always put my butt to sleep and then it gets all tingly and I can't stand up for nothing." His voice sounded old and abused beyond that of any old man's. It was as if his vocal cords were worn down with sandpaper. It

50

was above a whisper, but less than healthy.

"I'm sorry," Josh said. "But the viewing doesn't start for—

"What are you gonna do?" The old man's face squared up with Natalie's and looked up to Josh's eyes. "Throw me outta the chapel?" He looked back to Natalie. "You should keep your son under control ma'am." The tip of the old man's cane stabbed into the tip of Josh's wingtip as the old man pressed past the couple. "You should really get a room you know."

"Excuse me, but—

"Ssshhhhhh," replied the old man, holding up his two forefingers to quiet Josh. He stepped over to the casket. "They don't make 'em like they useta, do they?"

"I think you better leave," Josh demanded.

"Are you the brother," the old man asked ignoring Josh's outrage.

"Yes, I am."

"Where were you when this child was killed?" The man set his walking stick against the side of the coffin and leaned over Cracey.

"What difference does that make," Natalie interrupted recognizing that more tears were welling behind Josh's already tormented eyes.

"There it is. Thought for a moment I was going senile," the old man said. "Taking your time, aren't you?" He turned quickly, snatching up his cane, and without using it, made his way past Natalie and Josh toward the loud doors. "Let's see what happens shall we?" He stopped abruptly and turned back to the bewildered couple. "I have a feeling about you. This could be fun." He finished his retreat through the bellowing doors.

*   *   *

Here follows the tale of Oliver, a young-at-heart who plays a vital role in this story: Oliver was the little boy who sat in his backyard and watched the children play at the school behind his house. The children would throw balls and catch them. They would jump on each other. Sometimes they would hit each other, and every day Oliver wondered what it would be like to join them on their side of the tall fence, which kept him away from all their play. Oliver only played on his side of the fence with his friends the ghost man, mean man and the flying dog. Sometimes they would take him to see the talking kitty. Together they would dig holes and make mud sandwiches and they would laugh whenever they tried to eat one. All that Oliver knew was in his backyard, at the school with laughing children and in the secret clubhouse.

Oliver often cried as he leaned against the shiny gate, which a rusty chain held together. The gate led right into the exciting schoolyard. He could have probably gotten past it if he wanted, but momma said he had to stay at home because he was too big to play with the other children. More than anything, he wished that he were on the other side having fun with the other kids. To make sure everyone knew he was angry that he couldn't play with the other kids, some his own age, he stood by the fence and made little bonging sounds with his head and the fence posts. He wished that he could push his entire cage over. Children came and went over the years. They grew, but Oliver never did, and every day he sat in his back yard playing by himself or pounding his head against the metal poles enshrouded in chain link.

Once, a little girl appeared. Some of the other girls pushed her around on her first day of school and most days after that. She had thick glasses, metal teeth and wore brown ugly dresses. She had just run away from the mean girls and was leaning against Oliver's fence when he found her and knelt down behind her to see if she was all right. Startled, she turned and met Oliver face to face. He smiled at her to show her he was friendly, but she stepped away slowly and ran away crying. She never came near him again.

And so, Oliver never thought he would make any friends.

But one day, while Oliver was playing, a ball landed near him, not on the other side of the fence, where the other children played, but in one of his flowerbeds, for he eventually gave up mud sandwiches and learned how to grow flowers. He stared at the ball, wondering how such a glorious thing came to fall in his yard. He was just about to pick it up when he heard the most beautiful voice that ever spoke to him.

"Mister?"

Oliver turned, or rather jumped, at the sound. He stared at her. She was unlike the other children. She was nicer when she spoke to him. She wore blue overalls curled up at the bottoms and was barefoot. Her round face was freckled and straight, dark brown hair drooped down the sides of her head. Standing with her hands in her pockets, she shied away from the fence more than she shied away from Oliver.

"I accidentally kicked my ball into your yard, big kid." She stepped toward the fence. "Can I have it back, please?"

Oliver cautiously gripped the red ball between his fingers, carefully examining the small yellow star printed on the face and some squiggly lines in black. He carried the ball to the fence and held it out to the girl.

"You'll have to throw it over," the girl said politely. "It won't fit through the holes."

Oliver looked down to the gate, rusted now, like the chains and the padlock

52

that had been there since he was little like the girl who stood on the other side of the fence.

"It's okay, you can throw it over to me."

"No," Oliver replied.

"Why not?"

"Because the ball could get hurt."

"You can't hurt a ball, silly." The little girl started to laugh. "It's just a ball."

"Don't laugh at me," Oliver said.

"But you can't hurt a ball."

"Don't laugh." With that, Oliver hurled the ball toward the chain link fence, which, upon being struck, screamed out in a metallic pain and echoed through the tall posts. Oliver sat in his garden with his back to the fence and began to cry. Little kids were always so mean to him and he had no friends. Every day he watched children play and laugh with each other, and all Oliver had were his beautiful flowers and a dog that didn't come around to talk to him anymore.

"Mister," The girl said, poking Oliver in the shoulder with her gentle and petite finger. "I'm sorry. I didn't mean to make you cry."

Oliver pretended he couldn't hear her, but he really could.

"Please don't cry, mister big kid."

Oliver closed his eyes tight and wished the little girl would go away like all the other bad dreams that he wanted to go away.

"Do you want to play ball with me?"

He stopped crying. He didn't want to stop crying. He wanted to be sad. He wanted to make bonging sounds. He was good at it, but had he heard her correctly? She asked him to play. No one ever asked him to play. He looked back and the child was smiling at him, not the mean smiling that some children had done before they poked him with a stick to see if he was real.

Over the years, she got bigger and talked to him from across the fence almost every day. But, one time, the school bell rang and she left forever. Oliver knew the day was coming that she would soon leave. All the children left after a while. He didn't want it to happen to her. The next day, he started missing her.

More years passed. For some reason, Oliver's mother played sleep and never came home, but Man came to visit him and put a piece of paper into his hands. He told Oliver that he had a lot of money now. Oliver let Man tell another man to make more money with some of the money he suddenly got. All the while Oliver planted flowers in his backyard.

One day he was planting and he heard a voice.

"Hello, Oliver." Oliver turned and saw the most beautiful woman he had ever seen. She had long brown hair and wore a long brown skirt and a yellow blouse. She smiled at him and at once Oliver recognized the little girl from so long ago, but she wasn't little anymore.

He stood with a flower in his hand and smiled back. He too was different now. His yard was green and plastered with flowerbeds and rose bushes. "You came back."

"I teach here now Oliver," his friend said.

"You leaved."

"I'm not leaving for a long time."

The woman came to visit him every day, just as she had when she was smaller and discussed flowers and memories she shared with Oliver. She taught him to read and she let children help her. Sometimes they'd come out with big blocks with letters on them and help Oliver sound out words. He fell in love with his old friend. She was so nice to him.

One day, Oliver and the woman were talking and a group of children in the playground started screaming. A mean dog had attacked a small group of children and hurt one of the little ones. Oliver's friend ran to help the hurt child. She reached the dog and kicked it away. The dog quickly turned on her. Oliver saw blood on his best friend's face as she fell and screamed his name. The old rusty lock snapped into pieces as Oliver pulled the old gate open. He ran for the woman first but saw the dog charging for another child. Oliver kicked the dog hard in the stomach and the dog turned on Oliver, as it had done to his friend, but Oliver punched the dog away.

The teacher crawled to her knees and helped the injured child get as far away from the maniacal creature as she could. Seeing this, the creature lunged at the woman, caught her leg and threw her on her head. It leapt for her again, but Oliver met it with a blow to its crown from his large hard fist.

The angry dog had had it with Oliver. It regained its footing and took stance to fight, to kill Oliver. It leapt at Oliver, fought him and lost. As the dog dragged itself away, Oliver took his old friend in his arms and spoke to her for the last time before she slipped out of consciousness. She slept for many months after that and he stayed by her side at the secret clubhouse where his friends took care of her until she awoke. After that, she married him and began to teach again, but the wounds to her head caused her pain throughout her life. When she was thirty-eight years old, she died because of her injuries. Oliver buried her in his backyard by the fence where they first met. Years later, he purchased the school and all of its property. Oliver tore the school down and turned the land into a cemetery where his beloved could sleep with beauty all around, and he could care for the flowers of her gardens.

*   *   *

Josh joined his family and his friends on the front lawn of Oliver's Eden. They shared looks that needed no explanation.

"Let's go home," Josh said taking Natalie's hand. They ignored Barbara's grimace.

"She should be happy here," Stan remarked putting his arm around his wife and guiding her with the rest of the procession from the cemetery.

"So should Richard," Barbara replied.

For a moment, Josh had forgotten that Stan not only lost a daughter, but also a brother. The only brother he had known all of his life. And Josh lost his only uncle.

Cracey had entered the ground first while a neighbor who had tended her a few times sang a hymn. After the funeral proceeded from the cathedral, the tears began to flow from almost everyone in attendance. Barbara spent most of her tears during the past few days, so she cried the least.

After Cracey's golden brown casket disappeared into the ground, Richard became the target of the final eulogies. Officers in dress blues honored him with a twenty-one gun salute. Bagpipes played. A bugler honored the police chief with Taps. One officer released a crate of doves into the air. A police helicopter flew overhead. A man in police dress sang Amazing Grace. The mayor of Plattsville, dressed in his finest black suit and striped tie, sat between his wife and Stan and scowled at the lowering of the second casket into the ground.

In the back of the large lake of people, stood a lone man dressed in a brown suit, sunglasses and a dress hat wide enough to hide any identifying marks. The wrap around his broken ribs forced him to stand rigid. His breaths were painful and shallow. He wanted to salute as Richard's remains disappeared from his view, but the pain stopped him and he didn't want to draw attention to himself from the other officers. He stood quietly. No other officer would have wanted to be around him.

His superiors spent too many hours with vicious questions and didn't believe a word he had said about the events leading to Richard's death. No one believed him. Saying that Bricktain had been simply relieved of duty would be a kind way to describe how others treated him. A screaming mayor took his badge with no regard for how many of Bricktain's peers watched.

55

Bricktain walked to his car without aid from anyone to protect him from the insults and items other officers and staff threw and spit at him. No longer having the privilege of his patrol car, he had to walk home. Along the way, a few patrol vehicles drove past and kept a close angry eye on him, looking for any reason to harass him.

The worst blow came from all the comments and news stories run about the incident that put him in an unfavorable light with the members of his community. That's when the phone calls began, and people started throwing bricks through his window. His priest called him to pray for forgiveness.

He disappeared quickly before the funeral let out and the people began to disperse. He waited across the street of the funeral home for the right time to approach Stan and Barbara. As the group made their way across the front lawn, he made his move.

"Mr. and Mrs. Revlon," he said.

Josh's small group halted and gathered around Bricktain.

"You were relieved of duty, Officer Morris," Barbara observed.

"Yes ma'am." Bricktain reluctantly removed his sunglasses but left his hat in place while he eyed a few officers in the distance. "I was relieved of duty."

"What are you doing here," Stan asked with less hospitality than his wife offered.

"I just wanted to apologize for your loss."

Natalie wrapped her arms around Josh, trying to restrain him. Another girl in the group also clamped onto him, and a young man stepped between him and the ex-cop. Dustin helped Barbara hold Stan.

"You killed my family," Stan cried, swinging at the officer through Dustin. Dustin toppled back under the strength of Josh's father and landed on his back. Stan launched a blow for Bricktain, but his wife smacked his aim off.

"No Stan," Barbara cried. "You know it wasn't him."

"He left her in the trunk to die," Stan returned sharply.

"No."

"I swear I didn't know," Bricktain replied standing and stepping away from the posse holding Josh at bay. "I'm sorry, I shouldn't have come."

"You got that right," Dustin agreed just in time to see Josh break away from Natalie and the others. He reared back and threw his shoulder into Josh, knocking him to the ground. "Just stay down, Josh."

"You should go, Mr. Morris," Barbara urged. Stan and Josh greeted her with foul and bewildered looks. "I don't know if we can hold back everyone."

Bricktain followed Barbara's quick glance to the several approaching officers who obviously recognized him. He jolted away from the small group

56

of family and friends, and officers in unfriendly blue uniforms quickly gave chase.

"Pray he gets away," Barbara muttered, again greeted by awkward looks. "Don't blame him. A dog took Cracey. I saw it." She suddenly stopped and her eyes narrowed. Her finger rose and pointed out across the lawn. "That dog."

There it was, a golden cocker spaniel. It sat on the curb of the road as a bird perched on a tree limb. It stared in the direction of Josh's group.

"You sure," Dustin asked.

"That's the dog," Barbara spat out.

Josh got to his feet. "Let's go get it, Dust."

No sooner had the words left Josh's mouth than an old white pickup truck with rust spots and bald tires pulled up alongside the dog. A driver inside the truck leaned out the window.

"That's the old man from the chapel," Natalie said.

"That old man," Stand asked. "That's Jasper Zheeghan. He's harmless."

"Get in," Jasper yelled.

The cocker spaniel leapt into the back of the truck a moment before the truck sputtered and pulled away from the curb, leaving a black cloud of taunting smoke.

Barbara toppled. Stan moved quickly to catch her and laid her on the thick grass. Barbara's face was pale and thin, even her makeup couldn't hide the dark lines under her eyes from the lack of sleep and troubled mind.

"I have to get her out of the sun," Stan said repositioning his stance. He lifted Barbara. "I'm going to take her inside the funeral home. Get that dog."

"But Mom," Josh replied.

"I want that dog," Stan said. "I can take care of your mother."

"You sure," Josh asked.

"Yeah," Stan replied. "I think it's time we start taking care of this. Take your mom's station wagon, it has more room, and get the dog." Before Josh could argue any further, Stan was on his way toward the funeral home with Barbara draped in his arms. Two stragglers caught sight of Stan and rushed to help him.

*　　　*　　　*

Natalie's baby brother Nick refused to get lost and, instead of finding his own pack of friends, found he got along quite well with his sister's. Nick was eighteen, a senior in high school, in a Capoeira club and smart, even though he didn't realize it. He stood an inch or two under six feet and he liked to wear loose clothes. Mostly, he wore them because he didn't have any sense of style, which would explain the blue suit and orange plaid tie you see him wearing now for the funeral. That said, he was also self-conscious about his appearance. He worked out and it showed in the ring, but he used loose fitting clothes to hide his physique in normal settings. He had wavy auburn hair, which he thought was thick and gnarly. He had friends his own age, and once preferred to be in their company, but he had gotten used to this older group of friends. Cadence was the biggest reason he hung out with them, although he'd never admit to this fact.

Cadence hid her wealth well. She was also frugal and wise when it came to spending. She was a junior in college at twenty-two, studying art and theater. The summer following her high school graduation, her father died in a piece of farm machinery. A car accident took her mother a few years earlier. Now Cadence owned her father's successful farm. She hired a foreman to run it and let his family live in her parents' house as part of his salary. She lived in the two-room guest cottage behind the larger house, feeling the size suited her more and gave her more privacy. It was also less intimidating on some of her friends. There were truly people in the world who treated wealthy friends for better or worse and Cadence hated it. But that's not why Nick liked her.

Nick thought Cadence was beautiful. She was shorter than he was. Her dark, red hair streaked with blonde and flowed down her back like a rippling waterfall. Her dress was always stunning, slender, and casual, yet almost professional. She wasn't fond of wearing dresses. Today she wore yellow slacks and a suit with a white blouse buttoning almost to the neckline where she wore a thin silver necklace with a turquoise turtle. A small straight nose held up a small set of black rim sunglasses on her delicate, narrow face. Occasionally, she would pull them down to stare at Nick with her sparkling brown eyes for one of his stupid comments, and he liked it.

From time to time, a smile with perfect teeth brightened her face even more. When something struck her as amusing, her mouth would twitch on the left side forming a crooked half-smile. Nick especially loved to watch her when she talked about art. She was passionate about chalk drawing and even more so about drizzled paint. It all seemed like crap to Nick, but Cadence made any topic she spoke about holy. In secret, Nick saw as many of Cadence's stage performances as he could. She was strong on stage, not quite as some she'd worked with, but she held Nick's attention. Unfortunately, Nick couldn't hold hers. To Cadence, Nick was only her best friend's little brother.

"I'll call my dad," Dustin said taking out a cell phone while at the same time tearing off his maroon and black tie. "After we get the dog, we can take it to him to put it to sleep."

Josh and his friends piled into the station wagon—he and Natalie sat in the front and the others sat in the back. Nick found himself sandwiched between Cadence and Dustin. In a moment, the car drove off towards Jasper's house. Josh would have followed the old man all the way to hell if he had to.

"I've never been out that way," Nick said trying to get his mind off the fact he was pressed against Cadence and that her scent, in this confined space, was especially intoxicating. Not that he minded, but he was feeling nervous, and when he got nervous, he sweat, and he didn't want to sweat on Cadence

"Never," Josh asked. He thought it was every young person's duty to roam the dead lands in hopes of digging up one of the mythical ghosts and legends.

"I've never been there."

"Not even to cuddle cove," Cadence taunted Nick. She liked to taunt Nick.

"Are you kidding," Natalie answered, knowing without looking that her baby brother was blushing. She knew Cadence was baiting Nick for embarrassment. Natalie learned how to save Nick without showing she was rescuing him. "If mom ever found out that he went into the dead lands, let alone the woods beyond it, Nick would have died a young age."

"Not even to Plattsville woods," Dustin asked pulling himself from his cell phone for an instant. He eyed Nick as though he were some sort of poor soul.

"Don't worry about it, Nick," Josh said. "A lot of people haven't been out to cuddle cove."

"That's true Nick," Cadence said while rubbing Nick's knee in contempt. "A lot of people haven't. Maybe someday though, huh?"

Natalie turned abruptly and glared at her best friend.

"Your brother's so cute when he blushes," Cadence cooed.

Nick stared past Cadence and out her window. Plattsville disappeared. He stared toward the dead lands knowing that somewhere beyond them were the Shallow Woods. He thought about some of the stories he'd heard where campers disappeared altogether. He couldn't remember how many search parties had been called off because of other rescuers getting lost. The Shallows were that dangerous.

"Is it true about the cliffs," Nick asked. "I heard there are cliffs in the woods that drop into the earth for a hundred feet or so," Nick said.

"It's more of a gully really," Dustin replied, as he slid his phone into the pocket of his suit. "And it's more treacherous than any cliff."

"How do you know," Nick asked.

"I've been there," Dustin explained. "When I was younger, my dad took me camping."

"You camp?"

"Not anymore."

"What about the cliffs," Nick asked. "Do they drop as far as they say?"

"I told you they're not really cliffs. They're shale"

"Shale?" Cadence's eyes perked at the word.

"It's weak rock and you can't climb it. It breaks off in slivers and falls. Sometimes, if you're lucky, you might find a trusty handhold to support your weight, but good luck finding enough of them to climb out on."

"How big of a drop is it?"

"It's not really a drop."

"How? Not a drop?" Cadence found herself as interested as Nick was.

"It's more like a thousand-foot slide, and the farther down you go the denser the shale becomes. The problem is, if you fall, the shale eventually swallows you up and buries you. Kind of like a rocky, painful quicksand."

"I couldn't stand to be buried alive," Nick said. He made a nervous shift in his seat when he realized Cadence was actually listening to him.

"How did you and your dad survive camping out there?" Natalie joined the conversation. "I heard it's a maze."

"We got lost," Dustin answered and, this time, he turned to look out his window and watched the dead lands begin to overtake the houses. "I honestly don't know how we got out, but we actually stumbled onto the shale cliffs and if we hadn't taken rope with us to tie off to the trees, my dad wouldn't have been able to pull me out after I stumbled in. Rock just kept coming on top of me until my dad told me to stop squirming, but you know little boys. Somehow he managed to get me out."

"Were the woods as big as everyone says," Nick asked.

"I don't know." When Dustin turned back, his face had become pale. "But you'll never find me going in there again to find out. The trees and vine are so thick in some areas that you just get tangled up and almost can't move. I venture to think it's worse than quick sand."

The old farmhouse appeared out of the distance and slowly drew near. Josh pulled the station wagon to the side of the dirt road and parked in front of the house. It was three stories tall with two rows of windows above a covered porch and was white, except for sections where old brown and yellow broke through chipped paint. An old, wooden screen door sat crooked on the front of the house, unable to shut all the way. A long bench swing hung by a thin chain at one end of the porch. The white pickup truck parked to the side in a patch of tall grass.

60

The yard was large. The grass was brown. In fact, the grass was barely alive. The back yard appeared flat. The Shallow Woods lined the distance like fuzz. On the left of the house, green orchards sprouted and rose up the hill toward the junkyard road. Most of the fruit had fallen by now, but a few yellow pears and a few red apples dangled from branches. In an open section of the yard just to the side of the house was a freshly tilled patch of dirt. The yard didn't have a fence of any sort, but a cold, black, steel archway loomed over the four stone steps leading up into it.

Josh threw his dress coat around the backrest of the driver's seat. "Nata," he said. "We'll get the dog. Why don't you drive?"

"Don't you think we should call the police?" Nick asked leaning uncomfortably in his seat. "We can get arrested if we just steal his dog."

Josh's eyes narrowed upon Nick. "Yeah, we tried that already."

Natalie crawled behind the steering wheel as the rest of the car emptied.

"No one's going to blame you if you don't want to be here, Nick," Dustin said over the roof of the station wagon. He dropped the jacket of his suit into the back seat. "Just open the back hatch and wait for us, if you want to."

"No," Nick returned quickly. "Let Cadence get the hatch. I'm bigger, you'll need me."

Cadence smiled at the big dumb jock, who was sometimes intelligent, just not now. She threw her shin at the back of Nick's leg. Nick fumbled to the ground and watched Cadence disappear around the front of the car.

"Get the hatch, Nick," Cadence said. "And don't either of you guys open your mouths. Guys always mess things up. Let me do the talking."

By the time Nick was on his feet again and brushing off his blue dress pants, Josh, Cadence and Dustin were already climbing the small staircase into Jasper's yard.

Jasper, as it happened, was standing beneath a yellowing pear tree. He looked up into it. At first, he appeared to be shaking his walking stick at the tree. Or was he pointing at it? As the three friends approached, they could hear him yelling and was indeed pointing to something within the tree.

"No," He stammered. "And stop looking at me like I'm some sort of a joke. Now you get over there and you do what I told you to do when I told you to do it, and do it when I say do it."

Cadence approached the old man and the tree.

"Sir?" Cadence stopped a little more than arm's length from the old man.

"Now," Jasper cried. "Now. Now!"

Plop!

Cadence watched a yellow pear fall before her and splatter at her feet.

"You think this is funny," Jasper fumed at the tree. "It's not that hard. Watch. I'll do it." In a flash, Jasper smacked the length of his walking stick over the crown of Cadence's head. As Cadence grabbed her head, she caught a glimpse of Nick stepping away from the car with an upset look on his face.

What a dork, she thought.

The old man held the hook of his cane under Josh's chin.

"What are you doing in my yard," Jasper asked shoving Josh with his cane.

"We want the dog," Dustin said.

"What dog," Jasper asked.

"The one you had with you at the funeral," Dustin continued.

"Over my dead body." Jasper stepped away. "Shamus!"

All three friends flinched at the shriek from above their heads as a brown creature leapt from the yellow leaves and landed on Dustin's head. Dustin contorted into awkward positions, reaching at the figure of a small monkey, which was scratching and clawing at Dustin's face. The monkey's mouth opened wide and shoved its sharp teeth out the front of its face. Dustin tried to grab the monkey, but it swung around the back of his head and started pulling his hair and smacking his ears.

Jasper laughed, especially when Josh tried to help. He didn't appear to be prepared to let the stupid guest off as easily. Wherever Josh stepped, the cane managed to keep hooking Josh back. Cadence cuffed the monkey around the neck and flung him at the old man. Jasper's cane fell from Josh's neck as a ball of brown fur knocked it away.

"The dog," Cadence scowled.

The monkey scampered up the old man's arm and to his shoulder where he quickly launched himself at Cadence. This time Josh caught the monkey by the arm. Cadence grabbed it by the scruff of its neck again and pulled the monkey from Josh's grasp.

Dustin felt the sting from the scratches on his face. "Guys."

The growling began. Three dogs appeared: a small brown poodle with long hair, a black lab, and a cocker spaniel.

"You come into my yard and demand something out of me," Jasper asked returning his walking stick to the ground to hold his weight.

"The dog," Josh demanded pretending to ignore the approaching creatures.

"You're in no position to—

"The dog," Cadence ordered. She wrapped a hand around the monkey's throat. "Or the monkey."

Jasper's eyes ignited with hatred, but suddenly smirked. "You don't have it in you."

62

"I hate monkeys," Cadence returned sharply.

Jasper's eyes widened as he watched his pet struggle for breath as it dangled by its neck from Cadence's hand. He scratched at her wrists and arms, but Cadence held her grip. The dogs charged.

"Stop," Jasper cried, stepping in front of the poodle, which happened to be close enough to attack now. "Everyone stop."

The dogs halted, and the monkey began to breathe.

"Gin," Jasper called. "Come here."

The cocker spaniel ran to the old man's side. "These people are here to take you with them."

The golden dog bared it teeth and growled at the group of friends.

"Get Shamus," Jasper said.

The cocker spaniel leapt for Cadence, but Dustin swung a large stone down upon its head. The dog whimpered as it fell to the ground unconscious.

"Give us one," Dustin said. "Or animal control takes them all before the day's over."

"You're asking for trouble," Jasper said.

"That includes the monkey."

"Take the dog," Jasper said. "Let the monkey go."

Cadence set the monkey on the ground and kicked it before he could scamper back to Jasper's shoulder. Josh scooped up the unconscious cocker spaniel and started back for the car where he dropped the animal in the back storage section.

Dustin met Nick at the back hatch of the station wagon. He dropped the stone into Nick's hand. "Ride with it. If it wakes up, hit him."

"That could kill him," Nick argued.

"He's dead anyway." Dustin climbed in the back seat of the car.

Nick climbed into the back storage area where the cocker spaniel lay. He didn't want to, but he would crack the animal's head open with the rock should it prove not to be friendly if it woke on him. Josh dropped into the passenger seat as did Cadence. Natalie drove.

"How fast are you driving, sis," Nick asked not long after the car pulled away from Jasper's house.

"About thirty-five," replied Natalie and was about to ask why when she could see the reasons in her rearview mirror. A cloud of dust grew behind the car from the rear tires. At first, all she could see were shadows in the dust, but a black head appeared from within it and disappeared again.

"They're chasing us," Nick announced.

A brown face appeared at the window, only for a moment, but it glared at

Nick long enough to frighten him. The poodle left and bounced back into view, this time clawing at the glass as if trying to dig through the window. It got in only a few quick swipes before falling away.

Nick drew back startled. "What's up with this dog?"

The poodle appeared again and feebly scratched before leaving view again.

"That's right," Nick said. "Can't dig through glass, can ya?"

The black face of the Lab was suddenly in the rear window and barked loud enough that everyone in the car jumped, except Natalie who took the bark as a cue to drive faster. The Lab dropped and jumped back up to the window and slammed its head into the pane of glass. The glass crackled with lines as if a spider had woven a web into it. The Lab dropped down, bounced back up and hit the glass with its head once more and glass splinters flew into the car. The poodle also was suddenly in the window again trying to pull itself inside. Natalie jerked the car violently and the poodle fell out.

The dirt road improved into deteriorating asphalt and the cloud of dirt road dust disappeared. The two animals emerged from the cloud and managed to keep pace with Natalie's driving, which was now traveling at almost sixty miles per hour. The brown poodle jumped for the car and stayed in the air too long for Nick's comfort.

"Go faster," He cried.

"I'm doing sixty-five," Natalie replied.

"Well, they're doing sixty-six then," Nick said.

The car bounced over a pothole and the cocker spaniel's body shifted with the movement.

"If this thing wakes up, do we really want it in here with us," Nick asked.

"It's only a dog," Cadence said. "The ability to run doesn't make them scary."

The station wagon jerked and Nick found himself leaning out the window to see the poodle clenching the rear bumper in its jaws. Nick pulled back just as the Lab ran right up the poodle's back and leapt onto the car roof.

"It's on us," Nick yelled.

It felt as if the front of the car lifted off the ground. Two black legs dropped over the back of the car as the Lab struggled to stay on the roof. Meanwhile, the poodle snapped its head to the side, broke the rear bumper from the car and tossed the silver object to the side of the road. The car jerked.

"It just tore off our bumper," Nick said. He wasn't sure if he believed it, he wasn't sure if he saw it and he really wasn't sure if he was speaking anymore. The black feet crawled back onto the roof as the poodle's face flashed in the back window again. Its head bobbed behind the vehicle. The poodle began pulling itself into the back cargo area of the station wagon. Nick punched the side of the poodle's head and the poodle fell away once more. "Drive."

"Shut up." Natalie cried trying to see through the spider web that had now appeared in the windshield. The road had become a blur, she couldn't see very well beyond the web or the black canine hanging onto the hood of the car with every wild swerve she threw his way. Natalie swerved the car and the labrador continued to hold onto the hood, clenching his nails into the steel skin. It yelled at Natalie. When she stopped swerving the car, the Lab began striking the windshield with its paws and head. The spider web grew thick and white.

"Stop swerving, Nata," Cadence instructed.

"Have you lost your mind?"

"No. Take off your shoes, Dustin," Cadence ordered already in the process of taking off hers.

"What?" Dustin asked just as Cadence rolled down her window and began climbing out of the car. Dustin removed his shoes and followed the same suit with his window.

"This thing better not wake up," Nick cried.

"Shut up," Everyone cried back. Everyone left in the car, that is.

Cadence and Dustin now sat halfway out the back passenger windows of the speeding vehicle, which had slowed from all the swerving.

"Go faster," Nick cried after the poodle leapt up once more and punched a small clump of glass left in the panel into the jock's face.

Natalie pressed on the accelerator. She watched a black shoe pound the front of the car and ricochet into Josh's side of the windshield. Another shoe struck and the Lab caught it and tossed it to the side just as two more shoes struck the creature at the same time, one in the head and one on its arm. The Lab let go of the hood.

"Stop," Josh yelled.

Natalie stomped on the brake pedal and the labrador slipped off the hood. Dustin and Cadence both cried out. Unlike Cadence, though, Dustin hadn't been smart enough to hold onto the luggage rack on the roof. Josh managed to grab Dustin's pants and hold him in place. At the same time, he watched Nick unleash the stone he'd been given to beat the cocker spaniel with, hurling it through the back window directly into the poodle's face. The poodle fell and suddenly appeared in the window again and when it did, it hurled the same stone back into the car, narrowly missing Nick, Dustin and Josh. It bounced off the back of Natalie's seat. Nick let out some bizarre high school spirit-like war cry, grabbed the poodle by the head and slammed it into the car ceiling before throwing it out the back window. Nick mouthed the next word, but

Josh was the one who actually yelled, "Drive."

Cadence climbed back in through the window and helped Josh hold Dustin.

The Lab tried to dodge the station wagon, but the car was too quick. The station wagon struck the dog, flipping it near the front driver's side tire, before it drove over the animal.

The Lab stood and quickly scampered away.

"Stop the car," Dustin called from outside of the car.

"The poodle," Nick countered. "Don't stop."

"The poodle's down, whatever you did, it's lying on the road," Cadence replied.

Natalie stopped the car.

"Let me go." Dustin pulled himself through the window and ran up the side of the car past Natalie's window. He hunched down by the front tire. Nick watched for the dogs to return. The poodle rested lifeless on the road in the distance, the Lab was nowhere to be seen and Nick commented that the cocker spaniel began to breathe a little bit differently. Josh stepped out of the car and met Dustin at the front. Dustin's head was buried beneath the wheel well.

"Something got caught in here," said Dustin.

"You sure?"

"I watched it."

"What was it?" Josh knelt and slid his head under on the other side of the tire.

"Well, let me put it this way," Dustin explained. "As you are aware, dogs have four legs usually."

"Thank you for pointing out the obvious to me. I've seen a few of them."

Dustin pulled himself out from beneath the front of the car bringing something with him. "Ever see a dog with a leg like this?"

From beneath the wheel, Dustin produced the bloody arm and hand of a human.

5 ~ Things That Go Bump

The tweezers were long and thin and greased in blood. The pointed tips lifted a flap of outer skin before prodding around inside the mess of purple, soft tissue. The prongs leaned back and forth, twisted around and opened a hair's width. The latex covered hand pinched them tight again. Slowly and carefully, they withdrew a red jagged block of glass from Josh's wrist. Eric dropped the red chunk into a metal bowl. The red glass echoed through the metallic room. The instrument returned to the gaping wound and drilled again into the depths of crimson and flesh.

Eric returned on Josh's palm. He stirred the tweezers around a bit more before locking onto another hidden gem. "I think that's the last of it."

"Thanks, Dad," Dustin replied. He tightened a makeshift rope made of towels to a steel operating table. The rope wrapped around one of the hindquarters of the incapacitated cocker spaniel and held it to one corner of the table. Other ropes tied the front paws to other corners. He laid tight on the table in a sprawled out fashion. Other ropes secured the dog, belly down, around the hips and just below the shoulder blades. A noose encircled the cocker spaniel's neck and tied to the upper table edge.

"Bit off the bumper of your car, huh," Eric asked.

"My mom's car," Josh replied.

The dog's eyes scanned the yellow room, lit by fluorescent lights in white fixtures dangling from a tile ceiling. One side of the room held two tables for patients. Pictures of heartworms, fleas, medicines and bad animal teeth decorated the walls. One of the longer walls was filled with high and low steel counters and cabinets. A sink set in the center of them as a cleaning station for animals. The opposite wall held a plain, brown metal door and a small metal waste can. Josh sat on one of the operating tables while the veterinarian worked on him. Dustin stood with the other metal table and its prisoner in the center of the room near the sink.

"How am I supposed to explain this if someone walks in," Eric asked. "You know, I could lose my license?"

"Natalie, Nick and Cadence are watching the door," Josh tried to reassure, wincing as the tweezers continued to prod into his arm.

"Good for them." Eric yanked out another piece of bloodstained glass.

"They won't let anyone in. Besides, aren't you closed?"

"I shouldn't even be working on you." Eric dropped the tweezers on a tray and returned to Josh's arm with a brown bottle and white swabs. "I could go to jail."

"I doubt your friend is going to sue you for working on his son, Dad." Dustin slipped into a chair.

"He better not." Eric tossed a white bottle cap to the side and let it ricochet around the counter top. "I'll put the glass back in." He wet some swabs with the contents of the brown bottle and stopped short from contacting Josh's arm. "Sorry, but I'm not used to having people as patients. You okay?"

"It's not so bad," Josh lied. His pale face, lined with pain, told a different story. Sweat covered Josh's forehead.

"This'll hurt, but it'll numb it long enough for me to put in some stitches." Eric moved quickly and applied the soaked swabs to Josh's hand and arm. He started cleaning the blood away while, at the same time, painting Josh's injury and surrounding flesh a golden brown color.

Eric looked a lot like his son. His hair was the same color, but thinner. His cheekbones held the same depth and sharpness. His nose had the same curves. Even their eyes were as deep and with the same color. However, Eric didn't need glasses like Dustin. Even their smiles were similar. Eric was shorter than Dustin and most every other person he met. He stood just over five feet tall, and played a mean game of handball. Usually, he played handball with Stan. His and Stan's friendship went back to their college days.

After cleaning Josh's arm, Eric began to sew the gashes shut with a thick black thread on a hooked needle. "Almost done." And in a few more minutes, he was finished. A few seconds later, his latex gloves were in the trash.

"How are you feeling," Eric asked brushing a strand of hair back that he'd wanted to move for the last five minutes of his operating.

"I'm okay," Josh said examining Eric's handiwork. It was tight and clean. "Not bad for a vet."

"I'm not a rookie, you know." Eric swatted the back of Josh's head, stood up and turned serious on his son and his son's best friend. "All right, I don't know what to make of what you've told me," He said leaning back against the steel counter. "And I don't know why you would make it up."

"We didn't make it up," Dustin objected.

Eric held up his hand. Dustin fell silent.

"I know," Eric continued. "But I want you both to know that I don't think you guys approached this in the right way." He fell off into silent pondering and bit at his lip for a moment. "I don't know what else you could have done though."

"So what do we do," Josh asked.

"I don't have the capacity to run the best of tests on the arm, but I can still do something."

"And then what?"

"I can't keep the appendage around here," Eric said and kept chewing his lip. "And your dad's going to look pretty suspicious showing up to the hospital lab with a human arm in a plastic bag."

"We could put it in a brown bag," Dustin replied.

"Thanks, son," Eric replied. "But I've already taken care of it."

"What do you mean," Josh asked.

"I drained what blood I could from the arm and I took some tissue samples and I made some fingerprints," Eric explained.

"Good thinking, Dad," Dustin said.

"Yeah, thanks. Shut up. The blood and tissue we can give to your dad as is. As for the prints, if we take it to the police, maybe we can find out something from them."

"Without raising questions?"

"The police will always ask questions." Eric opened a drawer and withdrew a small syringe and a glass vial of tinted liquid. "Well, let's do what we're here to do." Eric pushed the needle into the rubber cap of the bottle, pulled the plunger on the syringe and watched the liquid fill the inside. He withdrew the slender needle and set the vial back in the drawer.

"Shouldn't we gas him first," Dustin asked.

"Would you let me work."

Eric stepped in front of the table. Dustin leaned against the closed door and Josh examined his new bandage a little more closely.

"That's a tad bit interesting," Eric said.

"What's that?" Josh looked up from his inspection.

"The needle won't go in," Eric said grunting. "I've never seen anything like this."

"What is it, Dad?"

Again, Eric grunted. He turned back to Dustin and Eric. "He bent my needle." He held up the syringe with a crooked needle to prove his point. "What kind of a dog did you bring me boys?" Eric moved back to the counter and dropped the syringe. He opened a cabinet and withdrew a larger syringe with a larger needle. He moved back to the dog. "Let's take a look at some of your blood." Dustin and Josh drew close and each peered over a shoulder. The needle stopped at the skin. "Come on, go in," Eric urged and finally the needle popped into the cocker spaniel's forearm.

The noose around the dog's neck snapped free from the table. The entire cart jumped off the ground and one of its wheels slammed down on Eric's foot. Eric stumbled and knocked Josh to the floor and Dustin into the door. The spaniel bit into one of the bindings around a front paw and tore it free from the table. It broke off the binding from its other front paw in the same manner. By the time Dustin regained his balance and Josh was on his feet again, Eric had leapt at the dog to restrain it. Unfortunately, the animal had managed to break the band around its shoulders.

Eric grabbed for the back of the dog's neck. The dog's head twisted and its jaws locked around Eric's wrist. Eric flipped into the air and over the table and landed hard on his back and against the wall. The dog twisted its body to reach for one of the makeshift ropes holding its hind legs. As it bit down, Josh kicked the cart and, and the creature bit into the table instead.

"It's loose," Nick cried out as he peered into the room from behind the heavy door.

"Get out," Dustin ordered.

The door slammed shut hiding Natalie's fear-struck face. Cadence, however, pressed into the room, took up the metal wastebasket next to the door, ran to the table, and struck the side of the dog's head. She leapt on the table and thrust the now-dented can over the dog's head. The dog's paws pushed to get the can off.

"Help me," Cadence cried.

"Kill it," Eric managed to choke out.

A paw struck Cadence in the gut and she lost her balance, but quickly recovered before the dog could escape the wastebasket.

Dustin and Josh both took hold of one of the escaped dog's forelegs and pulled him tight against the table once more.

"Help me get him to the sink," Cadence said struggling to keep the can over the dog's head by sitting on it. The cocker spaniel jerked violently, but Cadence managed to hold the can in place. Occasionally, she caught a glimpse of flashing teeth and she quickly adjusted her strategy to counter the dog's movements.

Dustin and Josh felt they were using all their strength to control the cocker's paws. They were relieved the animal's rear legs were still tied to the table.

"It's too strong," Josh said. Every time either he or Dustin tried to free a hand to grab the table and pull, the cocker spaniel nearly overpowered them.

"Find a different way then," Cadence's snapped. "This isn't working."

"Get off," Josh said. "We'll throw him."

70

"Okay," Dustin grunted. "Now."

Cadence flew off the table. Josh and Dustin vaulted the dog up off the table and onto its back over the front edge of the sink. The wastebasket fell off the cocker spaniel's head.

Cadence climbed onto the counter top.

"Hold him down." Cadence grabbed the sprayer nozzle from the wall mounted over the sink. The steel table, still tied to the cocker's rear legs, levered into the air and the dog's body slid off the sink to the floor, taking Josh and Dustin down with it. Cadence stayed in the sink doing her best to shield herself as the edge of the table catapulted straight at her. In the commotion, Josh lost his grip on the animal, but Dustin refused to let go. Cadence dived for the loose paw.

"I got him," She said stretching the arm out again before the animal could find a way to attack. "Take him."

Josh took the leg again. Cadence pulled the table back down and Josh and Dustin returned the animal back to the sink.

"Nick," Cadence called.

The door to the examination room opened and a frightened Nick entered.

"Stay out here, Nata," Nick said upon seeing what was happening, and shut the door again on his sister.

"Hold the table down," Cadence instructed.

Nick held the end of the table down and Cadence returned to the sink and pulled the sprayer hose from the wall.

"We're giving the dog a bath," Nick asked, stunned at the thought.

Cadence unscrewed softball-sized sprayer spout from the metal hose. She dodged the dog's head as it thrashed about and bit the air. "Can you get its head?"

With that, Dustin smashed the dog's paw he was holding against the counter top ledge. The dog stretched its head out as if to scream. Dustin drove his shoulder quickly under the dog's neck, somewhat locking the dog's head into a good position for Cadence's attack. The cocker spaniel fought even harder and nipped at Dustin's head several times, but to no avail. Cadence sat in the sink and clamped her knees around the dog's head. She thrust the hose into the dog's mouth and down its throat. She turned the water on and watched it gush like a psychotic fountain from between the dog's gums. The creature's body shook violently. Its strength suddenly tripled as it struggled for air, but so did Josh's and Dustin's when they realized the animal was almost finished. Its lungs filled with water and the dog's strength dwindled until he could fight no more and water gushed violently from his chops and rained down over the room. Cadence continued to hold the sprayer in the mouth while the others caught their breath. Finally, she turned the water off and removed the hose from the dog's mouth. Josh and Dustin threw the cocker back onto the operating table. Nick was shaking and wet. Without saying a word, he went outside with his sister.

"You boys all right," Eric asked softly crumpled on the floor.

"Winded, Dad," Dustin said

"How's the arm Josh?"

Josh realized he had managed to tear his bandages during the struggle. Fortunately, none of the new stitches had been broken. "I think it's all better now."

"Well now," Cadence said still sitting in the sink. "This can't be good."

It didn't take long to realize Cadence wasn't speaking about the dog, but about the dead man lying with his feet tied to the corners of the table.

"There's some ink in my office," Eric said without changing his position. "Print his fingers. Take them to the police if you feel you can."

"What about the body," Dustin asked.

"Your dad should see the body, Josh." Eric clenched his teeth for a moment and clamped his eyes shut. Slowly his jaw relaxed and his eyes reopened. "Burn him, Dustin. You know how. Hide anything the incinerator leaves behind."

"What about you," Josh asked. "You need a hospital."

"Call for an ambulance." Eric glanced over the room. "Lay the cart on its side and leave some water on the floor so it looks like I fell."

"We'll just take you to the hospital, Dad." Dustin took his father's arm and prepared to lift him.

"Don't move me."

"Want some pain killers first?"

"It's not that."

"Your shoulder's pretty bad."

"You can't move me."

"Dad?"

"He broke my back, boys."

72

6 – Homeward Bound

"Nata?"
Nothing.
"Nata?"
Shift.
"Oh geez, let me try." Cadence shook Natalie's shoulder. "Natalie!"
Natalie jerked awake.
Josh hunkered forward, his eyes cinched tight. "Good kick," he moaned.
"Bad aim," Cadence added. Unlike the others in the waiting room, she couldn't hold it. She started laughing.
"Oh Josh," Natalie said after realizing what she'd done. She jumped out of the uncomfortable waiting room chair. "I'm sorry." She hugged Josh's side and kissed his cheek.
"Our ride's here," Josh groaned.
"You sure you don't need to be taken to the emergency room first," Cadence replied and laughed even harder as Natalie glared at her.
"You need some ice," Stan asked smirking his concern.
"Crutches please," Josh answered.
Natalie clutched Josh tighter and almost finished apologizing a second time before she couldn't contain her laughter either. Her body shook as she laughed, and she couldn't bring herself to release her hold.
"Where's Dustin," Natalie asked upon noticing Dustin's absence.
"He's in recovery with his dad," Nick replied.
"He's staying here," Stan added. "But we're not. I'm tired, so let's go."
"Where's Mom," Josh asked.
"She's at home and not in a good mood either," Stan answered.
"Can't blame her," Natalie said. "Her wagon got trashed."
"Yeah," Stan agreed. He twirled a set of keys nervously in his fingers. "Honestly, I don't think she cares anymore."
"Don't say that," Josh replied.
"Let's go," Stan said.
The small party left the hospital. The funeral dress clothes were wrinkled and torn. Ties had been yanked off, jackets forgotten, and ripped shirts remained unkempt. Everyone piled into Stan's maroon wagon. Josh opened the front passenger door for Natalie and walked around to the other side of the

car before realizing he wasn't driving. He climbed into the back seat with Nick and Cadence.

"Please, watch out for dogs," Nick suggested. He rested his tired, heavy head against the cool door glass.

"Don't worry, we're not even going near Jasper's," Stan said while starting the car. "We're taking the canal road."

Plattsville was mostly farmland, but over time, farmers and ranchers sold to make clichéd room for new condos and houses. Some farms and ranches still stood today, most on the outskirts of the town where they didn't annoy rich snobs in the city council. These were the same rich snobs who moved into a farming community, complained about their pesticides and little by little strangled the farms into the far reaches of Plattsville's outskirts.

Plattsville was a round city. The main city was the central point. The business district was there along with the university and hospital. Residential zones surrounded all sides of the city like a clock. One main road led into and out of Plattsville and its suburbias. Beyond the north of Plattsville, nearly 80 miles of unusable jagged, stony and acidic ground stretched to the nearest small town of Applegate, an old silver mining town going bankrupt, but full of tourist attractions for anyone bored enough to travel to see them. It was like visiting the city of the world's largest hairball, which surprisingly some people actually find interesting enough to pack the family in a car for a thousand miles to see. Beyond Applegate, lies another hundred miles before the next town. The next city is a little more than sixty miles from there. To the south was forest, which stretched to the west, and a freeway, which went out of its way not to cut into any part of the forty thousand square miles of Shallow Woods, but attempted to follow the tree line instead. This freeway went eighty miles before it revealed a rest stop and another forty after that before a small gas station town appeared.

Josh and his family lived in the southeastern residential area of Plattsville. The northwest had a few similar areas and off these areas, smaller, yet richer, areas were under development, but the unusable terrain made such use nearly impossible and hardly anyone wanted to buy there. The south was mostly farmland. It was either very successful farmland, or it was unlivable. The west was the mysterious part of Plattsville holding mostly wheat farms. Three or four of them aren't wheat. One farm became Reggie's Junkyard, and another held the orchard of fruit trees for nearly a hundred years, which Jasper now controlled.

Through the middle of this area flows the Pen River, from the mountains well to the north and beyond Plattsville's borders all the way down to its

74

southern parts and into the Shallow Woods, where it supposedly disappears underground. These days, a reservoir slows the flow of this river. In the early years of Plattsville, when the entire city held only farms and small family businesses, the settlers built a canal system, which they could open and close on certain days.

The canal spanned the north side of the city and curved down around both west and east edges of the central part of the city following the borders of where old farms used to stand. They eventually gave it a concrete floor and walls. Today, the canal no longer had use ever since the construction of the reservoir and the installation of modern plumbing. The farmers preferred the canal still open, but yay for the snobs who know better than the people of their city do. They decided the canal was too dangerous for children who didn't live near it. They built another road parallel to it and did little to upkeep Canal Road. However, the canal and its tiny street still remain. The only drivers who use the canal road are commuting employees of the industrial funnel and the smart people who learned that all the red lights in the city actually make the drive to work longer than the narrow ditch road.

Stan's maroon station wagon pulled onto medical drive and began a five-minute trek north to the canal street.

"I want you kids to be careful," he said turning down the radio, some silly song by a young heart throb teenager who was discovering her fad days were disappearing and would soon be faced with having a bad marriage and a baby to redeem herself to her fans. "I have to admit I'm concerned. I'm not sure of what kind of retaliation could happen now."

"Retaliation?" Nick lifted his head. Whatever rest had once been trying to take hold of Nick's body during the long drive home, subdued. "You don't think any of those dogs could find us, do you?"

Stan drove in silence.

"Did you learn anything from the blood sample," Josh asked.

Stan was aware that all attention was now on him. "Not really."

"Great." Nick took to the familiarity of staring out the window into the cold black. Actually, he took his position of pretending to look like he was only looking out the window into the cold black. Really, he was watching Cadence. Every time the occasional streetlight passed, he caught her reflection in the window. He liked to look at Cadence. Her slender frame, the way she looked at him, even when she was teasing him, even when she thought he couldn't see the reflection of her in the window sneaking a look at him. For an instant, he caught her eyes almost staring into his own through the glass. How beautiful.

"So what do we do," Natalie asked. "It's not like we can go to the police or anything."

"Well we sort of can," Stan corrected.

"How are we supposed to do that," Josh asked.

"Morris."

"That cop," Josh said. "That guy who botched everything?"

"Yes."

"This whole thing is his fault."

"This whole thing is the dog's fault," Stan said.

"Isn't there someone, a friend of Richard's, anyone that would believe us?"

"You mean believe that the man you killed in Eric's clinic was really a dog first?"

"Guess that means no."

"I already did," Stan said. "Morris and he helped me look over the body before we incinerated it. He's trying to figure out how to check the fingerprints."

"Werewolves," Nick said.

"I think someone needs to get his head examined," Cadence replied.

"No, I don't." Nick turned to Cadence and instantly forgot the anger she had just stirred in him when his eyes met hers. "What else could it be?"

Silence.

"OK," Nick continued. "Maybe, just maybe."

"Maybe you're off your rocker," Cadence said.

"How can you say that?"

"Aren't werewolves supposed to come out at night when the moon is full, Einstein," Cadence asked.

"That's just about the dumbest thing you've ever said, nimdong." Natalie jumped into the conversation.

"Do you have a better explanation," Nick snapped.

"El Niño," Josh asked. "Maybe they have gas. Maybe the puppy chow isn't settling with them so well."

"Well this isn't good," Stan announced.

Everyone looked outside and watched as a white wall of film engulfed the slowing vehicle. The headlights reflected an almost blinding glare back into the car.

"Since when do we get fog," Natalie asked. "I mean, that is fog, right?"

Everything fell silent except for the pavement passing beneath the tires of the car.

Stan tried everything to see the road. Unlike his passengers, he had seen fog before. He knew the dangers lurking in the fog waiting for naive drivers. His high beams blinded him. His low beams weren't much better. Everything was turning too white to see. Finally, his parking lights alone offered some help. He could see the road move beneath the nose of his car. Being out on a dark road in this fog didn't add to his comfort. Somewhere to his left was the five-foot deep canal. To his right was the faint blur created from the lights of the city. He had to rely on memory, and he wasn't going to stop the car for even a moment, not after what happened with his son and his friends earlier that day.

Stay on the road, Stan thought. *As long as I can see gravel, I'm on the road.*

The minutes passed slowly and Stan's area of view to the road shrank closer to the nose of the vehicle. Stan could barely see. Natalie watched the road with him. Cadence also seemed to be entranced with the fog confining the station wagon. Could the dogs see in the fog? What would have become of her and her friends if they had fog as an obstacle earlier today?

The fog took on shapes and swirled in the gleam of the parking lights. Thick splotches of white would blend with blacker patches and turn gray. Fifteen more minutes passed. A shadowy patch crossed in front of the car. The vehicle bounced over a pothole. Another pothole and Nick hit his head in the bounce.

"Sorry," Stan apologized, feeling the sorrow of the dreary fog clasping onto his own nerves. "Bad road you know. Hopefully we stay out of the canal."

The pavement passed under. The fog encircled. The outside sounds whispered stifled silence into the car. Shadows passed and blended with each other and the fog. The mist shrouded the city lights.

And right above Cadence's head, the car's roof tore open.

7 – Case of the Munchies

Dustin stared into the belly of the machine, past his reflection and over all the price markers. Popcorn was a dollar; beef jerky, ninety cents; gum, fifty cents. This machine held snacks; ten flavors of chips and pretzels, boxed candy, wrapped candy, small cookies, big cookies, frosted cookies, frosted angel cake, chocolate cake, cupcakes, hard candy soft candy, and little round pink sour things he'd never seen before—all of it crap. Dustin jingled the change in his hand and glanced into a second machine. This one was more expensive, but sold real food; burritos, small pizzas, sandwiches and pizza pockets—if you could call that sort of food real. The 'out of order' sign on the microwave next to this machine told Dustin to keep contemplating the little round pink sour things.

He just woke up. He had dozed off for a minute, but his dad began talking to him, groggy from morphine. It was clear he was hungry. His dad wanted something, anything, just not hospital pudding. Dustin left his dad lying on the uncomfortable hospital bed. Eric's fresh, surgical scar stretched from mid-back to his hip. Stitches and staples held it together. It still wasn't certain if his dad would ever walk again. Dustin knew his dad should wait for the doctor's OK to eat, but his father asked. He wiped his eyes dry, punched in the code combination for jerky sticks, and watched the coil push a little package with two small sausages off the shelf. He took the sticks from the bottom bin and returned to his father's recovery room.

The bed was empty. The window to the room was shattered and a dark shadow quickly disappeared through it holding Dustin's father passed out over its shoulder.

Dustin yelled for security.

*   *   *

The claws appeared metallic as they peeled back more of the roof of Stan's station wagon. Nick cried out first when he caught a glimpse of green peering through the gap. The claws sliced at the roof over Cadence's head, continuing to widen the hole.

"Down, down," Josh cried, pulling Cadence as close into his own body as he could. "Get down."

A thick black paw, flared with silver curved razors, swiped for Cadence's head.

"No!" Nick threw his body on top of Cadence, blocking the blow from hitting her. "Get on the floor." He wrestled the paw under an arm and screamed even louder as he felt his skin tear. Cadence's body slid to the floor. Josh slid with her, his back against the door. Nick knelt in the back seat screaming at the monster's claw. Nick's head struck the roof of the car before the paw withdrew.

Natalie watched her brother fall with what appeared to be black needles stuck in him. Her heart jumped as she heard him cry out again. She saw the tears on his face. The silver claws reach into the back seat again, past Nick and straight for Cadence.

"Get away from her." Nick rolled onto his back and completely covered Cadence's body.

The car jerked to a halt.

"Keep going," Josh cried out smacking the back of his father's seat.

"I can't see the road," Stan snapped.

"Drive," Natalie screamed at the first sight of blood from lacerations covering her brother's arms. "Keep it straight and drive."

"I know what I'm doing." Stan's foot slammed the gas pedal to the floor. His heart raced. Shouldn't he know better?

The paw retreated from the attack on Cadence and Nick. Once again, it began widening the hole in the roof. The green eyes glared directly on Natalie. The roof of the vehicle screeched as a second set of claws dug into an undamaged section of roof.

"Stop swerving," Natalie yelled. "They just hold on."

"What is that thing," Josh asked trying to pull farther into the floor.

The claws returned inside the vehicle once again and this time retracted into the wooly coat over the monster's fingers. The thick, black paw batted Nick off Cadence and onto the seat.

Natalie reached for the black arm and quickly recoiled. Three thick hairs dug into her palm. Her hand burned. She grabbed the hairs and yanked on them. Three small, pink tears marked their places. "Quills."

The paw smacked back at Natalie and several more of the thick black quills stuck in the side of her face. Natalie caught a glimpse of horror on Cadence's face as the silver claws leapt from the black fingers once more and swiped for her even more feverishly.

"Stop it. Stop it. Stop it." Nick was over Cadence again. He caught the creature's open paw in his hands and struggled to keep it away. Natalie

79

couldn't count the number of quills sticking out from Nick's body.

"Under your seat." Stan pointed towards Natalie's seat. "My jump kit."

The claws pulled away from Nick's bleeding palms. They slashed through his left bicep. Nick grabbed at his arm and cried out.

"Leave her alone," Nick cried. He stared beyond the roof and into the green and dots that stared back into his own eyes.

Natalie fumbled with the emergency kit before finally discovering how to open it.

"The scalpel," Stan said watching the blur of gravel passing quickly under his car. "It's the long, thin package."

"I'm not moving," Nick screamed at the monster's head now trying to push down into the backseat of the car. Its face was large, its jaws wide, sharp and full of teeth that could probably destroy anything they bit. The opening in the roof was still too small for its head.

"You can't have her," Nick screamed. He grabbed the driver's seat to anchor himself. The claws retracted again and the paw grabbed Nick, trying to toss him out of the way a second time. "I'm not moving," Nick continued to scream. Suddenly, the monsters claws dug into his shoulder. "You can't have her." Bloody claws pulled away from the shoulder and the paw punched Nick's chest.

Natalie tore the plastic cover off the two-inch scalpel blade. She turned in her seat in time to watch the paw strike down on Nick's chest. The claws leapt out like switchblades, painted with crimson, and grabbed deep into Nick's chest, past cracking ribs and into his lungs. Still, at this moment, it occurred to her that her brother was all right, not because he was, but because she knew him no other way.

Pothole.

The car jumped. The surgical knife stuck into Nick's side, just below the rib cage. Natalie pushed the tears back and watched her brother wince from the jab she gave him. She heard his breath escaping through the holes around the claws imbedded in her brother's chest instead of through his lungs where he should have been able to breathe and scream. Blood trimmed his lips. He gripped the driver's seat harder and mouthed something Natalie couldn't understand. Natalie tore the scalpel from her brother's side and sliced again at the paw, which still held Nick. Quills sprinkled into the air as the scalpel sliced through the monster's wrist. Nick's body raised a little, sticking to the claws still imbedded in him, before falling away from the retreating paw. Natalie sliced again. The claws retracted. The monster shrieked in a most demonic way. The arm disappeared and the green eyes with swirling red vanished.

The car suddenly stopped.

The scalpel flew past Natalie's face and ricocheted between the dashboard and the windshield. Natalie fell back and smacked her head while Stan's face disappeared behind a yellow airbag.

*   *   *

The fog swirled around the battered station wagon. Only the car and the fog remained in the world. Beyond the vehicle was a sea of swirls and mist: thick, no stars. No sound existed, except the horrible, eerie song of the fog, sucking, swallowing, and eating all other sound that dared enter it. It had swallowed the city, it swallowed the road and it swallowed the car. This potion was concocted to dissolve any life of noise. It was a mist designed to catch the straggler's breath, thick in the lungs, able to block all strangers' screams and save them for exercise in hell. Scream, and the fog swishes in, drowns it, stretches it out, kneads it flat, pulls it apart and utterly mocks its every cause, diluting the scream with sheer and terrible silence. Like a virus, it suckles on the essence of sound to make itself stronger. It is a cunning, vile monster. It is a corrupted beast. The air was still. Only the fog breathed, and the station wagon was blind.

Click!

The rear door burst open and the fog began creeping inside to devour the sound of people struggling in the back seat.

Click!

The driver's door swung open.

Click!

Natalie's door.

The car was wedged into the canal. Its nose crumpled high against one wall of the ditch, headlights smashed to bits. Its tail end sat on the opposite ridge. It was four feet to the canal floor.

"It's still out there, Dad," Josh said.

"Sshh," Stan replied over his shoulder. He listened to Nick's wheezing lungs. "I have to try operating or he'll die."

"We should call an ambulance," Cadence said.

"If it found us at all, it wouldn't be in time," Stan said. "Natalie, try and find all the pieces to my kit."

Natalie was stunned, but she came back to reality, knowing her brother needed help. She started picking up pieces of medical equipment, now all

81

over the seats and floor, and returning them to the small plastic case.

Stan unfastened his seatbelt and slowly climbed down from the car. He stepped to the back door and reached up. "You're gonna have to hand him down to me. Hold him tight, Josh, and see if any of you can find the flashlight."

Cadence and Josh slid Nick's body towards the door. The prickly needles sticking out of Nick's flesh made it difficult to hold him, but they managed. They lowered Nick into Stan's arms. Stan stretched Nick out on the concrete canal floor. Cadence leapt from the car, followed by Josh. Natalie soon appeared with a flashlight and the medical kit, including the scalpel.

"Straighten that mess up," Stan instructed. "I can't use what I can't find." He took up the scalpel and held it out to Josh. "Find the alcohol and clean this. If that thing comes back, blind it with the rest of the alcohol."

Natalie set the silver flashlight on the ground, aiming it on Nick's body. It added very little light to the situation, but it was better than what the dim glow of the car's dome light offered. She forced herself not to look upon her wounded brother as she began organizing the contents of the medical kit for Stan.

Nick's eyes sealed shut, but bulged open again as if they were trying to pop out of his head to escape their body and pain. His hands tightened around Stan's fingers.

"The fog's clearing," Cadence said.

The canal began to empty quickly. The concrete walls appeared and the fog withdrew from around the party.

"Are we in a bubble," Natalie asked.

A bubble, in fact, had formed around the small party. The fog withdrew a small distance, but continued to swell above the canal, around its edges, and several feet away from Josh and his friends.

"Come on, Natalie," Stan snorted as he found a packet of surgical gloves. "I need this kit organized. Needles and knives here, everything heavy here. How's that knife coming ,Josh?"

"The knife won't be needed."

Natalie continued to arrange the kit for Stan, who was already tearing at Nick's clothes. Cadence and Josh sprang to their feet. Josh was now holding the flashlight and shined it around the canal to get a better feel for the surroundings. He flashed it over the wrecked car. He recognized the voice from earlier that day.

The fog continued to dissipate over the rim of the deep ditch. Cadence grabbed Josh's arm and gasped slightly. She was the first to notice the green eyes. Too many creatures lined both sides of the canal's ridge and looked down upon the small party within it. They swallowed the fog and watched the stranded group attempt to save one of their numbers. Natalie looked up and took the same frozen countenance as Stan; who didn't look up past Natalie's eyes, but instead watched down the alley to the tapping sound growing nearer.

Jasper emerged from the fog, his walking stick held tightly in his hand. The fog licked at his ankles and wrists as his body separated from the mist. The beam of the flashlight focused on his frail posture. Jasper's eyes reflected brightly. "About two hundred in all await my order to kill you." He tapped his cane against the ground and one of the beasts leapt from the top of a wall down to the aqueduct floor. Its fur flared like an angry cat. Its mass practically filled the trench and hid Jasper from view, but not his voice. "I had other plans for you tonight. Thought I could leave you a message to leave me alone."

The large black creature now towered over Stan's back and growled.

"You stay away from him." Cadence tore the flashlight from Josh's hands and threw it at the black creature.

The animal growled after the flashlight bounced off, hit the ground and stopped working.

Jasper laughed.

"Relax," Jasper said. "I want you to see something. I will not harm your friend. If you would be so kind as to move, Mr. medical man."

Stan felt the muzzle of the creature nudge his back. He had still not stopped working on his patient and hadn't noticed the black creature so near. He turned and caught his first glimpse of a set of sharp teeth.

"Your patient will not be harmed," Jasper said.

Stan moved, but only because the animal knocked him away. The creature's nose pressed carefully down upon Nick's bare chest, his blood stained dress shirt was in shambles. Natalie found the scalpel, and would have attacked with it, when the creature suddenly roared a fearsome and paralyzing bark inches from her face. The air filled with growling from above her head. She dropped the scalpel.

"Wise move," Jasper said.

Natalie knelt down next to her brother and took his hand. "It's all right," she lied. She took up the scalpel again and stared at the beast. "It will be all right, or you'll find this buried in your brain."

Again, Jasper laughed.

The dog continued to nuzzle his thick square nose against Nick's chest. It licked the blood away from the shredded skin and looked as if it was evaluating the extent of the puncture wounds in the rib cage. Fresh blood kept

83

seeping from beneath Nick's flesh. The monster licked a thick white tongue over the gashes before focusing on just one opening. It stuck the tip of its tongue against this opening over and over again. Nick screamed and tightened his grip around Natalie's hand and grabbed Stan's arms, digging his nails into Stan's flesh. The tongue folded and curled and the creature continued to use it to flicker around the wound. A section of white rib poked through the surface of the flesh. The tongue curled and stretched. It narrowed into half its original size and continued to curl and stretch and narrow until it was only a sliver of its original size, maybe even the sliver of a snake's tongue. It slithered around the wound like an angry wriggling worm and suddenly disappeared deep inside an opening. It flashed in and out rapidly. The blood stopped oozing from this and the other chest gashes. Nick continued to cry in pain. When he did stop screaming, it was only because he couldn't breathe; and taking in a new breath was torture.

The creature's eyes widened and it pummeled its head hard against the boy's chest. Nick wheezed and started breathing again. The pointy tip of the tongue poked up through one of the four other openings in Nick's chest. It was like a dying fish, flipping and twisting around. Little by little, it wormed its way back into Nick's chest and the wound sealed up behind it. The tip appeared through another of the other open holes. One by one, the lacerations disappeared, leaving trails of pinkish scars as the tongue licked at them from within Nick's body. The dog's head changed position, leaving its tongue inside Nick. Nick's chest squirmed and rolled as the tongue moved around under the skin. It was as if the flesh were on the early stages of a boiling. The broken rib disappeared beneath the flesh. This opening soon closed as well. After a few moments, the tongue slid from inside the remaining gash. The creature licked at this injury until it healed over as the others had done.

Nick found himself breathing more regularly. He clenched his sister's hand out of nervousness, as the creature's tongue attacked the claw marks over his arms and shoulders. It even cleaned the scalpel injury and began plucking quills from various places around his body. As it worked Nick over, it turned Nick's body, as it needed, to get at wounds on his back and sides. When it finished, it pulled away from Nick and rejoined a line of black dogs peering down from the tops of the canal walls.

"Do you see the power I possess," Jasper asked. He walked toward the group. The fog closed in behind him. For each monster on the wall he walked past, the breath of the creature turned into fog. As they exhaled, the fog filled the air, concealing them. "Do you understand now," He said as the fog kept close at his heels while the air remained clear before him, and around the group. "I give life and I take it away." He knelt down and placed his hand on Nick's forehead. "You may have a fever for a little while. The human body hates the dog's saliva." His callused fingers with their arthritic, bubbled knuckles felt around Nick's jaw and neck. "Your glands are already swollen. It's a side effect of the saliva, but penicillin will help clear that up and don't kiss any girls for at least a week."

"Side effect," Natalie asked.

"It's not fatal, but the penicillin will help his system flush it out. And he'll need a strong antacid within the hour."

"You tried," Nick mumbled incoherently.

"Sshh," Jasper stroked Nick's head. "Just relax. And don't worry, you won't change into anything."

"You tried to kill Cadence," Nick blurted.

"Yes." Jasper pulled himself to the top of his cane. "But you saved her, my boy. Such an act of chivalry can't go unrewarded." He smiled over Nick.

"Because we killed your dog," Nick asked.

"No, boy." Jasper laughed a little. "Dogs come and go." He turned his glance upon Cadence and his countenance turned from friendly to dangerous. "Monkeys are a different story."

Suddenly, Cadence was in the air. She stared down into the old man's eyes and gripped at his powerful hand, his fingers closing around her throat.

"I should make you feel what my Shamus felt," Jasper said. "Close off your air supply." He swung his cane with his free hand and Josh, who was embarking on an attempt to help Cadence, fell to the ground. "Watch your face turn purple and let you die, here in my hand." Another swing of the walking stick and Stan clenched his stomach and keeled. "Tend to the boy," Jasper continued, his eyes remaining on Cadence. "I don't like to hit girls." His eyes narrowed. "You hurt my monkey." He loosened his grip. "I would not spare your life tonight." He stepped back and looked down at Nick who was attempting to sit. His eyes were full of hatred for the old man. He crawled forward a step. "You owe this boy more than you owe me." He released Cadence and she fell. "I truly am sorry son. I admire you. Takes a love struck teenager to be a man." Jasper stepped back and fog suddenly filled the canal. "Sorry about your car, doc."

"What about my girl," Stan asked, finding himself running after the old man, but stopping at the sound of low growls overhead.

"Believe me," Jasper said. "She's safer with me." The fog swallowed Jasper and the sound of his walking stick.

8 – Safe Conduct

The hundred-year-old cabinet swung and smacked its outer wall, scarring the antique paint. The glass above it sang on the brink of breaking, but held its frame. Josh, Cadence and Dustin examined the contents of the tall arsenal in Richard's den.

"Well, can't say my uncle wasn't prepared," Josh said

"Do you know how to use any of this stuff?" Dustin held up a small handgun and studied it.

"Point and shoot?" Josh held a copy to the weapon in Dustin's hand.

"You're kidding, right," Cadence asked. She tore the fire arms from her friends' hands. "We'll start with something a little lighter for you two." She set the guns inside the cabinet, and lifted a long rifle off a set of hooks. "Watch me." She began a rampage of gun safety, demonstrating proper use of a gun.

"Why are we doing this," Natalie asked.

"You heard the old man," Josh answered sharply. "Cracey's not dead, and he has her."

"You don't know that."

"Then, why did he say she was safer with him," Josh asked.

Natalie studied Josh's face and finally nodded. "Then give me the Glocks and the twelve-gauge." She dug into the cabinet and took out the black guns Josh and Dustin held prior to the gun safety lesson.

"You ladies are just freaking me out a little bit too much here," Dustin said.

"Please, Dustin," Cadence replied pulling an underarm holster around herself. "I live on a ranch. I've taken Natalie shooting a lot of times."

"Does that mean you know how to shoot, Nick," Josh asked.

Nick looked up from a book he was reading. "No." He looked back down.

"He doesn't like guns," Natalie explained while digging through small drawers for ammunition and clips.

"Hercules is afraid of 'em," Dustin asked chuckling to himself.

"He doesn't like 'em," Cadence snapped.

"Oh that's just great," Dustin erupted. "When he can't wrestle with those things, he can throw his books at 'em."

"No he can't," A new voice said, intruding on the conversation.

"What are you doing here, Morris?" Josh's eyes narrowed on the police officer.

"Your parents called me," Morris walked to the gun cabinet. "Guess they thought someone with a cool head should keep you kids in line."

"And I guess you're the professional on this?"

"You need to get your hatred directed at the right place." Bricktain drove two fingers into Josh's shoulder. "Punk." He pushed the other shoulder. "You think you know the truth?" He pushed Josh. "You think the police told you what really hap—

Bricktain felt his knees buckle before he tumbled. He grabbed his knee and found himself looking up the barrel of the twelve-gauge right into Natalie's hateful quivering blue eyes. He barely noticed the other three faces peering down from around her.

"We've been friends a long time, mister," Cadence said taking Bricktain's attention away from Natalie for a moment. "I wouldn't try establishing authority here."

Josh's face appeared behind Natalie's and Natalie slowly pulled her empty weapon away. Josh held his hand down to Bricktain. Bricktain returned the gesture and groaned as he grabbed at his knee.

"Help him," Josh said dropping to his knees and pulling Bricktain's arm over his shoulder. "You been running from police all day in this much pain?"

Bricktain shook his head. "Two ribs and my knee aren't exactly happy tonight."

"How do you plan to fight, if we have to," Josh asked watching other hands help raise Bricktain to a sitting position.

"If we have to," Bricktain asked.

"Last night we were attacked."

"I heard about that."

"This morning my mother received a phone call telling her my sister's grave had been dug up. Her coffin was empty."

"I heard that too."

Josh helped Bricktain to a leather recliner. "We have a theory."

"And," Bricktain asked.

"Werewolves," Nick replied.

"I know we sound crazy," Josh continued.

"Four nights ago, I shot something, some four-legged dog thing monster," Bricktain explained. "It clobbered me and killed your uncle. Its fur sliced me open." He rolled up a sleeve to show stitched lacerations over the back of his arm. "I watched your uncle shoot that thing pointblank in the face with a shotgun. We found an axe with its edge half-melted away. There was nothing

87

left of the creature I know I saw or your uncle. Nothing sounds crazy to me, kid."

"What do you mean there was nothing left," Josh asked.

"I mean, this creature melted itself, bones, fur and all. All it left behind was a bit of mud."

"That doesn't make sense."

"I know," Bricktain said. "I've been through all of this with my superiors already, and no one believed it. I think your uncle caused more damage with the axe than with the firepower. I don't think you sound crazy, but I don't think they're werewolves."

"Why not," Nick asked.

"Well, don't werewolves only come out during full moons," Bricktain asked sort of chuckling. "I thought everyone knew that."

"We've had this discussion." This time Cadence's eyes narrowed.

Morris sat in silence.

"We've never met a werewolf," Nick replied. "And I don't think movies and fairy tales are the scholastic venue about this topic. I think the myths are wrong."

"If you think about it," Josh said. "No one knows anything about werewolves, real werewolves."

"But if you'd rather call them big, mean dog-monsters we can do that too," Dustin added.

"One thing is for sure," Josh said returning to the oak cabinet. "Werewolves or not, they obviously don't have to wait for a full moon, or night for that matter, to be a danger."

Bricktain Morris looked around the room to the angry faces and finally rested his eyes on Josh. "I'm sorry I couldn't save your uncle, kid."

"Kid," Dustin laughed to himself. "His name's Josh."

"No," Josh said without taking his eyes off Morris. "To the old, we are kids."

"Touché," Morris replied. "All right, we do it your way. What do you have in mind, Josh?"

"I don't know." Josh walked out of the room.

"You mean to tell me that you came all this way without a plan," Morris asked.

"Shush," Josh replied from the adjoining room.

"Did he just shush me," Morris asked. "We need a plan, boys and girls."

"He's thinking," Dustin explained. "Now shush."

"There's more that you kids should know."

"I swear if you call us kids one more time," Dustin snapped.

"What is it," Josh asked returning to the doorway.

Morris broke glares with Dustin and turned his attention to Josh. "I ran the prints on that hand you kids found."

Dustin opened his mouth to say something and decided that Bricktain caught his mistake by the apologetic glance he gestured to the people in the room.

"And," Josh asked.

"There's nothing."

"How did you run the prints," Cadence asked. "I was under the impression you were suspended or fired."

"It wasn't easy," Bricktain replied, subtly rubbing his knee.

"Well, there has to be something," Dustin said.

"I'm telling you, there was nothing on this guy," Bricktain continued.

"Well, no good sitting around here with nothing," Josh said. "We have to do something." he returned to the gun cabinet and began to dig through more small drawers. "Aha," He took a yellow envelope from one of the drawers and tore it open. A set of brass keys and a gold chain fell into his hand.

"What's that," Dustin asked trying to get a better view.

"My uncle showed me something once," Josh said as he moved around the back of a large desk that matched the hue of the gun cabinet. "Something he called his treasures." Josh sat down in a soft swivel chair and inspected the desk. "I used them once, and I know he kept the key with the shelter key."

"Shelter key," Bricktain asked.

"Oh, it unlocks a keypad and backup generator," Josh said as he continued to search the desk, lifting a pencil box, a desk lamp and a metal bin with memo paper in it. "There's a fallout shelter in the backyard."

"The chief liked to be prepared didn't he," Bricktain said.

"It's designed to sustain his family for an entire year," Josh replied as he pulled out the middle drawer of the desk. "He rotated the food every two years. It has oxygen recycling systems and air filtration systems, generators and solar panels that I have no idea how they're supposed to work. It has bedrooms, bathrooms, a kitchen, a dining center and living quarters with televisions and entertainment. He said he used the structural wall itself as an antenna so that he could keep up with emergency broadcasting."

"I couldn't handle being locked up that long," Cadence said. "I need recreation."

"Well," Josh said now staring at the desk. "There's a swimming pool, a bowling alley, and a fitness room. Or so I understood."

"You're telling me your uncle, with his low government pay, was wealthy enough to put that kind of equipment in his backyard," Bricktain asked.

"My uncle wasn't just a police chief. There it is." Josh lurched forward in his chair and grabbed an edge of the desk. He pulled at the desk and a section of the corner opened revealing a small console with three toggle levers and a key switch. Josh guessed and slid the smallest key into the switch and twisted it. A green light turned on inside the panel. Josh pressed a toggle and a humming sound sang from the opposite side of the room. The wall opened and a large safe door appeared. "There it is."

"Well, all you need now is the combination," Nick said.

"I know the combination." Josh stepped from behind the desk and to the safe. "It's my birthday Josh spun the dial feverishly stopping every so often at a number. He pulled the handle and nothing. "Weird."

"Sure it's your birthday, kid," Morris asked and realized from the unfriendly glances that he needed to redeem himself. "Sorry."

Josh tried again, nothing.

"Guess he changed it," Dustin said. "You could try a hammer, maybe."

"Try Cracey's birthday," Natalie suggested.

Josh began spinning the dial once more and pulled on the handle. This time, it opened.

"Nice call." Josh reached inside the safe and hefted out a red cedar box. He set it down hard on the desk, and cringed. "I scratched my uncle's desk." He fumbled with the set of keys once more and slid one into a keyhole. He lifted a latch and folded over a wide lid.

Yellow silk lined the inside of the box. Flowery impressions carved into the bottom exterior of the wooden case. Odd-shaped objects rested within the box. Josh inspected the outside of the trunk a little further and finally found a small drawer which he pulled open and withdrew a pair of thin black gloves.

"What are these things," Dustin asked before reaching down to one of two rectangular objects, about twelve inches long, buried in the silk lining.

Josh's hand blocked Dustin from reaching the object. "Sorry, bro, but you can't touch these with bare hands." Josh slid on the thin silk gloves and withdrew a black piece of silk from inside the same drawer. He opened the silk and set it over the desk.

"Why not?"

"It's the oil from your fingers," Nick answered. "It's not good for some metals. That is metal, right?"

The rest of the party moved around the desk to watch Josh as he worked. Inside the box, the items looked black, but as Josh took out a small moon crested object a little shorter than his hand, the color turned to a silver shade with a red glint.

"What's wrong, Josh," Natalie asked.

"It's been a while," Josh said. "What am I forgetting?"

He stared at the box for an answer before his eyes widened. "Oh yeah." He pulled out one of the rectangular pieces and lined up a groove on the rectangular piece with a tooth-like notch on the apex of the moon-shaped object. He twisted the two objects against each other until he heard a melodic tuning fork snap ring from the silver crest. He set the two pieces, which now made a single almost umbrella-shaped object, on the opened silk. He picked up the second moon crest and the other rectangular chunk of metal and repeated the procedure.

"I've never really cared much for guns," Josh said as his hands began to pull out more parts and attach them to the growing puzzle in his hands. "I did like archery and that sort of thing, you know, put a target on a bale of hay and everyone's smart enough to stay out of your way. That requires skill. Not like a gun."

Cadence snickered.

"Sorry Cadence, but guns are clumsy," Josh continued. "But with archery, it's more of an art." He dropped a slender cylinder into one end of the rectangle. "With a bow, you have to think about things like silencing the vibration of the cord after you shoot, and tension and well, there's just a lot more to take into consideration than aim and bang."

"That doesn't look like a bow to me," Cadence responded.

"They're not."

"They?"

"My uncle said he got these in Japan a long time ago from some antique dealer. He never told me where exactly. He always wanted to take me shooting, you know, sort of because he didn't have his own son to hang with."

He set the second object on the blanket of silk next to the first object and withdrew something resembling the shape of brass knuckles, but without the individual rings for holding each finger. The open knuckles snapped into one of Josh's puzzles. He dropped in some strange springs and rods and locked the hand grip into place. Josh pulled out a greenish cord about sixteen inches long with a small hoop on each end. He attached a hoop to each tip of the lathe on the far side of the weapon's body. He slid the loose cord into a notched block on the other end of the weapon "I told my uncle that the closest thing to a gun that I would consider shooting would possibly be a crossbow."

"So it's a crossbow," Bricktain said.

"With a bow that small," Nick asked.

"I don't remember what my uncle said these were called," Josh said reaching into the cedar box to pull out a second steel knuckle and a cord for the second puzzle waiting to be assembled. "But it's not exactly a crossbow. And I only got to shoot it once back when I was in the Boy Scouts."

"Where was I," Dustin asked finding himself enthralled in the majesty of the items that were set on the table.

"What do I look like? Your mother?" Josh set the puzzle on the table. Now, two small crossbows rested on the desk. In the light, they looked black, glistening red. "That's been a few years." Josh looked once more at the cedar case, which he had emptied of all but one of its parts. "Something's missing."

"Are you sure?" Natalie peered into the box.

Josh smiled. "Quite sure." He reached to the lid and pulled at the yellow silk. He folded the lining away and revealed about thirty cylinders, each about four inches long and a bit thicker than a school pencil. Whoever made them had sharpened one end of each to a fine round point, and notched the opposite end with a small hook. "My uncle told me that this thing is made out of some sort of Japanese steel, folded so many times, or something like that, which is why it has this reddish color to it." Josh set one of the cylinders into the groove on top of the rectangular shaft. He slid the notched end against the loose cord and continued to press the cylinder down the groove until the cord was taut. He let go and the cylinder remained in its place.

"You see," Josh continued. "The problem with the average crossbow was that it was generally made of softer material than this. And its user had to depend on their own strength to pull the string back before they prepared the bolt. The bow was wider, which made it easier for the average man to be able to pull back on, but there's something about this steel and the way the bow is formed that gives it a little more punch, if I remember my uncle right." Josh held up the strange crossbow-like weapon and flicked a switch on its rectangular shaft with his thumb. The lathe lunged forward and off the end of rectangular body, but continued to remain attached to a rod protruding from the front. The bow now curved back, the line taut, and Josh's friends felt the strong urge to move behind him.

"This puppy requires a key." Josh reached back into the box and pulled out the remaining two pieces. Each one was T-shaped and fit into the palm of his hand. He pressed the tip of the key into a deep star-shaped groove on the side of the crossbow's shaft. He left the T-shape in the shaft, took out another four-inch cylinder from the box and laid it in line with the first. He twisted the T-key and the cord began to stretch. The cylinders slid farther into the shaft with the cord. "The cord is some kind of metal, but somehow designed to stretch. You couldn't stretch it yourself if you tried. My uncle said it was like having a cord within a cord. So the cord stretches and that acts as one form of power behind the projectiles, bolts for those of you who don't speak crossbow."

"I know what a bolt is," Bricktain said.

The weapon clicked.

"I didn't say you didn't," Josh said.

He dropped a third cylinder onto the groove and twisted the key again. The cord stopped stretching and the small lathe began to bend backward.

"You want to use an archaic weapon in case we run into one of those werewolves tonight," Bricktain scowled. "I'm babysitting here."

Josh tore the key from the crossbow and inserted it into a crevice on the back side of the weapon. He took aim on the opened safe door. The steel crossbow clicked, the cord snapped and the safe door slammed shut and swung back open. The weapon was empty.

Cadence got to the safe first. "That shot straight through the door," Cadence said, her eyes wide.

Dustin and Nick also inspected the hole in the steel safe door. Dustin ran his fingers over the clean entry hole on the door. "."

"It also shoots one at a time," Josh said as he began to reload the weapon. "But it's not as powerful a shot and each one gets weaker."

"Check this out," Nick cried with his head buried in the safe. "That is, if I can get it out of here, it's in deep." A moment later, Nick pulled himself out of the safe and held out what looked like a miniature two-tier Christmas tree. "They smashed into each other."

"OK," Bricktain said. "Here's what I think we should do. We need to capture one of these things and bring it to the police."

The others shared uncomfortable looks.

"It would help us convince the police," Nick said. He tried not to make eye contact with anyone who might be glaring at him for siding with the cop.

"Exactly," Bricktain added.

"No," Josh returned.

Bricktain's eyes locked onto Josh.

"No," Josh snapped. "First, what good would it do? Second, I've seen what those things can do to cars and I'm not riding in any more with those things and third, no."

"Not to worry," Bricktain said leaning forward on the desk. "I have a truck. We can tie it down and if everyone keeps a close eye on it while we transport it—

"They'll pick off anyone that sits in the back of your truck," Josh replied. "You didn't see how many of these things there are."

"Then what's the plan, Josh," Dustin asked.

"Nick is our plan."

Nick stiffened. "Me?"

"He likes you," Josh said. "He thinks you're an honorable gentleman. He brought you back from the dead."

Nick touched his chest and caught Cadence frowning. She turned away when he looked at her.

"You're going to his house to thank him for sparing your life and apologize for offending him." Josh was actually prepared for the shocked faces that appeared around him. "Keep him busy, we'll look for any sort of clue leading to Cracey or Dustin's dad's kidnapping. You have to be convincing."

"I don't like that plan," Nick said.

"I don't either," Bricktain added.

"Josh," Natalie said. "I don't know if I do either."

"Neither do I, but Officer Einstein here hasn't seen what we've seen," Josh said, continuing to load the crossbows. "People are disappearing Nata, and we know something that nobody else knows or believes. I'm not going to wait for him to take you too."

"What if he takes Nick," Natalie asked.

Everyone looked at Josh, who now only stared at the desk, wishing he had a good answer.

"Then I'll blow the old man's head off," Cadence finally said. She pulled a rifle with a scope from the cabinet.

Josh thought about objecting, but didn't.

"OK, here's what we'll do," Josh said. "Morris, you drive, and we'll hide Cadence in the bed with the rifle. Park where she can get a clean view of the old man's front porch. No matter what, don't leave that vehicle and don't leave Nick. While Nick's keeping Jasper busy, the rest of us will check out the back."

"I don't think that's such a good idea," Bricktain said rapping the desk with his knuckles. "That's too close to where your uncle was killed. You're going to start a war with these things. Are you ready for that?"

For an instant, Josh thought of taking Morris's head and slamming it against the hard desk. Another image grew about firing one of the antique weapons darts right through the man's chest.

"I'd say we're looking in the right area then." Josh drove the special key into the star shape on the side of the second crossbow.

9 – Dogs, Strangers and Ghosts

Evil is the orchard, one apple hangs red, sweet and strong while ten weaker apples turn golden brown on the ground, their insides turned soft and mushy, waiting for ants, snails, worms and beetles to devour it. With the season changing, more apples littered the ground. The decaying insides sometimes leaked through holes in the dark thickening skin. Sometimes the soft apples would explode in the heat or pop under the weight of another apple falling on it, spraying its rotten juices everywhere. Sometimes an unknowing person would step on one of the dead apples and its putrid meat would spurt up the inside of that person's pant leg.

Dustin swore and shook his leg.

Natalie and Josh smirked.

Dustin kicked at a rotting apple, hoping to get even with his mocking friends by spraying them with its juice, but only splattered himself more.

The moon shined brightly through the dark cold leaves that had already started falling from their spindly branches. It was round and full and it filled the world with long creeping shadows. The orchard was dark from the tree silhouettes, but beyond the orchard, the land was gray and silver. The interior lights of Jasper's house crept into view as Josh, Natalie and Dustin emerged from a far end of the orchard into an open field, which was Jasper's backyard. The walk from the dirt road was long and stressful. Fast pulses and quick glances accompanied every step taken farther into dark shadows, as the friends wondered if a creature would leap from them. They feared the orchard with its canopy of leaves and giant trees, and it crept upon them subtly. A small tree popped up every once in a while and before they knew it, the group of friends found itself in the thick of the dark towering plants.

Dustin slipped and landed on his back. He couldn't count how many apples spurted onto his clothes.

He moaned while his two friends fought to contain their laughter.

"What a lovely adventure we're having." Dustin stood up while wiping apple guts from his neck and hands. He checked his belt to make sure he hadn't dropped his .40. He was hunched over, about to reach his full height when he heard the crackle of a branch.

The three friends stared silently at each other. A breeze whispered through the orchard branches, and the leaves applauded the three fools for entering the dark domain as if to welcome them to their deaths. Josh swallowed. Dustin looked everywhere. Natalie turned the safety off her twelve gauge.

"I think the joke's over, now," Josh said watching green eyes blink from under the dark boughs of one of the tree shadows. He directed the small crossbow toward the set of evil eyes.

A high-pitched whistle pierced the whispering night and the green set of eyes disappeared with the sound of heavy, trotting footsteps. The whistle trumped again. Heavy footsteps thundered from another direction and the small group turned toward those with weapons drawn. More footsteps pattered, and the friends spun again to face those. The ground grumbled and a violent storm of feet and massive black bodies appeared.

Dustin grabbed his shoulder and dropped his .40 as a large dark shadow ran past him and leapt over Josh's head. Natalie took aim with her shotgun, but the shadow disappeared and suddenly giants darted past the small group on all sides. Unable to move anywhere, the three friends stared at each other and occasionally tried to evade an oncoming monster only to have the beast dodge them instead. And suddenly the stampede was gone.

"They didn't attack," Dustin said as he again stood up from rotten apples.

"I don't think they cared about us." Natalie flipped the safety back on her weapon and reached down. "Here's your gun."

"They're headed for the house," Josh said.

"Nick's going to the front door," Dustin said. "Is Nick already there?"

Natalie darted off toward the flickering light of the old man's house. Josh and Dustin followed.

Natalie was by far the fastest of the group, although Josh should have been, and left her two friends behind. Nick was her main concern now and she couldn't let any of those things touch him. She flew with all the speed and agility of a human gazelle. She stomped down on apples and branches, slid once on some gooey leaves, and nearly fell when she stepped in a hole, but continued to run.

Josh did his best to keep sight of his girlfriend's shadow. He watched her stumble. "Watch out for the hole," he called back to Dustin just in time to jump over the hazard. He listened to Dustin stumble and swear. Josh ran and watched Dustin regain his composure. He was between his childhood buddy and the love of his life. He was afraid to lose either of them. Somewhere in the process of this thought, he lost the sight of Natalie and found himself on his face on dry ground. A moment later Dustin was tripping over him.

"You okay," Natalie's calm voice asked from beside Josh. She was lying in dirt and grass, pointing her shotgun in front of her over a stump.

"You fell too, huh," Josh asked trying to stand.

"Stay down," Natalie whispered. She forced Josh down again. Dustin quickly dropped as well. They had cleared the orchard. In the distance, they could make out the shape of the old man.

Many creatures, monsters and dogs alike, lined up in front of Jasper. One by one, they disappeared into the ground.

"Look at them all," Dustin whispered.

"Get in there," Jasper ordered smacking one of the large black beasts with his cane.

More dogs appeared out of nowhere and disappeared beneath the earth's surface.

Jasper whistled again through his fingers. He returned to herding the dogs and other monsters into the earth. He often looked up, herded a dog, kicked another, used his cane on the next and whistled again.

He kept looking up at the sky and stood up straight. He whistled and kicked and shouted and howled.

The last dog entered the ground yelping.

"Now," Jasper yelled.

"That's not Jasper," Dustin mustered the courage to whisper.

"That is Jasper," Josh returned. He wondered how an old man could suddenly sound so young.

Jasper's head turned to the tall dry grass where the three friends lay. The three friends remained silent and still.

Jasper's golden eyes glimmered at them. Josh noticed the moon for the first time. It was only for a second of a second in time, but the memory etched itself in his mind. Stars sprayed across the night's black cloak as if painted there by a graffiti vandal. A tinge of purple burned between the earth and the black heavens, void of any clouds. Josh could see all the stars, and the round moon, no, not just round, plump and full and ready to burst. It seemed to struggle to hold its magnificent weight so high above the ground.

"What are you doing," Jasper asked. His voice came at a higher pitch than it had only a moment earlier. "Think I can't see you?"

"Ba-roo," cried a monster from behind the three friends.

The friends snapped a quick glance over their shoulders and—

"Knock it off," Jasper cried. This time his voice grew higher toned with each syllable until the three friends were covering their ears by the end of the deafening sentence.

They each felt the wind graze their backs and watched as the large black shadow flew over their hiding spot. The monster rushed across the field to the old man who grabbed the creature by its wide throat and thrust it into the earth. Jasper began humming to himself as he swung what appeared to be a cellar door shut.

"Lock it up," Jasper yelled before he fell on his hands and screamed, not just screamed, yelled and cried, barked maybe. It was hard to tell.

The three friends watched Jasper and looked to each other to see if any of them had any answers to this scene.

"Let's take him," Natalie said breaking the code of quiet among the three friends.

"Sure," Dustin replied as quietly. "And we can all pet his little hamsters when they come out to snuggle with us."

"Guys," Josh interrupted. He was the first to see it, but the others soon sat upright when they saw Jasper's eyes staring in their direction again.

Jasper hummed, or growled. Whatever he did it was loud. "Shamus!" His head snapped another direction and he darted across the lawn.

The three friends looked each other over, until they heard the backdoor of the ratty house slam shut and the screen door chatter.

"Okay," Dustin said. "I vote to wet ourselves."

Suddenly, a cry bellowed from Jasper's house. It was if the very gates of hell were channeling through one man's inadequate throat, shredding every muscle and cord. The cry was long, swore only once, but quickly turned into a shriek, deep and ravenous. It yelped and screamed some more.

"I think you made a mistake, Josh," Dustin said as he found himself jumping onto his knees.

The shriek blasted again.

"Hey," From the dark cellar, a voice called. "Hey, hey hey hey!"

Josh stood up clenching the small crossbows. They were hot from how hard his fingers hugged their handles. "Did you hear that?"

"He's feeding them," Josh said, his voice quivered. "They catch the people and he feeds his animals in that cellar."

Jasper cried from the house once more and this time it was higher in pitch and smooth, almost bird-like and it wavered a moment before crying in a much lower range.

The sound paralyzed Josh and he stared at the house.

"Hey," The dark ground cried with more than one voice. "Run! Run!"

Josh jumped at the touch of Natalie's fingers on his arm.

"Jasper's the werewolf," Natalie said, looking up at the moon.

The house fell silent.

Several voices continued to yell from the cellar.

"He's the wolf," Natalie said again. "It's not the others."

"Oh please don't let him be a bad mother," Dustin said.

The voices continued to yell.

"We can't let them be eaten," Dustin said pointing a shaky revolver toward the darkness. "They probably have my dad."

At that, Josh stood and raced his two friends toward the cellar door.

The wooden screen door on the back of the house broke off its hinges and a tall skinny shadow with gold eyes charged the three friends.

Natalie raised the twelve-gauge shotgun only to watch its long barrel tear away from the rest of the gun. The butt of her weapon slammed into her chest. She never saw the attacker.

Dustin pulled on the triggers of his weapons, forgetting about the safety switches. He kept squeezing and couldn't breathe. But nothing fired. He saw the creature's eyes, gold and cold. He could probably have seen his reflection in those eyes if they didn't frighten him away from trying to find out. He kept squeezing the immovable trigger, until the barrel of the twelve gauge slammed into the side of his head and everything went black.

Snap!

The skinny shadow fell back growling.

Josh swung the second crossbow toward the shadow and took aim.

Knock! Knock! Knock! Knock! Knock!

The sound came of someone pounding away on the old screen door at the front of the house.

The gold eyes turned away from Josh, Natalie and the stooped over Dustin. It turned and darted in the direction of the knocking.

"Nick," Natalie cried. She stole the revolvers still clenched in Dustin's shaking hands and ran after Jasper's fleeting shadow. "Run, Nick!"

Josh ran too, forgetting Dustin, forgetting Dustin's father and the voices crying from the ground. All he cared about was Natalie. But, a small round shadow leapt straight into Josh's face and sank its teeth into his neck, and as Josh struggled with the shadow, he heard gunshots and Natalie's screams, from the front of the house, still ordering Nick to run .

*   *   *

While Josh, Natalie and Dustin were sneaking into Jasper's, Nick prepared to make his way toward Jasper's front door. He knew that Josh should never have asked him to play his part in this plan. He leapt from the truck and felt sick—he left proof of that on the road a mile back. He walked along the side of the vehicle and stopped at the open tailgate where he mustered a fraction of comfort from the dark lump that was Cadence crawling into a shooting position in the bed. She didn't look at him, or Nick didn't look at her. When he heard the ammo clip slide into the rifle, he began his walk down the dirt road toward the dark southern-style house.

What was a house like that doing in the middle of this town anyway? Who would have sold it to a lunatic old man, any old man for that fact? They should burn it down.

He heard an animal yelp and scream, and remembered his sister was counting on him to distract the old man and maybe his dogs. He walked, but a little slower than before.

The porch steps were the worst, they creaked and Nick could tell from the way they coupled around his foot that they were rotting. He hoped they wouldn't break beneath him. He wouldn't be surprised if he fell through them. The porch was different, solid and well cared for. It was a much larger porch than it appeared to be from the road.

The moon sure was full tonight.

He knocked on the paint-chipped door.

*   *   *

"Put that round part right up against your shoulder, sweetheart, or you're gonna rip your blasted arm off and break your friggin neck," Pete said helping his little girl pull the butt of the rifle into her shoulder. "You don't wanna let a single one a them dirty leg bumpers to get away, they make too many babies and they eat and crap and make more babies and all they do is eat and crap and—

Blam!

"Get them ugly little heads blowed off," Pete stood on his tiptoes and looked over the long patch of lettuce. "Just like that doodie, right there. Now you try, princess."

The child was only 8 years old. Every morning she watched her father burst through the back door, stomp through the kitchen and living room to the gun rack, where he tore down his favorite Mossberg twelve-gauge, and stomp back out the door before kicking it shut behind him, rattling the window within it. He always had the same words for the farmhands and more words for the varmints he was hunting. The little girl memorized the funniest words and would sometimes mimic her father.

"Those *dadgum* and *blasted* little *doodies*," she'd stammer, making sure

100

she didn't use her father's real language. Her mother heard her use it once and smacked off her face.

"We don't use language like that," her mother scowled with sharp piercing eyebrows and angry teeth. "Where did you learn that?" But before the little girl could answer, her mother was out the back door smacking the father who had innocently been working on a new door for the shed.

In a moment, the father stepped into the house and said, "Don't swear, dammit." As he left, he kicked the door shut and the glass in it broke.

A few weeks after her father replaced the glass, the child stood with her father's shotgun and greeted him at the door. "Can I come with you?"

Her father grumbled new swear words, stomped to the gun cabinet and returned with a .22 caliber rifle and snatched the shotgun out of his daughter's hand. "Don't tell your mother or she'll rip pieces of me off."

The shotgun was much louder than she expected and she was grateful for the smaller gun, for which she gained a quick sharp eye. She was twelve years old before she squeezed the trigger on a shotgun, but she didn't put the butt hard against her shoulder and ripped her arm out of socket. She thought she broke her neck. After her father passed away, she took to hiding out in the tree house that she and her father built in the back yard, a place where they would pick off the rabbits in the garden. The workers knew better than to step foot in her garden, while she was in the tree house, because they never knew when a bullet might zing over their ear and take out a rabbit.

Tonight, her practice would truly be put to the test, as Cadence pulled the butt of the rifle in tight to her right arm. She was adjusting her scope when she heard Nick's footsteps pass her. The scope blacked out as Nick crossed in front of her weapon. Nick wasn't too brilliant, stepping in the line of fire of a loaded weapon proved it, but he did have a lot on his mind. She brought the front door of Jasper's house into focus. She lifted her head and watched her friend disappear down the dark dirt road. It wasn't fair he was going alone. She listened to a monster howl in the distance, watched Nick knock on the door and emptied her ammo clip as she watched Natalie run around the side of the house chasing a monster, which sent a chill down Cadence's flesh.

"Run," Natalie cried, firing her weapons upon the monster that had decided to suddenly attack Nick.

*   *   *

Josh grabbed, but the monkey wouldn't take its teeth from his shoulder. Josh would have screamed if he thought it would do any good. The monkey

101

growled and smacked Josh's face. Even when Josh yanked on the tail, Shamus wouldn't let go. But, a dark hand appeared, cupped Shamus's head and poked two fingers down into the monkey's eyes. Shamus shrieked, flailed his arms in anger and ran off.

"Get on your feet," the stranger said pulling Josh off the cold grass.

"This one's out cold," said a second man. "Ugh, he fell in the apples."

"Natalie," Josh cried trying to run after her. He listened to her screams to run. He heard timbers break and more screams ordering Nick to run. Nick tried to follow, but other hands held him back. Gravel spit and Josh stopped breathing as he heard the sound of Bricktain's truck race away from the house.

"No," The stranger yelled as he gripped Josh's arm. "They're gone."

With tears in his eyes, Josh fought to chase Natalie, but the stranger overpowered him and carried him across the backyard lawn and down a flight of stairs, where new faces greeted him at the bottom. He watched two men carry Dustin in front of him. The cellar door slammed shut and men barricaded it with a large steel beam, chain and heavy bolt. A second steel door slammed tight and covered the first. The men sealed this door too. At the bottom of the stairs, they locked and bolted a third door.

"How's that one," Josh's rescuer asked.

"He's been hit hard," said another.

The strangers wore long brown robes, women and men, all of them bald.

"Who are you," Josh asked. "Where are the monsters?"

The room was large, with doorways leading to other rooms where Josh could see other faces peering at him. He caught the eye of one man looking up from a deck of cards, but couldn't see his opponents.

"Wake that one up," said Josh's guide before tilting Josh's head to the side and examining Shamus's bite marks. "He missed your jugular." He waved his hand towards someone behind Josh. "We don't have much, but we'll do what we can to help you. You're safe here for a few hours." He smacked Josh across the face. "No crying. You have to have your wits about you now more than ever. I'm sorry about your friends, but you will die if you don't come to your senses now. You screwed up, but your friends may still be alive. Pull yourself together."

"What is this place," Josh asked watching the stranger disappear through the crowd. "Where are the dogs?"

"Michael Banks," said a new face. Like the others in this dungeon, his head was bare and his face held no eyebrows or lashes. He led Josh to a bench and set him down. "Pitbull. Are you allergic to anything?"

"No," Josh said as Banks dug through a large orange tote and withdrew a needle. He watched a lady dig through a similar crate near Dustin while another man tried to rouse Dustin from his grogginess. "What is this place?" He thought of Natalie chasing the wolf and couldn't hold the tears.

Banks punched Josh in the stomach, and watched him hunker. "Get control of yourself. You cry and people die." He returned to his orange tote. "You're the only one who's made it this far. You're safe for now. We lock the doors from this side so he can't get in." He held up a syringe. "This will help keep infection down." He stabbed a needle into Josh's shoulder. "This is our sanctuary. It's where he keeps us when he loses his hold on us."

"Hold?"

"When he turns." Banks wiped blood from Josh's neck with a swab.

"Jasper?"

"The wolf, yes, and we are his."

"How did he do it?"

"No time for that," Banks dropped a filthy red chunk of cotton to the floor. "We only have a little while and you'll need your rest. I see this isn't your first bandaging up this week." Banks inspected the stitches in Josh's hand and arm. "Did you have a kindergartner sew these stitches?"

"Why do I need rest, I'm not tired?" Josh asked

The man and woman helped Dustin to his feet. Dustin held his head.

"Make no mistake, we will try to kill you when we change back and you must be able to run." Banks applied a bandage. "And your friend might not have his wits about him to help you much. Hold that there. We are his, Jasper's, some of us willing, some of us unwilling, and when he has control of himself he keeps us close. We change. We protect him and we take care of each other. We're not aware of what we do until we have control of our senses and we have the ability to feel regret. Did that hurt?"

"No, I'm fine," Josh lied. "You're not werewolf then?"

Banks laughed.

Josh wasn't amused.

"I'm sorry," Banks said. "I forget the curse of being ignorant." He controlled his laughter. "He can't make werewolves. That power belongs to another. He just makes dogs, but some of us in here can do that too. The fairy tales are wrong. He whispers to us and drives us mad and it changes us. He controls our sanity and our physical form. But the moon drives him mad, and when he goes mad he can't control himself, let alone us." Banks finished taping the bandage to Josh's shoulder. "And that allows us to be human for only one night in a month.

"Who was the cocker spaniel," Josh asked.

"His name was David Gin and I, for one, am glad that taskmaster's dead." Banks closed the orange tote and sat on it. "He was a child murderer and should have lost his head over it, but Jasper saw fit to save him. He's the one who took your sister. Now pay attention and remember what I tell you. Find a man, his name is Sir Thomas de Soleil."

"Who's that?"

A commotion of voices and movement erupted throughout the room. A dozen different people started shouting orders at each other. Josh suddenly found himself thrown to the ground and covered with robes.

"Put that other one in the trunk," said a new voice and something clanked.

Josh worked a small hole through the pile of robes over him. He didn't know what was happening, but he didn't want to be caught in this position if he needed to fight.

Josh wasn't sure at first about the commotion, but he was suddenly aware of the small brown shape of the maniacal monkey Shamus leaping from one man's shoulder to another man's head. This man reached for the monkey and Shamus shoved his finger into the man's eye and leapt to another stranger. Shamus continued to jump from one person to another and looked around new areas of the room, as if searching. His eyes suddenly locked onto the pile of robes on top of Josh.

Josh felt the almost insignificant weight of the little monkey land on him. He felt Shamus's hands prod through the folds of the robes. His hand found the small eyehole, Josh had created for himself.

"You know you're not supposed to be in here, Shamus," Banks yelled, swiping at the monkey to knock him off the folds of brown thick robes.

Shamus bit Banks's hand and leapt from the pile.

"You ain't nothing, Shamus," Banks yelled and backhanded Shamus off the robes and into the air. Shamus caught another man's head, and bit open a large gash on the side of his face. As the victim screamed and fell into one of his friends, Shamus disappeared into the end of a pipe barely large enough for his body to fit.

"I swear, one day, I'll kill you with my bare hands and chill your brains for dinner," the injured man cried out.

The commotion ended. The wounded men began cleaning and bandaging themselves as others brought Dustin and Josh from their hiding places.

"He's more dangerous when Jasper knows what we do to him," Banks said. "Good thing the old man doesn't speak monkey."

Josh sat up again and tried to remember what they had been talking about before the commotion broke out.

"Thomas De Soleil might be nobody," Banks said. "But some of the old ones here say he's a legend. Some believe in him and some don't. He's supposed to be an ancient hunter and the master lives in fear of him. We hear our master cry his name when he sleeps, yes even in his sleep he controls us. Supposedly, De Soleil serves England and is a highly protected secret of the queen. He's supposed to be a very powerful man. Find him, I don't know how, but find him and call upon him." Banks took out a small clear bottle. "This will help you sleep. It's a small dosage so you'll rest for a few hours is all. It'll take a few minutes to kick in."

"I can't sleep now," Josh said. "My friends need me out there."

"Your friends are probably dead by now," Banks said. "You certainly should be."

"But we survived," Josh said. "Maybe they did too."

"Well, then your going out there won't help them, trust me."

Josh trusted Banks for some strange reason. Banks seemed honest, had a sincere voice and fearful brow.

"I'll do my best to find this Sir—

"Thomas de Soleil," Banks assisted.

"But if I can't find him?"

"Then we're all trapped cuz we can't fight Jasper and we don't know how to direct you to find anyone who can." Banks inserted the needle into Josh's arm and injected the clear medicine. "We want him out of our heads. The child especially, we try to protect her from him and all the other deranged lunatics in this room. And we are tired that we can't control these visions of death that we cause."

A commotion arose behind Banks.

"Don't touch me," Dustin snapped and one of the bald men fell to the floor. "Where's my father."

"Who's your father," one of Dustin's guides asked.

"Eric Crank," Dustin shot back.

"Never heard of him, now keep walking or I'll give your head another welt."

"His father disappear," Banks asked. "I know most people around here, but I don't know that name." Banks handed two syringes also filled with clear liquid. "You're going to need these."

"What's this," Josh asked inspecting the contents of the syringe.

"Adrenaline," Banks answered. "It should be enough to help you run out of here when the time comes."

Out of nowhere Josh saw her. She ran straight up and wrapped her arms around his neck, holding tight. Tears ran down her cheeks. Josh looked up to see Dustin standing over him with tears in his eyes as well. Dustin fell to his knees and hugged back.

"Tyke?" Josh felt his own face flush.

"I want Mommy," she muffled into Josh's chest.

Josh ran his hand over Cracey's smooth head.

"It falls out," Cracey said looking up, her cheeks flooded with streams. "I don't wanna be bald!"

*　　*　　*

"Give me your hand," Cadence cried as she grabbed for Natalie. She helped pull her over the side of the truck bed.

Nick jumped onto the tailgate as the skinny brown creature crawled from beneath the timbers of Jasper's collapsed porch. His spindly frame and sharp face resembled the cat or wolf someone might find painted on a crumbling Egyptian wall. Its gold eyes locked onto the truck and the living hieroglyph made chase.

"Go," Nick cried.

Bricktain's truck jerked and threw dirt behind it as it began to speed away.

"We can't leave Josh and Dustin," Natalie said climbing halfway through the truck cab's rear window and startling Bricktain. "Turn here. We'll go back and get them."

Bricktain yanked the steering wheel and pointed the nose of the vehicle into the dark dirt road leading to the junkyard. Dustin's empty revolvers fell from Natalie's hands and her sides stung as she smashed into the aluminum windowpane.

Nick's head banged against the wheel well in the bed.

"A little faster on the turns would you please," Cadence cried out holding onto the side of the truck to keep from falling over.

The truck straightened out.

"Hit the bloody gas," Nick cried.

"No kidding," Bricktain yelled back, tempted to hit the brakes and let everyone topple just to teach them a lesson, but what he saw in the rear view mirror urged his foot down harder on the gas pedal.

He appeared out of the dark, the monster was faster than anything any of the passengers had seen.

"Shoot him," Nick yelled using his sister's leg as a rope to pull himself

106

against the back of the cab.

Cadence dug through the pocket of her jacket and pulled out a fresh clip of ammo. The old clip bounced around the steel floor bed and the new clip slammed into the rifle's belly. She fell backward after the truck bounced over a rut in the road and when she regained her stance, Jasper was right behind the truck. He peered down his long slender nose, taking a quick survey of everyone in the bed.

"Shoot him," Nick cried again.

Jasper's short, straight tubular nails sank into the tailgate and he started to pull himself up.

Cadence fired until she emptied another clip.

Jasper screeched, tore the tailgate from the back of the truck and threw it into the bed. A corner grazed Nick's shin. The other end careened past Cadence's head. The bulk of the gate struck Natalie's back and flipped out of the truck. Natalie slipped from the window and slid into Nick's arms, screaming all the way.

Cadence loaded her final clip into her rifle. She waited for Jasper's gold eyes and dark silhouette to resurface over the flat back of the bed again. She was suddenly aware that the mountains had disappeared and the road was open. It wouldn't be long until they reached the junkyard and the end of the road. She took aim on the shadow and squeezed the trigger. Jasper didn't stop. She fired. Again he didn't stop.

"Why didn't anyone think to get silver bullets," Cadence asked and kept firing, but nothing stopped Jasper.

Natalie dug her fingernails into Nick's arm as pain surged from her spine. She stomped the back of her heel on the floor in attempt to drive the agony from her body and attempted to sit up. "We need to get Josh and Dustin."

"We can't," Cadence snapped back. "That thing will follow us right to them. If we stop to pick them up, I think he'll get us all."

"Where are the other dogs," Nick asked.

Suddenly, Jasper was standing in the back of the truck. He stood as if human and looked down on the three friends. He was dark, colorless in the night and tall. He gurgled. His golden round eyes narrowed into slivers as he lunged for Natalie. White and yellow gunpowder blasted from the barrel of the shotgun, which Bricktain had shoved through the rear window. Jasper somersaulted backwards out of the bed. The shotgun kicked out of Bricktain's hand. The truck swerved and Bricktain yanked his right arm back into the truck, cursing his sore fingers.

This wasn't the first time Bricktain had returned to this road since his chief's death. In fact, he had returned every morning to look for any evidence to back up his story and get him back on the force. He still couldn't remember exactly what happened to him, but he remembered the monster. He found himself looking over his shoulder lately, expecting to see the monster. That creature, which nearly killed him, was a good dream compared to what chased him now. Bricktain kept his eyes on the dark road, in front of him, that would lead soon into a dead end and where the steel gates of the wrecking yard would alter the chase. It was a dumb idea to turn down this road.

The junkyard lights appeared in the distance, small and insignificant. For now, they were still a ways off. Bricktain knew he was going to have to find a safe place where he could leave the road, drive down the mountain back to Jasper's yard and eventually get back a better street. He was afraid of any old fence barbed wire that could be lurking in the dark waiting to wrap itself around the truck's tires and strangle their retreat. The junkyard was only two or three miles away. Most of the road was straight except for an incline where large tow trucks occasionally got themselves stuck when it rained. At least it wasn't raining tonight.

After Bricktain lost his shotgun, Natalie quickly gripped it. She'd never fired a sawed-off before. She handed the gun to Cadence and forced herself back up to the window despite the pain it brought her. "I have to get Josh, I have to get out."

"No," Bricktain replied.

"Fine." Natalie jerked away from the window, retrieved the shotgun from Cadence and leapt over the side of the truck bed.

Natalie didn't know the proper procedure to jump out of the back of a fast moving vehicle. Now, was she aware of the sharp air that would grab her, throwing her hair over her eyes. Her clothes filled like a windsock. In that moment of falling, Natalie didn't believe that a simple four-foot drop could hurt. Yet, she wondered about the dirt and gravel, how it might tear her flesh off like cheese on a grater. She wondered if the road would melt her skin and if the dirt would cauterize the wound. She wondered about broken bones, hitting the ground and rolling into snapping arms, legs, and ribs. As Natalie floated in the air, for that one moment, waiting for the ground to demonstrate the answer to all her questions, she remembered what a skydiver friend told her once.

"If your chute doesn't work," he told her. "You can try to tuck and roll if you hit the ground, but make it a tight tuck and a loose roll." He also told her it probably wouldn't work, but he said he would flap his arms if he thought it might help him fly as he was plummeting to the ground. Last resorts before death were always worth a try.

Natalie prepared her mind and body to roll. She wondered if she had turned on the sawed-off shotgun's safety so she didn't shoot herself in the fall. But, Jasper caught her in midair, his long, skinny fingers clasped right around her neck. Natalie could feel his cold fingernails. His needle shaped snout opened and bit at her head, but a blast full of lead hit Jasper in his chest and he screamed.

Natalie squeezed the trigger again, this time the shot hit Jasper's arm. He dropped Natalie, no rolling, no breaks, and no blood. She fired off another shot and ran. The headlights of Bricktain's truck blinded her as it sped back to retrieve her.

The truck swerved around Natalie, slammed into Jasper and threw him into the air. Jasper didn't somersault or flip, but he simply flew backwards, maintaining his fearsome posture, and landed on his feet. He immediately ran at the truck.

Nick and Cadence leapt from the bed and chased Natalie. Nick tackled her and the two tumbled.

"What is the matter with you," Cadence asked as she and Nick dragged her into a clump of bushes and grass for hiding. Bricktain's truck spit dirt out from behind it and again sped toward Jasper. This time, as the truck hit Jasper, its bed jerked into the air and the truck flipped over the creature, Jasper, and came down on its top. After it smashed down and flattened its roof, the werewolf let go of the vehicle's nose and he, himself, remained unharmed. He scanned the area and ran after the trio of friends hiding in the bushes.

Blue lights appeared. As they drew closer to the trio, their Cyclops beams turned from blue to white and blinded Jasper. The wolf stopped chasing Natalie and the others and evaluated the newcomers. Two dirt bikes sang past Natalie and the others. A full set of spectacles suddenly flashed bright from the front of a truck, followed by a crown of even more blinding halogens from the truck's roof.

BOOM!

Jasper tumbled to the ground and appeared to be fighting some invisible foe. The dirt bikes drove straight for Bricktain's demolished truck. The two riders leapt from the bikes before they had fully stopped. A big black dual cab truck kicked up a dust storm as its brakes locked and its body spun around in front of the hiding friends.

The side doors opened and a slender figure leapt down and nearly ripped Cadence's arm out of socket stuffing her into the back seat. "Hurry."

"I'm not leaving Josh," Natalie screamed as Nick and Cadence helped push and pull her into the cab. She fought, but the pain she had ignored for so long finally overpowered her and she fell into her brother, crying.

"If he's still alive, my brothers will get him," the girl replied. "Now get in."

"No, there are two more down at the house," Nick replied.

Both vehicle doors slammed shut and the girl was back behind the steering wheel.

Jasper continued to wrestle his unknown foe.

Bricktain had escaped the wreckage and was now climbing onto the back of one of the bikes.

The truck sped forward. The motorcycles whizzed past each side of the truck and disappeared into the distance as they headed for the junkyard lights. Bricktain sat on the back of one.

"How did you stop it," Cadence asked peering through the back window, past the red glow of taillights, past the strange tripod mounted in the bed and into the darkness at Jasper's fading figure.

"It's a fishing net," the driver replied. "He'll be out soon."

"Do you know how to kill him," Natalie asked.

"No," said the driver.

"What about silver," Nick asked.

"Grow up."

The truck raced back to the junkyard fortress at the end of the dirt road. Its steel walls were high and smooth so that no one could climb over. Razor wire and handrails lined the wall tops.

"One time when we don't have anything to do," Nick said as his sister cried into his shoulder. "Just once, we should try driving away from some freaky monster in somebody's car."

The wall surrounding the junkyard had already opened for the bikes and now waited for the truck. The bikes stood without their riders inside the gates. The truck entered the yard and skidded to a stop, its driver quickly jumped out.

"Get them spotlights turned on," cried an unrefined voice.

Cadence was the first of the friends out of the vehicle and got the first view of the huge junkyard. Although she couldn't see it all for the darkness and towering obstructions of obsolete machines, it was seven acres and all of it surrounded by the steel wall. A tall crane and high-rise office overlooked the compound from the front of the junkyard. A large flatbed trailer sat silent with three wrecked cars on its back. A rusty flat-nose rig with a cracked windshield and broken side mirror slept at the trailer's head. A four-car garage deteriorated away to the side of the crane and office, while another structure was under construction and already covered several other vehicles. Poor scaffolding, rusty-looking beams and conduit enclosed it. Several small piles of mutilated vehicles sat parked on one side of the compound awaiting their turn for the crusher, which sat silent and dark in the depths of the yard. An additional twenty acres of broken down junk heaps surrounded the compound.

A walkway stretched along the entire length of the tops of the steel walls. The driver of the truck was scaling a set of metal stairs leading to the catwalk where the two bike riders were already moving about. The steel gates whined and clamored together, sealing off the junkyard from the rest of the world. One of the bikers ran across a catwalk above the gates.

"'Kay, they're locked," he announced and darted back over the gates. The gates shook and the biker's figure stumbled. Suddenly, two figures appeared on the catwalk, the biker's and Jasper's. And Jasper quickly made two shadows from the single biker's figure. He threw the bottom half into the compound and left the top part on the catwalk.

The driver of the truck screamed and ran toward Jasper's shadow.

"Amber, no." He appeared from the shadows of the foot of the crane. His wheelchair drove forward, softly humming to the tune of a gas-powered engine. Lines dug deep into his eyes and forehead and he had a grisly beard. As he scooted over the bumpy terrain, he pounded his fist against the arm of his chair. "Let the lights have him."

The truck driver's silhouette stopped suddenly and fell. The second biker's shadow stood over her place and a blast of gunshot erupted twice.

Jasper fell back and howled.

Cadence grabbed her ears and noticed others had covered theirs as well. The female figure stood and leapt from the catwalk. She caught hold of something in midair and leapt in a different direction. She ran down the top of the handrail of the stairway and met the old man at the bottom. The biker's shadow leapt from the catwalk and, in midair, Jasper caught him and threw him into the razor wire where he stayed tangled and screaming. The monster jumped from the catwalk, into the yard and swiped at the female. The truck driver bent backward, avoiding the attack, and ran from the creature.

"Lights," the old man cried.

He whistled and the compound erupted with barking mongrels.

Jasper chased the girl and the mongrels jumped all over him.

The compound burst with bright lights from the tops of the walls. The whole area turned nearly blinding white. Jasper winced, leapt up to the catwalk and disappeared over the razor wire, leaving three animals dead and two that would soon bleed out. Two other dogs quickly disappeared into the compound to tend to their wounds.

The girl approached the man in the wheelchair. She bit her bottom lip.

"He won't come in now," the man said.

Amber stormed to Natalie. Her eyes were bulged with red hate and her cheek and lips twisted to a slight sneer. She cocked back her arm and punched Natalie's throat. Natalie fell backwards and searched for breath.

"Why did you jump out of the truck," Amber asked. She hoped the dumb girl would look up so she could hit her again. Instead, she kicked her in the stomach.

Amber wore a black baseball cap with a long blond ponytail stretching out the back; a short-sleeved black pullover shirt with a brown stain on the left shoulder and black jeans with holes sliced through the knees. Her black work boots made her look taller than she really was. In reality, she was maybe just a little over five feet tall, but the boots added an inch or two. "What were you doing up here?"

"Amber," the old man said. "Get some sheets."

"We'll talk about this later," Amber said and walked off. As she disappeared into the tall building, Bricktain walked out.

"I said the third switch in the control room on the bottom floor," the old man erupted through a voice shakier than when he had been giving orders. "It was clearly marked. Were the instructions cloudy? Surely you can work a light switch?"

"I moved as fast as I could," Bricktain replied. He held his side and walked slowly towards his comrades.

"Tell that to my grandsons," The old man's chair wheeled about and puttered into the distance. "We should have left you alone out there," He suddenly stopped and pointed his chair toward Natalie, Nick and Cadence. Natalie sat on the ground catching her breath. "What were you doing out there?"

Silence.

"Answer me," the old man snapped.

"If you don't mind," Nick said after a moment of awkward silence. "We've just been chased by an anorexic giant rabid Siamese dog thing and we'd like to let our pants dry out right now.

The old man ignored Nick.

"If you don't mind," the old man snapped back. "My grandsons are dead. Fifteen years we've kept those things at bay." The old man smacked the arm of his wheelchair. "Fifteen years we've minded our own business and they've never come in here. These lights will keep out this creature and the other dark ones tonight, but come morning those others will tear this place apart. We might as well walk through the gates and get eaten now."

"You," Natalie tried to speak, but her voice cracked. "You knew about the dogs?" She brought herself to her feet and forced out more. "You knew!"

"Who do you think you are," the old man snapped. "You don't live here and you don't know anything."

"People are dying out there because of those things," Natalie cried. "My friends are out there right now looking for answers to his five-year-old sister's death—

"The little girl," The old man interrupted. This time he stood silent. His chair turned and moved toward the lower torso and legs, of his grandson, lying at the front gate where he remained for three hours and sobbed. Amber returned with white sheets and covered the partial body. She threw another sheet over the razor wire after she couldn't get her strangled brother free, even with Bricktain and Nick's help.

A few hours later, Natalie laid in the bed of the truck with Cadence and cried. They listened to the occasional screams, which belonged to Jasper. Natalie screamed back as Cadence poured alcohol over the gashes on Natalie's shin and back.

The night grew cold and only the sound of the gas-powered wheelchair dared to break it. Amber walked beside the old man as the chair approached the truck.

"I'm Reggie Chambers," The old man said. "And this is my granddaughter, Amber."

Amber nodded her head at the ground to acknowledge Cadence and Natalie. In the distance, shovels scraped at the hard dirt compacted by years of heavy vehicle weight. Nick and Bricktain stood waist-deep in a hole.

"Seems we've caused each other loss," said Reggie. "We called the police. They don't believe us and they don't survive driving up here. They hide them, they always do. Those creatures'll dig up my grandsons come morning, but I'm still gonna bury them."

Natalie's tears had dried out but she continued to sob.

"Help us load up the truck," Amber said. "We have to get out of here and find some place to hide."

"Do you have anywhere in mind," Natalie asked.

"Maybe the woods," Reggie replied. "I don't expect to be alive by the end of the day tomorrow anyway. Might as well try there."

"I know where you can stay," Natalie said. "But I don't know if we can get in without my friends."

"Your friends are dead by now," Amber replied coolly.

"Then you will be too, come morning," Cadence said. She stood on the wall of the truck and took a moment to look down before leaping off. She hit the ground, gained her full posture, drove her knee into Amber's stomach, and watched the petite woman bend forward grabbing herself. "I think you know what that was for."

Amber returned to her feet and drew into a stance ready to fight.

"That's enough," Reggie cried.

"That is enough." Natalie was now standing in the bed of the truck. She called for Nick and Bricktain. Nick was already out of the shallow grave he was digging and charging toward Cadence.

"Where do you think you're going," Reggie asked, watching Natalie climb from the bed to the cab.

"We're going back out."

"No you're not," Amber rushed the cab and reached to the steering wheel for the keys.

Natalie's elbow hammered Amber's arm away. Amber recoiled, holding her wrist. "Stay here if you want, but we're taking the truck."

*　　*　　*

"It's time," Banks announced, peering from the cellar to the fading moon. He turned to Josh, who held a limp and sleeping Cracey in his arms. "Better shoot yourself up."

Josh nodded and held out one of the syringes of adrenaline to Dustin. Dustin stabbed the needle into Josh and injected him.

"Are we going home now," Cracey asked.

"No," Banks replied. "I'm sorry."

"That's not your call," Josh said.

"No," Banks said trying to take Cracey. "She's safer here. You're safer with her here."

"I want to go home," Cracey cried. "I want mommy."

"She doesn't want to stay," Dustin said.

"None of us want to stay," Banks said. "But I promise, when she turns either she'll kill you or you'll kill her."

"I want mommy!" Cracey's scream was so loud that it filled Josh's head with aching pressure as if to burst it open. He couldn't see and he thought for a moment that he went deaf. All he could feel was the ringing of Cracey's

114

voice between his ears. He didn't notice falling to his knees and dropping Cracey into Banks's arms

"Are you okay, Josh," Cracey asked throwing her arms around him and hugging his chest. "Did I hurt you?"

"She will kill you both," Banks said. "She will turn and she will kill you, or you will kill her. Is that what you want?"

"Can't we confine her someway," Josh asked.

"You don't have time to build anything strong enough to hold her," Banks replied. Josh could see the hurt in Banks's dark eyes. "She will eventually chew through any steel or chains you put on her."

"There must be something."

"Even if you could, he can see through her eyes. He will find you through her. And you can't fight him."

Josh felt it, he believed Banks. Dustin did too.

Josh hugged Cracey tight. "I know where you are,Tike."

"I want to go home," Cracey muffled into Josh's chest. "I want mommy." Her tears bled through Josh's shirt.

Josh held Cracey away from him and looked into her red eyes. "We're gonna come back and get you, okay?"

"Okay."

"You stay close to Banks," Josh said. "He's strong and smart and he'll take care of you, got it?"

"Okay."

Jasper screamed and this time, Cracey and Banks grabbed their heads for a moment.

"You have to go now," Banks ordered. His voice was suddenly rougher. "Go now."

"I wanna go with you," Cracey said, her voice gruffer as well.

"I'll be back,Tike. I promise." Josh turned his cheek to his small sister. "Cheek."

Cracey gave a small kiss. Josh turned his face to the other cheek. "Cheek."

Cracey kissed him.

"Now go inside."

Cracey nodded and stepped next to Banks, taking his hand.

Banks became sincere, his once friendly face became straight, his lips tightened and he eyes appeared sad. "Go wait for me downstairs, child."

Cracey turned and disappeared into the earth.

"If you hurt her in any way," Josh said.

"No one will touch her," Banks reassured. "We may be mindless creatures, but our instinct is still to protect our young. Many of us lost children of our own."

The high-pitched wail pierced the air. It was agony, pain screaming to deafen any ears listening to it.

A growl hummed, not from outside but from the bottom of the dark stairway leading to the den of human slaves.

"Go," Dustin pushed Josh so hard his shoulder should have popped out of socket.

"Run," Banks demanded, his voice no longer friendly or sincere. He pulled the cellar door over him and the braces locked into place. "Just run, boys," He continued to yell from behind the door.

Josh and Dustin bolted from the shelter.

The two friends darted across the open field of long grass. Dustin ran toward the orchard.

"No," Josh instructed. "They'll catch us in there."

The morning twilight brightened the hillside leading to the mountain road. The light blue of the early morning was fading and every running step Josh pressed into the ground reminded him that he was alive and could survive. More than that, he knew Cracey was alive and if anyone was going to get her back, it would be he.

"Where, then," Dustin asked practically stopping in his tracks. "We can't outrun them."

"There." Josh pointed.

A dull orange crown of headlights had been bobbing up and down farther up the mountain and suddenly stopped. A spotlight flashed from the side of the vehicle.

Something in the dark cried "Ba-roo!"

The two friends ran toward the truck. Dustin waved his arms through the air and shouted to the spotlight and the orange crown.

The spotlight scanned down the hillside and suddenly twisted as if something else had caught its attention and the truck sped away.

Josh and Dustin stopped suddenly.

"We have to find another way," Dustin whispered.

"I know," Josh replied. "You were right. We'll have to go through the orchard."

10 ~ Bitten

Josh and Dustin trudged towards the chain link fence. Dustin kicked the gate open and Josh stumbled as they entered Richard's backyard.

"Keep moving," Dustin said pulling Josh to his feet. "Where is it?" Josh struggled for the words.

"Where, Josh?"

"The garage," Josh forced out, but still only mumbled.

The two friends muddled through the backyard, one dragging the other.

"You can't stop now," Dustin said. He found himself guessing the steps remaining until he reached the single door leading into the side of the white garage that appeared big enough for perhaps two vehicles. "Help me, Josh."

Josh fell limp and Dustin lost his grip on his friend.

The sharp, dewy blades of grass pricked Josh's face. "I'm tired."

Dustin reared back and kicked his foot into Josh's stomach.

"What was that for," Josh coughed.

"I'm sorry," Dustin replied glancing from one end of the yard to the other. He rocked on his feet, having learned to jump at the slightest sound. "I don't have any adrenaline shots to give you. Get up."

Josh tried to stand and stumbled again. "I can't," he said. "I'm so tired." He tried standing again, but still couldn't find the strength. "The key's in the flower pot. The password to the elevator is 'tyke'." Josh's chest was heavy. He'd have breathed in every bit of air between him and the sky if his chest would let him. Every vein in his body trembled. He was tired, his head spun, but he could see his friend was doing better.

Dustin's face streaked with sweaty dirt and scratches. His head bled from where he'd hit a rock. "Help me, Josh."

Dustin pulled Josh to his feet and tossed him over his shoulder. He continued toward the garage with Josh leaning against him. He found the flowerpot and searched inside.

"There's no key."

"It's inside."

Dustin looked around the thick leaves of whatever plant was growing inside. He reached into the pot and small barbs clung to his skin.

"It's not there," he said, tearing his hand from the pot and swearing at the small pricks left behind.

"You have to dig," Josh continued mumbling, barely able to breathe.

"Can't anything be easy?" Dustin kicked the round clay pot and pieces of ceramic and chunks of dirt flew everywhere. With Josh still slung over his back, Dustin began breaking the dirt clumps in his fingers until the sharp teeth of a jagged key appeared in his hand. He wiped the key clean.

"Run," Josh tried shouting, but only spoke. He held out the silver crossbow and pulled back on the trigger. He wasn't sure how, but somehow, the crossbows remained tied to his sides with thin rope. He knew he had bruises from the number of times they had banged against his legs. And he had lost the special silk gloves.

"Don't shoot," Bricktain cried and apparently believed that holding his hands in front of his face would shield him from any projectile Josh's antique weapon was capable of shooting at him.

"It's empty," Josh said and started laughing.

"Where have you been," Dustin asked as he set Josh on the small step leading up to the garage door.

"Looking for you," Cadence replied, using Nick as a crutch to limp towards her friends. "What happened? We thought you were dead."

"He looks dead to me," said a new face that Dustin didn't recognize.

Her hair was long and blond, half remained wrapped in a ponytail and the other half matted around her tired and plain face. A wheelchair puttered through the gate, shooting exhaust out the back. The chair coughed and tried to stay alive while the old man sitting in it jerked back and forth on a small knob, swearing the entire time.

"Who are you," Dustin asked.

"Who is this," Amber asked.

"Where's Nata," Josh asked.

Cadence didn't mean to, but Josh knew her too well. Her eyes flashed, not angry, but to the ground and her brow frowned.

Josh felt the darkness closing around him; his eyes hurt, but he asked again. "Where is she?"

Cadence finally looked back to Josh with her worried eyes and knew she'd already said too much. Her head rested on Nick's shoulder; she looked like a rag doll trying not to topple over. "I don't know." Suddenly, her eyes grew wide and for a moment, she stood on her own. "Josh, what are you doing?"

Josh pulled himself to his feet, grimacing the entire way.

"We have to get her," he said hugging an arm into his chest. He hunched forward and fell on his face. "We have to find her," he said as he rolled onto his back and his eyelids closed.

Dustin pulled up Josh by the front of his shirt.

"What happened to you guys," Cadence asked.

"What happened to us," Dustin asked back. "We were chased by dogs. What do you think happened to us?" Dustin propped Josh against the side of the garage door once again, slid the key into a deadbolt, and twisted. He reached for a doorknob but found none.

The door clicked once and swung open on its own, revealing a second blockade made of steel. A chorus of digital beeps followed.

"Password," the door said as a gray panel suddenly shifted, revealing a full-sized keyboard.

Dustin stared at the buttons, but realized the stare wouldn't open the door. "Oh, come on. What's the password?" He shook his incoherent friend. "How do I get us in, Josh?"

Josh didn't move. Dustin shook him harder.

"This was a great idea," Amber said.

Reggie rebuked her.

Dustin threw a hateful glance at the new girl who appeared to be as beaten and weary as the rest of the group. "Any ideas," he finally asked.

"How about some smelling salt," Bricktain said.

Cadence replied, with a roll of her eyes. Smelling salt would be a great idea if, in fact, any of them had any smelling salt.

"Pick him up," Reggie ordered.

Amber obeyed instantly and stepped forward, but Dustin was the one who pulled Josh straight up and leaned him against the steel door, which Dustin had revealed. Dustin smacked Josh and yelled in his ear.

Josh's eyelids fluttered open, staring straight through everyone his eyes scanned over, focusing on nothing and no one.

"Did he say something," Amber asked.

"I didn't hear anything," Reggie replied.

"Just kick the door open," suggested Bricktain.

"He said 'tyke'," Nick said.

"No he didn't," Amber growled.

"Yes, yes he did," Cadence said. "He said 'tyke'."

"Oh yeah," Dustin said. "He said that already." He punched in the code.

The door, clicked, banged and clicked again before dropping straight into the ground, catching everyone off guard and causing Dustin to stumble forward while trying to keep from dropping Josh through the doorway. Cadence rushed to help.

For the first time, Dustin got a good look at Cadence's face. It was a mess, painted from her crown to her chin with a trail of blood. A small black pearl glued itself to a crack in her lip. The white of her left eye was also tattooed with an explosion of blood, which stabbed into her perfect brown iris like a rose thorn. Her hair was knotted, gnarled, torn from her temple and pressed with more blood against her face and head. He could smell the hours of clotting and weariness poisoning her flesh.

"Nick was bitten," Cadence said in a hushed tone, as if surrendering to any hope she had left to survive the night.

"Let's talk inside," Dustin said. He directed the others inside Richard's garage; where they discovered a small elevator door with a numerical keypad. Josh quickly figured out that the password was Josh's name. The elevator took two slow trips into the earth to bring everyone to what they hoped was safety.

Reggie disengaged his gas motor, as he always did when indoors, and rode down with everyone in the elevator. The elevator opened into the darknes and with the help of the green L.E.D. Light on Reggie's chair, Amber was able to locate the outline of a light switch hiding on the wall. Lights flickered overhead a moment before remaining constant.

"What kind of place is this," Amber asked looking over the room.

Everyone stood in a living room with a black leather couch, two matching recliners, yellow carpet, and a flat plasma screen television hanging high on one of its five walls. The room held three paintings of people who appeared to be hunting, but no one was really in the mood to examine them.

"See if you can find a medicine cabinet or something," Dustin said as he laid Josh on the couch.

The living room connected directly onto a dining room with a spiral staircase and a wall-sized liquor cabinet. Beyond that was a kitchen with bright red walls and black cabinets and countertops. One hallway led from the living room and another led from the other side of the kitchen. Amber went down the spiral staircase while Nick and Cadence each went through one of the arched hallways upstairs.

At the bottom of the staircase, Amber found a second living room with television, couch and chairs. It was the same layout and nasty furniture as the upstairs room, but the walls were brown and the carpet was white. Two hallways led off this room too: one led to a large bathroom and Jacuzzi room, the other hallway led to four bedrooms, each large enough for a double bed and a small dresser of drawers. In the bathroom, she found a medicine cabinet filled with bottles of isopropyl alcohol, bandages, and little package of medical knickknacks and envelopes of all sorts of medicine. She returned up the spiral staircase.

Upstairs, Nick found a washroom and three bedrooms that were nicer and larger than the ones Amber found. He also found an office, an exact clone of the office in Richard's house. The antique cabinet in this office held more guns, however, and it didn't have a safe. Nick assumed Richard felt the underground bunker was safe enough. Beyond the kitchen, Cadence found a greenhouse where natural sunlight somehow flowed into the earth. On top of that, the greenhouse was alive. She also found a pantry jam packed with more food than Cadence conceived of needing in a lifetime. She returned to the living room to report her findings.

"Did he get Natalie," Dustin asked, without breaking his concentration on a gash that revealed itself from beneath Josh's collar.

"I don't know," Cadence replied. "We thought we should stop and get some clothes and food, things we thought we might need if we were going to hide and, what was that?"

"What was what," Dustin asked looking up from Josh's wounds.

"You rolled your eyes at me. Don't roll your eyes at me," Cadence said. "We didn't even know if you were alive, and we sure didn't know if we could find this place or not and then if we found it, we didn't know how we were going to get in. We made it to my place and packed a few things and were loading up the truck when a dog attacked us."

"Jasper?"

"No, one of his mutants. This was a white wolf, as big as a bear and wide like a horse, and gold eyes—it had gold eyes like Jasper. It bit Nick."

"You're bit," Dustin asked.

Nick cradled his arm under a piece of clothing, which Dustin recognized as a T-shirt Cadence had worn on a date a few weeks ago. It was dark with blood and rivers ran dry clots to the canyons of his fingers. "I'll be all right," Nick said.

"What happened to Natalie," Dustin asked, returning to bandaging the battered Josh.

"There was a cry," Cadence answered. "A howl, and the creature ran off and three more of those black wolves came out of nowhere."

"We managed to net one of them," Reggie said, looking to Amber who quickly looked away.

"It got away though," Amber said. "I might as well choose a room." She quickly retreated through the archway.

Dustin watched her leave. He studied Reggie a moment and turned to Cadence, who had begun unwrapping Nick's arm to clean it. He opened his mouth to ask about the two new members of the group and decided it didn't matter. "So what happened?"

"Natalie found a rake and started beating the dogs," Nick replied.

"She fought two of them," Dustin asked. His body suddenly sank. "So they got her?"

"Ha," Reggie burst out. "She got them. And it was three of them"

"What," Dustin asked. "How? And what do you mean you net one of them?"

"I've never seen anyone fight like she did," Reggie said.

"But they got her, right?"

"Hardly," Reggie said sounding delighted. "She smacked the snot out of those things, just –Wham! Wham! Wham! She didn't even let 'em up, just laid into them all, like some mad, crack-head. When another dog appeared, and started for her, we netted that one too and she pounded on it before it managed to get away. The other creatures tried to withdraw, but that girl just kept at them and when they ran off, she ran after them."

"She went after them," Dustin asked.

"That girl was out for blood," Reggie replied.

"She was out for vengeance," Cadence said. "She thought Josh was dead."

"What happened to you two," Bricktain asked from one of the recliners.

Dustin worked quietly on Josh.

"Dustin," Cadence asked.

Dustin continued to work. "Tired, Brickface?"

Morris looked up.

"Why don't you use that elevator and see if anything's below us."

"You go do it," Morris replied from behind closed eyelids.

"Get out of that chair and help or I'll drop you down the elevator shaft."

Morris sat up again. "Look, kid, I did things your way and now I'm tired and I'm hurt from spending the entire night getting spanked by dogs and digging graves. Since our fearless leader isn't exactly alert to give us any more wise instruction, I'm going to sleep and try to have nice dreams of him and me and a secluded spot where no one can hear him scream."

Dustin stood up and a moment later tore Morris out of the recliner and threw him across the room and against the sealed elevator doors.

"Do not," Dustin snapped, "start with me."

Morris, like the others in the room, stared dumbstruck at Dustin. He returned to his feet and, a moment later, the elevator swallowed him. Dustin returned to Josh and began picking up empty bandage wrappers. A hand rested on his shoulder and Dustin looked into Cadence's face.

"What happened," Cadence asked.

"We found Cracey."

"You found her?" Cadence didn't know whether to feel relieved or be worried.

"Is she all right?"

"No, she's not all right," Dustin answered. "She's bald and she's the only child in a den of thieves and murderers and who knows what else. We couldn't save her. And that's only part of it."

"Tell us then," Cadence urged.

"We got to Josh's home and it was awful. You could smell the air was sour as soon as we walked in. Everything was destroyed: furniture, lights—even the walls. And blood everywhere. No one was home."

"Stan and Barbara are dead," Cadence asked.

"I imagine they are," Dustin replied. "There was just blood. And this white dog was there, and before it ran off, it bit me." Dustin held up a wounded hand to show off the bite mark. "Maybe it was the same white dog that attacked you. Anyways, we got away, I don't know how but we did and we ran all the way here."

"We're trapped here, aren't we," Reggie asked.

"Why would we be trapped," Nick asked.

"The dogs are out there, we're in here," Reggie said. "We're stuck, aren't we?"

Dustin didn't have the answer. His thoughts dwelt on the blood splatters on the walls of the living room in Josh's house and the big screen television broken over the arm of the recliner. The banister leading up the stairs had been broken and splotched in red. The carpet was torn. Kitchen tile and countertops were all damaged and bloodied to some extent. The house was no longer the warm safe haven Dustin had come to regard it over the years.

Dustin finished bandaging Josh. He sat on the floor and leaned against the couch, dwelling on everything that happened in the past few days. He thought about Josh and his family. He wondered about his own father and wondered if he was all right, and he wondered how easily Jasper's army of dogs could find them buried in Richard's bunker and dig them up. He was suddenly aware of someone in his head and woke up.

"I found a pantry, a movie theater and what appears to be a jail cell two floors down," Bricktain explained. "I also found a swimming pool, a weight room with a billiard table and there's a door that I can't figure out how to open."

"Did you try the doorknob," Cadence asked.

"There's no doorknob."

"Then how do you know it's a door?"

"It looks like a door," Bricktain said. "Something smells good."

Dustin smelled it too, the scent of fresh steak waiting to be grilled over a healthy flame like he had never smelled before. The aroma of blood tantalized and brought Dustin to his feet. He followed the savory air, breathed in all he could and let its succulent flavor fill his body and destroy his taste buds. He could taste the blood. He was aware that he knew how fresh and raw the meat was. He imagined walking into a kitchen and seeing a nice thick steak waiting on the countertop with blood oozing from its center. Strange, he never realized how keen his taste was to meat and blood before—and he was hungry, which made what he sensed all the more invigorating. The more he tasted in the air, the hungrier he realized he must have been. He ran from the living room, through the open adjoining dining room and into the kitchen where he found Cadence stirring over a steaming pot and Reggie sitting at the table chopping fresh vegetables. He looked around and found a large open package of oriental noodles sitting on the counter next to the four-burner stove. He was confused.

Amber stepped out from the pantry with Nick. She was startled to see Dustin and Bricktain. Nick looked pale.

"Look what's in this garden," Amber said holding up an armload of corn. "I don't know how this uncle did it, but it's a real garden and we have fresh produce."

"I could have sworn you were cooking steak," Dustin said.

Nick suddenly looked to Dustin and color filled his cheeks.

"Sorry, no meat," Cadence replied.

However, Dustin still smelled bloody raw meat. He walked to the oven and pulled on the door.

"Uh, excuse me," Cadence said side-stepping out of the way.

Dustin found the oven empty. "I could have sworn it was meat." He stood up and met an angry Cadence face to face and suddenly realized the source of the meat. He smelled it on Cadence, the blood pumping through her veins feeding her bones and tendons, her ribs and muscles. He could see her flesh pulsate as the blood pumped through her. Cadence was the raw meat, Amber and Reggie too. Dustin stepped away and noticed Nick standing far off. He wasn't standing protectively close to Cadence as he had been doing for the past few days.

"You smell it too, don't you," Dustin asked.

Nick didn't say anything, but looked frightened.

"Whatever it is," Bricktain said. "It sure smells good. I love Mexican food."

Reggie stopped chopping. "Smell what?"

Dustin didn't know whether or not to answer the old man who was now sitting on a hardwood barstool at a long bar countertop, which separated the kitchen from the dining area with its rectangular table. He noticed a different look of fear on Reggie's face and suddenly his scent was different. He was sweeter. Reggie was afraid. Dustin didn't know how he knew it, but the old man was afraid and Dustin liked it.

"You're one of them." Reggie pointed the blade of his knife at Dustin.

"What are you talking about," Cadence asked.

Now Dustin felt sick.

"That one too," Reggie said. "No wonder he looks ready to puke it up."

"They've been bitten," Amber replied and realized what her father was talking about. "This stuff's real, isn't it?"

"You can't stay here," Reggie said, his voice quivering. He dropped his knife and reached for a control knob that wasn't on the barstool. "You have to get out of here."

"They can't go," Cadence replied. "Those dogs are out there."

"*They* are those dogs," Reggie said and squirmed in his chair. "Get them out of here, now. Get them out."

"Dad." Amber ran to her shaking father.

"Get them out of here."

"We can't turn them out," Cadence said. She turned to Nick. "He can't own you."

"We kill them," Bricktain said.

Cadence could only open her mouth.

"That's an option," Amber agreed.

"You'll go first," Cadence replied. "They might not turn. No. No."

Amber shook Cadence. "If we let them stay, they will kill us when they turn."

"Unless we kill them first," Bricktain took up Reggie's fallen knife and was immediately struggling with Cadence who was trying to take it from him.

Cadence recoiled and held her arm. Blood dripped from it, onto the white tile floor. Suddenly, she found herself trying to hold Nick back from attacking Bricktain. Bricktain held the knife and stared at the blood on the floor. Dustin tore the blade from the officer's hand and stabbed it through the marble bar top up to the handle. Everyone, including Dustin, stared at the knife handle sticking up from the top of the counter.

"You can't stay here," Reggie said.

"What about the cell," Dustin asked. "You said you found a holding cell downstairs, Morris."

"It won't be strong enough," Nick said. He didn't know the cell wouldn't be strong enough, but he felt Cadence's blood sticking to him. He wanted that blood. He was hungry for more and he knew if he hungered much longer that no cell would be able to hold him back from food. He held his hands tight around Cadence to keep from fulfilling this new desire to taste human flesh. He wondered if he would have to fight Dustin for her. Dustin kept glancing back at Cadence and making eye contact with Nick. "What if we break out?"

"I won't let them kill you," Cadence cried.

"You have to," Nick replied. "You're the only ones who know about Jasper. You can't let him win. Don't let him use us to finish you off."

"No," Cadence cried and started hitting Nick. "You're so stupid. You always have been. You know that? You're so stupid."

Amber pulled Cadence away from Nick.

Cadence broke away and embraced Nick once more. "I'm sorry, I should have noticed."

This time Bricktain pulled Cadence off Nick.

"Don't touch me," Cadence screamed.

Nick wanted to tear Bricktain apart, but understood why he couldn't.

"Come on," Amber said. "You need bandaging." She started to pull Cadence from Nick, which wasn't an easy task.

"Wait," Nick said. He pushed Bricktain out of the way and took Cadence by the hand. He stretched out her arm to reveal where the knife had cut from Cadence's palm to midway down her forearm.

Cadence winced.

"Remember what they did to me in the canal," Nick said. He licked at Cadence's hand. He felt his saliva build one moment and in the next, tasted the sweet-bitter sensation of Cadence's blood on his tongue. He wanted to taste more, but he couldn't imagine hurting her. He loved her too much.

Cadence pulled her hand away. A pink line of flesh, where the knife cut her was all that remained of her wound.

"I guess there's some benefits of having a dog that can do that huh," Nick said. "Either you kill us in here, or they take us out there. At least out there, we won't regret fighting those who try to hurt us."

"Wait," Reggie said a bit calmer now. "Maybe there are benefits."

Dustin smiled. "We're stronger. Maybe we can fight back."

"We could spy on him," Nick said and suddenly he was smiling.

"Or spy on us for Jasper," Bricktain said. "You know how to get in here.

You don't think he'll use that on us?"

"Then change the codes," Nick said. "When Dustin wakes up maybe he'll know how to change the codes."

"If we go out there, Cracey won't be alone," Dustin explained. "And maybe we can learn something to help all of us."

"That could work," Reggie said and he too was grinning. "Hide for as long as you can. Maybe, he won't attack you since you're his now."

Cadence held Nick. "Don't kill anything, not even to eat. We could leave food out for you."

"Yeah, we'll leave a bowl of dog food on the step," Bricktain said.

"Don't be like the others, and bring Cracey with you," Cadence said. "Who knows what she's been eating."

"Don't ever go outside," Nick said. "Don't leave us food. Don't endanger yourself. Stay inside.

Dustin winced. "That voice." His eyes clenched. "We have to go now."

"Come back to me," Cadence said and held Nick one last time.

*   *   *

"And just how long have I been asleep," Josh asked.

"About ten hours," Cadence said.

For a moment, Josh wondered if the ceiling was decorated with Styrofoam egg cartons painted bronze. He decided it was foam.

"The first thing we have to do is get some more ammo for the guns in the den," Bricktain said. "Cadence and Amber should go into town and do that."

"The first thing we need to do is get rested and slow down," Josh replied.

"You're in no position to call the shots anymore, kid."

"I'm in no position?" Josh sat up on the couch for the first time since he had entered the bunker. He asked the question again, stood and walked to the elevator where he opened a keypad and punched in a code. "Now no one leaves unless you know the code. How's that for a position, you arrogant moron? No one leaves until I think it's safe up there, least of all anyone you want to send to do the work you're too afraid to do yourself. We're all staying right here."

Josh left everyone dumbstruck and walked into the kitchen. His uncle brought him down every so often to help restock the pantry. He never went anywhere other than the pantry, mostly because he never had any reason to. He always thought his uncle was eccentric for building this elaborate hideaway. Did his uncle truly believe that some foreign leader would really

127

drop a nuclear bomb on Plattsville? Was there really enough fear among the people of this city to justify creation of private bomb shelters in backyards? Or did his uncle, with his vast fortune, somehow just need a hobby? Where did his uncle get enough money to build something so high-tech anyway? Whatever his uncle's reasons, Josh was glad it was here now. He was tired of bad news. He was tired of the sight of blood. He was tired of losing everything that meant something to him: Cracey, Natalie, Mom, Dad, Richard, Dustin, Nick. He was tired of it all.

He tossed open a cupboard over a black kitchen sink and slammed it. He opened another and another until he found what he was looking for. He pulled down a tall narrow glass and filled it with water.

"What are you thinking," asked a voice Josh had heard but didn't recognize. "We're not your prisoners, now open the doors. As far as we know, we could be sitting in a deathtrap."

Amber ducked in time and dodged the glass Josh hurled at her. She felt its broken shards and water shower upon her. She stood back up and watched Josh pull another glass from the cupboard. She ran at Josh with an elbow bent and fist drawn back to strike.

"Amber, stop," Reggie cried.

Amber swung, but Josh struck. His fist blasted the side of Amber's head with hard, firm knuckles. She toppled and caught herself. She held the side of her burning head. More than anything, she wanted to lay down where she stood, but she forced herself to regain her balance. Cadence helped her. Reggie and Morris appeared paralyzed in the adjoining dining room. Amber looked up, angrier than before. She wanted to beat this punk and must have tried to a second time, because Cadence's grip tightened around her arm and restrained her. She held her ground and watched Josh move to the liquor cabinet in the dining area where he tore down a square bottle filled with gold liquid. The bottle slammed against the rectangular dining table as Josh set himself in one of the wooden chairs behind it. He twisted off the cap and poured a small bit into his new glass. He glared at Amber with red eyes and quickly knocked back the drink. When he looked at her he wondered why the stranger was here but not Natalie. His eyes filled with tears and his glass with more of the golden liquor, this time all the way to the rim, leaving the bottle half empty.

"No one else dies today," Josh said.

At that, Amber realized Josh had lost much that night and she remembered her brothers' torn bodies left in the ground and in the fence. She couldn't protect them after they had protected her all these years, and now they had left her the responsibility of making sure her grandfather was cared for. With each drop of saddened dew breaking from Josh's eyelids, Amber felt herself more able to reel in her own losses the previous night. She knew he was right. Enough people had died. Still, he hit her. As she watched him drink, somehow her hatred seemed to flush away with her own sadness of her family. Yet, somehow, she felt sad for Josh too; whom she had learned had no family now. Who was this man? What made his friends respect him enough that they would travel through the hell of the previous night, for him? She felt sorry for herself and for him and didn't know why. She stood and started for the hallway leading to the bedrooms. She wanted to punch Josh out. This was his fault. She despised him.

"What is your name," Josh asked as if he were asking the gold liquor in the glass he held.

Amber stopped and answered without turning.

"Well, Amber," Josh said before taking a long draught from his glass. "I need a computer to email someone, find one."

"There's an office down the hall," Amber replied. "Find it yourself."

"We have one ally on the outside," Josh said avoiding eye contact with anyone in the room. He felt his grip tightening around his glass. "Thomas de Soleil. He's supposed to be some sort of hunter in the Queen of England's royal service. We need his help. Email every English government department you can, and then start looking for other avenues."

"I'll rot before I do anything for you," Amber replied and disappeared the room.

Reggie watched his daughter leave the room and rolled his chair up to the table. "You and me are gonna have a little talk about this later."

"No, we're not," Josh replied and matched Reggie's sharp brow with an even sharper one. "You knew." Josh drank from his cup. "You could have stopped all of this. We're here because of you. My family is gone because you're a coward. Now wheel yourself down that hall and do what I say."

And she was there again, this time tears filled her cheeks. "You're wrong," Amber said standing behind her father's chair.

"No," Reggie replied. "He's not." His chair pulled away from the table. "We'll try and find this Thomas de Soleil."

Reggie and Amber left the room together.

"You're such an inspiration," Bricktain said. "When we all get out of here, you and I aren't going to talk. I'm just going to pound you."

"Why wait," Josh asked, leaping out of his seat and nearly knocking over the drinks on the table.

Josh shoved past Cadence and Bricktain and returned to the keypad. A moment later, the elevator door opened. "You want a fight? Lets do it. The winner returns and you get knocked out."

Bricktain and Josh entered the elevator with Cadence between them.

The three tumbled out of the garage and eventually into the dark backyard. Security floodlights flashed on. No one seemed to notice that night had fallen once more. Bricktain swung first and missed Josh completely. Josh stood and swung but fell to the ground and he watched Cadence snap her foot into Bricktain's throat. Bricktain grabbed at himself and fell forward.

"This conversation is over," Cadence said. "Do you understand, yet?"

Bricktain brought himself to his feet.

"Dog," Bricktain yelled.

Josh and Cadence barely had time to react before a black creature leapt from the garage roof, knocked Cadence off her feet and pinned Josh to the ground.

Josh wanted to reach for his crossbows, which were actually on the living room carpet next to the couch, but found himself reaching for his aching sides instead. The creature snapped its teeth at Josh, raised a paw with flared claws, but fell over as two smaller and lanky black dogs appeared out of nowhere and fought it away from Josh. Bricktain and Cadence began pulling Josh away.

The smaller dogs were slender and wore the brown masks of the Doberman pinscher. They bit and leapt at the black monster, which dwarfed them both many times over. One Doberman bit into the monster's forearm while the second scaled the monster's back and latched its teeth deep into its shoulder. The three dogs cursed at one another. Josh was on his feet before he saw another monster approaching just outside the chain link fencing.

"Inside," Josh ordered. As he turned, Cadence and Bricktain were already on their way into the garage, and he followed closely when he heard a familiar voice, which forced him to stop.

The others heard it too and looked just as surprised to Josh as he felt.

Josh turned and watched as the monster just outside the fence struggled with a slim shadow that turned the right way in the light to reveal Natalie's face filled with hatred. The monster lunged forward, but fell back with a long silver pole stuck in its neck. The pole yanked out and a spurt of liquid leapt from the creature. Its head jerked to the side and flipped up as Natalie thrust the pole up through the creature's mouth. The monster spun around with the pole stuck in its head and kicked Natalie down before it retreated into the darkness, pole and all.

The monster fighting the Dobermans managed to break free of them and moved quickly for Natalie's shadow as she ran through the gate and into Richard's yard.

Josh called to Natalie as the two Dobermans flew through the air and tackled their opponent one more time. Natalie's shadow fell, rolled and stood back up as the three dogs began their fight again. Natalie hurled an object at the largest of the dogs. The object smacked against the ground and the creature fled. Natalie suddenly turned on one of the Dobermans and kicked its side. The dog cried.

Natalie ran for Josh and, the masked dogs chased her. One bit at her heel, but didn't get a good grip. They suddenly stopped and ran into the surrounding shadows beyond the chain link. Natalie reached Josh and collapsed into his arms.

"I went to your house," she stammered and quickly found that spot, which fit the contours of her face to Josh so well. "I saw the blood. I thought you were dead."

Josh wanted to hold the moment forever, but was fully aware they still stood in the open backyard, vulnerable and in danger. He held Natalie tight and led her towards the safety of the garage door. "We'll be safe inside." But Josh was forced down into the cold grass and Natalie screamed as a new monster tore her away from him. She cried for Josh and Josh scrambled after her but was no match for the speed of the white creature dragging Natalie back into the darkness. Josh's only concern was to free her from the vicious jaws of this new beast. Natalie kicked and swung fists and threw tufts of grass at the creature's eyes. Josh ran after her with outstretched arms as if he believed he could reach his Nata faster that way, but other arms wrapped around and held him. Amber and Cadence held back Josh. Bricktain appeared with a shotgun and a blast of light erupted from the muzzle into the darkness. Josh broke Cadence's grip, and nearly threw Amber into Bricktain. He threw the muzzle up, forcing the next shot into the air.

"Don't shoot, moron," Josh cried. He felt Cadence and Amber's arms lock around him once more and drag him toward the garage. Josh's strength was useless as he helplessly watched the white wolf drag Natalie off into the cruel depths of the night's shade. Bricktain soon blocked Josh's view as he stepped backward with Josh into the garage, with his shotgun poised to fire. Josh heard Natalie's pleas for help before the slam of the garage door silenced them.

11 — A Mean Drunk

Josh looked to the worm for help.

Jack, it seemed, had become a new best friend too.

Josh sat in the lounge chair by the pool and drank as much of his friend's advice as he could, straight out of the bottle—fewer steps that way and no need to dirty a glass. It seemed Richard must have been fond of the drinks too, because half the liquor cabinet was stocked with nothing but whiskey and tequila. Wine, a bottle here and there of rum, brandy, and brands of drink that Josh had never heard of before because they weren't labeled or appeared foreign and old, filled the other half. The bottom of the cabinet held three cases of beer: Greymeister, Chums and D'ublin. Josh tried the beer and when he emptied the case of Chums, he started on the Greymeister, and after he emptied that case, he opened a D'ublin and spit it all over Bricktain who, of course, was grateful for the compliment and stormed out of the billiard room shouting some of his own. Josh threw can after can of the unopened D'ublin into the swimming pool to try and drown their horrid taste. After realizing he was out of beer, he nearly drowned himself trying to get the cans off the bottom of the pool. That's when he made best friends with the two bottles, Jack and the one with the worm. For fun, he brought along a shotgun to sit in his lounge chair and blow away empty beer cans and bottles on the opposite side of the pool.

He held the bottle around its neck and stared at the still yellow worm lurking in the shallow remains. He hadn't been able to bring himself to drink his little buddy. It wasn't the worm's fault it was thrown in the bottle. It was probably a family worm returning home from work or school, having a good time trotting through dirt or sewage before some jerk took it and dumped it in a bottle to see if it could swim. It couldn't.

The darkness would come again. Josh was used to waking up now in places and positions that he couldn't remember finding. Soon, he would sleep and he would see his loved ones again. Natalie still smiled at him and held him when Josh thought he was sleeping, Cracey had hair and his mom prepared her gourmet dishes that still enslaved every one of Josh's six senses. In most of his dreams, wolves didn't exist, dogs didn't exist and the idea of Jasper wasn't even the shadow of a shadow on the dark side of the moon. Everyone was alive. They were happy. He played video games with Cracey

132

and watched her run in circles every time she got excited. He slid a ring over Natalie's finger time and time again and his mom finally saw past her own pride and accepted Natalie into the family.

It wasn't until Josh became aware of his surroundings, the pain in his head, the echoes of real sounds and voices that he returned to the real world. When he did return, he tried his best to hold onto the glimmer of images he remembered from his dreams. That's when he drank himself back to sleep again, back to the better of the two worlds. He would have traded the heavens and earth for just five more minutes of fantasy to be reality. He wanted to return to the way things were, back when Cracey outsmarted him, Mom still hated Natalie for no good reason and Josh remembered worrying about grades on final exams. Sometimes, he could still see everyone dear to him, as if they were still there. And out the windows of his house, he might see Jasper and his dogs circling in on everything. Sometimes dreams were good, but sometimes Josh woke screaming. He couldn't die in bad dreams and the good ones made the nightmares worthwhile. Sleep was good. Passing out was better. Josh drank and sleep lasted longer. Jack saddled the worm and made more of it possible.

Mustering all of his strength, Josh brought himself to his feet and shuffled towards the edge of the pool where he emptied part of his stomach onto the concrete ledge. A moment later, he emptied more on his feet.

"See what you make me do," Josh said holding the bottle with the worm and tapping it. "You ever throw up? Hey, wake up."

Of course, the worm threw up. It had to, in all that tequila. That's probably what made the tequila so good, the worm's vomit. It probably just sat in the bottle drinking and puking, and along comes some idiot who thinks it tastes pretty good and he drinks it and throws up. Josh wondered if anyone would drink his throw up. How funny would that be? Josh tipped the bottle and watched the remaining contents drizzle from the narrow mouth into the pool. The worm fell with the last remnants of tequila.

"If I have to wake up, you have to wake up," Josh slurred. He watched the worm hit the water and sink. The worm sank deeper and deeper and farther from Josh's sight straight to the bottom of the swimming pool where a can of Dublin happened to rest, right from one bottle straight to the can. Josh realized the worm didn't want to wake up. It wanted a beer.

"Hey," Josh said. He yelled and threw his empty tequila bottle at the water where, unlike the worm, it fought to stay afloat like a cheap buoy. "That's my beer."

Josh returned to his lounge chair and threw a blanket off the side to reveal the pump-action shotgun he had been using to blow up empty liquor bottles and cans. He pumped the gun once and returned to the water, nearly slipping in his own vomit.

"Get away from that beer." He fired off a shot at the worm and the water erupted into his face like an angry geyser trying to slap Josh away from the poolside. Josh cursed the water, pumped the shotgun and fired again, this time at the water for spraying him. He fired off three more shots, each time creating a fountain, which he also needed to shoot, before he noticed the buzzing in his head from the gun shot echoes.

"Josh!" Cadence clenched a cue stick as she quickly walked toward Josh. "Put that thing down before you kill someone,"

Josh stumbled a little turning to Cadence, but managed to maintain his balance. "Oh good, Cadence. I need your help."

"To what, kill somebody?"

"Yes, the worm's after my beer."

Cadence still wasn't accustomed to Josh's stupid and destructive behavior over the past four months. Everything had changed. Every day she watched the Josh she knew disappear. His eyes dimmed with each bottle he downed. She wanted to help, but she didn't know where to start. Did she start by saying she understood? Did losing a father and mother count towards her ability to understand losing a father, mother, sister, girlfriend and best friend? For four months, she didn't know the answers to any of those questions and for four months, Josh grew worse until no one was brave enough to be around him. They might have all left the bunker were they not afraid of the threat that waited outside for them.

She missed Natalie so much it hurt, and she cried herself to sleep every night for the first month and then off and on for the following three. Natalie was her best friend, the closest thing to a sister she knew. She wondered if Natalie was dead or turned into one of Jasper's minions. Poor Natalie. And what about Nick, she had spent so much time seeing the little brother that she never admitted what his feelings could have been for her, or what her feelings were for him. Now she'd never be able to tell him. Cadence drank the first night after Natalie was stolen, even stayed up late with Josh until they both fell asleep, passed out really, in the living room. When she woke, her head pounded. Her own pulse bruised her brain against the inside of her skull with every heart beat. She might have actually drank more, but she watched Josh wake up, stumble to the liquor cabinet and wash down a beer to calm his headache. He looked awful, and he barely noticed anyone.

The others hated him. Bricktain continued his grumbling, but that was just

Bricktain. He'd been a clumsy thorn ever since he joined up with the group. Amber and her father pretty much kept clear of Josh. Amber's bruise disappeared from her face and Reggie placed himself between his daughter and the drunk whenever Josh was present. Cadence wanted to hate Josh, but couldn't bring herself to it. She wanted to convince everyone else that Josh's behavior was just a phase, but no one wanted to hear it. Cadence felt sorry for her only remaining friend.

"Get away from my beer," Josh screamed and fired another shot into the water. He pumped the gun and took aim again.

"Josh, stop it," Cadence screamed and cupped her ears as she listened to another shell empty into the pool and water lash up in rage. "That's not going to bring any of them back."

Josh pumped the gun again and a red shell leapt dead from the side of the barrel. He stared at the water for a moment. "I need a drink." He turned back for his chair where several empty bottles rested on their fronts and backs and sides.

"No, Josh," Cadence plead. "This isn't good."

"Leave me alone."

She thought about leaving him alone, even stepped away, but for some reason stayed with him. She stood her ground and watched Josh dig through blankets and towels for a sign of a bottle with any liquid in it. He was pathetic.

"You need to eat, Josh" Cadence said. "You need to get some sleep."

"I need a drink to sleep." Josh prodded empty bottles away from under his chair with the barrel of his gun.

Now, Cadence found herself thinking of Natalie. How would Natalie react? What would Natalie say if she were still alive? "Natalie wouldn't want you hurting yourself like this."

Josh shoved the end of the barrel through a bottle with the black Jack label on it, breaking it to shards.

"I know it's hard, Josh. I know it. I miss her too," Cadence said. "And I can't think for a second that this is what she'd want for you. Neither would your parents or Dustin or Cracey."

"You shut up," Josh yelled and pointed the gun at Cadence. "You don't say anything, you're not even worthy to speak their names. You were supposed to protect them. You're the deadeye and you couldn't even shoot an old man. This is your fault."

Cadence wasn't even sure if she heard anything Josh just said. She stared down the hollow barrel of the shotgun while Josh stabbed it, with every other word, at Cadence's chest and face. "Don't point that at me."

"Don't tell me what to do."

"Please, put it down."

"You want my beer."

"No I don't, just please put it down."

"Why?"

"Because you're all I have left," Cadence screamed. She fought to take in a breath, but managed to take in a long drought before exploding with: "Natalie wouldn't put up with this behavior and you know it."

Josh's eyes and nostrils flared and he bit his bottom lip and jerked back the shotgun trigger.

Cadence screamed at the click of the empty gun.

Josh dropped it and stumbled backwards. He didn't know why he did it, why he pulled the trigger. He heard Cadence's voice and Natalie's name and all he could think about was that Natalie wasn't with him anymore. He didn't hate Cadence, felt like he wanted to, but certainly didn't hate her. No one else could be blamed for Natalie, Dustin and Nick. Someone needed to be blamed and Cadence was the only one who could be responsible. Josh didn't know the other people. Bricktain already held the blame for Cracey, but who was he in Natalie's abduction? The driver? Cadence was the one who swore to protect Nick. She should have been able to protect Natalie as well. Every day he saw Cadence, he saw her best friend Natalie. They were always together, and he still imagined them as such. He knew Cadence was only trying to help him cope with all that he had lost, but he kept seeing the terrified look on Natalie's face as she begged him for help as the white beast dragged her away. Someone needed to pay for that and Jasper was too strong and sober to take the blame.

"Cadence," Josh whispered.

"Don't," Cadence replied. She looked as though she had more to say, but stepped away instead. "Stay away from me." She looked at Josh in a way he'd never imagined possible, full of hurt and anger. "I was the last thing you had left." She suddenly ran off, wiping tears from her face.

Josh screamed at the ceiling, took up the gun and started smashing bottles and the chair with its butt. An instant later, he flung the empty shotgun into the pool. He picked up empty shotgun shells and threw them into the pool. When there were no more to dispose of, he hurled in the chair he had been sleeping in and the dirty blankets he'd slept under for the past two weeks. Last of all, he threw in the towels. Suddenly, he felt sober and he was angry, not just at what he lost, but angry with himself. He needed a drink to make all the

136

pain disappear, but first he needed to set things right with Cadence. He started after her. He ran and as he ran, slipped. His ankle twisted and he stepped off into the pool. He slipped, hit his head on the concrete edge of the pool and rolled unconscious into the water.

*　　　*　　　*

Dear Sir,

We have sent off several emails with hope that you truly exist, but to no avail and so I write this letter and take great risk in sending it. I anticipate I won't survive getting this letter to a mailbox, but people depend on what aid this letter may bring. We know little to find you and I pray one letter gets through so that you may come to our aid. My name is Amber Chambers and for several years, I have tried my best to ignore the deaths that have taken place around my family and home.

Recently, I'm ashamed to say, I witnessed an atrocity that altered the course of several lives and destroyed many. A young child was abducted by a dark and evil creature. I had it in my power to fight for her, but I have spent my entire life ignoring the cries of others in order to keep the vengeance of the beasts away from my home and family. My slothfulness has been repaid upon me, for now my father and I cannot return to our home. We have been taken in by a Josh Revlon who has lost his entire family and most of his friends. He has since turned mad. But it is his generosity that protects us all and his leadership that allowed him to learn about you and some extent of the nature of the creatures that now hunt us and hold his sister as one of their own.

We are holed up in some sort of bomb shelter that these monsters have been unable to penetrate. We are five in number, but we used to be eight. We have not contacted the police because they've been unhelpful in the past. We tried to contact a few family members, but none have responded and now we remain unable to contact anyone outside anymore. We fear pursuing contacting people for we don't want to bring the innocent into our situation, nor do we want anyone to try and drag us out of the only safe haven we have. We know now that no one is in any position to help us, no one except maybe for you.

We no longer have use of our phone or internet and I am the only one I feel sane enough and skilled enough to be able to survive venturing outside to send this letter off as a final attempt to contact you. We are all truly frightened and we request your aid. There must be something we can do to regain our freedom. You can find us at the following address, we will know when you arrive.

Sincerely and at your mercy,

Amber Chambers

*   *   *

Josh touched his head. Everything was dark and muffled. He pulled a small towel from his face and tried to sit up, but found the venture more tedious than should have been. He felt stiff. Every muscle in his body either was tight or wouldn't respond.

"Bad news," Amber said. "You're still alive."

Josh kept trying to sit up and found his tongue wasn't as eager to work either. So, he moaned.

"Take it easy," Amber said.

She appeared over Josh, kneeling beside him. Her hazel eyes gouged into his soul like no others had. Here, hate truly held a home for him. Yet, she seemed both welcoming and frightening at the same time. Her hair fell down the sides of her face and she quickly became annoyed with it and reached back to tie it into some kind of a knot. She helped Josh sit up and didn't worry about being gentle about it.

"You hurting," She asked. She wore a plain white T-shirt and the same black jeans she wore when the two first met.

Josh grunted as he rose to a sitting position. "No." He found himself on the red shag carpet next to the pool table. "Shaky. Thirsty."

"You want a drink," Amber asked. She disappeared around the end of the pool table, leaving Josh hunkered over in his own pain and bewilderment, and

138

reappeared with a glass of water. "Drink this."

Josh did.

"You're lucky," Amber said. "We hoped you wouldn't wake up."

Josh dropped the glass as the memories of the shotgun and Cadence filled the foremost thoughts in his head. "Cadence?"

"Her too," Amber said picking up the empty glass. "Let's take a look, here." Amber turned Josh's head and scrutinized a wide abrasion on his forehead. "How do you feel?"

"Shaky," Josh replied.

"Anything hurt?"

"Everything's tight."

"Well, you've been asleep, off and on, more than two days."

"Two days," Josh asked. He tried to stand but gave up just thinking about it. "I'd kind of like a drink."

"I'll bring you some more water," Amber said standing up.

"No, something else," Josh said. "Something to alleviate the pain."

"I've disposed of all the hard stuff," Amber said.

"What about the rare stuff?"

"Everything."

Josh felt the last bit of strength leave his body and he slumped forward. "I just want to forget."

Josh tried not to cry, but the more he thought about not talking, the more he thought about why he didn't want to talk or why he didn't want to remember anything. Natalie's face flashed through his mind. Cracey also flashed through his mind with her bald head and her tears. And Cadence filled his mind and the sound of the shotgun trigger snapping forward into nothing, but all he heard was the explosion of gunpowder and shotgun shrapnel.

Amber forced Josh to his feet. "You need to exercise."

"I killed her," Josh said barely audible, but Amber heard.

"Cadence is alive," she replied.

"She might as well be dead," Josh said. "She would have been if I hadn't blown the last shot."

"True," Amber said. "But you would have been too."

"How so?"

"If there had been a bullet in that gun, I'd have let you drown."

"I fell in the pool?"

Amber was silent, just stared at and hated Josh.

"You should have let me drown."

"You're not getting off that easy."

Josh didn't know how to respond, but the tears seemed to be response enough.

"What do I even say to her now," he asked. "I'm so tired."

"No one cares," Amber replied. "You don't talk to her, you hear me? You're alive and that's all I care about, my debt's repaid as far as I'm concerned. There's been enough death and torment in all of our lives, and you've been the cause of all of it, and so am I."

Josh looked to ask why, but didn't have to. And something else caught his attention.

"What is this," Josh asked reaching to Amber's side where he could clearly see gauze padding and white medical tape beneath a tear in her T-shirt.

"We'll never be that good of friends," Amber said smacking Josh's hand away. "I had to leave the shelter."

"What made you do a stupid thing like that," Josh asked.

"Your orders," Amber replied. "Believe me, I'd rather I hadn't, but you were right. We need to find this Thomas de Soleil if he can help."

"You did that because I asked you too?"

"Call it a moment of weakness and don't expect it again. Those people followed you into a fight that you weren't prepared for and because of it your friends are gone, my brothers are gone and Cadence has never felt so alone. All she wanted was for you to come back to your senses so you could give her some hope, and you hurt her."

"She hates me," Josh asked.

"It wasn't easy to keep her here. She was ready to let those things take her just like they took her friend, Nick. But for some reason she stayed. Don't ask me why."

"But I locked down the elevator."

"You don't remember a thing do you?" Amber gripped Josh's arm, trying hard to twist his stitches as much as she could, and drew close to him. "Listen, Cadence is a good person and I don't believe for one second she would look up to a drunken pooped out sack, such as you, if there wasn't some sort of redeeming quality in you. You deserved her respect once maybe, but I swear I will do whatever it takes to keep you away from her until I think you're no longer crap."

Josh didn't try to protest.

"You're not the only one who's hurting," Amber said. "But you're the only one who treats everyone else like they're not allowed to feel pain and we're not taking it anymore. If that means getting rid of that poison you drink, so be it. From now on, I stand between you and anything that makes you take it out on the rest of us."

Josh could say nothing. She was right. All of it was true. Amber's nails dug tighter into his arm before she finally tossed it against him. She stood and walked away.

"Amber," Josh said.

"What," she asked from the other side of the pool table.

"I hit you," Josh replied. "I'm sorry." He still didn't know what to say and he almost let himself fall backward so he didn't have to try and stand any longer, but Amber was at his side once again. "Natalie's always been my compass," he continued. "Some people have consciences, but I had Natalie. I've never hit anyone in my life."

"That doesn't excuse it," Amber said.

"No," Josh replied. "It doesn't. And you're right, I am crap. That's why Natalie made me better. I'm sorry. I really want a drink."

"How about a walk instead?"

"Okay, but you'll have to carry me," Josh said.

Amber drew Josh's arm around her shoulders. "You stayed in the same position the entire time. No wonder you hurt."

"You know, you're not supposed to let someone with a concussion sleep," Josh said. He groaned as he did his best to walk under his own strength.

"Like I said," Amber replied. "Everyone was hoping you wouldn't wake up."

"Sorry to disappoint you."

"I'm not disappointed. I punched Natalie after I blamed her for the deaths of my brothers," Amber explained. "I think I understand a little."

The two strolled around the billiard table a few times before Josh felt his joints loosen and his strength somewhat return to his legs. Josh continued his discussion with Amber and learned all about what had transpired with Natalie the night the foolish party marched on Jasper's house. After a few more rotations of the table, Amber suggested a walk around the pool. She didn't appear as the same angry person that she had been a half an hour before.

They wandered into the pool area where everything was clean. Floating beer bottles and cans no longer polluted the water. Plaster and glass no longer covered the floor. Amber explained how everyone pitched in to clean up because they had a sudden urge to swim, since Josh occupied the billiards room and no one wanted to swim in the filth he left behind. And no one cared enough to help him to his own room. As Josh and his host completed their first full rotation around the pool the elevator doors sprang open and Cadence stood in a black one-piece swimsuit with a brown towel over her shoulders.

She glared at Josh from behind stranger's eyes.

"Don't," Amber said when she believed Josh was about to say something and she forced Josh to keep walking. They passed the elevator doors and watched them conceal Cadence.

"Will you talk to her," Josh asked.

"No," Amber replied.

The two continued their pace in silence until red and yellow lights suddenly flashed overhead and an alarm screeched.

"We have company," cried a voice through speakers.

Josh turned to run for the elevator, bumbling a little over his feet. Amber helped him recover and he watched the elevator doors suddenly reopen revealing Cadence in the exact same position she was in when the doors opened the first time. Josh tried his best to ignore the alarm. He wanted to say something, anything to Cadence, and he couldn't decide which was more important: his apology for his behavior or the urgency of the alarm ringing in his ears. He was afraid to enter the elevator, but an abrupt shove from Amber told him to get a move on. He stepped into the elevator and the doors closed again.

He tried not to look at Cadence as he felt the carriage make its slow journey upward. He found he couldn't bring himself to look at her. Amber stood between Cadence and Josh, which helped make the trip more bearable. No one said a word until the doors finally flew open and Bricktain stood posed with a revolver pointed right at Josh's head.

"Intruder," Bricktain cried out as the hammer on the .45 drew back. Josh felt Amber slam against him and all three passengers fell against the steel wall and slid to the floor as the revolver belched into the air and ricocheted throughout everyone's eardrums.

Josh looked Cadence in the eyes as she continued to pin him and Amber against the wall.

She glared back. "Doesn't feel so good, does it?"

12 – Speatsh Cheatham

The grass was gold, long and gold. Occasionally, different dogs passed through the view of the camera and eyed the entrance to the garage, their warm breath frozen by the cold air. Dobermans and chihuahuas, terriers and bulldogs all made some sort of appearance for the security cameras. Average-looking dogs appeared all day and dark ones appeared at night.

"I saw it," Reggie said holding down some keys on the computer keyboard. The camera panned across the back yard. "It was a big gray one with two dogs and they walked right into the yard but I lost them."

"Doesn't look any different than before," Bricktain said as he peered over Reggie's shoulder at the computer monitor. "Dogs everywhere, which is why we can't go outside without fearing for our lives every time we've tried."

"You figured that out after only three and a half months, huh," Cadence asked.

A Labrador marched with its head held up high near the steel drop-down door.

"It's been that way since we came here," Reggie said. "They're waiting for us. They know we can't stay in here forever."

"At least, they haven't marched on us," Amber said.

"You said this place could hold us for a year, right," Bricktain said.

"It wouldn't matter if we could stay in here for one year or a hundred," Josh explained. "They may have more time and patience than we do. Besides, we haven't exactly been rationing our food, have we? We'll run out sooner than we should I'm afraid."

"We'll still be okay on food," Bricktain said. "You haven't eaten anything that hasn't come out of a bottle."

"Why would the alarm wait to go off 'til now, if they've been out there the last few months," Josh asked.

"We're sitting ducks," Reggie said.

"Not yet," Josh replied.

"I told you," Bricktain said. "We should have never come here."

"It's too bad we don't have a back door," Amber observed.

"Maybe we do," Josh said. "We should try to open that door downstairs again."

Reggie frowned at this and frowned at the white bandage wrapped around his hand. The cut was still deep from the broken jigsaw blade.

"That door's not opening," Cadence said. "And I doubt if you knew how to open it, you could remember how."

"Well, there has to be a key some place," Josh responded. "Let's search the place again. I'll start with the door."

"Yeah, check the rest of the place while you're at it," Bricktain said.

"Or you can help look and maybe we'll find a solution sooner," Josh replied.

"Well, look who's back from the dead and ready to take charge," Reggie said.

"Go back to your cave," Bricktain said and he walked out of the room. "Let the big boys work."

Josh remembered his body was sore. "Like me or not, we have to find something and now." Josh left the office without realizing Amber and Cadence were following.

The three approached the elevator in the living room and hardly paid any attention to Bricktain who, if they had been paying attention, would have been too scared and too stupid to signal that something was wrong. He was still. Josh, Cadence and Amber waited for the elevator before Bricktain decided to speak.

"The elevator's coming down," Bricktain said.

Josh listened to the distant hum of the carriage as it lowered from above.

"Someone called it to the garage," Bricktain said.

"They got in," Cadence said and in an instant was gone.

"We were just looking through the cameras," Bricktain said. "How did we not see it happen?"

Josh didn't know how, but someone or something called the elevator and now it was coming down. How did it happen? Josh thought he changed the bunker access password since Dustin used it when they first arrived at the underground bunker. But then he did unlock it when he went outside to fight Bricktain, didn't he? So, what happened? Jasper couldn't have the code. Of course, Jasper did have these past four months to learn how to break it. Maybe it wasn't Jasper at all. It couldn't be Josh's parents, could it? One or both? No it couldn't. He remembered the blood defiling his home. How many dogs could fit in the elevator? He felt something silky and cool slide into his hand. He gripped it and recognized the texture of the gloves. He dropped them and knelt down to a box Cadence set on the floor. Cadence, herself was loading the very shotgun that had almost killed her more than a month before. Amber

144

too was loading some sort of weapon, but Josh didn't have time to pay attention to what it could be as he quickly snapped the crossbows together and packed them full of silver cylinders. He wound them both and turned to the elevator. Bricktain held a floor lamp, oblivious that it was still plugged into the wall.

"What are we doing, Josh," Cadence asked.

"If it's Jasper, kill him," Josh replied. "If it's a dog, don't let them out of there alive, unless it's Dustin or Nick."

"How will we know if it's Dustin or Nick," Cadence asked

"Wait for them to attack us," Josh asked. He wasn't sure.

"I'll bash them good if they do," Bricktain said, shaking his lamp at the elevator doors.

"Yeah, you do that," Josh said.

The doors opened.

Josh ran the scenario through his head, but nobody moved. It wasn't Natalie or Josh's parents. The man's face was stubbled with gray and his eyes were dark and deep. He wore what appeared to be the small pelt of a brown bear around his shoulders and down half the length of his arms. A thin coat made of other furs draped to his knees. He wore plain blue jeans and black boots. If Josh had time to decipher more details, he would have noticed that they were good motorcycle boots with thick zippers up the side, and a metal ankle brace encased one of them. He had two Dobermans, one on each side, sitting patiently. Josh didn't recognize him and he waited for the man, or the dogs, to make a move.

Bricktain lunged first, shoving the lampshade into the old man. The Dobermans leapt. One tore the lamp from Bricktain's hands and broke it. The other tackled Bricktain. Josh took aim on the dog over Bricktain and squeezed the trigger, but the crossbow flew out of Josh's hand. A sharp pain shot up his fingers as a smooth laceration appeared on his wrist. Josh ignored the spurts of blood for the time being and quickly aimed the second crossbow at the intruder. The mountain man threw what appeared to be a large flat, hollow disc straight at Josh. The ring toppled through the air and slipped right over a side of the crossbow. It encircled the front of the bow and suddenly jerked the weapon from Josh's hand.

The old man limped from the elevator and his metal-braced right leg forced Josh to the ground. The ring flew in the air in such a manner that the crossbow fell from within it. The flat ring appeared be held to the end of a steel-like whip, yet it seemed to spin where it was attached. Each time the intruder cracked the whip and sent the ring in a new direction, it whistled softly. A second ring appeared at the end of a second steel whip. The old man snapped that whip and the ring sliced apart Cadence's shotgun. Amber stood still as one ring flew past her head and stuck in the wall and the second ring spun at Reggie who was sitting in his wheelchair with a rifle. The ring hovered a moment before it coupled over the barrel of the rifle and jerked it away from its wielder's hands as it had the other weapons.

"Sit," the stranger ordered. The Dobermans pulled back from Bricktain and took a seated position behind the old man. "Put it down, I'm not in the mood."

Amber dropped her gun and flinched as the ring tore away from the wall, and a tuft of her own blond hair fell before her eyes. The rings curled back into the old man's hands and quickly disappeared beneath his robes. He turned to Josh and reached down with a soft leather glove with a back lined of a soft fur. The intruder exposed Josh's wrist. "Lick it."

One of the Dobermans approached Josh and started licking his wrist. It licked until all the blood was gone, becoming more aggressive the more blood it washed away. Josh could feel the dog's teeth scrape harder and harder against his skin as if begging to tear the flesh apart rather than heal it.

"That's enough," the old man demanded.

The dog kept licking and gradually began gnawing.

"I said that's enough." The mountain man kicked the Doberman away from Josh. "Sit."

The dogs sat.

"You in charge," the gray man asked as he towered over Bricktain.

"In a way," Bricktain replied.

"Yeah, whatever you say, Falstaff. Everyone else has a gun, and you start the fight with a lamp," The old man said. "I know village idiot when I see him." He turned to Josh and peered down through red and black eyes. He brushed a large hand with thick fingers over black-gray stubble, which painted from his ears and down over his neck. Suddenly he turned on Josh. "You're supposed to wear gloves with the fangs." He took up Josh's small crossbows and frowned at them and Josh.

"The what," Josh asked.

"You don't even know what they are," the old man asked waving the silver crossbow in Josh's face. "Fangs, they're called fangs."

"Are you Thomas de Soleil," Cadence asked.

"Thomas de—that suck bag," the stranger cried. "No, I ain't and you all lucky too cause he's nothing but a ruthless killer who wouldn't give a second thought to usin ya fer food. You don't want his help."

Josh felt something inside of him freeze as he watched the old man's eyes

146

suddenly open with what could have been fear.

"You sent for him, didn't you," the stranger asked.

Josh realized he didn't know.

"We did our best to find him," Reggie said.

The stranger slowly curled a smile at Reggie, who was still shaking in the wheelchair. He held a hand out to Josh. "I'm Speatsh Cheatham. Your uncle called me the night your sister disappeared."

Josh didn't believe him.

"Thomas de Soleil will come to help you," Speatsh explained. "But he's a vampire, and I don't mean that in a metaphoric sense neither. The buzzard is older than dirt and should be fartin a weathered tombstone. We've crossed paths before. He hunts what chases you and he will feed on each of you, one by one, to give him the strength he needs to fight the monsters you fear 'til he can't kill anymore of 'em."

"What do you mean feed," Amber asked.

"What do you think it means? Feed? Food? He eats you. You're in his belly and when you're gone, he leaves, and maybe he makes a quick stop at a doo-doo room. He wants the wolf and he doesn't care about humanity, and you just called him to you." The intruder pressed toward the kitchen and suddenly stopped. "Who drank my sack? And where's my mead? I came all the way from North Korea and you snot bags drank my drink?"

"I threw it away," Amber said. She was beginning to wish she hadn't flushed it all.

"I got that mead from Aristotle's yes man and you threw it away?"

"I held onto a few cans of beer," Bricktain said.

"Well, hoo-dan-poo-pa-doo for you," said Speatsh. "I can make that myself."

"We had to throw it away," Amber quickly replied.

"Why?"

No one really wanted to answer. Bricktain almost did.

"I became violent," Josh finally said.

"I'm ready to become violent," Speatsh said. "That mead was nearly two thousand years old. Violent, how?"

"I hit someone."

"Hit? Who?"

"Me," Amber replied.

"And he nearly blew her face off," Bricktain said gesturing to Cadence. "When he turned a shotgun on her."

Josh tried not to look at Cadence, but he caught her returning the familiar hate toward him. "I was drunk."

Josh keeled forward. Speatsh's braced foot hooked under Josh and kicked him onto his back. He looked ready to stomp, but instead lowered his foot. "You may never know how lucky you are." He helped Josh to his feet a second time. "Come with me, all of you." Speatsh made his way back to the elevator. "You two, behave yourselves."

The Dobermans continued to sit and watched Josh, Amber and Cadence join Speatsh in the elevator.

"Meet us downstairs," Speatsh said before the doors concealed the small group and the elevator sang itself down to the lowest floor.

"Planning to take a dip," Speatsh asked.

"Huh," Cadence asked, when she realized that she was still wearing Barbara Revlon's one piece swimsuit. "Oh, yes, I was."

"Sorry I interrupted your plans."

The doors opened and no one moved.

"After you," Speatsh said gesturing to Cadence.

Cadence felt uncomfortable, but she exited first and Speatsh followed. He quickly took the lead as he marched past the swimming pool toward the empty hallway, leading past the weight room and to the pair of plain doors that had proven to be impenetrable.

"We don't have a key to the room," Josh said. "It's impossible to open."

"There's no key to the trophy room," Speatsh said as he stopped at the larger than normal and doublewide metallic doors. "Did you try knocking?"

"Oh, why didn't we think of that," Josh asked. "Of course, knocking." Josh smacked an open palm against the doors and they echoed with a hollow ring. "Excuse us, could the nobody on the other side of this door please let us in." Josh stopped knocking and turned back to Speatsh. "We don't have a key and there's no code. We've tried everything."

"Who's there," a distant voice called from behind the doors.

"It's me," Speatsh replied.

"Me," the raspy voice asked. "Me who?"

"I come bearing gifts," Speatsh said, "Now open the doors or I'll kick them into your head, you little fur ball."

"Fur ball," the voice called back. "This fur ball's got a few tricks up his sleeve."

"Just open the door," Speatsh ordered.

"What are you doing here?"

"Richard called me."

"Where is Richard?" the door asked. "I don't take this attitude from anyone. You want in? Get Richard."

"Richard's dead," Josh blurted.

"Who's that," the door asked.

"My name's Josh. Richard was –"

Click!

The door swung forward and the fur ball stepped out. It clenched a small oak walking stick. "Richard's dead? How?"

Josh found himself unable to answer. He stared down at the white longhaired cat. He looked almost Persian, but his nose wasn't set far enough into his face. He looked up at Josh through white eyes.

"That's a cat," Bricktain announced, peering down over Amber's shoulder.

"I'm no cat," the cat shrieked and suddenly leapt into the air with a distorted face full of long fangs and angry brows. It gripped its walking stick and looked ready to strike Bricktain Morris. He stopped midair as Speatsh's hand gripped the animal by the scruff of the neck.

"I see you still have your temper, Bogi," Speatsh said, holding the cat in front of him.

The cat's eyes flared and Bogi struck the point of his stick into Speatsh's throat. Speatsh dropped Bogi.

"I see you still have that weak spot in your neck," Bogi replied, using his crutch to stand himself up on his hind feet.

"Your name's Bogi," Josh asked.

"No, that's just what they call me. My name's Jae Quincy Woof."

"Woof," Bricktain asked. "You mean like a dog? Woof, woof?"

"Was the world maimed while I've been in here," Bogi asked. "Did you bring me the town dipstick," Bogi suddenly stopped his tirade. "So they finally got him? And you're here, Speatsh, and the town dipstick's here which means we're training?"

"Right."

"Do they know," Bogi asked looking over the group and resting his eyes on Josh.

"Know what," Josh asked.

"That means no."

"They knew enough to send for Thomas," Speatsh said. "And I told them what he was and that he would feed on them."

"You did?"

"He was the only name we had," Josh said.

"Besides, we couldn't find him," Reggie said. "We tried, but we've heard nothing."

"He's not coming," Amber added.

"Oh that's where you're wrong," Bogi said. "He's coming, you can't assume he isn't. When he comes, you better be able to defend yourselves or he will drain each of you dry. Isn't that right, Speatsh?"

"That's right," Speatsh replied.

"Well, good then," Bogi said. "Besides, he has a score to settle with your uncle, young Josh Revlon." Bogi pushed a large door inwards and hobbled his way into a large well-lit room. "Well, at least I know who's been making all the noise and keeping me awake. The garden better be alive and the place better be clean. I haven't kept it clean all these years to be destroyed."

"Why didn't you say something, if you heard us out there," Bricktain asked.

"You didn't knock," Bogi replied. "And I have responsibilities when enemies are nearby. And what moron was firing off the gun at all hours?"

No one answered.

Bogi huffed at the silence. "What year is this?"

"Two-thousand-nine," Speatsh replied.

"Again?"

Josh was overwhelmed by the room. Crystal chandeliers, not fluorescent fixtures, hung from the ceiling and softened the white walls, walls covered with portraits of men, women and wolves encased in dark wooden frames. Also around the walls were trophy heads of animals such as elk, deer, bear and wolf, many kinds of wolves and dogs. However, the large figure in the far corner of the room was the item that caught Josh's attention. He broke away from the group and made his way to the corner, where he found himself staring at a scene of stuffed figures around one larger creature.

More than a scene, it was a bigger-than-life diorama. Tall trees, shrubs of all sizes, grass, fake rock and other woodland details made up the scene which appeared to go on forever into the monstrous room. A large waterfall stood high above the scenery and spilled from the tall ceiling into the dark reaches of the diorama. Where it fell to wasn't visible, but a stream ran up to the front of the forest scene where it spilled into a decorative grate. It was difficult to tell how large the room truly was because of the unknown size of the indoor forest diorama. Even the floor of it was earthy. The rest of the room was lined with cabinets of all heights, fat and short, thin and tall. Glass covered tables and cabinets made a circle in the center of the room. In a corner near the doors leading to the pool stood what appeared to be a workbench. Various large doors led out of the room. Josh approached one of the creatures standing a ways into the diorama.

"These are our kills. This was your uncle's last kill," Bogi said, as his weight against the leafy diorama floor announced his presence alongside Josh. "And that was his first," Bogi said pointing to a large familiar black creature with silvery black hair. "He was sixteen years old at the time. He's obviously smaller than the others, but he was an honorable warrior."

"How is this possible," Josh asked.

"Your uncle was a hunter, Josh," Bogi said. "He hunted us, and he was skilled, the best I've met and I've killed a lot of hunters. When he gave up the hunt and finally settled down, it was a shock to all who were his friends and allies."

Josh broke his gaze with a large white wolf, the size of a horse, with silver eyes. "Why?"

"One attacked him once and he barely escaped with his life," Bogi said. "And it set a fire inside him that led to the total annihilation of numerous clans. He went after them all and he took their belongings, after they were dead, to fund the hunt. He guised himself as an antique dealer, sold useless items at high prices and kept the items that helped him hunt for himself. Your uncle was a very smart and very rich man."

"And he hunted these wolves?"

"Wolves, but not wolves," Bogi corrected. "The common wolf you know is a wild dog that can't be tamed unless you speak their language. Beneath this world lies another world that's been here a long time, respectful of humanity. For thousands of centuries this hidden world and its people honored human life. It was their religion. Though no one ruled them, they looked to what you might call a queen. She was wise beyond the others and they looked to her for counsel and heeded her wisdom, but she would not put herself above them. They were her equals, though they didn't see her as equal. They saw her as a goddess. Thirty-two came from one set of parents, and the one the others considered queen was the oldest of them. We call them the ancients. Not only did they honor life, but they understood nature. They understood it so clearly, they could actually use some of its natural elements. They are the parents of those monsters you hunt from this day forward.

"About seven thousand years ago, against the counsel of his family, one of the ancients left his home to search out others like them. He searched for three thousand years and found nothing. Then, one day, legend tells that his hunger became insatiable when he couldn't find prey to feed upon. He came upon a human and quickly devoured him. Afterward, the guilt of this atrocity drove him home, but his spirit was tainted. The other ancients could smell the death of human on him and they cast him out. He was furious and he fought them,

151

but lost the fight in the end. Enraged at his family, and wallowing in his guilt for the murder he committed, he became a hermit. For years, he thought only about vengeance on his family, and he learned a way that he could enslave humans to his mind simply by biting them and transferring certain parts of his being through his saliva.

"He learned that he could make others just like him, but he couldn't have others his equal who could rise up and destroy him, so he only gave out a degree of power and to some of those he gave power, they too could give some power and he called them his generals. He created an army and returned to his home where he slaughtered many of his ancient siblings. The youngest of the ancients sacrificed her eternal safety to allow the queen and eleven other survivors to escape the onslaught. And she did this because she had sworn to protect the queen always from any harm, and she did, to the end of her ancient days. By a fluke, the youngest ancient killed the rogue's army."

Josh realized Speatsh was standing beside him after he cleared his throat upon the last comment.

"What happened to the ancient and his army," Amber asked.

"He was angry," Bogi said. "He set out to find those ancients who escaped and he still hunts them today. The queen didn't make it easy for him though. She and her ancient siblings managed to stay in hiding, but never in peace. This rogue ancient, set on destroying his family, rebuilt his army and sent his generals as spies in all directions of the earth to seek out his brothers and sisters.

"But one day a human discovered one of the ancients in hiding, feeding on his cows and he attacked it, but the ancient wouldn't fight back because it honored human life. The human nearly killed him. The human felt compassion for the creature and, upon learning the ancient's history, led the surviving ancients to a secret cave beneath a lake. Here they went into hiding, where legend says they remain today. They built a temple to honor their kin who were murdered and raised a great garden in honor of their dead. There, most of the survivors remain, hidden and protected to this day. Only their greatest allies know the entrance to the cave and the rogue continues to hunt for it."

"But I have yet to tell you the worst of this story, and I can tell you have more questions by the way you keep opening your mouths like dumb fish and have tried to interrupt me so many times. Knock it off! I'll tell you."

"The rogue learned that the humans played a part in hiding his family and he vowed to use and destroy them all. He declared war on all humanity and he's been placing his servants throughout the world, biding his time for the right moment to strike. He will conquer the humans because few of them know he exists. Those who know otherwise hunt his slaves down one by one and some hope to find the rogue. Other hunters just hunt wolves ignorant of the full story. These idiots are an embarrassment to those few of us aware of the larger picture."

"And that's what my uncle did," Josh asked.

"Your uncle, next to Thomas de Soleil, was the most wanted hunter ever and his name's not even Richard Revlon. Your name is not Revlon."

"What's my name then?"

"None of your business. Your family has been in hiding ever since your uncle gave up the hunt. Your uncle built this underground fort to keep your family safe from the rogue and his army. Your uncle was a very dangerous man. He was responsible for destroying nearly a third of the ancient's army around the world at one time and he nearly killed the rogue ancient himself. He's the only hunter outside of the wolf family who's ever seen the cur."

"What would happen if the rogue were killed," Cadence asked.

"Anarchy," Bogi said. "All his generals would have no master to keep them from running rampant, trying to dominate each other or hunting in ways you don't want to consider. At least with the rogue in charge, he understands the need for humans as a source of food, and knowledge. He knows there are humans who know where his family hides. He won't attack humanity until he learns where that hiding place is. And yet, as he lives he attacks the human race, enslaving some, feeding off others until the day he can conquer and destroy it all."

"Don't look so distraught. We also have an army. The queen knew there was only one way to fight the rogue's army, and that was to build her own. But building armies is difficult on an ancient who is trying to stay pure. You see, the blood is key. We need it to rejuvenate and giving your essence away weakens you. The ancient craves its taste and that hunger passes with their power to the next in line. The queen started by passing her power on to others, good people, giving them equal power, but the rogue hunted them down and destroyed all she made. While her siblings hid themselves from the world, she attempted to hide among the humans to watch for the rogue's progress in locating the family of ancients."

"With progress in the human race, it wasn't long until she too was drawn to a taste for human blood. But unlike the rogue, she found the strength to turn her back on all taste for any kind of blood. In her journeys, she fell in love with a human, denounced her blood thirst and she grew old."

"How do they just turn their power off," Josh asked.

"Why am I talking, if you won't listen," Bogi asked. "It's the blood, animal and human, it mixes with wolf bodies, ancient and slave alike. The chemical reaction elongates their lives. An ancient ages one year for every four hundred of your human years. At least that's the best we can measure so far. When they don't feed, they age just at about the same rate as humans. The blood is the catalyst of all their powers. And human blood is the only forbidden blood."

"What about the moon," Cadence asked.

"The moon," Bogi asked. "Oh, the change? Yeah, that. The ancients, you should know, have a high sensitivity to nature. They can feel the moon's spirit and the earth's spirit and they live harmoniously between both, but their generals, or their most powerful slaves, haven't learned to understand those spirits—they're just too young. When the moon is fully alive, generals can't understand the nature and it drives them mad. The mingling of the earth's spirit and the spirit of the moon surges through them and their confusion of both spirits, drives them mad, wild and free. It turns them into a form that both moon and earth argue over controlling. Or that's the easiest way I could describe it to you in terms you would understand. Only the ancients have learned to channel both spirits harmoniously. But that's not what's important. What is important is that the queen stopped feeding. She began to age and she had a family and she had those who would protect her. After falling in love, she realized a deeper respect for humanity than she ever knew. She knew if she wanted to save her ancient family, she also had to save humanity. Thus, she hid herself among the humans and turned her back on her powers. She sacrificed herself, knowing the rogue ancient would never find her in her human form."

"And where is the queen now," Josh asked.

"The rogue found her," Bogi suddenly stopped and closed his eyes. "I've been forbidden to say any more. You've come a long way since Barbara and Stan let me play with you in your crib."

"You knew my parents," Josh asked. "My parents knew what he did?"

"Yeah," Bogi replied. "They didn't like it, but they knew. You should really ask them about it."

"I can't," Josh said. "They're dead."

Bogi closed his eyes again. "I understand now." Bogi's face turned angry. "What you have to understand is that when your uncle was still very young, he rescued your father from a hungry wolf. The wolf killed your grandparents and since that day, your uncle set out to exact his vengeance on those creatures. Your father obviously knew because he was there when the attack happened that started your uncle's hunting days. Your mother had a difficult time with the family secret, but eventually didn't mind your uncle's strange friends. But after you were born, your parents felt it best those strange friends stayed away. Your mother didn't want you growing up following your uncle's ways, thinking they were normal. Hunters tend to invite those they hunt. If you want to save your sister, you'll have to learn how to hunt now." Bogi walked away. "If you'll excuse me, I must mourn." Bogi disappeared behind another set of large decorative arched doors.

"Listen up all y'all," Speatsh announced. "You've got a lot to swallow here, and we gotta get a move on. So, here's how it is. The creatures you see here, we managed to preserve them by giving them lobotomies and severing their spinal cords, otherwise they'd all be in human form. They're as brain dead as a Democrat, but they are very much alive and paralyzed. In this state, they can't handle even the faintest whisper of even the earth's spirit, so they're constantly in their animal form. Bogi, here, injects them with just enough blood to keep them from aging. We needed something to train with. Bogi watches them to make sure they can't get out of line."

Speatsh took a stance near a longhaired terrier, a Labrador and a Saint Bernard.

"These ones that look like regular every day dogs are called scouts. They don't have power to turn creatures. They're strong, smart, agile as an Olympic Japanese jackrabbit and their purpose is to locate food and even bring it in for these large black ones."

Speatsh moved away from the average-looking dogs to the statuesque, black wolf.

"That's what killed the police chief," Bricktain said.

"We've seen them," Cadence replied.

"These things bring bad news," Speatsh continued. "They're in tune with nature enough to use the elements sometimes—any of them are, but these puppies especially. They can walk on water, practically fly, spit venom and disappear completely in a shadow. Their claws are stronger than steel and slice through practically anything and you'll never see them coming because they're clear and practically invisible.

"Their fur is laced with quills that will shred your skin if you're not protected. Ultraviolet rays burn them, and long exposure can kill them, but they're strong and smart and agile too, and their whole purpose is to protect the general, this guy right here," Speatsh approached a slim Egyptian-like creature with a tan and gold short fur coat and spindly and narrow features. Along the backside of each leg was a row of sharp clear spines. "These guys

155

are the ones that the rogue has turned himself and he's given them all the power they need to independently build up a clan to serve him. If we're gonna bring one of these down, we gotta be good. These things generally need to lock their slaves up at a full moon so they don't inadvertently kill them. You can usually find out who's disloyal to him because they're the ones who'll open the doors to their jail to you, and usually the loyal ones are the first to jump out and attack you, so it's easier just to burn everybody inside. Getting your sister back is gonna require a little bit different of a tactic."

"Is that one an ancient," Josh asked, pointing to the large white wolf."

"That's an old friend, and yes," Speatsh said. "Enjoy this evening. Tomorrow, I start teaching you how to kill these things."

No one really knew how to leave the room, they were too interested in the artifacts and they continued to investigate.

Josh stayed at Speatsh's side, but only because Speatsh dragged him away from the rest of the group. He wanted to stand and be mesmerized with the frozen ancient, but Speatsh didn't give him the choice.

"Josh," Speatsh said. "Those dogs upstairs are your friends, Nick and Dustin. I've been helping them. You should know I used to be a general. I have enough of my own voices in my head to deal with without having to train you and your pathetic friends, so you have to lead better than you have been." He turned around and glanced over the others in the room. "Your job is to protect them, if you're to lead them. Personally, I'm not impressed and I think you're a coward. The Richard Revlon I knew would have gutted you for what you've already done here." Speatsh disappeared behind the same doors as Bogi.

13 – Tools of the Trade

Josh hated the smell of the greenhouse so he didn't hide out in here ever. He did tonight and stayed as far away from the trophy room as possible. The circular tubes overhead that somehow reflected sunlight into the stronghold were dark, telling Josh it was night out again. The humidity annoyed him, but not as much as the circulated air he'd grown used to during their long stay underground. The plants made the air fresher in this room, but the humidity was too much for Josh's taste.

What did being a hunter mean? And how long did Richard know about these creatures? Was his uncle honorable or the cause of Josh's misfortune? Josh held a yellow blossom in his hand. The petals were all crinkled and cracked now with brown lines. He needed a drink.

"I didn't realize anyone was in here," Cadence said, startling Josh.

Too many things ran through Josh's head that he wanted to say. He'd wanted to say them since he saw Cadence earlier by the pool, but he kept biting his tongue because when it came right down to it, he didn't know what to tell her.

"I'll leave you be," Cadence said, drawing the plastic door after her.

Josh found himself running after her.

He caught up with her in the kitchen. Bricktain sat at the table playing with a bowl of green olives and Amber sat in the living room talking with her dad while the Dobermans slept nearby.

"I messed up," Josh cried out. "Everyone's gone, and the only ones left are you and me."

"No," Cadence replied. "There's only you. You made that clear."

"I know and I'm sorry," Josh continued and thought he knew what to say next but Amber suddenly appeared over Cadence's shoulder.

"I told you not to say anything to her," Amber said.

"Then when," Josh asked. "After she's dead or turned into a dog?"

Cadence turned and started away again.

"If anything happened to you, Cadence, I couldn't live with myself," Josh said after her. "Everything that's happened, happened because I dragged everyone I loved into this mess. The only person left I owe any loyalty to is you and I can't keep hurting people." And with that, Josh walked past everyone and called for the elevator.

"Yeah, go swim," Cadence called after him. "You're pretty good at hiding from us down there."

"I'm not swimming," Josh replied waiting for the doors to close.

"What are you up to, son," Reggie asked.

"I'm going for a walk." And the doors closed over Josh.

The elevator carried Josh away before anyone could say anything more. When the doors opened into the garage, Josh moved quickly to the exterior door and punched in the security code to leave. The door dropped into the ground and Josh started for the doorway into the backyard. Dogs waiting beyond the doorway were already eyeing him, but the door slammed shut again. He punched in the code once more and a red light flashed as the console beeped at him.

"Don't be stupid, kid," a voice called from over an intercom.

"Let me go, Cheatham," Josh demanded. "I can take care of myself."

"It's suicide," Speatsh said.

"Then let me die," Josh yelled. "Maybe then no one else will."

The doors remained shut.

"Josh," another voice spoke. "It's Amber. We may not appreciate it, but we owe their lives to you because you brought us here."

"Yeah, well not everyone made it, did they?"

"Oh get over yourself, kid," Bricktain's voice said, softer than the rest.

"Will you go taste test some poison or something," Speatsh said.

"Josh," Speatsh said. "If you want to go, I'll go with you, but you'll never help Cracey if you give yourself to Jasper."

"I don't want anyone else to die."

"Then don't go," Cadence said from the elevator. Josh didn't even hear it travel. "If you want him to stop, then let's learn how to stop him together."

"It's not fair," Josh said. "I dragged you into this."

"Leaving isn't going to fix things with us," Cadence said. "I don't know if anything can. Someone has to fight. Don't make me do this without you. You think I trust that Bricktain bozo to back anyone up?"

"But you won't forgive me, will you?"

"Nothing could make me consider it."

*   *   *

"The fangs are three hundred and fifty years old and you forgot to wear the gloves when you handled them," Speatsh set the reddish crossbows on a glass case and tore the silk gloves out of the wooden box. "These never come off your hands." He threw the black thin gloves at Josh. "When you're readying to fight, these are the first things you put on. When you go outside, you're wearing these. When you use the fangs, you use these. You're a hunted man, Josh, and at any time you might be tempted to reach for the fangs. Just for that, maybe I won't teach you how to make more ammunition for them. And I'm not going to give you anymore from the stockpile." With thick gloves, he took up the small antique crossbows and handed them to Bogi. "Can you repair the damage?"

"I'll do my best," Bogi replied. He took the fangs and made his way toward the opposite side of the trophy room where he climbed up to a full-sized desk, turned on a light and pulled open a cabinet full of bottles.

"You can't get those at Hick-mart, kid," Speatsh continued.

"Don't call him kid," Bricktain said. "He'll yell."

"What is this, kindergarten," Speatsh asked. "I'm twenty-five hundred years old and I'm wiping noses. Look, I'm not your mom, I'm not your dad, I'm not your best friend and I just don't care. In fifty years when you're all wearing old person Pampers, I'm still going to be out there trying to teach snot-nosed infants like you how to hunt the rogue-ancient and his generals."

"And what makes you so important," Bricktain asked.

"All these people in your group got caught by Jasper and somehow he missed Bartleby the rain man, here," Speatsh replied and in a flash punched Bricktain's nose for blood. "I'm better than you—that's what makes me so important."

Speatsh hobbled toward the diorama of dogs and wolves. The claws of the bear pelt drummed against the white fur sleeves covering his arms. He stepped up next to the frozen body of the guardian. "There's only one thing that can kill these guys."

"Silver," Josh answered.

"Have I mentioned how much I love breaking in newbies," Speatsh said. "No! Force, lots and lots of force. Wolf flesh is thick and resilient, and their organs are just as resilient. Most guns can't penetrate it. Silver is soft. That myth was probably started by some moron lucky enough to puncture a wolf with a silver-plated butter knife. I promise, whoever made that statement was full of crap, probably got killed soon after too. Silver breaks apart on wolf skin. Shotgun blasts can't do it either, but they're annoying and they'll slow a wolf down long enough to allow someone to get in a killing blow. The soft points are here at the clavicles, under the jaw and the pelvic area. You can cut their stomach but they'll only chase you down and put you in it. The hardest place to get at is through the rib cage, and you have to thrust straight in or have a magic bullet that can punch through that shielding. You can slice away at it, hack and slash style, but you're gonna have to go deep to get the kill. Don't try for beheading or cutting off limbs, go in at angles and straight and you'll bring these critters down. Then you can worry about cutting off heads and whatnot. You probably won't need to do that, but it sure does feel good sometimes."

Speatsh stepped away from the diorama and clanked his way toward an oak cabinet and threw the doors open. "I'm not sorry if I don't prepare you with suitable gear, but I've only seen you fight once." He reached into the cabinet and drew out what looked like a conglomeration of leather rope. "Come here, Cadence."

Cadence walked up to Speatsh and found herself dragging Josh along with her.

Speatsh smiled a little. "How interesting." His hands were suddenly on Cadence and he was buckling the leather straps to various places around her body from head to toe. The straps went over her shoulders and around her forearms and buckled across her chest and abdomen. Speatsh latched four hooks along Cadence's spine. A thick strap buckled around her waist and four smaller straps buckled around each leg. She was belted down from shoulder to ankle. Speatsh glanced over her.

"Good," he said. "Too tight?"

"I think it's cutting off the circulation in this shoulder," Cadence replied.

Speatsh cursed, undid all his work and started over. This time Cadence approved of the fit, not because she was afraid to say it was too tight, but because she actually felt comfortable wearing it.

Speatsh turned back into the cabinet and pulled out a sort of wire cage. He pulled some of it apart and slid it over Cadence's head and down over her shoulders until it covered her chest and part of her upper torso. Speatsh locked it together and fastened it to the leather outfit at her chest, waist and back of her shoulders. Next, he placed two smaller cages over each forearm. Again, he went back into the cabinet and this time pulled out two narrow long, black plastic tubes. He attached one to the outside of each thigh, stretching from the knee halfway up her thigh. Next, he found and connected several thick cup-shaped pouches along the belting.

"Heavy," Speatsh asked.

"Not really," Cadence said.

Speatsh dragged Cadence to a large cabinet without doors and made entirely of cubbyholes. He looked around before reaching for a compartment and withdrawing a pair of black sawed-off shotguns. He slid them into the

160

tubes he had just attached to Cadence's legs. He twisted an end of the tube and something snapped. Speatsh pulled on each gun, and they remained in the holster. He returned to the cubbies and found two small pistols, which he quickly tucked into two strange holsters near her ankles. He pulled out two more guns. These had flat, smooth edges all around and were about a third the width of the average handgun. Speatsh attached one directly to the small cage around her right forearm. He forced the gun into the cage until it appeared to lock in place.

"Open your hand like this," Speatsh said while flaring his fingers.

Cadence mimicked Speatsh's movement. The slender weapon launched forward and made a few people jump. Cadence cautiously closed her hand over the grip of the weapon as if it were waiting for her to do so.

Speatsh attached the other slender, silver gun to her left arm and it too flew into Cadence's hand when she flexed.

"Now do this," Speatsh said opening his hand and lowering his arms straight to his side.

Cadence did as Speatsh instructed and the silver guns folded back into their armlet cages.

"This is a little something Richard and I came up with," Speatsh said returning to the cabinet and searching for another cubicle. "He got the idea from a man in the Congo where a hunter he met used something similar for blow guns. Richard had the idea and I developed it further. Ah, here they are. Heavy yet?"

"I'm feeling a little of the weight now," Cadence replied.

"Weight lifting'll fix that right up," Speatsh said and he turned back with an armful of Glock .40 handguns. "The idea was to create a walking arsenal. Turn around for me."

Cadence faced away from Speatsh.

Speatsh clamped one of the guns onto a small track made of chain, hooks and slender steel plates, within the cage. He pushed down on the gun and it held in place with its hand grip standing straight out from Cadence's shoulder. He pressed again and the small track ratcheted from the top of Cadence's shoulder to her back. He clamped on a second gun and pushed again. The track clicked again so that the first gun he placed moved around to her side and the second was now at her back. He locked on a third Glock and left it alone.

"All you have to do is reach up and pull it off now. The others won't move back on their own. When you empty a gun, push it into the system at the side, like this. This pushes the loaded weapons back to the top of your shoulders for easy access while unloading your empty ones at your side like this. You're gonna have to practice this 'til you get the feel, or you could drop a gun and the system won't work because you won't be able to reach the next gun. When you holster the weapon on the system, push it and it will push the next gun up your back, got it?"

Cadence reached up to one of her shoulders and found the grip of the .40 Glock sticking straight up from her shoulder, perfect for the grab. She tore the gun away from the system.

"Now stick it back in the system," Speatsh said. "Put it in your other hand for now. Think of an "X" across the front of your body. Left hand takes from the left shoulder, loads it into the system on the right side, under your arm and vice versa. No clips, just fresh guns."

Cadence placed the gun in her left hand and reached across to her right side. Speatsh helped her recognize how to line the Glock with the small track in the system. Cadence shoved the gun and the system jerked on Cadence's petite frame. The rail of guns running up her right side ratcheted and clanked and a new Glock handgrip appeared next to her head. She let Speatsh walk her through the holstering process some more. She felt clumsy, but Speatsh was careful to help her understand how it all worked until her head jerked and she screamed.

"Yup, that's gonna be a problem," Speatsh explained. "Have to cut your hair or it's gonna catch and tear out."

"Can't I just tie it up," Cadence asked.

Speatsh slid a slender knife behind Cadence's head and cut her long hair in one smooth stroke. "Whatya say," Speatsh asked. "The hair should work its way out of the system." Speatsh loaded three Glocks onto her left side before turning back to the cubicle. He took out a long rifle with a scope and slid that into the cage along Cadence's spine. He returned to the first cabinet and took out two belts with holsters. He put them around Cadence so that a holster rested on either side of her diaphragm. He took out a thick belt with pockets, strapped it around Cadence's waist and returned to the gun cabinet where he withdrew several round reloader clips. The reloaders slid into the pockets. He dragged her back to the cubbies and withdrew two .45 revolvers and slid them into the empty diaphragm holsters.

Finally, he stopped and looked Cadence over. "Heavier?"

"Much," she answered. "This is a lot of work for something that should be simple."

"You'll like it and be thrilled," Speatsh said unhappy with Cadence's remark. "I call it the system. You can call it your new husband. It's designed so it doesn't harm your back, alter your spine—that sort of thing. It won't let you bend wrong. There's eight shots in each shotgun, thirteen in each ankle shooter, thirty in each one in the system itself. That includes the two that slide into your hands."

"Glock clips don't hold that many bullets," Bricktain said.

"The pansy ones you police officers use don't," Speatsh replied. "Open your mouth again and I'll punch your teeth out your butt." He turned back to Cadence. "You're gonna have to learn how to coordinate everything so you don't have guns flying into your hand while your reaching for one over your shoulder. The revolvers are six shooters, classic but powerful to kill under the right circumstances at point blank range, especially if you can nail the dog right in the eyeball."

"Now, your shotguns don't pull out of their holsters, they're only good up close, anyway. They'll create an arm's distance between you and whatever you shoot if you need more room to work. Nice thing is they're automatic and you don't have to pump to reload, but don't hold down the trigger or you'll empty. And once they're empty they're done for the rest of the fight, so be wise when you use these. This way, it's only a matter of raising your leg and pulling the trigger. You're gonna have to learn how to aim with your knee and how to stay in control of your balance. I've seen these things blow out ligaments just from kick. Oh, and forget kneeling, or you cram the barrel with dirt and crap."

"I hate it," Cadence said already overwhelmed with the weight of the system and the dexterity she'd need to use it.

"If Josh hadn't screwed up your life, you wouldn't have to wear it," Speatsh replied. "So get used to it."

Josh wanted to hide, but Speatsh was right.

"Your job is to stay out of the fighting and to keep the wolves from escaping us. Understand?"

Cadence nodded.

"No hand-to-hand fighting," Speatsh ordered. "None. We need you to shoot."

"So basically, I'm a sniper," Cadence said.

"I thought you said guns couldn't hurt these things," Amber said.

"These can," Speatsh said holding up a strange, slender and practically invisible bullet. "Gun powder is too weak to give us the punch we need to break skin and organs so each bullet is packed with a special mixture of nitroglycerin."

"Are you kidding," Bricktain asked. "Cadence will blow herself to bits with that shaking all over her body."

"It's under control," Speatsh snapped. "Now, look at the bullets." Speatsh held the bullet closer to the friends now huddling together for a better look. The bullet was clear and a small amount of clear liquid sloshed around inside."

"What kind of ammo is that," Reggie asked as his wheel chair moved to give him a better look.

Speatsh let Reggie take the bullet. "They're diamond, shells and bullets alike. These are flawless diamonds made only for Richard and a select few of his friends. We have access to a diamond mine and a particular craftsman makes only this because he is so devoted to our cause. When we're done fighting, we try to find the shells and the bullets so we can reuse them. The head is special, it has teeth and as it spins, it can literally saw its way through the wolf flesh and bone. But because they're so slender, chances are, just one of these won't drop guardian. And boy, do these babies give a kick." Speatsh tossed the bullet into the air and quickly snatched it again. "Boom!"

Everyone flinched, but nobody was impressed. Bogi shook his head and Speatsh tucked the bullet away in a furry pouch hanging from his side. He stepped under the eyeless head of a lion.

Three masks hung beneath it. One looked like an old samurai warrior mask with its wide mouth and sharp fangs. Another mask was a thin full-face that looked a bit clownish with its dark, rouged cheeks, shiny red lips and brown circles around the eyes. Speatsh took down the third mask, a dark brown one with darker wood veins running through it. It had a nose, an oval for a mouth and it curved a chin, but everything above the nose was empty. Speatsh flipped it over and untied some leather straps.

"Our friend, Bogi here, takes excellent care of everything in this bunker," Speatsh said. "This is the original leather." He stood in front of Cadence and gestured for her to face away from him. "You need eyes to see what you're shooting at in the dark." Speatsh reached around her, positioning the mask, without directly placing it over her face. He remained that way.

"Am I supposed to do something," Cadence asked.

"No," Speatsh replied. "No. Just, try not to be so impulsive, okay?"

"Impulsive?"

"Remember who you are and stay focused," Speatsh instructed. "Don't let anyone tell you what to do."

"I never do," Cadence said.

"Good," Speatsh said. "Then there shouldn't be a problem." Speatsh continued to hold the half-face mask out in front of Cadence. His lips moved but he didn't make any sounds.

"Is something wrong with the mask," Josh asked. He felt worried for Cadence. Speatsh spent the last ten minutes throwing a strange outfit onto Cadence without a care, but now he was hesitant.

Speatsh's eyes darted to Josh. "No." He pulled the mask over Cadence's face.

Cadence's hands reached towards Josh and the two silver, flat guns jumped into them.

"Hackmanyatoya," she screamed.

Both gun hammers reared back and slammed down.

Speatsh quickly pulled the mask away. "We'll have to work on that." Speatsh stood wide-eyed. "Lucky for you, Josh, they're empty."

Josh couldn't speak. From the look he saw on Cadence's face, he knew she was stunned too, more than stunned. She was horrified.

"Take this thing off me," Cadence said.

"It's OK," Speatsh said. "We'll try again later."

"Take this thing off me," Cadence snapped, her voice quivering. "I am not putting that thing on my face again."

"Yes you are," Speatsh said. "You just have to learn to be in control of yourself."

"What control," Cadence asked. "I did not do what just happened. I am so sorry, Josh."

"Guess that makes you two about even now, doesn't it," Bricktain said.

"That's not what this is about," Speatsh said. "This mask is about the oldest thing in this room, and probably the most dangerous. It takes a strong mind to use it."

"And you gave it to the person who has such brilliance when it comes to choosing her friends," Bricktain said and chuckled to himself.

"You weren't really a cop, were you," Speatsh asked. "The great-grandson of a hunter gave this to Richard. Richard's partner used it, and barely mastered it, but it works. An old aborigine possessed it. The story is that the aborigine hunted for his village at night and learned to see shadows within shadows. Apparently, when he was out hunting, one of the rogue's clans attacked his village and killed the hunter's family. The hunter spent his remaining days trapping and hunting the wolves, mercilessly. He designed a mouthpiece that he used to spit poisonous darts, but we'll wait on that one. He eventually adopted a family of children, after their parents died, and went into hiding. Unfortunately, the wolves found him and killed him and his new family, miserably I might add, but one son escaped and managed to find a way to tie the hunter's spirit to the mask.

"So the mask is haunted," Bricktain said.

"Isn't that what I just said," Speatsh replied. He handed the mask to Cadence. "It can see shadows you can't and will point them out to you. It knows your thoughts and has a habit of making you act upon them. Be careful the grudges you hold. Your companions don't need you shooting them. We'll practice with it more later. For now, don't wear it, but take care of it."

Cadence dropped the mask, ran to Josh and realized the system kept her from hugging him. "I didn't mean it, I didn't mean it."

"Hey, stupid," Speatsh said.

No one answered.

"Are you talking to me," Bricktain asked.

"I must be. You're the one who answered." Speatsh reached deep into his pockets and pulled out a black bag the size of his hand. He loosened the drawstring and withdrew a semicircular pair of glasses. "Put these on." Speatsh had to direct Bricktain how to slide them over his face.

"What is this," Bricktain asked.

"You don't wear contacts, yes," Speatsh asked.

"I have twenty-twenty vision," Bricktain replied.

"Good," Speatsh said. "But we'll have to get your eyes measured for contacts or you're gonna have problems soon. I designed these myself. Don't break 'em."

"Everything looks weird," Bricktain said after sliding them over his eyes.

"I just gave you three hundred degree peripheral, give or take a few degrees." Speatsh held up his hand. "Can you see my finger?"

"I see a stick. Everyone's thin."

"Well, you're only able to comprehend so much," Speatsh explained. "These glasses are lined with diamonds. They let you see more around you, but they fold everything in on itself too, make everything you see seem skinnier."

"Much skinnier."

"Tell me when you can't see my finger anymore," Speatsh slid his hand past Bricktain's ear and finally stopped when Bricktain said he couldn't see it after it disappeared somewhere near the back of his head. "Good, take a walk, don't fall into the pool. Take them off in twenty minutes. We'll measure your eyes later for contacts. They'll be ribbed to counter the folds in the glasses."

"What are these for?"

"To make you dumber than you already look," Speatsh said. "Just get used to them for now, and get out of my face."

166

Bricktain turned and slowly began walking toward the pool area. His feet fumbled occasionally, but it was more because he seemed unsure of where to step. He reached out four or five times as if feeling for something that wasn't there.

Speatsh burst out laughing.

"This isn't funny," Bricktain said tearing the glasses off his face.

"Hey! Put those back on your face and start walking, moron." Speatsh waited for Bricktain to put the diamond glasses back on. He started laughing again when Bricktain immediately stubbed his toe on the floor. Speatsh continued to watch for his own amusement and once Bricktain made it out of the room, which seemed to take several minutes, his face suddenly looked different. Josh thought it was concern, but when Speatsh faced Amber, he looked angry again.

"Your father tells me you have interesting balance," Speatsh said.

"You grow up running around on rusted cars, you learn not to fall," Amber replied.

"She ran up a stair railing when we met her," Cadence said.

Speatsh smiled. "Don't know too many cars with poles that need to be run over."

"When I was little, I wanted to be an acrobat," Amber explained. "Used to bet my friends I could run up the banisters at school without falling."

"And did you fall?"

"I was in a coma once for three days."

"And that didn't stop you from acting like an idiot?"

"No," Amber said. "I just found it more of something that I had to do."

"And you did?"

"I did."

"Do you still fall?"

"I never fall."

"You do it barefoot, I assume."

"Barefoot, in sneakers or in heels."

"Heels?"

"I've done it in stilettos. Lets me run on my toes. Great for inclines. Thought it might add to entertainment novelty."

"Why would you ever need to run up poles in heels," Speatsh asked looking bewildered for the first time.

"Why would you make a pair of glasses that can see all around you?"

Speatsh turned sharply and trudged to a new cabinet lined with drawers. He pulled one of the drawers out and took a small bundle of black leather rags. He opened the cabinet doors and revealed coiled up chains, cables, ropes and other loose bundles of materials, all hanging in different manners. He pulled down a coiled rope. "Ever used a whip?"

Amber shook her head.

"We'll start you on an easy one then," Speatsh said and held up a coiled leather whip. He tugged on a small loop at the fat end of it. "This is the wrist loop, hand goes through like this. Don't use this thing if you don't have it attached to your wrist." He held his hand out for Amber to see and pointed at a large ball making up the thick end of the whip. "The ball goes in your palm so it can pivot. Don't just hold the cane." He rolled his eyes when Amber appeared to be confused. "That would be the handle of the whip. If you hold it by the handle you're going to hurt someone, probably yourself. Do you understand?"

"The loop goes over my wrist," Amber said. "The ball—

"Call it the knot," Speatsh corrected.

"The knot goes into the palm of my hand so it can pivot."

"Good," Speatsh said. An instant later he unfurled the glossy leather whip to its full nine-foot length in one motion. The rope lurched backward and suddenly snapped forward, arcing and biting the air as it cracked an almost deafening sound. It wriggled like a snake before it lunged behind Speatsh. It swung around and cracked once more as its tip suddenly reached forward to a wooden figurine in the shape of a horse on top of a nearby table. The small statue kicked into the air. While the horse floated, the whip cracked again and smacked the horse.

"Hey," Bogi cried from his desk in the corner of the room. He rubbed the back of his head. "I'm trying to work here."

Speatsh snapped the whip back and caught it in a way that it wrapped around his forearm and when it slid back into his hand, it was perfectly coiled again. "I'll show you how to do figure eights and all the fancy cracking techniques, but our goal is not to impress the mongrels with our cracking talent. We wanna smack the dumb out of them. Now look here."

Speatsh held up the thinnest part of the whip to its end where a thin strip, different from the rest of the weapon, extended the whip several inches. From this strip, a piece of steel cable meshed into the leather and finished the whip off with a tip of flared out wire.

"This is a modification," said Speatsh. "This wire allows you to create ultra sonic sound that deafens dogs. Nick and Dustin are gonna hate these. Even though you'll hear a crack, it's the sound within that crack you can't hear that's gonna be a valuable weapon. Use this puppy right and you can slice a tree open. We'll start by getting you to knock the little horsey out of the air like I just did." Speatsh handed the whip to Amber and showed her how to hang it from her belt loop. "Get this down and we'll let you play with two. Get those down and we'll give you something that can do a little more damage." Speatsh reached under his robes and donned the silver razor disks attached to the steel whips at his sides.

Amber looked the leather whip over. She didn't know anything about whips. This one was a beautiful one, braided tightly together, soft and shiny brown. A silver cap crowned the knot of the whip.

Speatsh appeared before her holding a pair of yellow safety glasses in one hand and a football helmet in the other.

"Wear these when you practice for now," Speatsh said. "And stay away from me while you practice. I'll show you more tomorrow."

"You really think I can just learn how to do that," Amber asked.

"You don't have a choice," Speatsh said.

He pulled Amber to a table with a glass cover. He opened the cover, retrieved a bundle of soft leather and pulled the clump into two pieces.

"These are wind-riders," Speatsh said.

"They look like moccasins," Amber said.

"Exactly, if moccasins are knee high," Speatsh replied. "They're thin but durable, and they're surprisingly warm in the winter. They tie up the back here and they're awful to put on, so I'm not going to do it now. You can do it. They need to be tight and secure, but not too tight."

"What are they," Amber asked.

"These babies let you walk on air," Speatsh said. "So long as there's even the slightest breeze, which there always is to some degree. The human foot is an amazing thing, filled with so many nerves. Some people say feet are the map to the entire human body. Once you put these on, these things will amplify the sensation of the breeze so you can actually feel it, climb on it and run on it. Oh, it's the mother of all balancing acts. Your falling days have just begun. The only person to ever use these successfully was the Cherokee woman warrior who enchanted them. Everyone else has fallen on their faces."

"Some have died," Bogi added.

"What," Amber asked and suddenly looked beyond frightened.

"This oughtta be fun," Speatsh said smirking. "Why don't you go out by the pool, make a will and put them on. I'll be out in a few minutes to see if you did it right."

"I'll come with you," Reggie said wheeling his chair to follow Amber.

"You're not fighting," Speatsh asked.

"How," Reggie asked. "I'm sixty-four years old and this chair wouldn't let me maneuver enough to fight against those monsters anyway.

"How about if we make you a better chair," Speatsh asked.

"I could live with another chair," Reggie said. "But I can build it if I have the tools. I'm pretty good at building things."

"How about a chariot," Bogi asked from the desk.

"Don't be stupid," Speatsh said.

"You just sent his daughter out with the wind riders and already promised her the orbits," Bogi snapped back. "The girl could rip herself in two and you think the chariot is absurd?"

"What's the chariot," Reggie asked. "And what danger are you putting my granddaughter in?"

"We keep it locked away so it doesn't make a mess of things in here," Bogi explained.

"I think I could be more use helping out in other areas," Reggie said. "I'm a mechanical engineer. Maybe I have something to offer. I could help build and repair equipment."

"That could be interesting for you. We'll play with the chariot idea later though," Speatsh said. "Go help your daughter."

Reggie drove his chair from the room. He'd gotten into the habit of using the backup battery as the chair's only source of power. He still had a little gas, but he didn't want to pollute the bunker. He wasn't sure how many more charges the old battery had left in her.

Bogi leapt down from his desk. "You must wear the gloves," Bogi said. "Or you'll disintegrate the stability of the weapon. I was able to clean the fangs before any more damage was done." He walked up to Speatsh. "They're on the table when you're ready."

Speatsh looked over Cadence and glared at Josh. He moved for the first cabinet where he found the system for Cadence. "Come here, you."

Josh followed and was surprised when Speatsh turned on him. "And what should we give you?"

"Just teach me how to fight them hand-to-hand and I will," Josh replied.

"You're not getting off that easy," Speatsh said. "Your uncle was an admirable man. You see everything in this room? Your uncle didn't have it handed to him. He found it, all of it. Why should a punk kid, who disrespects his own friends in so many ways, start out with more?"

"Because you forget, it's mine," Josh replied. "Richard left everything to me and my sister. It's all mine. If you don't want to train me, that's fine. I survived one battle. I'll just have to do something different next time. If I have to fight these things with a pair of tweezers, that's what I'll do, but no pompous wolf man is stopping me. There must be vengeance and protection and I'll fulfill both."

"You'll be fighting alone," Speatsh said.

"No, he won't," Cadence replied.

"Do you think the others will stand with you," Speatsh asked. "Where do you think their loyalty will be when you find yourself facing death and they have the choice of a guaranteed escape or to risk their lives for you? Do they trust you enough to know you'll risk your life for them? Have you shown them your will? You want your vengeance, but all you think about is your problems and what you can do to make things right."

Josh didn't know what to say.

"Do you trust him to save you," Speatsh asked Cadence.

Cadence couldn't look at Josh while she contemplated.

"Your friends follow you because you're their friend and they respect the people who are gone," Speatsh said. "But you don't lead them, you follow them and tell them what you want, not encourage them to do. They give an order and you follow. They say feel guilty and you do."

"So how do I fix it," Josh asked.

"Use your head," Speatsh cried at the ceiling. "Think. Don't ask."

"Shouldn't a leader know when to seek counsel," Josh asked.

"Do you call a timeout and ask for counsel when you have only seconds to react while you're fighting? No. Counsel's good, but eventually you have to decide an action or the others will act without you—foolishly if they must. Right now, they're acting without you. You need to think about what is right for them. Their lives aren't the same any more, just as yours. Your uncle was lucky, he found a reason to stop hunting, and I'll bet it surprised him when he found a clan in his own backyard.

"Nothing will ever be normal again. You're going to find your world isn't as safe as you thought it was. And these aren't the only people you'll find you need to learn how to lead. You have no idea how important you are. Hunters you've never met will expect something great from the paladin's kin. That's what they called your uncle, the paladin. He's the only hope some hunters have in believing it's possible to take the wolves down.

"Like it or not, you have a responsibility to keep that hope alive. It's chaotic out there. The rogue is closer than ever to discovering the ancients. He will make this his world. He won't end by enslaving humans. He'll destroy them. And how, pray tell, does someone like you take on such a responsibility of protecting the world from that?"

Josh wondered how to answer that. He looked to Cadence and realized she didn't have his answer for him. Speatsh was right. Cadence couldn't tell Josh what to do, and he didn't picture Bricktain staying and fighting on his behalf anymore. How far was Amber willing to go? Cadence just pulled a gun on him, just as he had done to her. Was she still there for him, or there to survive?

"You'll have to teach me then," Josh said. "It's the only way they'll see someone they can rally to in a fight. Cadence has a good eye for shooting and I trust her, but I want to fight these things up close, hand-to-hand if I need to. If they catch me off guard and jump out of the bushes, I want them knowing they made a mistake. Give me a sword."

Speatsh remained still.

"Give him Wolf's Breath," Bogi said.

"You're screwed now, Josh Revlon," Speatsh said and not only smiled, but seemed to enjoy this particular smile. He limped to a cabinet that was different from the others. It was thin and tall with tinted door glass. Speatsh peeled the double panels apart. A cloak hung inside. Its shoulders appeared wide and it draped to the ground as if made solely to be kept behind glass.

"That is Wolf's Breath," Speatsh said. "Go ahead. Take it."

Josh hesitated a moment. Wolf's Breath was dull black and it looked like an old Victorian-style dress cloak. Was there a proper way to pick up something so refined? A shawl capped the shoulders and fell to just above the elbow and a set of wide, gaping sleeves drooped from beneath this shawl and thin sleeves fell even farther from within these. The inside appeared smooth like silk. He reached into the cabinet, slid the cloak from off a silk-wrapped hanger and suddenly dropped it. The cloak fell, crumpled to the floor and left Josh's fingertips and palms bleeding through several small lacerations.

"This isn't funny," Josh snapped and clenched a fist to stop the bleeding. "If you wanted to insult me—

"We're not insulting you," Bogi replied.

"Are you bleeding," Cadence asked.

"Yes," Speatsh replied. "Now, put the coat on, or we have nothing more to discuss."

"More to discuss," Josh asked. "What's more to discuss? I get the point. I'm useless and I deserve all these kicks, but how does me cutting myself open for your enjoyment help this fight?"

"Hunters have given their lives to find that cloak," Speatsh said. "Put it on,"

Josh looked at his hand and watched as blood coated and filled the natural lines and creases throughout his palms and fingers. Red drops fell and

172

disappeared against the back of the coat now lying at Josh's feet.

"Josh," Cadence said.

"Isn't this justice," Speatsh asked. "Doesn't he deserve this?"

"No," Cadence replied.

"Then he'll do it because it's the greatest protection a hunter can have," Speatsh said. "And it's nastier now that it's all crumpled up."

"Give him something else," Cadence said. "Get something else, Josh. You said it yourself, you own it."

"Then I leave and Bogi closes the door," Speatsh said. "I can teach you to fight, but if you don't pick that coat up and put it on, I walk out and you hope you become good enough to fight those things on your own. And when the time comes you find you need food, hope you survive going outside. Sure, maybe you can do it on your own, but what happens if you fail again."

Josh decided he hated Speatsh.

"Show what these people mean to you," Speatsh said. "Give them the best training they can get."

"This is dirty and childish," Cadence said. "Don't do it, Josh."

"You want these people to see what they mean to you," Speatsh asked. "To see the devotion a leader puts into his own training? So he can aid them? Then put on the coat only a leader should wear or I leave now." Speatsh made his way for the door.

Josh noticed strange braids on the backside of the cloak, tangled in the clump. He thought about kicking the coat open with his foot, but found his hand reaching right for it instead. Maybe he and the others could figure out how to fight with the new arsenal, like Speatsh said, but Josh didn't want to answer for any more deaths. He clamped his fingers right into the ruffles of the cloak and thought he saw Bogi cringe. He felt small sharp edges cut his hands even more. The folds of the coat and its braids ripped at his arms as he lifted Wolf's Breath off the floor. He gripped with his other hand and noticed how the coat clung to his flesh before leaving behind clean lacerations. Everywhere his flesh touched, the cloak sliced into him. Blood coated his hand and oozed from his arms to his fingers as Josh fumbled around and found the smooth insides of the cloak, but it kept sliding from his greasy red fingers. Every time it slid, Josh cut his fingers more as he looked for other ways to grip it. Speatsh pulled Bogi and Cadence away from Josh only a moment before Josh swung the coat over his head and behind him so he could stuff an arm inside.

Something shattered. Josh turned to look at what broke and felt the back of his neck cut open on the cloak's collar now set against one side of his neck.

173

His neck burned. The coat draped over only one side of his body and Josh hurt. Josh wondered how a portion of one of the tinted glass doors managed to drop a large triangular piece off the bottom. Cadence's eyes and mouth were wide. Bogi stared. Maybe he was smiling, but it was hard to tell if a Persian cat smiled. Speatsh was most definitely smiling, more in his eyes than his lips. Josh fumbled with the coat and felt his flesh open with new cuts before he finally slid his other arm into the remaining sleeve.

"At least your uncle remembered to wear the gloves before he put Wolf's Breath on," Speatsh said. "And it helps if you fold down the collar first too.

Josh felt himself blush as he looked at the floor where he somehow managed to drop the silk gloves when Cadence drew on him. Cadence took up the gloves and was about to bring them to Josh when Speatsh stopped her. He looked at Josh. "Turn around."

Josh turned.

"Faster," Speatsh said.

Josh turned faster.

"Take the rocks out of your pockets," Speatsh ordered. "Do it. Now."

Josh threw his arms straight out and used his heels to spin his body around. In less than a full revolution, the cloak flared out in all directions. Countless braids and tassels flared out and across his back, from beneath the shawl-like shoulder cap, and whipped the air. As the revolution ended, the cloak's cabinet doors fell from halfway down and chunks of sliced wood clattered against the floor and walls. A glass display case shattered as one of the chunks crashed into it. The top of the tall cabinet began to topple. Josh reached out to catch it, but a low edge of Wolf's Breath snapped forward and sliced it apart. The whole thing crumbled down around him.

The cloak settled at Josh's feet. Blood now made decent puddles on the floor and broken wood and fallen glass. Josh stepped from the mess. Smooth lacerations filled his face and neck, making no effort to hold back their trails of red stains. Even more blood trickled from his fingers and palms and he mustered all his strength to keep from screaming in pain.

"I'll call the dogs before he bleeds to death," Bogi said and left the room.

14 — Training Day

Cadence's shoulders hurt, the left one more than the right. The pain pulsated and burned down to her elbows, but she continued to push herself away from the ground one more time. The floor was hard and cold on her palms and she felt like she was pressing every drop of blood out of them. Still, down and up she went—down to the floor until her forearms seemed to turn to rubber and up until her shoulders reminded her why some people wanted to die. Her arms shook more with each count. On her way down, she wondered if they would collapse. And on the way up, she thought she would fall flat on her face.

One more, she kept telling herself on the way down, and one more managed to keep pressing her up.

On the other hand, Josh lay on his back and stared at the ceiling. Sweat stuck through his hair and dripped thick on his neck. He didn't care what anyone said, he was done. All he could do was breathe deep, listen to Cadence groan next to him and stare at the ceiling. One of the light bulbs needed to be replaced, but he didn't care to climb up the thirty feet to do it. He couldn't move anymore. His arms died nearly three minutes ago, he was merely waiting for someone to come along and cut them off so he could go to bed. He didn't hurt, but his chest was heavy.

It was only the second day since Speatsh gave everyone a strict workout schedule. Although Josh hadn't finished with his workout routine today, his body was finished and Cadence's was ready to collapse beside him, which was odd since Cadence and Josh were so physically active with their sporty activities. Strangely, Amber took right to the workout schedule. She did her pushups and sit-ups as well as her weight training. She ran her five miles of laps around the pool without any difficulty, as did Bricktain. To Josh's chagrin, Bricktain had no problem with his workout routine either. It seems Bricktain had already been following a daily workout schedule, running around the pool and using the weight room. Now, Bricktain was off somewhere else in the house doing whatever he did with his new glasses because he was already finished with his session, and Josh was dying on the floor. Cadence grunted out her last breath and she finally collapsed. She didn't even bother to roll over, just stayed on her stomach. Josh could hear her taking in the same short, stocky breaths as he was. Together, they listened to the constant whisper of a locked oscillating fan from the opposite end of the pool.

"Now can you feel that," Bogi asked.

Amber giggled, giggled louder, stopped and finally burst out laughing. "I'm sorry, it tickles."

"Really," Bogi asked. "Let me see your foot."

"Ow," Amber cried.

"Does it tickle now?"

Josh stared at the ceiling and Cadence stared at Josh watching the ceiling.

"Now," Bogi tried again. "Can you feel that?"

"Yes," Amber replied.

"Good," Bogi said. "As long as there's any bit of a breeze you can learn how to hold yourself on it. Move your foot around. Can you feel any pressure?"

"Sometimes," Amber said. "It goes away and comes back."

"Very good," Bogi said. "Now move your foot until you can feel that pressure constantly. The trick to is move your foot so that no matter where the breeze turns or how weak it gets, you don't fall. It might take a while, so—.

"OK," Amber said. Her voice heightened. "I got it."

"You do," Bogi asked. "Really? Already?"

"Yeah, it still wavers, kind of, but there's always a pressure," Amber said. "Like it's solid."

"That's what you have to learn to balance yourself on," Bogi said. "Try the other foot."

Amber squealed.

"Don't worry," Reggie said. "I've got you, honey."

"You'll have to learn to control that," Bogi said. "You don't want that to happen when you're forty or fifty feet up. Now, find that pressure again."

"I have it," Amber said.

"And try to get it with the other foot again."

By now, Josh's eyes were closed. His breathing grew easier. He even thought about trying to sit up, but felt so much more comfortable on the ground. Cadence said nothing.

"I have it," Amber replied.

"Constant," Bogi asked.

"Yeah."

"Strong?"

"I feel pressure, if that's what you mean."

"A little pressure is the same as being strong," Bogi said. "Can you feel it

176

under all of your foot?"

"Yeah, but only if I hold my foot like this."

"Then that's the way you should hold your foot. Can you push on it?"
Amber yelped.

"I've got you," Reggie said.

"Don't touch her," Bogi said. "Use your other foot, if you have to, Amber, and catch yourself."

Josh no longer felt pain. Things around him seemed dark, shaky dark, and his mind started wandering into a blackness with ambiguous shapes of shadows and familiar sounds.

"Josh," Cadence said.

Josh opened his eyes and turned to Cadence. He still hadn't grown used to her new haircut.

"Look." Cadence pointed out across the pool.

Josh let his head roll to the side and found the strength to sit up slowly. He watched Amber's face twist as if in pain. She bit and re-bit her bottom lip. Her feet twisted in all directions and her knees bent and straightened. Her legs split apart and in an awkward fashion came back together. She looked like a marionette hanging in the air, struggling to find the right string that would hold her body up. She continued rising into the air.

"Careful," Bogi said. "Don't keep pushing against it, or you'll be falling from the ceiling before you know it."

"This is some balancing act," Amber replied. Her whole body swayed in every direction possible, but somehow she stood about two feet off the ground.

"You're doing well, my dear," Bogi said. "All you have to do now is learn to walk level without turning into a contortionist."

"You think it's easy," Amber said. "You try it."

"Your goal is to walk across the pool and back," Bogi said. "And don't fall in, water makes you heavier. Propel yourself off the pressure under one foot and then find it again stepping forward, and always maintain your balance."

Amber struggled in the air. She lifted her foot to take a step and, a moment later, fell, flat on her knees.

"Ready to try again," Bogi asked.

Josh listened to Amber cry and watched her roll on the concrete to her back while tucking in one of her knees to her chest. Suddenly, his arms didn't seem so lifeless and he stood up. Cadence too, it seemed, had regained her strength and looked Josh over.

"You know," Cadence said. "She could have left, but she told Speatsh she wanted to fight."

"That happens when you have nothing to go home to," Josh said.

"It had nothing to do with going home," Cadence said. "Speatsh promised her and her father he could get them somewhere they would be safe, somewhere they wouldn't have to worry about being hunted, but she wanted to fight?"

"Why would she do that," Josh asked.

"Why do you care," Speatsh asked hobbling around behind Cadence. He held Wolf's Breath on a hanger. "Put this on."

Josh reached for Wolf's Breath, but remembered the silk gloves in his back pocket and quickly put them on. He slid his hands beneath the inside collar, pulled the cloak from around the hanger and carefully twisted it until he could slide his right arm through one of the sleeves. His left hand searched along the smooth insides until he felt it slide into the other sleeve. The collar didn't cut him today. Maybe it was because he had learned to put the collar down, or maybe it was because this time he wore the turtleneck shirt that may have been made from the same material as the insides of Wolf's Breath. He'd cut himself enough over the past two days that Speatsh decided to throw him a bone and give him the shirt.

"Once Richard got his hands on this beauty, and stopped cutting himself, he never went hunting without it," Speatsh said. "I think it came from Spain. If I remember correctly, it was originally designed by a matador who became a hunter. He passed it on to his protégé and the student redesigned it with a rare fabric immune to the acid the wolves could spit, but for that to work, it has to be wet, which means more weight you have to carry for it to be effective."

"So I'm supposed to get it wet before I start hunting," Josh asked.

"No, then it requires more effort to use," Speatsh replied. "But you want to start paying attention to where the water's at when you're hunting." Speatsh stepped to Josh and reached to the cloak. He still wore his gray fur-backed gloves. He reached inside the lining of Wolf's Breath and slid out a leather strip with a metal pin through its end and he stuck the pin through a metal ring on the other side of the cloak's collar, tightening it around Josh's neck. He attached a second pin and ring at Josh's chest. Josh felt the fabric form against his shoulders. "Even mud can help if it's wet enough and if you can't find water, but then you have mud flying everywhere." Finally, he found a third set of straps and pulled the cloak tight around Josh's torso. "This is the last time I help you get dressed." Speatsh looked over Josh and stepped back, pulling Cadence with him. "Spin around once with your arms out again, and this time

178

stand up straight like I've been telling you."

Josh twirled around, although he didn't want to, with his arms fully extended and once again, the cloak opened up into two tiers and hovered through the air. When he finished his turn, the fabric crumpled against itself and fell back to his sides.

"Good," Speatsh said. "You didn't cut yourself and you didn't destroy anything. You're getting better. Spin around again, start with your arms out and bring them into your chest like a boxer."

Josh twirled and the tiers formed again. He made fists and brought them into his chest. The top tier lifted from his shoulders and drifted up around and above his head, taking on the shape of a cone. As he stopped, the fabric once again settled in a crash of rifts and folds.

"The edges of the cloak are what you'll be learning to use," Speatsh said. "The first move is a simple defense. If you're surrounded, simply turn like you did and you should slice open anything within reach of the fabric. There's forty-two inches from the bottom of the cloak to the lowest strap there on your torso. That gives you a total span of about eight feet when it's fully stretched out. Release that low strap and you'll add two feet to it, but it's harder to control because it comes so close to your arms."

"How do I release it," Josh asked.

"Not until you master the small range. For now, do only as I say," Speatsh replied. "The second spin you did is useful to shield you from acid. It will still cut anything in range, but you can't see a thing because you have that huge funnel up around your ears. The last thing you want is to open up from this spin and have a wolf take your head off, so be wise using this one. Now, spin again and this time, tuck in one arm, like this, and throw a right hook, but stop when you get to here. Keep that other arm straight. And how many times do I have to tell you, stand straight?"

Josh spun as Speatsh instructed. As he brought in one arm, the bottom tier of his cloak opened and tilted, as if using Josh's waist for an axis. He formed a fist and hooked his arm. He stopped turning and threw the fist around and in front of him, forming a type of hook punch. The bottom corner of the tier snapped out at a point and Josh flinched. He felt his hand fall into the lining of the fabric and the sharp point suddenly snapped back into his face.

"Don't reach," Speatsh yelled. "Don't move a muscle." Once Josh looked like he wasn't going to move, Speatsh finally approached him. He quickly pulled the straps loose and let the cloak fall from around Josh's shoulders. "Let's go have the dogs lick your face and we can start again." He turned to Cadence. "Go put on the system and take a few laps around the pool."

Speatsh nudged Josh towards the elevator. As they walked, a giant splash burst from the swimming pool. Josh looked in time to watch Amber resurface with her blond hair matted flat against her head. She swam to the side of the pool where her father and Bogi waited.

"Very good. You did very well," Bogi said. "Now, get out and do it again, but with less water and more air, my dear."

As she pulled herself out of the pool, Josh couldn't help notice the way the water-weighted clothes clung to curves that she had done well to keep hidden. She wore the same black shirt she had worn the day she came to the bunker. It was torn. Josh could see her side through the tear. He realized he never thanked her for saving him from drowning. He'd have to do that some day. Amber sat on the edge of the pool before standing up again and for a moment, her eyes met Josh's. Her glance turned from nonchalant to concern when she saw the curtain of blood draping down his cheek. For a moment, she looked beautiful. Though Amber stood in front of him, Josh saw Natalie in his mind and he turned to the elevator so he didn't have to look on Amber anymore.

He and Speatsh stepped into the elevator.

"If we're going to work together, you need to know something about me," Speatsh said as the elevator began to lift them. "I belong to the line that swore guardianship to the queen. I thought I had failed."

"You were injured," Josh said.

Speatsh pressed a button and the elevator stopped moving . He turned abruptly. Even the brown bear's head seemed to glare from Speatsh's shoulder.

"I was left alone," Speatsh said. "And yes, I'm maimed. I can't fight like I used to. You can thank your uncle for that."

"He got you hurt?"

"Something like that," Speatsh replied as he ran his leather fur-backed fingers around an ear of the bear. "Actually, he helped me protect the queen's family."

"I should get my face taken care of."

"You're fine," Speatsh said. "The queen had a daughter who survived, Josh Revlon. You tell no one, you get me, Josh Revlon?" Speatsh squared up his face with Josh's and backed him into a corner. "Only a handful of us know, and we didn't know she survived until recently, but I'm of the line left sworn to protect the family. My mother was the youngest of the ancients, the one who swore to protect the queen."

"You're not going to help us get my sister," Josh said. "Are you?"

Now Speatsh ran his fingers over the bears head.

"Perhaps," Speatsh said. "When the time is right."

Josh felt it again. For once, he had felt hope in helping Cracey, but it was gone now. Even he believed he could learn how to fight Jasper with Speatsh's help. He threw all of his weight into Speatsh and watched the old man fall back into another corner of the box. "I thought you came to help us."

"I did," Speatsh said. He looked surprised, perhaps because Josh caught him off guard. "But I came looking for help too, your help."

Josh didn't understand and Speatsh must have been able to tell.

"I could ask other hunters, but they wouldn't have the loyalty you offer."

"I have no loyalty to you," Josh said.

"You owe more loyalty to me than you realize," Speatsh said through tight teeth. "And how about to your friends? To your two friends turned into dogs? To your Natalie? To your family? And the others?"

A frightening realization hit Josh. "Will they lead Jasper to us?"

"They don't belong to him," Speatsh said. "He has no power over them."

"Yours?"

"We've been fighting this war a long time," Speatsh said. "You're going to find that you have allies you never even knew existed beyond these walls. Nick and Dustin are warded to me, and I have trained them to overcome certain new instincts. I give them to you because they are loyal to you and will fight for you. They will fight because they understand the grander scheme of things now, things you don't know, which are forbidden for my kind to speak. But I can tell you this, and you never utter a sound about it, understand?"

Josh didn't.

"After I tell you what I need to, your life can never be the same, not just because you're a hunter now, but because of loyalty and what you know, which will be little to what you may eventually learn. Are you ready to hear?"

"I don't know if I am," Josh replied.

"The queen met a mortal man," Speatsh said. "She loved him and abandoned her powers so she could grow old with him and they had nine children. When the rogue attacked them, the youngest ancient, the queen's guardian, managed to save one child, a daughter. The guardian ancient told no one, not even her most trusted allies, of the child. The guardian ancient hid the child, but the rogue sensed her and he sent scouts to find her, which they did, but they didn't find the daughter who had grown considerably by then.

"Like the queen, the daughter went into hiding, married and also had a child. She knew the scouts were looking for her, and that it was only a matter of time before they discovered her. She never told her daughter, the queen's granddaughter, about her heritage. She made sure her daughter would never want for anything and then she destroyed herself so that the rogue couldn't use her to find her family. The rogue shares a mental link with the other ancients and it was through this link that he was able to hunt them down and kill them. It was the same way he found the queen and killed her and discovered her daughter and searched for her. The instinct of the wolf lies dormant in the queen's grandchild. If the child should ever learn about her heritage, the instincts may awaken and the rogue ancient will feel her and could use her to find the other ancients and then destroy them and the human race. She's the key to finding the rogue's siblings. That's why he hasn't set his plan into motion yet."

"If he has a link with the ancients, why does he need the queen," Josh asked.

"The link to the ancients is through her," Speatsh said. "It's in her awareness. If she dies, he'll never find them."

"Then why did he kill the queen?"

"He didn't understand how it worked then. All his life he'd had this link with his family, but when she died, the link disappeared and he understood why. But the queen's blood lived in her daughter and so did the power of the link. The queen's daughter knew her family past and she also denied her powers, but the rogue found his link through her because even though she denied her powers, the wolf in her was yet alive. The wolf part of her was aware and that was all the rogue needed to make his connection to her. He knew she had a child as well. That's why she never told her daughter the family secret so that the wolf in her could never awaken. The ancient must remain in dormancy so the rogue can never establish a psychic connection and use it to find the others. The ancient grandchild must never awaken. I am of the line of the youngest ancient who swore to protect the queen. She must live to become a banner of hope and strength to preserve the human race and the race of the ancients."

Josh didn't know what to say.

"Cadence is the grandchild my family is sworn to protect," Speatsh said. "While I've been occupied tracking down leads to find the rogue, she's been here right under Richard's nose. Not even the queen's own family knew who Cadence was because her mother kept her so secret. I would have been here sooner, but it's harder to stow away anymore. Richard was one of the few mortals who knew much about the ancients, which is partly why he was so hunted. But the rogue's general found him and flushed him out by attacking the one weakness he had, you and your sister. When he called me, I had to give up chasing my lead on the rogue and return home. The rogue knows who you are, Josh, and he will not risk coming after you because of the tools he knows you have at your fingers to fight him. But if he ever learns about Cadence, all the armies of hell at your disposal won't stop him from storming on you and this town with his very last slave. We don't want to be here if that happens. As far as he's concerned, you're just a naïve hunter who learned a dark family secret that you don't understand, and he's not going to risk coming into the open over you. He doesn't know about Cadence or who she truly is. And you better hope he doesn't learn anything from Cracey."

Josh wondered how his world had turned so quickly. He remembered Cadence's parents and always thought they had died in accidents. He thought about all he lost again. He was both happy and scared knowing that Nick and Dustin were still his allies. Even still, how could he protect Cadence? She, herself, was learning to fight.

"What would happen if something happened to Cadence," Josh asked.

"You mean, like if she died," Speatsh asked. "Then we hope that buys us enough time to find him first because if he ever found out he'd have no reason to keep his existence secret anymore. He'd wreak havoc in war this earth has never before known, and he'll probably win."

This is about when Josh thought about locking Cadence in the bunker and never letting her out, but would she forgive him? What kind of life would that be for her?

"So you're not leaving then," Josh asked.

"Only if it's with my queen," Speatsh answered. "And I doubt she'll be happy going into hiding. I'd end up spending my days chasing her rather than protecting her. So, I have two choices, tell her the truth and wait for the end of mankind, or let her stay here and be surrounded by friends."

"If she's the queen," Josh said. "Why not teach her to lead, instead of me?"

Speatsh smirked and pushed a button that started the elevator moving again. "Because she listens to you."

"She fights for Nick now," Josh said. "There's nothing I could say to stop her."

"She has Nick," Speatsh said. "When she learns that, she'll fight for you. You have to help me, Josh. I'm not the warrior I once was. I'm human and every day I fight to push the wolf back. I know the taste of human blood. I can smell it in the air here. Cadence is the only thing preventing the genocide of humans."

"I'll protect her," Josh said. "And we'll hunt every one of those things that we can in the process."

"Thank you," Speatsh said. "Remember, you can never say anything."

"If the time comes I need to," Josh said. "I will tell the others. We may need to."

Speatsh was silent.

The doors opened into the second floor living room and Bricktain stood in front of a wall of more than thirty television screens, all showing different pictures.

"Who's there," Bricktain asked, holding a toy gun in each hand. He aimed the gun at one of the far screens and a gunshot rang out over speakers.

"What is this," Josh asked. He had been in this room yesterday and none of this equipment was here. Bricktain was the only one allowed in the room at all since Speatsh appeared.

"Hard to explain," Speatsh replied.

"While you guys get to learn to fight," Bricktain said as he fired off two more shots at two different screens. "I have to play games."

A large commotion of metallic sounds erupted from the speakers.

"You are dead," Speatsh's voice announced from the televisions as the screens turned black. "Good job, loser."

"Why am I doing this," Bricktain asked.

"It'll make sense in due time," Speatsh said. "Where's the dogs? I told them to keep an eye on you." Speatsh whistled.

The Dobermans' heads appeared over the back of the black couch.

"Come," Speatsh ordered.

"Stop," Josh said. "They're still my friends. We don't need to treat them differently."

"I don't think you have any more friends, kid," Bricktain said and another bang rang over the speakers.

"Get back to work," Speatsh snapped and once again, Bricktain fired.

Josh knelt down and looked over the two Dobermans. Which was which? They looked the same, black with brown masks and brown paws. The dogs stared back.

"They may be your friends," Speatsh said. "But they're wolves now."

"I won't treat them differently," Josh said and continued to look them over. He remembered the first time they licked his wounds and Speatsh pulled them off.

"Dustin," he said kneeling. "I cut myself. Can you give me a hand?"

The Doberman on the left stood and walked over without making a sound. It looked over the gash, which reached from under Josh's right eye and spread around his cheek. The Doberman sniffed at it and pulled away. It sat and

184

stared at Josh, and looked to Speatsh.

"What," Speatsh asked.

"Dustin," Josh said.

The Doberman looked back to Josh.

"Can you clean it, please?"

Dustin stood and again returned his nose to Josh's face, licked and bit down. Josh pulled back and Speatsh kicked Dustin. Josh felt his face grow warm with more blood.

"Nick," Speatsh cried. "Lick the wound, and don't bite."

"No," Josh said. "Dustin, this doesn't help Cracey."

Dustin's ears folded down and he stepped slowly toward Josh, watching Speatsh every bit of the way. He sniffed the wound, licked the blood, and opened his mouth. Josh snapped his head toward Dustin and glared. Dustin pulled back and Josh allowed Dustin to lick again. Dustin cleaned the wound without further incident. Josh returned with Speatsh and the dogs to the swimming pool.

Amber stood at the elevator doors as they opened. She held a towel to her face, littered with familiar red abrasions. "I'm supposed to have the dogs lick my face."

Speatsh laughed and stepped out of the elevator.

"Nick," Josh said.

One of the Doberman's ears perked and looked up to Josh.

"I don't want them touching me," Amber said. "But this really hurts."

"If you bite her, Nick, I'm telling Cadence," Josh said. Josh reached up to pull Amber's hair to the side and get a better look at the wound.

"I almost made it to the other side," Amber said.

Josh watched closely as Amber knelt down and Nick licked her head clean. Nick seemed to have less of a problem fighting the wild urge to have at more blood than Dustin. When he was done, Amber stood.

"Time to injure myself again, I guess," Amber said turning away. She stopped. "Josh?"

Josh held Amber by three fingers. He wasn't aware he had done so, but deep down he didn't want her leave and so he held her. When he realized what he'd done, he pulled away. "I'm sorry."

"Is something wrong?"

"No," he replied. He wanted to thank her for saving his life, but when she looked at him, he realized how simple and stupid his gratitude would sound. He forgot because she looked at him. She looked through him. She still smiled just a little before she turned and walked away.

15 – Out on the Town

Reggie found Richard's chore list in the antique desk in the office near the computer. Every Monday, the swimming pool area needed to be squeegeed so no one slipped and mildew didn't grow and pollute the circulated air. The generator located behind the weight room had to be refilled every 72 hours. The generator hadn't kicked on yet, so everyone assumed the city still provided electricity. Of course, who knew if the city still took automatic payments from Richard's, now Josh's, bank account? If the power should shut down, twenty thousand gallons of kerosene waited to be used, and when that was gone, it would be time to leave the bunker to get more.

The water kept coming too, but if it stopped, Richard had left instructions about how to operate a filtration system that turned the swimming pool water into something drinkable. There was also something about the water in the diorama, but until recently no one knew what that meant. No one had to do that either yet. However, the sunlit windows feeding the greenhouse had to be cleaned every day to keep condensation from interfering with charging the emergency batteries. Since the windows were too bright and too hot to clean in the day, everyone took turns each night. Bricktain hated cleaning them more than anyone, but Bricktain hated everything.

Once a month, someone had to check the elevator hydraulics. No leaks yet, but if any were found, the only way out of the bunker was by climbing up the ladders inside the elevator shaft.

Air filters needed changing every three months, and the computer needed updating each time someone used the internet. Since no one could get online anymore, it wasn't necessary to keep clean. Reggie didn't take long to take over the computer once he found Bricktain talking in chat rooms about events and telling strangers about their situation. Reggie figured he didn't need idiots trying to find them.

Bricktain had a difficult time. The diamond glasses were his worst enemy. He now wore them four and a half hours a day. Speatsh left the bunker from time to time and brought in electronic gadgets and closed boxes. More and more stuff came into the bunker and went straight to the trophy room where Bogi would work with Speatsh and sometimes Reggie. They argued a lot. They took Bricktain down and shoved his face in front of a machine that flashed a photo of his eye and nearly blinded him. Four days later, they returned to the room and Bogi forced a full-sized contact lens into Bricktain's eye. It wouldn't have been so bad except that one of Bogi's hairs got caught under the lens and Bricktain refused to let Bogi help him remove it and he ended up tearing the lens taking it out. Three days after that, Speatsh put new contacts in and when Bricktain said he felt like he needed eye drops, Speatsh spit in his eye. Bricktain hated the contacts but he had to wear them whenever he wore the diamond glasses. They were supposed to help his eyes maintain their correct vision. Bogi said they were ridged to match the way the glasses folded the world into strange thin images. The first day of wearing the contacts, Bricktain rubbed them through his eyelids and couldn't wear them for three more days because his eyes were swollen shut.

Why he had to sit in front of the television screens didn't make sense, but Bricktain continued to do so. He wanted out of the bunker. The others understood why they had to learn new skills, but Bricktain felt left in the dark shooting at now nearly eighty twelve-inch television screens all connected to one computer. With his glasses on, it was difficult learning who everyone was. Everything was so much thinner and his friends all looked like sticks. The dogs looked like short barking sticks and Bogi looked like a tall white pencil walking with a wire. The images on the television sets were even more difficult to comprehend, but he was starting to be able to decipher the white round targets that floated like balloons across the screens from the square targets that grew and shrank. After a while, he began to see contours through the glasses and nearly shouted for joy when he was able to tell when one of the slits he saw was Josh. He didn't, because he hated Josh.

For now, Bricktain looked for toilet paper. He always worried they would run out, but the rolls continued to remain in supply in the large pantry just off the laundry room. He took out a few rolls and this time paid particular attention to the fact they were down to the last three packages. He took one of the packs and left the pantry.

"We're running out of toilet paper," Bricktain said as he passed Josh who was dropping articles of clothing into a beige washing machine. "We have less than a case left."

Josh didn't drop the last piece of clothing into the washing machine. He knew time was short and that they were running out of everything. They had only been there nine months. They just weren't good at rationing supplies. "Maybe we should ask Speatsh to do some shopping."

"Ha, good one," Bricktain said leaving the room.

Bricktain was right. Josh knew it, but he was afraid of what that meant. He didn't tell anyone, but he was afraid of the wolves killing his friends, afraid of the wolves killing him, afraid of himself tearing his limbs apart with Wolf's Breath. He had more control over the cloak now, after five months of training with it, but still he cut himself from time to time. He didn't like to use spinning moves because they made him dizzy and it was hard to hit the targets when he used them. He also learned how to fight using the clump of braided leather straps on back of Wolf's Breath to his best advantage. He never saw them work, but Cadence told him he puffed up like a hedgehog whenever he flipped in the air or somersaulted across the floor. Once, when he moved too quickly, Speatsh fell back grabbing his leg and holding his shoulder. Speatsh disappeared into the trophy room for the rest of the day and came back wearing a type of round knight's shield over his right forearm to protect himself.

Josh stared into the washing machine. He held Amber's black shirt and put his finger through the tear on the side. It reminded him of his own exhaustion that night he went to Jasper's, the exhaustion that forced Dustin to carry him to the bunker. He never knew such weariness and he wondered if he was up to surviving that a second time. He tossed Amber's shirt into the washing machine and pulled the last box of detergent from the shelf. He turned the box over and let the remaining crumbs fall onto the clothes. It was time to shop.

He went straight to the wooden box in his room and took out the black gloves. He put them on, took Wolf's Breath from his closet and wound it around his shoulders. He assembled the fangs and locked them at his sides onto a belt he didn't know was hidden in the box until Speatsh revealed it to him. They were difficult to reach right now, but Speatsh said he'd learn how to grab at them without throwing Wolf's Breath into his face. His next stop was the office where he found all the account numbers he would need to access his inherited funds. When he walked into the living room, he called Dustin, Nick and the elevator.

"Training again," Reggie asked.

"Going shopping," Josh said. "We need supplies."

Reggie jerked. "Just like that? Going shopping?"

"Who's going shopping," Cadence called from down the hallway, but suddenly appeared in the main room and didn't look too happy.

"We're out of detergent and we could use some food and other things," Josh replied.

"So, you *are* going shopping," Bricktain asked, running up the spiral staircase into the living room. He was trying to tear the top off a can of Vienna sausages. "Don't forget toilet paper."

"Hold it," Reggie said. "I don't think it's a good idea."

"I'm tired of stinking," Josh replied. "I'm tired of no deodorant and I'm tired of no soap because we used it all because we're out of deodorant. I'm tired of the way Bricktain smells and I'm tired of this whole stinking place. I'm going out and I'm taking the twins with me."

Josh had gotten used to referring to Dustin and Nick as the twins since he couldn't tell them apart.

The elevator doors opened and Speatsh started out of it. "No more training today," he scolded. "I'm tired."

"He thinks he's going shopping," Reggie said.

"Are you stupid," Speatsh asked.

"We need supplies," Josh said. "I'm taking Nick and Dustin and I'm going shopping."

"Pick up some resin, will you," Speatsh said. "I'm working on a project."

"I'm going with him," Cadence said.

"No," Both Josh and Speatsh replied.

"Oh, I'm coming," Cadence said and was clearly unhappy.

"That's great, Cadence," Josh said. "When you walk down the streets with the system and we get stopped by the police for all your hardware, we'll just tell them we need it because very bad things are after us."

"Then I won't wear it," Cadence said.

"No one goes out with being armed up," Speatsh scolded.

"Try and stop me," Cadence replied.

"You'll put him in more danger in the daylight wearing the system," Speatsh said. "It's not prudent and he'll have the twins with him."

"Well, it's all right if I go," Amber said, storming into the room with a leather whip swinging from each side of her waist. She had proven her ability enough with the whips over the past five months that Speatsh started teaching her to fight with two. She pulled a bulky, brown coat over her shoulders and Josh immediately knew it was one of the articles of clothing from one of the closets, which didn't fit anyone. Everything in the closets were there to fit members of Josh's family.

Speatsh scowled and made sure Josh saw it. "Take these." He pulled back his gray fur-covered sleeves on his right arm and revealed a silver armlet. In a moment, he pulled a cage, similar to the ones Cadence had around her wrists, from off his arm. "I was going to give these to you later, but you might need them now." Speatsh reached under the large fold of Josh's right sleeve and folded it back so he could attach the armlet and the cage to Josh's appendage. He pulled a second armlet from beneath his other sleeve and attached that to

Josh's left arm. He folded the sleeves back down until they tightened around the cages, careful not to let the sleeve drape over the front of the silver metal armlet.

"Make a fist and flex your forearm," Speatsh said.

Josh did and two narrow, steel plates launched out from atop each wrist and from within each of those plates lunged a second and third until two short needle-like swords were fully erect.

"They'll pull back in when you stop flexing," Speatsh said. "Be careful. You can pull a muscle easier than you think with these, but with as light on your feet as you have to be with Wolf's Breath, you should learn how they can work together. Try not to kill the cashier when you swipe your card, don't stab yourself reaching for the fangs and make sure you squeeze the triggers rather than flex or who knows what you could do to yourself," he said before suddenly turning on Amber. "And you."

Amber jumped.

"Be careful. There's no swimming pool to catch you if you fall."

"Why don't you come with us," Amber asked.

"He can't," Josh replied before Speatsh could.

Speatsh glared at Josh. "I can answer my own questions," he snapped. "I'm too well-known around here. It could put you both in more danger than is necessary.

"Then let someone else go," Cadence said.

"There is no one else," Speatsh yelled. "I can't go. You can't go. Wheels can't go and Bricktain'll get himself killed. And we need supplies."

"I would feel much better if I was coming with you," Cadence said.

"Would you like us to pick up anything in particular," Amber asked.

"Bring him back alive," Cadence said and left the room.

Josh, Amber and the Doberman twins stepped into the elevator and a few minutes later they stood in the garage looking over Josh's inherited Chevy Silverado. It was white and had a black cab. The word 'Hickerbilly' was painted in small silver letters over the driver's door. And the words 'I hate dogs' were painted on the front lip of the truck hood.

"That color's ugly," Josh had said once to Speatsh. "I should paint it black."

"You're separated from your friends, you're tired, you're beaten, you're fighting at night in the dark and you wanna look for a black truck," Speatsh asked. "That truck is your lifeline to escape, don't make it hard to find."

"I still think Hickerbilly's ugly," Josh said.

Amber agreed.

Josh walked to a small locker and punched six digits into the number pad. The locker opened and Josh pulled out a key ring. He put his fears of tearing up Hickerbilly's seat with Wolf's Breath to rest when he realized the fabric on the seat was made of a thick material similar to that of the insides of the deadly cloak. He climbed behind the wheel and Amber pulled herself into the passenger's side. Dustin and Nick scrambled into the back.

"Are you ready," Josh asked.

"Guess we'll find out," Amber replied.

Josh pressed a button on a remote on the visor above his head and the garage door lowered into the ground. Josh threw his foot against the floor and the truck screamed as it raced backward. The truck cleared the garage door, which immediately closed as Josh backed down the driveway. The twins did their best not to slide around in the bed as the truck pulled out of the driveway and the nose spun around and faced an empty street. Josh waited, looked around and waited. Nick and Dustin stood with their ears cocked. They looked in all directions.

"Do you see anything," Josh asked.

"Nothing," Amber replied.

A few cars a couple blocks away sat on curbs and a group of kids threw a rugby ball around in the middle of the street, but there didn't appear to be signs of dog anywhere.

"Where are they," Josh asked.

"Do you think they gave up," Josh asked back.

Josh didn't know, so he wasn't sure how to answer.

Josh shifted into second gear and started towards the business district.

Josh made a quick stop at T.C's National Bank. His uncle took him when he turned 18 and put him on the account. Richard told Josh he felt there might be times he might need Josh to run errands for him. Josh never did run any errands for his uncle. He checked his available funds, nearly had a heart attack and returned to the truck with Amber.

"Some antique dealer," Amber said.

They stopped at Grady's Hardware and picked up some resin for Speatsh.

The next stop was the supermarket. The Silverado parked and took up more than its share of surrounding parking stalls. Josh stepped down from the cab and instructed Nick and Dustin to keep an eye out, but to stay in the truck. If something appeared wrong, they were to find him and Amber inside the store. If anything else went wrong, they were to return to the bunker. Josh and Amber made their journey toward the front doors. Still, they watched for anything strange.

Josh and Amber weaved in and out of aisles and the cars parked in them. Josh felt weaving in and out of the aisles would help them hide better. More than once, it crossed their minds that something could jump out from under or behind a car at any moment. They stayed close to each other. Amber was afraid her whips would be useless in such cramped conditions. Josh wondered more about the damage he would cause both outside and inside the store if he had to defend himself.

"Josh," Amber said.

Josh stopped and turned, expecting to have a mongrel pointed out to him. He listened to the blades of his right arm open before he looked upon Amber.

"Be more careful with your coat," Amber said.

Josh saw the blue Volkswagen with large streaks of scratches down the side. Perhaps using cars to help hide them wasn't such a great idea.

As he and Amber approached the automatic sliding glass doors, he attracted the attention of a large round woman toying with a small Pekingese at the end of a thin, pink leash. The Pekingese danced on its hind legs and its front paws swam through the air reaching for both the woman's long gray skirt and the piece of jerky she had just pulled out of a bag above his head. The Pekingese barked and the woman praised the dog for being cute, small and stupid. The dog dropped to all fours and immediately leapt back up on its rears in a second attempt to bring down the jerky. Josh fought back the urge to let the blades open again, but the dog paid no attention, so Josh assumed he wasn't wolf. The woman finally dropped the small piece of jerky to the Pekinese, who didn't catch it, but let it bounce off its flat face and eagerly licked it off the ground, grunting through its short snout as it chewed and licked.

Inside the store, Josh asked a clerk for a couple of flat bed carts with as many cases of toilet paper as they could each hold. Josh eagerly paid for them and returned to the truck where he tossed them up to Amber who packed them tightly into the bed while Nick and Dustin climbed on them for a better view of the parking lot, which they watched closely.

Next, they loaded one flatbed with detergents, bleach and fabric softeners and the other with cleaning supplies and air fresheners. These they paid for and loaded into Hickerbilly's oversized bed as well. They hauled out boxes of tampons, deodorant, shaving cream, hand soap, body soap, face soap, razors, shavers, toothpaste, dental floss, and many kinds of medicine. They also loaded up on food: fresh and dried vegetables and fruits, canned and frozen meat, flour, sugar, cornmeal, cake mixes, cereals, frozen dinners, frozen pizza, juices, soda and anything else that stacked neatly on the flatbed cart. Josh loaded up a few cases of whiskey and Amber put them back on the shelves. Again, they paid and packed their supplies out. They returned to fill two shopping carts with as much as they could of anything else they wanted.

Josh was pulling blasphemous numbers of jars of pasta sauce from the shelves and Amber unloaded an entire shelf of turkey stuffing, in one sweep, when she surprised the terrier staring at her from the back of the shelf. Amber jumped away and clenched her whip under her coat when she caught more movement above her head. Another dog sat poised on the top of the shelves watching her. She saw the other two standing over Josh's head monitoring him.

"They've been watching us the entire time," Josh said as he dropped packages of noodles into his cart. "We might be in trouble, here." He left his cart and pulled one of the boxes of stuffing mix from Amber's. He looked down the aisle, saw no one and suddenly the set of blades leapt from his right arm and he held their points against the terrier's throat. He pressed the animal against the back of the shelf.

"They're moving," Amber said.

The terrier struggled to climb from under the pressure of the steel swords. It whined, but struggled not to make a sound.

"Stop following us," Josh said before eventually pulling away. The terrier huddled against the wall of the store shelving, flashing its teeth. Josh knew the terrier understood him. He placed the box of stuffing over the open gap on the shelf.

"You should have killed it," Amber said.

"They'd be stupid to fight us in here," Josh said loud enough for the dogs overhead to hear. "That could lead other hunters to Jasper, especially when the news reports that dead naked people were found in a local supermarket."

The dogs continued watching, but with less aggressive behavior.

"Besides," Josh said in a softer tone. "That could have been my sister."

Josh and Amber filled their carts and were soon back at the truck. Nick and Dustin were now still and intent with perked ears and statuesque stances. Josh and Amber covered the bed with a tarp.

The Dobermans leapt from crates and took new stances in a hollow depression in the canvas. In a few minutes, the truck was back on the road heading back the direction it had come. Amber felt relieved, but not completely at ease, knowing it would be a fifteen-minute drive before they were all safe in the bunker again. She hadn't said much the entire trip, and she could see Josh was already too tightly wound up to enjoy conversation.

He gripped the wheel, thinking he could probably tear it from the column if he needed an additional weapon. He didn't even sit all the way back in his seat. His eyes bounced from one side of the street to the other, straight ahead, to his side mirror and back to the sides of the street. After four or five miles of driving, he remembered to shift into third gear. They approached the street that led to the bunker, but Josh continued driving past it. Amber didn't feel relieved any more, and was too afraid to ask why he kept traveling. Ten minutes of tension passed before Josh drove the truck into a larger parking lot and stopped at the south end of a round shopping mall.

Josh was out of the truck and barking orders to his mutated friends before Amber knew what to do. She followed him across this parking lot and through more automatic doors into a Sharber's Clothing Outlet.

"Why don't you pick out some things to wear," Josh said.

"I have clothes," Amber said.

"You have clothes meant for my mother and you share those with Cadence," Josh replied. "You should have more than a pair of ratty jeans and a shirt that's torn up."

"I don't need anything, really."

"I know you stayed, when you could have left," Josh admitted.

Amber tried to wipe her eye without looking like she was trying to wipe it.

"You saved my life," Josh said. "And you stayed even after I hit you. How do I apologize for something like?"

Suddenly, Josh couldn't breathe. She looked at him, not past him like people do when they're in an awkward situation, like when a guy professes his love to a girl who doesn't love him in return, and she searches the walls behind him to find a way to let him down easy. Amber looked right at Josh and he felt himself smile even after she looked away.

"You don't know what you're saying," Amber said.

"I know I'd be alone in that bunker, or dead if it wasn't for you," Josh said.

She looked back and allowed herself to smile back.

"OK," she said. "But I'm not the only one you owe apologies to."

"Would you pick out some things for Cadence," Josh asked. "Apparently, I could buy a small country."

"So can I," Amber replied and she pulled a slender black envelope holding a single plastic card from the back pocket of her beige slacks, which were clearly not the right shape or size for her. "But I'll let you pay." She returned the card to her pocket.

Together they searched racks. Both quickly sorted through the gigantic display rings filled of hangers holding shirts, pants, sweaters and jackets. They found men's jeans and button up shirts for Bricktain, or at least they looked like the type of shirts they thought Bricktain would wear, in other words, they picked the ugliest shirts in the men's clearance rack they could find—the kind of shirts that would look better as curtains or couch fabric than they did as clothing. Amber picked out jeans and slacks for her father as well as the plain color T-shirts and polos he liked to wear. Josh found brown leather gloves for everyone and a dozen pair extra as well as socks and warm hiking boots. He bought himself a pair of black steel-toed boots and extra laces. He chose some sunglasses, watches, ties, sports coats, winter coats, thinner coats that were on a clearance ring hidden in a far corner, and some black jeans for himself to wear beneath Wolf's Breath.

As his shopping cart overflowed above and beneath, Amber's filled slowly. Her cart was barely half-filled with jeans and slacks, a few flannels and other button-up shirts, a variety of pullovers, belts, bras and panties, which reminded Josh he better load up on under garments for the guys. While Amber gently set silk pajamas in her cart, Josh forced several packages of undershirts, boxers and briefs into the bottom rack of his. Nothing more could fit in the top. Amber continued to drop clothes into hers, skirts and blouses and jackets to match.

"We need swimsuits," Amber said.

"We can look if you want to," Josh said.

They found three designs of suits on another rack, all of them ugly. One was a two-piece that looked like someone threw up the bad part of a half-eaten banana split on it, and the other two were one-pieces: one with purple frogs and the other with blue glitter.

"Well, they've got to be better than wearing your mother's swimsuits," Amber said and dropped them into the cart. She threw down hair ribbons and chose some cheap jewelry. She also found shoes and guessed at Cadence's size, just as she had been doing the entire time, and stopped.

"I keep forgetting I won't need a good pair of shoes anymore, huh," Amber said as she held a pair of dark boots to her wind riders.

"Get them anyway," Josh said. "We have to have time for ourselves once in a while."

Amber smiled and slid the boots alongside other boxes of footwear beneath the bucket of the cart. She led Josh and his overflowing carriage towards a wall with leather trench coats. She took down one of the coats, as well as articles of clothing from surrounding shelves and bins, before disappearing into a fitting room. Suddenly, Josh felt awkward. He hadn't noticed any of the creatures following them in this store as they had in the other. He looked toward the ceiling and frowned at the way the dressing rooms were open near the top. He imagined the creatures climbing along the tops, watching and even waiting for Amber in one of the rooms. He listened to a door close and the lock click.

"Amber," Josh called out. He entered the dressing room area, ignoring the awkward glance a female customer threw his way. "Amber?"

"I'm not going anywhere," came Amber's voice from a door deeper into the dressing room than made Josh comfortable.

"Umm, OK," Josh replied.

"Sir," a woman's voice addressed from the entrance of the dressing area. "You know better."

Josh pretended not to hear the woman.

"Sir," the woman said.

"Josh," Amber spoke through her door. "Don't worry. If something's wrong the entire store will know it."

As much as it frightened Josh, he left Amber and the scowling dressing room manager. He waited for what he thought was too long before Amber reappeared. She had slicked her hair back and tied it into a tail with a black ribbon. The purple trench coat reached just above her ankles and an interior vest fastened the coat together across her chest. A black rounded collar climbed from beneath the top of the vest and stood sharply around her neck. A pair of black jeans barely seemed noticeable within the lower folds of the coat. Amber's hands were working beneath the coat and behind her back, Josh knew she was tying down the whips. When she pulled out her hands, the coat fell down and hugged her sides. She was even skinnier than he realized.

"I have got to cut holes in these things," Amber said bending her knees. "There's no way I can stretch in these."

She walked past Josh and began pushing her cart and suddenly stopped. She reached up to a wall of baseball caps and found a leather one. She took it down, tore off the barcode and adjusted it onto her head, being sure to pull her ponytail through the hole in the back.

"Do I look as intimidating as videogame heroines created by men," she asked.

Josh nodded and laughed a little.

"Might as well have some sort of fun with this whole mess," she said and started pushing again. Josh followed and nearly didn't see Amber stop at a rack where she took down four or five pairs of black stretch pants. Finally, Amber stopped in front of a rack with dresses, thumbed through and pulled out a white one. She immediately curled it into a ball and dropped it into her cart.

"Okay, we can go now," She said.

Amber led the way to a cashier's station where a young male was eager to announce the cost of the clothing, sales tax, store profit and his commission all rolled into one generous number. He tried flirting with Amber but she ignored him, and to get even with him told him she wanted everything gift wrapped. He disappeared to get wrapping paper and mumbled something about not being paid enough. Josh and Amber quickly retreated to the parking lot before he could return. They found Nick and Dustin watching the entire world intently from atop Hickerbilly. Amber and Josh dumped everything into the back of the cab and drove away from the mall.

Josh took a different way home, not because he wanted to tempt fate, or because he wanted to prolong the trip home, he wasn't even sure if he wanted to spend more time with Amber, but he didn't mind and it confused him. He steered Hickerbilly deeper into the city and closer to the campus of the university, he had invested so many hours, and soon found himself staring at Natalie's apartment building.

Her apartment was the one on third floor, second from the corner, the one with the light pink curtains that would never have belonged to Natalie. The stuffed ducks lining the sill and the plastic window stickers weren't Natalie's either. He knew at once, Natalie wasn't there anymore.

Josh started the truck and started back home, taking the canal road. He thought about the last time he was on this road.

"What was she like," Amber asked.

Josh wanted to answer, but he knew who was asking the question and he wondered if he could tell her the truth without feeling weird.

"I mean you don't have to tell me," Amber said.

"We were going to get married," Josh said.

"Oh," Amber said. "She must have been something special."

"Yeah," Josh replied. "My mom hated her, but my sister, Cracey, she loved her. What?"

"Huh?"

"Are you okay?"

"What do you mean?"

"You just looked like," Josh decided Amber grabbing her head meant nothing. "It's nothing."

"Josh, if there was anything I could do to bring either of them back," Amber said. "I would."

Josh looked at Amber. He was smiling. He knew he was smiling and she smiled a little too, but quickly looked away and Josh looked away. He heard the siren of the police car following him and saw the flashing red and blue lights in the side view mirror.

"Is the registration expired," Amber said as she started folding down visors and looking for papers.

"I didn't even think about that," Josh asked.

Hickerbilly pulled to a stop and the police truck pulled up behind it.

"He has ten years of registration papers in here," Amber said as she rifled through a small stack of papers, from the glove box, until she found what she was looking for.

"For a police chief, my uncle sure knew how to break the law." Josh waited for the officer to approach the driver's door. "Afternoon, officer," Josh greeted the uniformed man.

Sergeant Chandler requested the usual documents for those being pulled over.

Before Josh could turn to Amber for the papers, he found them in his hands. He handed the papers and his license to Chandler, who accepted them coldly while he stared at Josh through his bronze tinted glasses. He looked over the license and the papers.

"This isn't your truck," Chandler said.

"Actually, it is," Josh replied. "I inherited it from my uncle."

"Your insurance doesn't cover you."

"Yes it does," Josh replied. "That's my name right there."

"Why don't we call Richard and see if he knows where his truck is today," Chandler said.

"I told you," Josh said. "I inherited the truck, I can provide documentation of that fact. This truck is mine, I just haven't registered it in my name yet."

"You mind if I take a look inside your truck?"

"Yes, I do," Josh said. "You know, my uncle Richard Revlon was your former boss. I do know a thing or two about the law here."

"Why exactly are we being pulled over," Amber asked.

"Please step out of the truck," Chandler ordered.

"Why," Amber asked placing her hand on Josh's gloved hand. "We have a right to know why you pulled us over."

"I think we'd like to have another officer present," Josh requested.

Suddenly Chandler had his gun drawn and pointed at Josh. "Driver, step out of the car with your hands where I can see them."

"This is illegal," Amber said.

"I believe you're right," Josh acknowleged.

"Out of the car now," Chandler yelled.

The gun aimed for Josh's head.

"I will shoot," Chandler said before he heard the growling and looked up to the back of the truck. Chandler stepped away and whistled. Josh heard the nails of the German shepherd racing toward the truck and, just as the body appeared in the window of the driver's side door, the Dobermans fell upon it.

Chandler retreated around the front of the truck. He slowly lowered his weapon as he watched the Dobermans bite into the German shepherd.

"Call them off," Amber said. "They'll kill the dog. It's a cop."

"Knock it off, you two," Josh ordered.

The police dog broke free of Nick and Dustin, flipped into the air and bit down on one of their backs. Josh couldn't tell which one of his friends took the attack. The shepherd twisted around and threw the Doberman it held onto. The Doberman hit the ground, rolled and jumped right back at the police dog, which was now sparring with the second Doberman. One bit and the other bit, their teeth flared and they swiped at each other, but the German shepherd struck the Doberman down and took up fight with the returning twin. Josh was out of the truck now. "How long have you had this dog?"

Chandler didn't answer.

"How long?"

"Five years," Chandler replied.

Josh grabbed the edge of Wolf's Breath and snapped the folds forward. It slashed out like the blade of a knife, in front of one of the Dobermans, and cut a gash into the German shepherd's shoulder. Josh heard the crack. The dogs all flinched at the sound. Amber's whip circled around the police dog's neck and pulled it flat. The dog stood up and bit cleanly through the whip. Amber snapped the other whip as she tumbled backward and the German shepherd caught that one in its mouth as well. One of the Dobermans bit down around the snout of the shepherd and the other gripped its throat. Together, they pinned Chandler's dog onto its back. Josh drew a fang. The shepherd suddenly jerked and tried to bark, but the fang's darts had lodged into its chest. The shepherd was still. He bled, but breathed. Josh now stood over the dog with an empty fang. He clenched his fist with the other hand and stabbed the blades through the shepherd's neck. He pressed hard, but the skin wouldn't break. The dog managed to kick. Josh recoiled and shoved his blades down a second time with a power he never knew before.

The blades entered and the German shepherd eventually stopped moving.

"Get back in the truck," Josh ordered Nick and Dustin. The blades and the fang disappeared into Wolf's Breath.

Chandler approached the dead dog and peeled his bronze glasses away from his face. He still held his gun, but it pointed at the ground. He kicked the dog and it flopped onto its other side.

"That's for five years of hell," Chandler cried. He aimed his weapon and emptied its clip at the creature and when all the bullets were gone, he threw his gun at the lifeless body, which looked more human with each passing second.

"Go now. You're in danger," Chandler cried handing back Josh's license and papers. "I don't know who you are, but you know how to stop them. Please stop them all. I'll try to delay them."

As Hickerbilly sped away, Josh watched the police vehicle, in his side mirror, spin around and drive in the opposite direction. A pack of dogs appeared and gave the patrol car chase.

"Did anything happen out there," Speatsh asked upon Josh and Amber's return to the living room. He looked different than he had. He looked worried. Cadence looked not only worried, but angry too. The twins found the places on the red couch they had come to like. Bricktain moved out of their way.

"Something happened," Amber said.

"Yeah," Josh replied.

"What," Speatsh asked.

"They're using humans against us," Josh said. "We killed a police dog."

"It wasn't really a police dog," Amber added.

"Yeah, they do that," Speatsh said. "But that's nothing new."

"Then stop holding punches and get us ready," Josh snapped. "I'm not hiding anymore, and I want my sister back. Before we declare war on the rogue, I need to know where she is. Will you get a move on and train us right, old man?"

Josh returned to the elevator. The doors closed and Amber and Josh made their way back up to the garage in silence. They returned to Hickerbilly and began removing the tarp. Something was different. Suddenly, Josh wasn't just angry anymore. He had ideas and plans running through his head, and one of them didn't include staring at Amber. It didn't contain coming face to face with her at the back of the truck and it didn't include his soul falling into her eyes and gently grabbing her face. It didn't include kissing her either, so he let go and dropped the tailgate instead.

16 – A Change of Plans

He slept. And while he slept, he dreamt. And while he dreamt, he wept tears, which couldn't be felt, not hot, not cold, not sticky, but he wept. He stood before the elevator doors and looked over the pool. He watched Amber swim. She was graceful and gorgeous and as she swam, the water rolled to the side and climbed to the ceiling where it could watch her play with the same awe and wonder as Josh held for her. She climbed out of the pool and the water dripped from her curves as she walked toward Josh and when she approached him, she was wearing the jeans and shirt she wore when they first met, and they were wet and clung to her body. The water stood as tall tidal waves in the pool, and they washed over her back as she approached Josh and she took his hand. They both walked to the elevator, and the elevator opened before them and as they started to enter, Natalie stood inside with those admiring eyes of hers. She looked to Amber and cried.

Josh shot straight up in bed. He looked around the cold room and decided he needed to tell the worm, but that friend had been taken from him too.

* * *

"Are you kidding me," Amber asked. "You cook?"

Josh lowered the black lid over the large pot. He held a wooden spoon brimming with a red sauce sparked with green toward Amber's mouth. "You pick up a few things."

"She sounds pretty amazing," Amber replied before dipping her finger.

"She was the best," Cadence replied. She was wearing a blue button up shirt with a pair of brown Dockers that Amber picked out for her at Sharber's those three days earlier. She wandered up to a barstool and sat down. She winced.

"Arm still hurting," Josh asked.

"It's not so bad," Cadence said.

"I'm really sorry about that," Amber said.

"I know."

"I could have killed you."

"At least the wolves can't bite through the orbits," Josh said as he pulled a lid off a smaller silver pot and stirred through the steam that rose from it.

"Well, until I get more practice, don't come within eighteen feet of me, or I'll cut your arms off with those things," Amber said.

"You," Cadence asked. "What about me? Every time I put on that possessed mask, I try to shoot Josh."

"That mouth piece thing scares me," Josh said. "At least when you draw, I can hear your arms clicking and dodge before the hammers pound."

"Yeah, I don't care what Speatsh says, I'm not wearing that thing anymore," Cadence said. "The mask is bad."

"What is that language you speak anyway," Amber asked.

"What do you mean," Cadence asked. "You can hear me."

"Yeah, we can hear you," Josh said. "But we don't understand you."

"I hear a voice," Cadence said. "It speaks and I speak."

"What is it though," Josh asked. "What is Hackmanyatoya?"

"I don't know what that is," Cadence said laughing.

"You say it," Amber said.

"No I don't," Cadence replied. She looked between Josh and Amber. "The voice screams in my head, it says 'death to the traitor.'"

"Death to the traitor," Josh asked. He held a colander over the sink and shook it. Water dripped.

"Does it," Amber started to ask but stopped when she noticed the way the others looked at her. "Never mind."

"No, what," Cadence asked.

Amber was silent.

"Does it have something to do with what I did," Josh asked. "Is that it?" He emptied the contents of the colander back into a silver pot before throwing the strainer into the sink.

"I'm sorry," Amber replied and before Josh could turn around, she was gone.

Josh thought about going after her, but only thought about it.

"She's right, Josh," Cadence said.

"I hate that I did that, more than anything," Josh said. "And it's hard for me to concentrate when it gets thrown in my face."

"It's hard for me to forget that my friend almost blew my face off, but that's the reality" Cadence replied. "Somewhere in the back of my mind, I hate you for that, and I can't stop it."

Josh didn't know what to say.

"The spirit in that mask sees that part," Cadence said. "I swear it knows things. I don't know how I know, but I feel it. It talks to me and sometimes it controls me. It knows me, probably knows things about me I don't even know. We hold conversations. It knows how I feel about you. That I love you and that you're one of my best friends and that you tried to end my life when I was trying to be yours. Part of me wants you to feel that same pain over and over, but the mask wants it to happen to you for real, I think."

"Things have changed," Josh said. "I want you to know that my priority now is making sure none of my friends get hurt anymore, you more than any of them."

"I feel the same way about you," Cadence said.

"And yet you won't forgive me," Josh said.

"I don't know," Cadence said. "Have you forgiven yourself?"

"How can I?" Josh said. "I had a responsibility to you."

"What about Amber," Cadence asked. "Don't look at me like that. You think I don't know you well enough to know your eyes smile when you're around her."

Josh felt that smile flicker.

Cadence reached across the counter and took Josh's hand. "Natalie would approve."

"Why would she do that," Josh asked.

"Because of the way Amber looks at you," Cadence said.

Josh left Cadence at the counter, left the pasta in the silver pot on the stove, but off the burner. He went down the hall to the bedrooms. He stopped at the second door, and knocked. Amber didn't respond.

"Are you in there," Josh asked. "Amber?"

The door cracked open and Amber tried her hardest not to look at Josh. He wasn't prepared for how she appeared. She'd just been in the kitchen standing right next to him and he still wasn't used to how beautiful she could look. Her hair draped over the front and back of her shoulders. It was wavier than she allowed it to be when it was pulled straight back or hidden beneath her hat. This close up, and without the scents brewing over the stove to interfere, she smelled so different. Her new perfume wasn't flowery at all, but savory. Savory?

"Are you hungry," he asked. "Would you like something to eat?"

She didn't say anything.

"I'm sorry," Josh continued. "I'm mad at me, not you."

"My brothers made me a balancing beam once," she said. "They took two cars and welded a flagpole to it. I was so excited and I practiced for days. I was six years old and what my brother's didn't tell me was that the flagpole was from school. They wanted me to have it so they cut it down and brought it home. My dad was so mad, but he couldn't bear to take away my balance beam. When I got good, really good, my brothers moved the flagpole to the top of two buses. It was a joke at first, but, when I started crossing it, my brothers got scared. Once, I got scared because of how high I was and I slipped. My oldest brother, Bruce, he caught me. They died trying to protect me because they always thought they had to catch me."

"I'm sorry," Josh said.

"I'm the one who said it. It was my mistake. Don't ever think you have to catch me, not even when the mistake is mine," Amber said. "It could screw up your actions. That's how my brothers died. And I don't want to lose you too."

She didn't want to lose him. She did love him, though she didn't say it. Josh knew it, and he wondered if Amber knew how he felt about her. He thought it would be harder, should be harder, to love again. Did he love again? He thought he did. Maybe he didn't know what love was. Maybe no one really knew love until love was lost. Losing Natalie would surely have been a big step in knowing what it was to love and lose. But to have Amber standing in front of him, was that love?

He missed Natalie. She'd know the answer.

"When we start hunting," Amber said. "Don't you look out for me. You fight and you stay as far away from me as you can, and you fight to stay alive. You hear me?"

"Why, do you care so much," Josh asked.

"I don't know," Amber replied. "But I'm better around you."

All of a sudden Josh found himself kissing her, pushing the door open and enveloping her into his arms and he felt her arms tuck him down into her as she kissed him back. When they finally pulled apart, he saw it in her face. She did love him. Someone new, someone alive now stood before him, and he loved her. More so, he felt safe loving her. He missed Natalie—that would never change—just as he would never stop loving her, but he had to face reality now.

Josh had spent too much time thinking about what his life could have been like, if Cracey hadn't disappeared. He thought too much about his could-have-been perfect life with his should-have-been perfect wife, whom his mother would someday have been forced to accept and someday swap recipes with. And together they could be angry about the people their children and grandchildren would someday date. He often wondered the type of person that Cracey would have grown to date and love. He still imagined ways that he and Dustin could embarrass her prom date. He thought it would have been funny to sit on the front porch with Dustin, cleaning a fifty-millimeter cannon for Cracey's first date. That would keep any punk in line.

His life was barely recognizable now. His sister and best friend were dogs. His parents were dead. He shared a bunker with a mountain man and a cat-like wolf. Psychologists locked people up in nice padded rooms with white walls for imagining such things. He thought about how he needed to move on, and maybe that was why he started to see Amber. He didn't have to explain anything to her, she knew exactly the things that haunted him. His mother probably wouldn't have liked her either. She was next to perfect, and grew better each time he was with her. He was as ready as he would ever be to move on with her, and he couldn't do that if he didn't let go of the what-could-have-been.

The bunker started screaming as the alarm cried from every room. Josh caught the red flash of the circle of L.E.Ds on the ceiling in Amber's room. Amber saw it too and looked to him with the same question about what was going on. They ran back to the main room and found Cadence looking just as confused.

The elevator doors sprang open with Speatsh, Nick and Dustin inside. The Dobermans were through the doors before they had finished opening. Speatsh followed but stumbled as something loud crashed against the roof of the carriage. The carriage dropped about six inches and Speatsh was suddenly holding a small silver bugle. The mouthpiece appeared to be normal in size, but the horn itself was about the fourth of a real horn. He blew into it and no sound came out. The Dobermans whimpered and tried to bury their heads beneath their paws as something screeched from above the elevator.

"Brooo!"

"They got in," Speatsh cried.

"How'd they get in," Josh asked.

"Do I look like I know," Speatsh snapped back. "Get your gear on."

Speatsh dropped the bugle and it disappeared beneath his coat of animal pelts. He withdrew a pair of brown leather gloves lined with curved spikes across the knuckles. He pulled them over the gloves he already wore. Another crashing came and the elevator dropped a few more inches.

Chunks of metal fell. Growls and yaps groaned from above Speatsh's head. A large black paw swung down at him and disappeared.

"It's on," Speatsh cried and leapt at the ceiling and pulled a guardian down into the carriage. Nick and Dustin leapt out of the way. Speatsh pinned the black monster against the wall. In return, the guardian pinned Speatsh and Speatsh struck the guardian and pinned it again. More black paws reached into the elevator and pulled Speatsh through the roof.

205

17 – Dark Thoughts

atalie could hear the blood bubble in her lungs. As fast as she could cough it out, it filled her up again. It just wouldn't stop, and it kept blowing over her lips and ran in warm streaks down her face. Some of it had already clotted over her skin. When she noticed she couldn't hear the chirping of crickets in her right ear as well as the left, she wondered if she had gone deaf or if her ear was full of her own blood. She could hear the bubbling in her lungs through both ears, so she decided her ears were indeed filling with blood.

Who knew how long she laid there looking through the thinning branches above her. The dead leaves were hard-soft beneath her and the new moon looked on her through holes in the tree leaves and branches. She could still smell the lingering of breath that the white creature left behind before it suddenly left Natalie alone on the ground for reasons unknown.

Please help me, Natalie prayed as if she were begging the moon for help. She was hurt more than she realized. If Josh were there, he could help her, but he was too far behind her for that. The wolf who stole her from Josh would have suffered Josh's wrath.

The white animal must have dragged her a half a mile before it finally let go of her. She thought it would have killed her right there, but it only stared at her through liquid gold eyes. The white wolf did nothing, and quickly disappeared. Natalie stood just as another black creature appeared. The black wolf seemed as surprised of Natalie's presence as she was of its. Natalie took up a branch, screamed at the beast and somehow found the strength to crush the monster's head, but not before the monster sank its claws into her lungs. The white wolf appeared again and finished off the black creature without ever making its presence known to its victim. Natalie fell and swung her branch at the white wolf. She swung feebly as she tried to stand again, but the white monster stepped back and waited for Natalie's strength to fail even in lifting the branch, but Natalie still had a lot of fight in her. She knew that any creature she killed was one less in the world to hurt Josh or anyone else. Only, Natalie's dying body disagreed and she dropped to her knees.

What do you want, Natalie wondered as she wished she could crawl a space from the white wolf. Something was different about this dog. For the first time that night, she realized the mortal danger she had been in. If she had killed any of the wolves she fought earlier, she wasn't fully aware of it. She fought, that's all she did was fight, and she did so without mercy for the aggressive dogs. When they attacked her, she unleashed every ounce of anger she held. She cared nothing for compassion as she attacked any monster that crossed her path. And she did it all to keep any of them from getting to her friends, Josh most of all. No, that's not true. She did it to exact her vengeance on those she believed had helped murder Josh in the night.

This white wolf was different though. It watched Natalie. Strange, Natalie was more aware of her mortality, yet didn't feel as threatened by this creature. Still, she refused to drop the branch, her only weapon. Natalie finally fell backward and stared up at the sky, let her ears fill with blood and listened to the blood bubble in her lungs. The wolf sauntered toward Natalie and stared into her eyes. Natalie could see only the gold. Its breath even smelled different from the stench that she smelled on the other monsters.

The creature suddenly lunged and snapped its teeth into the bare flesh of Natalie's forearm. Even over Natalie's punctured lungs, the bite stung, and the creature wouldn't let go. Natalie smacked her palm against the wolf's head, but the animal still forced Natalie to the ground. She kept slapping and wished she had her branch.

No, Natalie heard.

Or thought.

Or felt.

Or felt she thought she heard.

She wasn't sure where the voice came from, but felt she shouldn't fight this monster. Her veins filled with fire. Her forearm burned. The heat spread into her fingertips, up past her elbows, to the depths of her biceps and flowed around her shoulders. Her neck itched and burned. And her face burned and her head, and suddenly she couldn't breathe as the fire encircled her chest and her lungs filled with hot. Her stomach felt hot and Natalie saw her. The woman stood in Natalie's mind, or rather the idea of her stood in her mind. If the woman spoke, Natalie couldn't tell, because she couldn't see the words appear nor could she hear them, but she understood that she shouldn't fight what was happening. The woman in her thoughts told her everything would be all right. The fire pierced Natalie's heart and she screamed, but the only sound that escaped her was the popping of blood in her throat as the last tiny bit of air left her body. She felt a tear break from one eye. She felt a second surge of heat erupt from the depths of her heart and it pumped into her system like thick grease. It was so powerful that the first flame she felt in her forearm was nothing compared to this inferno building within her now.

She was becoming aware of something moving about her wrist, not just moving, but wriggling. It was sticky and it flopped around like a dying snake. She thought about the thin tongue of the black creature flopping around her brother's chest. Was this dog healing her? She felt a poke, a sharp poke. The tongue crawled inside her arteries, and slowly crawled into her arm, thick at first and painful. Natalie tried to pull away, but the wolf refused to let go. She felt the tongue twist and puff and push its sharp point, letting it creep farther into Natalie's burning veins. It pressed toward her shoulder, prodding and stabbing its way deeper along the insides of her ducts of blood. But the pain somehow stopped. The wriggling and the puffing up of the snaky prod was still at her wrist, and Natalie could still feel it under her skin using her circulatory system as a guide.

Her heart skipped a beat. It beat twice and stopped beating. Natalie felt something, something tickling inside her chest and something inside her heart. She couldn't breathe and when her heart suddenly jerked at her chest three times, Natalie lurched. Her heart beat, stopped, beat again and stopped. Over and over, it beat, eventually stopped all together. While it stopped, Natalie felt nothing inside her, and she couldn't breathe. Her head felt light and she watched the night grow darker as her head grew hotter.

It beat.

Again, it beat.

Faster and faster her heart pounded inside her chest, the wriggling tongue tapping out and commanding a new rhythm, from within it. Her body jerked and the insides of her chest continued to stomp this new fierce pattern. The cadence picked up pace and it howled like a powerful drum inside Natalie, working harder than ever before to force blood into the smallest capillaries of her limbs. With each burst, fire spread from her chest and into her brain. Her breath slowly returned, stronger and deeper and she felt the snake withdrawing from her vascular organ, up through her shoulder and out of her arm. The white wolf let go and Natalie felt at peace as she sensed that she somehow belonged to this creature.

In an instant, Natalie was alone. She felt exhausted, but invigorated by the churning of fire in her blood. Her arm appeared to be all right as well. The holes and punctures had gone from her skin. What just happened? Why was she on fire? She coughed more red liquid out her mouth, but she felt her heart beating new into her system. She saw the stars and listened to the cracking of fallen leaves. She should have climbed to her feet and run, but she rested and let her body burn inside.

It grew lighter outside. Bright silver stars shone through an emerald sky.

208

The stars seemed brighter and stronger. They started to move above her, but she realized she was the one moving beneath them. The earth slid beneath her and something had hold of her leg. She coughed and listened to her lungs fill with sweet night air. She found the strength to spit rather than cough out the blood. It was sweet. Still, she felt it fill her lungs, but it became easier for her to spit it out, and it became easier to breathe.

Shadows of branches passed between her and the green sky with silver stars and she was overwhelmed with this new sensation inside of her. The heat swelled within her. She thought, and she became aware of how precise and clear her thoughts had become. She recalled the creatures she beat to death and thought she could remember the smallest drop of blood each one lost to her. She saw Josh trying to cling onto her as she was pulled away less than an hour ago. She held that thought of Josh and she felt her blood grow even warmer.

She cried out at whatever dragged her, but didn't recognize her own voice. She couldn't believe she was making the sound she heard now. That sound filled her and when she screamed she felt more at ease and somehow it reminded her that she wasn't dead. She knew if she died now, Josh would be alone and so she held onto an image of Josh, more than an image even. She felt his touch on her skin. She remembered his soft breath on her shoulder. She felt his heart beating through his chest and pounding against her, and she lost herself to listening to his song. She heard his heart over the feverish pounding of her own. Here, she found her strength and knew she had to return to him. No matter what happened to her, she belonged to Josh. She was his and he was hers.

With that thought, she reached out and grasped a large stone which she felt pass beneath her leg. She tore the rock from its nest buried in the earth and sat up. She threw the rock and the large, black creature's head bounced forward and its body keeled to the side. Natalie stood and waited only a moment for the creature to regain its balance and when it did, she slapped it and watched the monster's face tear open. She swiped again and the monster fell to the earth. She watched the wolf begin to turn into its natural human self, never to breathe again. In a few moments, the creature was no more, except for the dark shadow of a naked man face down on the earth as if trying to nurse on nature herself.

That is why I chose you, someone whispered from the back of Natalie's mind. Before Natalie could hear anymore, Jasper had her by her throat and pressed her against a tree. He was no longer in his fearsome slender form, but he was every bit as frightening to her.

"Where is she," he asked.

Natalie couldn't breathe as Jasper's fingers dug into her neck. She felt the urge to spit. The amazing sensation was building inside her to vomit and Jasper was too strong for her. She inhaled.

Don't, the whisper she belonged to commanded. *Never do that.*

Where is she, Jasper asked again, and Natalie recognized the voice was in her head and not in her ears.

Suddenly, nothing was there. Natalie saw nothing, remembered nothing and imagined nothing. Her mind was empty and she knew nothing about herself.

Jasper stood.

"I'll find her," he said and began dragging Natalie by the throat across the ground.

I must not be discovered, her master's voice whispered. *You are strong now. Stay strong.*

Who are you, Natalie wondered.

I am yours and you are mine, the whisper replied. *I emptied your thoughts, and you must remember that sensation for when you must remember nothing on your own. The rogue must never know them.*

The rogue, Natalie asked.

Not now, the whisper in her head, now becoming more of a voice, replied. *Your feelings for the one you love make you strong.*

Can't you save me, Natalie asked.

Yes, replied the voice. *But I won't. Endure for now Natalie Meade.*

Jasper dragged Natalie to a structure and Natalie recognized the back of Jasper's home immediately. He pulled her down a set of wide earthy steps. Natalie could smell the mold growing, but there was something else she could smell and couldn't quite identify. At the bottom of the stairs, Jasper threw open a heavy door. Nothing was dark to Natalie. She saw no difference in the light, the green, bright hue around her lit up everything. She was now in a windowless room built of strange brick. A light fixture dangled from the ceiling in the center of the room. Really, it was a light bulb hanging on a wire. It wasn't turned on. The strange smell was stronger in this room.

She felt something cold clamp around her neck and listened to the cold scratching of a steel pin locking it tight. As soon as Jasper pulled away, Natalie lashed out and her neck jerked back.

"It'll take more than that to break that chain, little one," Jasper said.

The way he peered at Natalie from behind his thin, round glasses drove her mad. He didn't flinch when she lunged at him a second time.

I'll tear you up, she thought as she watched him stand just out of her reach. She was aware of a new strength, which she hadn't felt or noticed moments earlier. She still felt hot, but the heat was a part of her now. She noticed that it no longer merely surged through her veins; it drove her. When her heart beat, it wasn't just pumping new blood into their arteries. Each time she felt the heat pulse from the center of her being, she felt her anger build to match the look of glibness on Jasper's face for capturing her. Chain or no chain, she would get the old man. She leapt again, this time twisting her body and kicking out at Jasper. When she recoiled, Jasper stood back a few paces and his glasses were missing. He was also wiping orange streaks from his face and before she could kick once more, Jasper's hand was back around her throat and he was not amused. Hatred burned behind his eyes and he grinded his teeth.

"You'll never be strong enough," Jasper said. "I am a ruler of hundreds like you that cower at the thought of me. I break each and every one who betrays me, because that's what my master expects. I will get your thoughts if I have to crack your skull open to get at them. I must know what I hope lies in that head of yours."

Old man Jasper's eyes sparkled with gold and stared past Natalie's, and into her brain. She felt him too. The pressure starting at the front of her head, just behind the bridge of her nose, was this old man. He bore deeper and finally her surroundings became dark to her. The pain hit and she cried out as her brain felt like it was trying to burst through her skull. A presence of anger and hatred, such as Natalie had never known, continued to hold darkness over her mind, and she knew it was Jasper. Her own thoughts diminished. If she could recall any strength she may have had inside her body, she might have been able to stand up to the old man, but all she knew was that he was powerful inside her head.

"You can't hide your thoughts from me," Jasper said. "I'm invincible to you." He let go and Natalie fell, but not before he shoved her right hand into a steel band and locked it around her wrist. Soon, thick shackles and chains held her legs, wrists and neck to the wall. "You'll help me find her or you'll rot an eternity in this room." Jasper, holding his face, marched out of the dismal dungeon and closed the door. Natalie sat in green black and realized that she recognized the strange scent hidden in the brick. It was blood. This room smelled of death.

Much depends on you now, Natalie heard from the back of her mind. *Help will come. Josh will need you more than you know.*

18 – A Lesson in Art

Natalie sat in the green darkness listening to the sounds of scratching somewhere beyond the walls. Whatever they were, their numbers were large, he knew that much. They were probably rats and she hated rats, hated their tails, those long, twisting, winding, balancing, scaly, serpent-like tails. She hated the way they crawled around on those little feet with their little claws, scratching and pattering through hidden tunnels. She hated the way they crunched their little teeth together. She especially hated those little blackball eyes that stared at everything and nothing at the same time. She was afraid of the diseases they carried. All she cared about was that they stayed behind the walls. Of course, who knew, maybe they weren't really behind the green walls, and maybe they were afraid of her. Maybe they weren't really rats and maybe she was just hearing things. Regardless, she wanted to get away from the rats, away from the strange smell of her deranged cell, away from the scratching sounds and away from even the thought of the fuzzy, little beasts.

What time had it become? Sometimes streaks of daylight tried to creep under the thick door, which sealed her into the room. It was bright and she had to shield her eyes from its blinding rays, and with just that little bit that made its way into the room, her entire body felt warmer. However, this warmth was peculiar, uncomfortable and hot, not like the hot that had taken over her physical being, but painful and searing hot, like it tried to burn her. She wondered if what she saw was actually daylight. She watched it come and go three times. The strange light stayed for a few hours, went away and returned for a few hours. It must have been cloudy outside. Feet came near the door regularly. One set was light and sometimes accompanied a heavier set. The heavier set would stand at the door and do nothing. The smaller set paced back and Natalie wished she could reach through the crack and swat the unholy prowler away.

These events repeated constantly, and kept her awake. She knew she should sleep. That's what the body did, it worked and it rested, but she couldn't sleep. She thought of her bed, the blankets with their soft cotton sheets and her feather pillow. That soft pillow, flattened to the point of almost needing replacement, would feel delightful this moment. She needed rest, but the feet kept her awake: feet of the rats, the small feet at the door, the heavy feet too. The blinding light constantly creeping and burning every few hours didn't help either. She wanted to be tired. She wanted to rest.

She closed her eyes and hoped dreams would carry her away, but nothing came except for the footsteps and more flashes of light, which she began to recognize even through closed eyelids. As the hours waned on, she grew anxious and angry. Who couldn't sleep after a day of brutal beatings? She kicked the wall behind her at the thundering rat feet hiding within it. No matter what she did, she couldn't sleep, so she just stared into the darkness, the green, bright darkness.

The room became too familiar with Natalie than she would have liked. At first, it appeared to be nothing more than an empty room, not large, but not cramped. The large bulb hung at the end of its long cord from the ceiling. The floor, the walls and the ceiling were large corroded glittering brick that were all slapped together with grayish mortar. A small circular drain dimpled off-center of the floor, but there were no faucets of any kind in the room, so the drain might have been useless. Sticky mildew buried most of the floor and a large puddle of black consumed one of the far corners of the prison cell. The whole place was rank. Natalie stunk too and wanted a bath, but first she needed to sleep.

She closed her eyes to force sleep, but still it didn't come. She started counting bricks. She saw Josh in her head, sometimes tried to imagine him leaning against the wall talking with her, or holding her while she leaned against him and enjoyed his presence. Was Josh safe? She knew about Richard's bunker and had once seen the elevator, which led into it. If a place existed where Josh and everyone could be safe from Jasper and his hordes, it must be the bunker. Still, she wondered if the bunker was impenetrable. She imagined conversing with her friends. She missed them, and she missed her brother. Was he all right? Who would watch out for Nick? She knew he would watch out for Cadence and that everyone would look out for Josh, but who would look after her baby brother? She thought about Nick's brutal beating earlier that week and his resurrection in the canal. The monsters beat him once, they could beat him again, especially with how headstrong he was to be around Cadence. Was Cadence still marked for death for harming a monkey? Would Jasper fix him again or let him die? How was Cadence? Josh. Josh would protect Nick.

And what about her and Nick's parents? What would they think had become of their two children? Someone needed to contact them.

Natalie had a choice; she could give up, or she could try to return to her friends. She tugged at one of the chains holding her to the wall. It was strong, even though it jiggled on the large bolt holding to a weak-appearing brick. She pulled again, but the wiggling bolt held fast. She pulled with all her might, but it wasn't enough. The bolt moved, but it wouldn't break. She went ballistic, screamed at the chain, yanked it and bit it and hit and coiled it around her body and ran from the wall, nearly choking herself in the process. She screamed for Josh and screamed for Nick and her mom and dad, but the bolt didn't care. It held.

She'd smash her hands and pull them through the shackles. That's what she'd do. She placed her unrecognizable hand on the floor and contemplated the best way to snap herself free. If she broke her own hand, could she use it to pull the pins holding her shackles to her.

Stop it, the voice came again from the back of her mind.

Why, Natalie asked still searching for what she thought would be the softest bone in her palm to fracture.

You need to stay if you want to help your friends, The voice replied.

What's going on?

I can't tell you, the voice said. *Your friends are fine for now. Help will come for you soon. I promise.*

When, Natalie asked. Suddenly her mind felt dark and the presence of the being in her head was gone.

A clank at the door tore Natalie's concentration away from her conversation.

There's more to this than Cracey, the voice suddenly returned. *Find his master. You should find him in Jasper's mind, just as Jasper will try to find me in yours.*

What's happening, Natalie asked.

Find him, answered the voice. *Keep Jasper out and find him.*

The presence disappeared once more.

The large steel door opened and Natalie felt alone again. Natalie's thoughts spun and in an instant, she burned from the heat of the sunlight flooding the stairwell and overflowing into the room. Her eyes hurt and fell blind from the overbearing white. She listened to the heavy footsteps enter the room. The door slammed shut and gradually Natalie's vision returned so she could watch Jasper set up an art easel and small folding stool.

"How do you feel," Jasper asked, as he raised a canvas to the tripod and blocked the top half of his frame from Natalie's view.

"Let me go," Natalie screamed.

"You don't want to do that," Jasper said. "You don't have the vocal control you're used to. Just think and I'll hear your thoughts."

But the voice warned her that Jasper would try to get into her head.

"So you've been warned," Jasper said. He opened a silver briefcase and began squirting paints onto a white plastic slate. Jasper chuckled. "Well, fight me if it will help you feel like you're accomplishing something. I'll just paint." He looked up from what he was doing. "You don't mind if I paint do you?"

Natalie shook her head.

"Good," Jasper said from behind his crooked grin. He had a new pair of glasses too. "I find it helps me relax. Do you do anything to help you relax, Natalie?" Again, he looked up. "Do you mind if I call you Natalie? Or would you prefer Nat, Nata or Daddy's little gnat?"

Natalie only thought about it a moment, her dad calling her little gnat from his large recliner. It wasn't even a full thought, just a flicker of a memory. How did Jasper know it?

"I've done this a few times," Jasper replied. "So, how's your brother?"

Leave him out of this, Natalie thought.

"Very well," Jasper said. "I won't talk about your brother. But if you won't tell me where she is, I will need to know how to ask your friends where she is. Maybe one of them knows. Unfortunately they're locked away in a pretty impressive underground building." Jasper disappeared behind the canvas with a large paintbrush and a pallet full of thick globs of greasy paint. He reappeared suddenly. "At least we're having a cordial conversation this time, right? I'll leave Nick out of this. I'm so glad he's still alive after those unfortunate events near the canal."

Natalie's mind went dark and she felt her thoughts wander back to Nick and back to the events of all that had happened the previous night.

"That's the right mixture," Jasper said from behind his canvas.

Her thoughts turned to the way Josh stood guard above Nick's body as the fog had rolled in, but suddenly Nick wasn't there anymore. She was alone with Josh and remembered him holding her in Richard's backyard. It was the day he told her about the bunker. She remembered he was going to show her a keypad near the garage door, but that didn't happen the last time she saw him. That was another time. The thought was wrong, all mixed up. How did the two memories become one? She didn't want to go with these thoughts, but Josh led her towards a keypad and Natalie did want to go with him. She walked with him to the garage door and the keypad. Just then, she remembered the image of Josh fighting to reach for her as her master dragged her away and her thoughts instantly jumped back to following Josh to the keypad and the white wolf wasn't dragging her away anymore.

215

Nat, a more familiar voice cried. Natalie knew it wasn't Jasper's and for a moment believed she remembered Nick.

Natalie did remember Nick, remembered the night in the canal.

"What did Josh show you, Nat," Jasper asked.

She wanted to remember. She remembered some. The image of Josh reaching for her flashed through her mind once more.

"Who keeps doing that," Jasper asked. The canvas jerked.

Again, Natalie found her thoughts trailing back to the keypad with Josh. But again Josh was reaching for her, and the canvas rocked on its easel and a paintbrush fell to the floor. Natalie knew Jasper was, in fact, inside her head. He had managed to creep into her mind, following her thoughts from one to the next to find what he wanted. He used her own thoughts to betray. She had to stop him. She couldn't let him get the code. She was standing with Josh at the keyboard. He reached and pressed the first digit, '1'.

Stay out of my head, old man.

Jasper laughed and she remembered Josh talking to her as before. Once again, Josh was reaching for her and her master's jaws clamped around her leg and dragged her away from him.

Jasper swore.

Josh stood at the keypad and pressed the '1' again, just like he had before. The thought jumped again and Josh reached for her as she slid away from him, reaching for him. But, Josh led her back to the keypad, and she knew she was safe in his presence, but she felt the creature as it began dragging her away and Josh reached for her once again. He started for the keypad again, but Natalie let the white dog drag her away. Again, he tried leading Natalie to the keypad where he pressed the '1' again and Natalie was being dragged away so she couldn't see the rest of the code and Josh was reaching for her.

What are you after, Natalie wondered.

Natalie thought about Nick and remembered the last time she spoke to him in Reggie's truck, but suddenly he was talking to her from behind Josh who was now reaching for her as she was being dragged away from Richard's backyard. Josh led her to the keypad before turning and reaching for her. He reached for her and she reached back and suddenly, nothing dragged her away. She was just reaching as if enchanted to stay in one position, frozen in time. Josh stood still too, reaching for her. They reached for each other and didn't move anywhere. The creature didn't take her away this time, and Josh wasn't leading her to the keypad. She understood now. These weren't confused memories. Jasper wanted the code to the bunker and was manipulating her thoughts and remembrances to get it. Natalie wouldn't let him have it. She

216

wasn't sure if she even knew it, but she wouldn't let her sub-conscious betray her friends. She focused on Josh and that image of them reaching for each other. She wondered how the image stayed in her head. She also wasn't sure that she and Jasper were the only ones controlling her thoughts.

"How long do you think you can focus on that image," Jasper asked.
She thought about replying, but found Josh leading her back to the pad where he stretched to press the '1' and once again Natalie and Josh froze and reached for each other.

"Why don't you focus on a happier moment than that one," Jasper asked. "I'm sure there has to be something better than that."

Are you and Josh gonna get married, Nata," a new presence asked.

Cracey, Natalie asked.

Did you get a ring?

Natalie did get a ring. She remembered opening the velvet box and being so happy at the sight of the square diamond that she cried. She remembered running her fingers over the velvet, almost too afraid to remove the diamond from its religious groove. She remembered Josh's hands on hers and asking her again if she would marry him. She relived her answer, and he asked her to follow him and led her back to the keypad where he punched in the '1' and the '7'.

This was all wrong.

Suddenly Natalie felt herself dragging away and she froze reaching for Josh as he reached for her.

Natalie, Cracey asked. *Do you remember—*

I remember being dragged away, and Natalie screamed still unable to recognize her own voice.

"Trees, shadows, wolves, wedding rings," Jasper said. "Math, Nick, Dustin, Josh, Flowers, Sun, God, dogs, truck, your daddy can help you."

Daddy, Natalie cried to herself. She saw each image as Jasper shouted them out, but it was her image of daddy that she dwelled on.

Daddy always protected her. She slipped in the creek when she was little and Daddy pulled her out. He stopped her from choking on the cookie when she was thirteen during one of their cookie-eating contests. She remembered being happy with him. When she was even younger, she thought she would marry Daddy. She couldn't imagine life without him. But she matured and met Josh, who proposed to her and started leading her to the security pad where he punched in '1' and '7' and tried to punch in another number, and again she reached for Josh like a statue.

"Mommy, diamond, paint, school, babies," Jasper began reciting again.

Babies? Cracey was a baby and Josh tried to save her, but first he had to tell Natalie the code to the keypad and she watched him punch '1' and '7' and he became that statue reaching for her again.

"Kitties, paint, ear, chair, light bulb, flag, Abraham Lincoln," Jasper continued.

Natalie continued to see each image appear in her mind but she fought to hold onto reaching for Josh. Jasper was too crafty in mixing her thoughts into Josh. She needed to fight back.

"Legs, windows, VW bugs"

Natalie hated bugs, she felt them on her when her white wolf master dragged her away, but she wouldn't stop reaching for Josh.

"Tears, birds, music."

Josh, Natalie replied in her own thoughts, recalling her frozen image of him reaching to her.

"Water."

Josh.

"Children playing."

Josh!

"Enough!" The canvas fell and Jasper kicked it at Natalie. A moment later, his hand clamped around her nose and mouth and held her face to the floor.

"You want to know why you can't sleep," Jasper asked. "You don't need to sleep. You don't have the kind of metabolism to sleep. You're one of us now, but you still have human tendencies don't you?"

Jasper stared into Natalie's eyes, his appeared to smile.

She saw gold, gold in his eyes, gold on the ring, the ring Josh gave her.

Josh, she thought.

"No," Jasper yelled. "He's dead."

That's a lie!

Jasper released Natalie and began picking up his art supplies.

"You still think you can talk," Jasper asked. "You think you need sleep. Humans go crazy if they don't get sleep, but you're changing. You've been here three weeks and you don't even realize it. You will come around, but maybe not before you go mad. Then you won't keep me out, and I'll find her. And all because you crave sleep."

Jasper, now holding his tripod and canvas, leaving his paints and brush on the floor, returned to the door where the sunlight peeked through the bottom. "Ever wonder why the sun feels so warm in such a small dose?"

He kicked the door open and light seared into the room. Everything went black and Natalie was warm and grew warmer. Her skin burned and the room filled with a horrid stench. She cried out. She tried to roll, roll away, roll over, but the chains holding her wouldn't allow her to move far enough.

"Do you understand now," Jasper asked. "You are not who you were."

Natalie's joints burned, every inch of her ached. Her brain boiled. Her flesh peeled open with white-green smoke.

"You need blood," Jasper said. "You need meat. The sun will destroy you. You are only learning the power you possess and the day will come that you will hunt your friends because they will become nothing more than familiar images that haunt and torment your sleepless existence. But not before I get inside that head of yours. My master has interest in whoever made you. Your evolution was too quick."

The door slammed shut and Natalie ached. The green light slowly returned. Needles stabbed her all over. Smoke rose from everywhere the sunlight touched. It hurt to breathe. She waited a while before she tried to stand again. Unable to, she stayed on the floor before she realized she wasn't alone.

The monkey sat still, mistaken for a shadow. The beating of his heart and the whisper of his breath made Natalie realize it was more than just a shadow. She wondered what it was. She stayed motionless on the floor, staring at him. Shamus finally stood and crept toward Natalie. He chirped at her, sniffed her, slowly reached out and touched her snout.

His touch felt as a handful of salt on her freshly melted skin and Natalie leapt to her feet. She yelled and bit at Shamus who scooted just out of her reach. He shrieked at her and poked her nose again. Natalie pulled at the chains. She would destroy them. She would kill the monkey. She'd eat him. And for the first time since she'd been locked up, she realized she was hungry. Her belly was getting cold. She smelled Shamus and she wanted him. She bit at him several times, but the monkey simply sat and stared at her. Shamus scampered away and took up one of the tubes of paint, which Jasper had left behind, and returned to Natalie.

He squeezed the tube and paint burped into Natalie's eyes. It stung and she felt Shamus's hands rub it deep into her face. She couldn't see, but bit at Shamus anyway. His little hands and feet scampered around her body tearing out hair and squeezing paint over her scorched body. How did he do it without getting hurt? He leapt off and Natalie could hear him scuttle away. A moment later, he trotted back to her and started squeezing more paint onto her. She screamed as Shamus's featherweight body attacked countless nerves by tearing out handfuls of Natalie's hair and rubbing gobs of paint into the open patches, blisters and melted wounds on Natalie's skin. She screamed as the burning paint seeped into her open flesh. Again, Shamus left her and again he returned and continued squirting paint over her body. She tried to fight back, but he managed to elude her every move, using her, the chains and the wall as his personal jungle gym. Finally, he finished and left her for good, but he remained in the room. Natalie could hear his breath.

She heard the scratching again, the scratching behind the walls, and it grew louder. Shamus howled and shrieked. The scratching sounded different from before. It wasn't just scratching she heard, it was clicking and ratcheting. It grew louder still. Shamus continued to howl. She heard the sounds as if they weren't behind the walls anymore. She felt movement. Something crawled on her foot, and her foot hurt. Another something crawled on the same foot and she screamed at the sensation of the tiny legs scaling her flesh and spelunking through her hair. More came, clicking and shrieking and biting, eating the mixture of paint, thick hair and flesh. Two or three fought over the same spot on her body to dine. In fact dozens, hundreds, thousands even, now fought and fed. She felt as if they had covered every inch of her, crawling into her ears and screaming at her eardrums. She stood, screamed, threw her body back and forth. Some flew off and some held on. Natalie smashed some but most were eating her. She slammed her body against the brick wall and cried.

And Natalie remembered hearing these types of clicks in her apartment. The sounds she once thought belonged to rats, she realized belonged to cockroaches. They came out at night at her apartment and disappeared when the lights turned on. The building manager relented to help, but only after Natalie had bought every brand of roach trap she could find. Finally, he got an exterminator to get the clicking cockroaches under control. She had almost forgotten the sound, but now she recognized it. Now, the roaches climbed on her. She slammed her body against the wall again and felt one of the bolts cut her side open. Immediately, the wound filled with little feet and numerous tiny mouths. They prodded at her nose and lips. She bit at some, swallowed some, but they kept climbing her, biting her, chewing the paint and eating her. She shook her head often to throw bugs away that took too close an interest in her eyes.

Shamus's shadow opened another tube of paint.

19 – Shamus

She was tired of fighting, tired of cockroaches and tired of Shamus. He came back every time the sun appeared and threw rotten food, paint and other crud at her, and the cockroaches dined every couple of hours. And she'd heal and the process started all over again.

She laid on the floor and watched the door. Strength failed her, sapped away by the tortures, but she couldn't sleep, just felt herself die without dying. When she thought she couldn't die anymore, Shamus returned with a stick or a cattle prod or a motorcycle battery, just to show her how wrong she was. She hated him.

The white sun's glimmer disappeared from the door. And this time, as it disappeared, something different happened. Everything tensed. Her body arched and her teeth clinched and every muscle and tendon within her tightened. Every bone in her body cracked, shifted, and bent almost all at the same time. The flesh grew cold and hurt, but tickled. Muscle spasms collided into each other and her flesh bubbled as tendons and ligaments twisted into old familiar human positions. If she could have screamed, she would have, except her jaw and tongue were too busy, shrinking and popping into a different place to allow her the luxury of human voice. As suddenly as it started, it stopped and Natalie felt the cold mildew brick against her flesh. She opened her eyes, but it did no good. The room was pitch black.

All the pain had disappeared, not just the pain she lived, but all the injury Shamus had inflicted upon her. She stood up and she felt one of the shackles slide from one of her hands. She removed the clamp from her other hand. Her head was small enough to fit through the clamp around her neck now too. She tried to remove the ones from her ankles, but they still managed to hold. She screamed, and this time recognized her voice. She fell against the wall defeated.

"Hello," the voice called again. "Can you hear me?"

"Yes," Natalie cried, relieved this voice was real. "I hear you."

Several voices cheered.

"Can you get your shackles off," the man asked.

"Not all of them," Natalie yelled back. "Can you help me?"

"No," the man replied. "The brick can't be broken."

"It's so dark in here," Natalie said. "And there's roaches."

The voices began shouting behind the wall, but Natalie couldn't decipher their meaning. The clutter of voices fell silent.

"Cover your eyes."

"My eyes," Natalie asked.

A blinding geyser of flames burst from the drain in the center of the room, as if pouring liquid fire straight upon the ceiling of the room.

"They hate that," the man yelled.

The door opened. A dim light fell down the stairs and died a few feet into the room. It was night outside. Shamus's shadow entered and closed the door behind it. He disappeared into the black of the room.

Tink! Tink! Tink!

Natalie heard the tapping and wondered what created the sound. The noise continued against the brick floor. Natalie remained silent, listening only to her breath and the light tapping before her.

TINK!

A small white gleam sparked a few feet in front of her. Another spark flew and another, each accompanying the same tapping sound. Natalie recognized what she believed was the sound of a hammer striking the brick floor. The hammer struck repeatedly and more sparks flew with each smack. The sparks drew closer to Natalie, growing brighter and larger until finally she could make out the small silhouette of Shamus appearing within each strobe. Jasper's monkey approached, creating flickers until Natalie could sense his breath on her feet. She could see nothing and dared not look away. The hammer struck again and this time didn't spark and didn't make a deep cold tapping sound either.

Instead, Natalie's small right toe cracked loud, but not nearly as loud as her own screaming and before she could finish releasing her scream, her second smallest toe busted under another strike of Shamus's hammer. She dropped to the ground, continuing her screaming. Her body coiled as best as it could, under the confines of the chains around her ankles, and tried to hide her feet from Shamus. She felt small fingers touch her foot. She kicked them away and they smacked the broken toes. While Natalie cried again, the small hands pressed her foot flat against the floor and her middle toe suddenly shattered.

"What's happening," The man's voice cried through the wall.

Natalie couldn't answer through her screaming.

"It's that monkey," the man's voice called. "Shamus, you foul creature. Leave her alone."

The hammer smacked at the wall and suddenly smashed Natalie's second largest right toe.

222

20 ~ Painted Horses

Jasper walked into the room and Shamus perched on his back leering down on Natalie. The door crashed against the wall and Natalie didn't even bother to indulge Jasper with a reaction. She just laid on the floor, locked in her chains and closed her eyes to the blinding light coming down the stairs. She was tired of not sleeping and tired of changing forms. As the monster, Jasper punished her every time he tried to get into her head. When he couldn't accomplish what he wanted, Shamus found ways to make her miserable. The cockroaches fed on her flesh more. Eggs grew in her skin and their babies became more and more comfortable with chewing away at her, even when Shamus wasn't throwing goo on her. When she turned human, her soft skin pushed the eggs out and she stomped all she could. When she was human, the bugs feared her, but Shamus always came with his hammer, and broke her in many places. Those places all healed when she changed back into her monstrous self. All she had to look forward to were the few minutes of conversation she held with Cracey and the other voices on the other side of the wall before Shamus inevitably appeared. When she was a beast, she was in agony and when she was a human, she wanted to die. Jasper's smile upon entering told her he knew how she felt.

"Moon's up tonight," Jasper said. He started setting up his canvas. "That'll make nine times won't it? Used to it yet? Sometimes I still don't think I am."

Natalie knew how many times she had changed. She counted and held onto the memory of each time that she suffered the severe metamorphosis. She feared it. She hated it. Compared to lying on the floor, eating roaches and the dead rodents thrown her way from time to time, the actual change was a nightmare. She craved food now, meat and blood, the fresher and the warmer the better.

She thought often about Josh. It helped her fight, and Jasper had given up trying to use the memory of him to enter her mind. The image of Josh helped her remember there was a greater purpose in all her torment, even though she still didn't understand what that purpose was. But, what a meal Josh would make right now.

"Nine months and nine full moons," Jasper said. "One more and you could win a free sandwich and a cup of coffee." He set his stool behind the canvas and began to work as usual.

At once, she felt him in her mind, dark, just as he had always been. He learned to steer the ravines of her mind as if he had forged their trails himself. Sometimes he bent her thoughts to his will. Sometimes she beat him back. Occasionally, he pried out thoughts, which Natalie thought she had forgotten, tried to use them against her and even created great hallucinations. He succeeded at getting three digits to the code, but there was one left. When she fought back, he got angry and he'd let Shamus prove it to her. Jasper's mind was dark. She felt his darkness and tried to follow it. Once, she thought that she had entered his mind. If for a moment only, she saw images, which couldn't have belonged to her, but Jasper screamed and she felt herself thrown from that dark place. And Shamus would proceed to throw cockroach food at her. Last time, he used old eggs. She expected something similar to happen today. Jasper was a cruel old man who refused to give up.

"I think you might be tired enough for a different approach," Jasper said.

Jasper's darkness webbed through her mind at once, plucking at every memory and emotion tied to it. He was almost everywhere. He never tried this tactic before. Natalie feared that this strategy might just work. Especially since, she was tired, still couldn't sleep and he was so strong. She soon found herself staring at Josh's fingers poking at an alarm pad. The same three digits appeared and almost a fourth when she decided she was indeed too tired of this game with Jasper.

No more, Natalie thought.

"We don't have to do this," Jasper said. "Give me what I want, and I'll end your suffering."

I'm not giving you anything, Natalie replied.

"You will," Jasper said. "I thought I had what I wanted once before. He lasted five years in those very chains."

A little more than four years and you'll owe me a sandwich.

"You're trying to change the subject," Jasper said. He laughed a little. "Let's just get this over with."

I'm not in the mood.

"You're not in the mood?" Jasper leapt from his chair and was quickly on his knees in front of Natalie. "You've wasted enough of my time already. I know you have a link to the information my master wants. I don't have to be patient with you. I'll turn your mind to mush and spend a year picking through the images to make sense of them if I have to. And then I'll find your friends and hopefully her."

Now he had Natalie's attention. Her eyes met his.

Turn my mind to mush?

224

"It's easy," Jasper said. "But it's easier if you just give it to me rather than force me to put together the world's worst jigsaw puzzle."

Natalie stood. She felt her lips quiver and she clenched her teeth together.

Not today, old man, she thought and felt her head burst with pain. She continued to stand.

"Mush it is," Jasper snapped.

Natalie fell to the floor. He was in her mind. Who was she? Was she Jasper? She must have been because she couldn't remember being—what was her name? Her mind was his and it was like ice. She saw Jasper's tubes of paints laying on the floor. What was it people called them? And what were they used for? She couldn't remember anything about the items, but she should have been able to. She remembered what they looked like and she remembered their colors. Maybe, if she looked inside the tubes she might remember what they accomplished. She imagined the tubes suddenly squeezing their colors into the air over the back of Jasper, and envisioned the stains splashing down in front of him, creating a wall between her and him. They swirled into each other, the red and orange, the yellow and green, blue and purple. Lavender dots and turquoise stars blotted areas and she remembered the names of her hues.

She remembered painting a tree in first grade. She started painting it again now in her mind with all those vibrant shadess erupting from the tubes of paint on the floor. Brown sprouted and exploded with a green woolly and leafy afro. Yellow birds flew to the head. An orange rope fell from a branch, and a black tire appeared and she watched her stick figure self swing back and forth. Her father made her the swing, she remembered that, and she imagined painting her father pushing her on it.

Jasper's face appeared in the colors and he tried to blow the tree down but the tire swung against the wind and smacked him away. Her mind was light, she felt happy and she knew she was stronger than Jasper. Jasper was strong, but no one was stronger than her dad and the tire swing. The bright colors pushed him out of her mind and it was hers once more.

"Shamus," Jasper cried.

The colors suddenly crashed to the brick floor of the small room and Natalie saw Jasper holding his head and pointing at her. Shamus screeched at her and ran for her with Jasper's paintbrush clenched in his tiny fingers. The paintbrush stabbed into Natalie's shoulder, and she gave the agony that came with it a voice. He rammed the point of the brush into her again and would have gloated but this time Natalie was faster. She bit down on him, bit through his collarbone and popped his chest open in her teeth. He made no sound, and Natalie cherished his surprise as she felt the last of his air rush over her gums. His sticky savor filled her mouth and down her tongue. She drank him, devoured him and gave no heed to Jasper's deafening screams for her to stop.

The old man backed Natalie into the wall, kicking and hitting her. He pulled at her ears and tore out handfuls of hair and quills without getting pricked. He screamed and cursed at her. He beat her with his cane and suddenly, he was in her mind again.

I'm tired of this game, Natalie thought and imagined Jasper's presence as a pool of black paint. She dived into the pool and the pool bled red, yellow and blue as she entered. She swam towards the center of it. *Where are you?*

He wasn't there, but she saw the black, she felt its coldness and she swam with it. She grew colder and darker and the farther she swam with the current, the fewer colors appeared around her and she saw an image. A girl with long blond hair, someone she didn't know appeared. She saw other faces too, some smiling, some screaming and some bleeding. Another face appeared, it felt warmer than the others did. Natalie watched it for a moment.

I'll kill you, Jasper's voice cried from the depths of the black.

Then get on with it, Natalie replied. She imagined herself swimming into the thought of the warm face, a woman with red hair and dark eyes.

"Father, what's wrong," The woman asked. She stared as if she was speaking to Natalie. Who was this woman? A man appeared behind her. He was handsome, dressed in robes and Natalie feared him for some reason. He pushed the woman and yelled as he threw objects around a small room. A bright flash appeared and Natalie leapt into it where she watched as the man now knelt over the woman and beating her—no, not beating—feeding off her. The red-headed woman laid on the floor at Natalie's feet. Natalie felt the fear of the moment and felt the emotion as the man dressed in robes turned his attacks on her. Something about the emotion she suddenly felt made her want to stay with this image. There was something she needed to protect. A child, a child not much older than Cracey, a child with the same red hair as the woman, and Natalie protected the child from the man as he beat at Natalie's back. Natalie was overcome with the feeling that this child was worth dying for.

"Give me the child," a man asked.

Natalie didn't want to.

"Give me the child," the man yelled.

Suddenly, Natalie was running through night, a small hand held hers. Trees shielded her from torches burning in the distance and she heard something

226

behind her. She was scared and she watched the dark woods spin around. She found herself lying on her back. A child screamed, and the large white wolf with gold eyes was on top of Natalie. It bit her and she relived the sensation of the dog's tongue forcing heat into her veins.

You're not mine, Natalie heard and the white face fled. *Jasper, retain control.*

Natalie swam after the white beast and it began to change before her eyes. This image felt different from Jasper's usual presence. Natalie chased it. Was this what was required of her. Is this the one she was supposed to touch? She leapt over and through obstacles familiar and surreal to follow him.

Do not hunt me, the voice said.

No part of the voice was pleasant. It was angry, hateful. Natalie swam at it, leapt at it, felt his soft hair in her hand and suddenly felt herself fall on the floor. Her head hurt and all was green again. Jasper's body stretched before her and sweat ran down his brow. He rose to his feet.

"If it's any consolation," Jasper said. "You did good."

He stepped toward her and stopped. He grabbed his side.

"Time flies," he said. He broke into a terrible scream.

The change had begun again. Natalie felt her own body spasm and lock. She realized the sun had gone. She began the pains of turning human and knew Jasper was becoming his dangerous wolf self. Now, she would die. She wouldn't put up much of a fight in her human form. After the change, he would move with god-like reflexes against Natalie's slow, human body, which was chained to the wall. But she couldn't think about any of that as a bed of nails slammed into her body and tore at every place her ligament glued itself to any bone. She felt her bones shift all at once.

She didn't know how she sensed him, but she knew he was there. He touched her shoulder, not Jasper, but someone else, someone who wanted Natalie to know he was there. His hand was gone again and the pain rampaging through Natalie's body was disappearing. Something struck one of the chains and Natalie felt it reverberate into her ankle. The reverb sensation rose up her other foot and she felt his hand grab hers and she felt the clamps fall from her wrists and from her head. She was free of the chains.

In the next moment, she found herself flung over the stranger's shoulder, and the last effort of pain from the change left in her body dissolved. It was light around her again, light from the moon and night sky, not the horrid green she had grown used to seeing. She recognized the stairwell Jasper used to bring her to the dungeon. She welcomed the sight of it as well as the stars overhead as the stranger carried her out of the room. How she missed them

227

these nine months. The dark man pulled the door shut and Jasper screeched from the other side, scraping and clawing.

"Take her," the stranger said.

Her rescuer lowered her to the ground. A set of hands quickly unfolded a robe and draped it over her. After the torture, after all the anger and torment, she thought she was finished. Yet, she wasn't finished. And it hit her; she remembered the power Jasper had. Nothing could fight the monster Jasper. He'd find her no matter where she went.

Jasper clawed and roared from the bottom of the stairwell. The stranger stood between the door and Natalie.

"My dear," said the stranger. "Please run."

When Jasper cried again, Natalie was running across the open field behind Jasper's house.

"This way,"said a man wrapped in robes similar to those draped around Natalie. His was the voice from the other side of the wall. He quickly led her away with three other men.

She ran through the yard. Other people stood around, all wearing robes. Some watched while others rushed to help her in the darkness. One small one ran to her.

"Natalie," She said. "Come on, the horses are over here."

"Horses," Natalie asked and realized who was speaking to her.

"He brought them."

At first, she didn't see the horses hidden in the shadows. Both had black in them, but one had white splatter marks, while the other had brown. Neither wore a saddle, but both bit into a bridle. Natalie's escorts stopped near the horses.

One man shoved a pair of sweatpants and a T-shirt into Natalie's hands and she quickly put them on under her robes.

"It will make the ride more comfortable," the man said.

"Time for everyone to get underground," called the voice of the one who freed Natalie and she watched his shadow emerge from the stairwell.

"Good luck," said the man whose voice Natalie knew from speaking through the wall of her dungeon. One by one, the people in robes quickly disappeared into the ground.

Jasper screamed.

"Get on a horse, milady," the stranger called as he approached in the distance.

Natalie turned to the brown and black horse. Thanks to Cadence, she knew how to ride, but she never mounted bareback before. She reached for the mane, but the horse dropped to its knees before she could pull herself up. Natalie straddled the horse and nearly jumped when a bundle appeared in her arms.

"Please take the child," one of the robed men said. "Maybe you're strong enough to help her."

Natalie stared at the bald child she once knew with long blond hair. She felt her own head, realizing how smooth it had become.

"I have a hat, when I don't like my head," Cracey said, pulling a small black knitted beanie from a pocket on her robes. "This lady made it for me, but it itches. Would you like to wear it?"

Natalie hugged Cracey.

"She stays," the stranger announced. He stood alone now in the dark. "She has to get underground."

"Try to take her," Natalie replied.

The group of robed men had disappeared from around the horses and into the earth.

The stranger kicked at the ground and the heavy door swung shut. He flipped over the other cellar door. "Lock it up."

Another sound echoed and Natalie's horse climbed to its feet. Natalie grabbed the reins and watched the familiar wiry outline of Jasper leap from the stairwell. He ran for Natalie and Cracey's horse.

Natalie clenched her fists. She didn't know how she'd fight, but she wasn't going to let Jasper take her or Cracey back without making him regret it. Jasper leapt through the air, flying over the stranger, from the house. He landed right in front of Natalie's horse. Jasper's claws stretched and the brown and black horse Natalie sat on reared back. Even though she was surprised, somehow Natalie managed to hold the reins and keep her and Cracey upon the horse. They slipped a little down the horse's back, but neither fell. The brown painted horse smashed its hoof against Jasper's face. The black and white horse appeared and pounded both hooves against the back of Jasper's head. Jasper jerked about as both horses continued to snap him with their front hooves.

Jasper bayed at the bizarre pugilists. The white painted horse toppled just as Jasper snatched the hoof from beneath it, but Jasper suddenly grabbed his wrist and fell away. Natalie and Cracey's horse backed away. The white and black horse rejoined them. The hero stranger stood straight and tall in black pants and a red jacket with tails falling past the back of his knees. Gold trim glistened off his shoulders. He had long hair, neat and down the middle of his back to just above his waist. It appeared black in the night, but Natalie thought it might be white. He held something, but Natalie couldn't see what it was. He stabbed it toward Jasper and Jasper fell back grabbing his shoulder.

Jasper growled and leapt upwards. He came down on the stranger, pinning him to the ground, but rolled off grabbing his stomach. He lunged for the stranger and the stranger snapped his head and reeled his shoulders. His hair flared out like a white dandelion, and Natalie thought she saw several shiny objects flicker as the stranger twisted his hair into the monster Jasper. Jasper backhanded the stranger. The stranger fell onto his back, but somersaulted to his feet and leapt onto the back of the white and black painted horse as if it were a prepared act. The stranger grabbed the reins and appeared to be pointing a finger at Jasper. Natalie saw he held a small sword; its outline glimmered, but held no center. The stranger's hair was definitely white and had fallen neatly against his back as if it hadn't been disturbed. His face was narrow with a sharp light brow, sunken shadowed cheeks, and a barely noticeable chin. He was middle-aged.

"Go, Petruchio," The stranger ordered.

Natalie's horse jerked around and darted into the orchard.

Jasper roared and ran after Natalie and Cracey.

"You'll not have them," the stranger yelled and was gone as the brown and black paint escaped with Natalie and Cracey into the orchard. Natalie looked behind her to see if Jasper followed. She saw only darkness.

Jasper yelled, a horse whinnied and Natalie and Cracey were free.

21 – The Silver Bullet

Speatsh's cries bellowed throughout the apartment. A monster screamed from above the elevator and Speatsh's voice yelled back. The guardian in the elevator seemed unable to take its eyes off whatever was going on above its head. It leapt up and half the body disappeared, but suddenly fell back down against the elevator carriage floor.

"Will somebody take care of that thing," Speatsh yelled. "I have enough to deal with up— Ow! Don't do that." The sounds of scuffles and wild dog yells accompanied Speatsh's blasts of obscenities.

It was Josh who finally managed to get in the deadly blow on the intruder. The monster had put up a mighty fight with everyone, while Speatsh fought in the shaft to the garage. It was as the monster was charging Cadence that he finished loading a fang and discharged all three bolts into the monster's head. The monster fell and Josh and the others suited themselves with their weaponry as quickly as possible and rushed to help Speatsh.

Once inside the elevator, Josh could see half the roof was missing. Speatsh straddled the hole, moving with an awkward agility. He moved carefully and quickly. At first, it appeared Speatsh was struggling with a guardian, but it became clear that he was struggling with three. He punched his clawed glove at one, dodged a blow, kicked, leapt against the wall and rebounded with another kick and slash, and still managed to keep from falling through the ceiling.

"Speatsh," Amber called up the shaft. "Clear it."

"What's wrong with your brain, woman?" Speatsh snapped back.

Amber grit her teeth and threw an orbit again, taking off a black paw swiping at Speatsh.

"Clear out of the way," she screamed.

Speatsh kicked, swung and leapt down through the hole in the ceiling. One of the guardians tried to follow, but Cadence, who now stood in the elevator, fired several harmless shots at it. Perhaps if she had been given the glycerin, diamond tip bullets, she might have had something that could have done damage. However, she was still training and Speatsh hadn't found the need for her to waste the diamonds yet. She fired at any animal body part that appeared.

"You trying to kill me," Speatsh asked.

Josh punched a button on the elevator control panel. The carriage jerked upwards.

"What are you doing," Speatsh asked before blowing his bugle at more dogs appearing on the elevator roof.

"Taking this fight outside," Josh replied cupping his ears under more explosions of the nitroglycerin bullets.

"Could you have at least remembered Nick and Dustin?" Speatsh said. "They could have helped."

The elevator stopped.

Cadence withdrew the mask from a small pouch on her hip. She glanced at Josh, knowing he was every bit afraid as she was of her putting on the dangerous mask. The guns were all loaded this time.

"Good luck," She said, but still didn't draw the mask over her face. Instead, she stared straight into the elevator doors.

The doors lurched open and two guardians instantly fell from Speatsh's deadly, quick attacks. Cadence started out of the elevator, but Josh pulled her back.

"That's not your job, remember," Josh said.

He ran out of the elevator ,spun around and swiped his blades for the first dog that got in his way, which was a black great Dane, but Speatsh was the one who ended the dog's life. Another dog was tending its own wounds and Speatsh made sure it didn't have to worry about finishing the job.

Josh looked for anything else to attack. The next thing Josh noticed was the open steel door leading into the side of the garage. Speatsh stood in its frame and struggled with another creature, the blackness of the backyard loomed beyond. Josh wondered how the door had fallen into its groove below ground and allowed the breach of the bunker.

"The outside keypad's been destroyed," Speatsh announced. "We have to change the code."

Josh scrambled to an interior keypad next to the door and slid the faceplate down. Before he could press in any numbers, Speatsh fell and rolled with a guardian over the floor, his brace clanking with each roll.

Another guardian appeared in the doorway and Josh found himself fighting to keep the creature from entering the garage too. The monster moved fast, dodged every blow Josh threw at it. Although he didn't realize it, Josh managed to dodge every swipe the guardian threw at him also. A second smaller dog began fighting Josh too, fighting around the guardian's legs, swiping through any opening it could get through. Josh stabbed the mutt. The dual blades on Josh's right arm speared into the mutt's shoulder. They dug in easier on this monster than they did on the police dog, and he withdrew quickly in hopes he wouldn't kill the animal. Speatsh was correct about the area being softer. Josh twisted the blades through the mutt's muscles and cracked through a bone.

"Stop pulling punches and kill that thing," Speatsh yelled.

Josh kept swinging at the guardian, but kept missing. A type of hunting dog took the place of the mutt and a third animal joined in the onslaught and tried to get a nip in at Josh every so often, but Josh found he was fast enough to dodge the bites.

"Josh, move," Amber called from behind him, but Josh wouldn't move. In fact, he couldn't move.

"Kill those things," Speatsh yelled.

"Josh, move," Amber called again.

Josh felt a burst of wind kick past his ear and one of the dogs keeled backwards and fled into the dark night. Josh continued sparring with two dogs and another one managed to find its way into the battle.

"Cadence, kill them," Speatsh cried. "Put on the mask."

Josh heard the system ratchet behind him.

"Move," Cadence ordered.

"No, don't shoot," Josh yelled back as he barely dodged yet another bite to his leg. He slashed his blades around wildly and narrowly escaped the guardian's attempt to sink its teeth into Josh. He felt the silver orbit spin past his head and watched another dog fall, this time it didn't get up and again a third dog joined in the fight against Josh in the doorway to the garage.

"Stop it," Josh yelled, and he swung one of his sets of blades into the interior control panel. He launched himself into the onslaught of dogs and avoided the steel door as it shot up from the ground and sealed the others inside the garage.

The yard was dark, but Josh could make out shadows and reflective hateful eyes of dogs and guardians. He continued to dodge the blows of the three dogs, but others soon surrounded him. He threw his blades in every direction and snapped his cloak to fend off a few attacks. He even felt himself reach for the fangs a time or two before reconsidering. He remembered his first day of training and spun on his heels, pulling his arms into his chest. He watched the collar fly up over his head and the animals disappeared from his view. He heard a few cries and as Wolf's Breath settled down, he thrust a set of swords into the throat of the first creature he saw, a large and extremely surprised guardian.

Josh took a stance and looked over three wounded animals and several others standing out of range of Wolf's Breath. Dogs leapt at Josh, but a guardian got to him first. This guardian bit into Josh's shoulder and shook him like a rag doll.

The guardian screamed and its own blood oozed over its jowls.

"Hurts, don't it?" Josh found himself laughing as he kept fighting.

And suddenly Speatsh was at his side helping him fight while dragging him away. He blew his bugle.

"Did you forget what you were supposed to do?" Speatsh complained. He dragged Josh around the corner of the garage where Hickerbilly's open passenger door awaited him. "Get in."

Amber sat behind the wheel of Hickerbilly and Cadence stood in the bed with a .45 revolver in each hand. Josh he began to climb into the cab while Speatsh fended of more beasts.

"Hackmanyatoya," Cadence yelled. The revolver fired and Josh fell against the door and flopped to the ground.

"Josh," Amber cried.

"Are you stupid?" Speatsh yelled, tearing Wolf's Breath from around Josh's shoulders. "You shot him." Speatsh stuffed Josh onto the seat and threw Wolf's Breath on the floor. He slammed the door, kicked a dog, leapt into the bed with Cadence and punched a guardian off the cab roof.

"Go now."

"What were you thinking," Amber asked.

"I was keeping everyone safe," Josh replied trying to adjust his weight in the seat without aggravating the pain that was seeping from his right shoulder where the guardian bit him and his left shoulder where Cadence shot him.

"Well, don't do that."

Speatsh banged on the roof of the truck. "I said go."

The truck squealed. One of the twins leapt through the back window and immediately began looking over Josh's wounds.

As the truck pulled away, a collie bounded onto the hood and over the cab. Speatsh grabbed him and threw him behind the truck where Hickerbilly ran him over instantly. Explosions rang out from the six-shooters, dogs cried and the truck spun out at the end of the driveway, nearly throwing Cadence over the side.

"What are you doing?" Speatsh cried.

"Stuff it, grandpa," Amber yelled and drove the truck right into a ditch.

Speatsh banged the roof of the truck. "The road's over there. We don't drive trucks in ditches."

Josh felt the Doberman's tongue crawl into his wound and feeling began to

234

return to one of his shoulders. His whole head throbbed as the truck suddenly stopped and Josh slammed into the dashboard. Cadence toppled over the roof, and rolled from the hood. Speatsh chased after her. Josh reached for the door to follow him and felt the pain that remained in his arm from the gunshot. He stumbled out of the cab, drew a fang and shot a guardian dead right there.

"Get back," Speatsh ordered. Josh ignored him and watched all the dogs emerge into the view of the headlights. Speatsh carried Cadence back over the cab of the truck. Josh had difficulty climbing back into the cab, but the twin who had been working on cleaning his gunshot wound helped pull him.

"Plow 'em over," Speatsh yelled and hammered the roof.

"That's nice and all," Amber screamed. "But we're in a ditch."

"Then get us out, you doobie," Speatsh yelled back.

Amber moved the gearshift and stepped on the gas. Just what was a doobie? The truck rocked back. She slammed the gearshift forward and the truck rolled forward. She swore that Speatsh just had to make words up. The truck bobbled back and forth and Jasper's dogs crept in closer and closer. The guardians watched. Josh wanted to reload one of the fangs, but he couldn't move his right arm and he actually felt a little dizzy. On top of that, he was feeling a little flu-ish.

The truck bounced out of the ditch and began driving again.

The passenger's window shattered and glass rained into the back seat. Josh took aim on a dog crawling through the opening with an empty fang and suddenly the dog tore away as a flash of gold carrying Reggie and Bricktain sped past it.

"Dad," Amber asked.

The hood banged again. "Go faster, you daffy dame."

"I know what I'm doing, doobie." Amber screamed.

"You don't even know what that means," Speatsh yelled back.

A small golden cart spun around in front of the truck and sped back toward it. A grey wolf lunged for the cart. A Doberman's head appeared from within the chariot barking at the oncoming wolf just as Reggie swung something at the attacker. A long silvery-white blade leapt from whatever Reggie swung, but disappeared when the weapon stopped moving. The wolf fell. Bricktain blasted another dog with a shotgun.

A third being stood at the front of the chariot, clenching reigns and yelling at six spectral horses. The tops of the grey horses' heads pulled the reigns tight. If they had legs, they might have been digging them into the ground. The chariot darted past the other side of the truck and began to circle around again. Reggie clenched what appeared to be the silver hilt, which should have belonged to a long sword.

The truck sped right at two guardians, which evaded the vehicle. Josh watched the ghostly horse heads run up alongside his window, followed by the chariot. The driver yelled at the horses and cracked an invisible whip. The other twin leapt from the carriage and through the window upon seeing Josh bleeding.

"Are you all right," Reggie asked.

"Way to screw things up buddy," Bricktain yelled.

"Drive now," The spectral driver cried. "Yell later." The golden chariot fell behind the truck and Reggie continued to swing and force a long silver blade from the sword hilt he held.

"Do you know where Turpin's is," Speatsh asked, leaning through the rear window.

"Who's Turpin," Amber asked back.

"What do you mean, who's Turpin," Speatsh asked.

"What do you mean, what do I mean," Amber snapped back. "Obviously, I don't know where they live."

"It used to be a dance club."

"The only dance club I know of is Bam Bam's," Amber said.

"Who names a club Bam Bam's," Speatsh asked as he withdrew from the window and slamming it shut. He jerked it back open. "Go there."

*   *   *

When the truck finally stopped and the pursuing creatures had given up the chase, Speatsh leapt out and Josh joined him. He was still sore, still a little sick, but his limbs all worked again and the wounds were closed. He cautiously gazed to Cadence, who no longer wore her mask.

The parking lot was bright from neon and about a dozen street lamps. The club sang and rumbled from beneath two flashing bulls' heads blowing smoke from their exaggerated wide nostrils.

Speatsh slammed Josh against the side of the truck. "How stupid are you?"

"I'm bit," Josh said.

"We'll give you a rabies shot," Speatsh said. "You have nothing to worry about. See, no holes in Wolf's Breath, it's like Kevlar to wolf teeth. What were you thinking?"

"There's a security measure on the pad that locks the whole place down if someone tries to break into it," Josh replied.

"So what."

"So, how did they breach the outside panel and get into the garage," Josh asked. "It should have locked down. Someone knew the code."

"You could have been killed."

"I thought you'd all be safer."

Speatsh glared.

"Well, once again you've fed us to the wolves, you moron," Bricktain said hopping down from the chariot.

"I hate to say it, but he did the right thing," Speatsh said and slapped Bricktain across the face. "Why do you always have be so mean?"

"So now what," Amber asked.

"It's obviously not safe underground anymore," Speatsh replied.

"What about Bogi," Josh asked.

"Bogi can take care of himself," Speatsh said.

"So, now what," Amber asked again.

"Richard was a strong man," Speatsh said. "The best." He continued to stare Josh eye to eye. Compared to Josh, Speatsh was a giant. He began stroking the bear's head. "You're not the best and you're not your uncle, but neither was your uncle when he first started."

"Him's uncle vas a pansy-man," the chariot driver said. "Vy ven ve met, e vet imself."

He appeared large and bare-chested except for a leather girdle wrapped about his chest. An elephant appeared on the girdle and on his thick wristbands as well. A thin rope hung around his neck and his long blue hair was unkempt and matted. The chariot concealed the rest of him. The ghost floated down from the chariot. When he touched the ground, his feet appeared wearing strange sandals, but everything above his ankles and below his navel were invisible.

"Thank you Aggon," Speatsh said.

"I amember acuz of dun smell dat e pooted."

"Shut up Aggon."

"An I tawt e vould do more uva mess acuz—"

"Aggon!"

The specter fell silent and vanished, but suddenly reappeared in the Chariot holding his horsewhip. "I dun av to put up vid dis, I ave my own tomb."

"Your tomb was desecrated, you stupid bonewack," Speatsh replied.

"Oh, yeah," Aggon replied and disappeared again.

The six half-horses snorted among themselves and stamped their hooves against the blacktop of the parking lot, now they had hooves. Like Aggon, they were invisible from above their hooves up to their quarters.

"And take the horses," Speatsh said. "Real world, remember."

"Sorry," Aggon replied. "Come, girls."

The horses whinnied and were gone. The chariot stood like an empty bucket. It was long and slender, large enough for maybe four people. The unmistakable half-image of the sun peeking over a horizon embossed one side of the chariot. It was a simple image, but Josh recognized it at once. The wheels appeared to be some sort of bronze metal. Long, barbed, thick nails stretched from the axle beyond the sides of the chariot wheels. Reggie sat in the back in his wheelchair and held his strange sword pommel.

"Well, now that we're in the open, now what," Reggie asked.

"Bricktain," Speatsh said.

Bricktain jumped at the sound of his name, or at least at the way Speatsh pronounced it.

"You're free," Speatsh said. "You can go."

Bricktain was silent. He held the strange crescent-shaped glasses in his hand. "And do what?"

"You've been whining since the day I met you," Speatsh said. "If you wanna go, this is the time."

"I have nowhere to go," Bricktain said.

"Then you hunt," Speatsh asked.

"I hunt," Bricktain replied.

Speatsh faced Bricktain. "Where we go now, your attitude can kill. If you betray us, you worthless pus bag, I'll tear your tongue out through your cuticles."

Speatsh glared and didn't blink.

Bricktain tried to return the stare. Strangely, he believed Speatsh could perform such a task. "I'm tired of being a screw up."

"That won't change," Speatsh returned. "But the blame game does. We're not here because Josh led you into a battle unprepared. There's no doubt in my mind we're here because you made a mistake backing up Richard and that mistake killed him. He may have been old, but he was resourceful enough to kill a guardian and the only reason he would have failed is if someone screwed it up for him. And since you were the only other person around, it must have been you."

He turned his attention back to Josh.

"Richard was the most dangerous man I've ever met," he said. "He had more enemies than any hunter, that's a fact. A hunter has many adversaries. There's the wolves and humans. Most hunters trust no one. And there are those hunters who will attack any who trust you, just to teach them a lesson.

You need to protect your friends from that. You are a hunter. You must be the most feared hunter or you will not be respected. And the day may come that you have to call on those hunters to respect you, fight for you and trust in you—something most hunters cannot do."

"Most hunters chase wolves only because they've lost everything that meant anything to them. As far as they're concerned, you're just as selfish and hateful as they are. They don't have the luxury of friendship like you have and they forget everything except anger and the hunt, or their souls have been so mutilated that they can't recognize good if it happens. Courtesy does not go beyond this group when it comes to hunting, or people here die, Josh. You're no longer Josh Revlon. You're a hunter, the meanest, most hateful man on the face of this earth and when your name is whispered people will fear you. You have to start showing them why. Do you understand?"

"I'm not sure," Josh replied.

"You will," Speatsh said. "There's only one rule, never brag about who you are or what you've done, people will challenge you and at this stage you will lose. You must be prepared to hurt anyone who hurts your friends without remorse. You're not only above the law. You make the law." He turned and started clanking away from the group. "All of you, come on."

"What about the truck," Reggie asked.

"Watch it, Aggon," Speatsh called back.

"Can I drive," Aggon asked, reappearing in his golden chariot.

"No," Speatsh replied. "And hide that chariot, will ya."

The group followed Speatsh toward the club and into a narrow alley beside it. It was dark and Josh felt vulnerable. He still hurt from the attack, but with Wolf's Breath back around his neck again, and the fangs loaded once again, he felt more confident. Josh's friends followed behind him as he, in turn, followed Speatsh into the dark of the alley. He looked to the roofs and found himself watching the dark skyline of buildings overhead for moving shadows that could pounce down at any moment. He was glad Speatsh was leading and glad Speatsh was there. Speatsh began to lower into the ground and Josh followed him down a dark set of stairs where they stopped in front of a steel door and a large landing with two picnic tables and 5 benches.

"It's your show, they won't let you in if they don't believe you're a hunter," Speatsh said. "Don't let us down." He pounded on the door.

A narrow slit suddenly appeared in the door and dark eyes peered at Josh from what appeared to be a fat face.

"We're closed," the man said. He stared for a moment and slammed the sliver of light shut.

Speatsh slapped Josh and pounded on the door again.

The sliver opened again. "Go away."

"We'd like to come in, please," Josh said.

Speatsh kicked Josh's shin.

"Now," Josh said and realized he sounded unsure.

The eyes stared a second or longer and slammed the sliver shut.

"You'll get us inside," Speatsh scowled softly. "If it means I have to shove your head through the slot to do it." He pounded again and the sliver immediately opened with the same angry eyes.

A second slot opened lower on the door and Josh felt the end of a double barrel shotgun poke into his stomach.

"Git," the man said.

Speatsh shoved Josh into the stairs, clasped the barrel and pulled at it. The end of the barrel screamed with two explosions. Speatsh shoved the gun back into the door. The man behind the door groaned and Josh found himself back on his feet and pointing a fang at the man's fat face.

The man's eyes widened and the shotgun disappeared and so did the second sliver.

Something large and metal slid from the other side and suddenly the door swung into Josh and knocked him into one of the picnic tables. Josh threw himself back against the door, Speatsh helped. The door slammed shut and the angry man cried out from behind it. The eyes and steel slit returned. Josh made sure the man saw the two slender blades shoot from the back of his right wrist before he pressed them through the slit.

"Forgive the boss," Speatsh said. He was suddenly smiling and he politely stepped between Josh and the door. "Will you please let Thug know the greatest of hunters is here."

The eyes stared deep into Speatsh's. "He'll want to know who that greatest hunter is."

Josh kicked the door and tried to shove a fang back in the man's face. Speatsh politely held Josh's hand back and smiled once again through the sliver.

"Tell thug the paladin is here," Speatsh said. "The new paladin. And he is in need of food and drink because of his latest victory in destroying an entire clan this very night."

The man's eyes glanced to Josh and studied him for a few minutes.

"He sounds pretty scary," the doorman said.

"I've never met his equal," Speatsh said. "Why, he saved my life and the life of every person who accompanies us. Why, if I didn't hold him back, he'd make mincemeat of you and this door and any other rookie hunter in there feeding his fat lazy face instead of helping this noble warrior fight. He's gallant and powerful, and most patient, so we can wait while you take your fat lard into the kitchen and tell Thug he has company."

The eyes narrowed even more, but not toward Speatsh, toward Josh.

"Stand back," the man said. Josh and Speatsh stepped out of the way and the door slowly opened. Light flooded the landing and Speatsh quickly looked to Josh as if looking for approval, but abruptly stepped through the doorway. Josh followed.

The room wasn't too large. Four tables sat along a wall and a bartop with six stools sat along the other wall with a large open window and a steel counter. As Josh entered, he notice three doors opposite the entrance; one door said restroom and the other two were unmarked. The man behind the door was large, as Josh suspected. He wasn't taller than Speatsh but he was definitely wider. The man could pulverize Josh. A stool and a table sat at a small one-person booth beside the door. The wall above the table was filled with guns and blades. Josh tried not to stare and simply followed Speatsh inside. Three customers were inside, one at the bar and two together in the same booth, and so was a man who appeared to be the bartender, who stood behind the tall brown counter. He was dressed in an apron and a white shirt with brown and yellow stains. Another man stood behind the steel countertop behind the bar. All but the doorman aimed weapons at the newcomers.

All Josh remembered was that he had to be the meanest hunter. Speatsh told him to be mean and he needed to be, but could he do it? Could he hurt humans now just to gain their respect and not regret it? Did he want to know what that feeling was like? Whether he liked it or not, the world around him had changed yet again. It wasn't just wolves and monsters picking off humans for food and soldiering for their generals. Josh knew the time to be mean was now, but didn't know how to go about it. He stepped past Speatsh, stared right down the barrel of the rifle the man behind the window aimed at him and slid into a barstool. Before he knew it, he jumped up and slammed the head of the bartender against the counter while shoving a set of telescopic blades under the chin of the customer sitting at the bar. Is this what Speatsh meant to do?

"I am not in the mood." Josh looked over the other customers and watched their guns fall as they realized Amber had uncoiled her strange whips and stood ready to fight. Cadence also had drawn weapons.

"How do you have Wolf's Breath," the man from behind the window asked.

"The paladin bestowed it upon him for his loyalty and profound wisdom,"

Speatsh said. "Now tell your new bellhop to drop his gun or I'll show him one really mean bear."

The man behind the window smiled and lowered his rifle. The fat doorman and the others followed suit.

"Would you be so kind as to help my friend at the top of the stairs," Speatsh said.

The doorman disappeared through the entrance.

"We need her, Thug," Speatsh said, pushing his way farther into the room and setting himself down at the farthest side of the bar beside the customer already sitting at it.

"Is that who I think it is," Thug asked.

"He's the new paladin."

"What happened to the old paladin?"

"He's dead."

The customers all stood. Two raised beer bottles while the other raised a whisky. The bartender grabbed a rope hanging from a silver bell.

"May he rest in peace," Thug said.

"May the beasts burn," the others cried.

The bell rang.

"I believe I read something about that in the paper," Thug said. "Have something to eat," Thug set some plates filled with meat and gravy on the steel window counter.

The bartender slid one plate in front of Josh and another in front of Speatsh.

"Mine's the one without the steak," Speatsh said.

The bartender grabbed the steak with a grungy hand and slopped it onto Josh's plate, which held only steaming potatoes and white gravy with brown and black speckles.

Josh threw the steak into the bartender's face and smacked Speatsh's plate of thick white gravy into the bartender's chest.

"You treat my friends with respect," Josh said. He threw his plate at the bartender. "Try it again."

The bartender clenched his fists and looked angry enough to swing at Josh, but instead turned back to the window where a laughing Thug dropped down more filled plates. He concentrated on his work, but each time he looked at Josh, he laughed even harder until he wiped tears from his eyes.

The bartender set the plate with steak in front of Josh and the plate with just gravy and potatoes in front of Speatsh.

"I'll get her ready for you," Thug said and he disappeared from the

242

window, walked through one of the unmarked doors and disappeared through the second unmarked door.

Amber, Cadence and Bricktain filled the final three barstools. Cadence set one of her Glocks on the bar.

"This belong to you," the doorman asked. He set both Reggie and his chair on the floor.

"We're not all in, boss," Speatsh said.

"Might as well come on in, guys," Josh called out.

The Dobermans walked into the room.

"You bring this filth into our solace," the doorman asked.

"They're mine," Josh replied. "They eat at my table."

Josh heard the clicking of a hammer on a gun.

"Dustin," Josh said.

One of the Dobermans tore one of the men at the booth from his seat. His companion took aim on the Doberman, but dropped his gun, realizing his mistake after Nick huffed at him.

"Perhaps your hunting days end here," said Josh as he tried not to look at the men.

The entry door slammed shut and locked. Josh didn't look away from his plate. He wanted to, but he wondered what a mean person would do. He wondered what a hungry mean person would do. He didn't know and he didn't want to look at anyone so that his eyes could betray his deceit. Speatsh continued to sit and neither Amber nor Cadence moved from their seats so Josh assumed the customer disarmed himself.

"How do you know the paladin," the customer at the bar asked. He was short and his leather jacket bulged awkwardly. Josh wondered how quickly the man could draw whatever weapon he concealed beneath the zipper.

Josh wanted to answer but a subtle glance from Speatsh told him to hold his tongue.

"The paladin was the best there was," the doorman said. He walked up close behind Josh so that Josh could feel him breathing on his neck. "Are you the best now?"

"I'm eating," Josh said with a full mouth and remembering what Speatsh had said about not bragging..

The doorman stayed and breathed.

"He saved our lives tonight," Speatsh said. "There's not a hunter alive that can hold a candle to this young boy. You'd all do well to learn from this kid. He has more reason to boast than any of you cowards, I reckon."

"I might challenge that," the doorman said.

"It's like high school in here, isn't it," Cadence said through laughing.

"Not high school, little girl," the doorman said ,leaving Josh. Josh didn't know what he saw in the look the doorman gave the bartender, but the bartender saw it too, only the bartender's reaction was to step closer to Cadence on his side of the counter. He reached for something under the bartop.

"You respect us here, girl," and the doorman pulled her head back by her hair. Cadence screamed. Josh watched the bartender aim a sawed-off shotgun in Speatsh's face and pointed Cadence's Glock at Bricktain's. Small divots scarred his forearm. Josh knew they had to be from the guardian's quills.

Amber reached for an orbit and the doorman backhanded her off her stool to the floor. Reggie sat still in his chair. The two customers in the booth dropped strange metal nooses, which made electrical sounds, over Nick and Dustin's necks. Both dogs cried and fell to the ground.

The doorman leered at Josh, smiled and punched Cadence in the back through the system. Cadence screamed out and tried to jump out of her chair. Her face turned redder the louder she screamed. Josh wasn't sure if she screamed more from the punch to the back or the way her body twisted in the system.

The customer at the counter did nothing.

A set of blades shot back out.

"I'll blow someone's head off, kid," the bartender said.

"Is this the high school you were talking about, girlie," the doorman asked. "I've fought in three wars and hunted wolves all my life. Don't come in here and call me juvenile. This is the real world, sugar. You need to learn that."

"How's your food," Josh asked the customer at the bar. He still clenched a fist allowing one set of blades to remain drawn. "That tequila?"

The customer at the bar said nothing, but risked a smile and nodded. Josh decided he wasn't a threat.

"I could sure use a drink of that right now."

Speatsh ate his food and glared at Josh, but Josh recognized that the old wolf wasn't angry with him.

"Learn who the best is, sugar," the doorman said. "It's important."

"Let me tell you the way I see it," Josh said.

He didn't know what a mean angry hungry person would do in this situation, but he knew what he wanted to do. Wolf's Breath snapped out straight and sliced the bartender's wrist open. The Glock fell from his hand. He spun on his stool, cautiously so as not to cut the customer or Bricktain. He leaned forward and sliced through both metal nooses with the other edge of

244

his cloak. The fangs were in his black gloved hands and before he could shoot, Reggie's ghostly sword slashed through one customers' gun and he turned to the other customer as if to hold his sword under his throat, but the blade disappeared. The customer laughed, but started swearing as Reggie's fat rear wheel drove over his foot. The customer swore and Reggie went to punch him with the sword still in his hand. The silver blade leapt out at the customer. The customer fell back and grabbed his chin, which now bled.

"Ha," Reggie said more out of surprise than for glory. "Ain't so funny now, is it?"

A shotgun blasted and by the time Josh turned to the sound, the bartender had dropped his sawed-off onto the bar, stepped back and grappled his bleeding thigh. Cadence sat in her chair with her hand on the trigger of one of her leg shotguns poised directly at the counter.

The doorman struck Cadence again. Cadence screamed and Josh leaned across Bricktain and stuck his blades into the doorman's fist. And he realized he didn't care because no one hurt his friends anymore.

The doorman didn't make a sound.

"That's not how we treat women," Josh said and he twisted the blades in the doorman's hand. "Let your hand be testimony that the new paladin won't stand for it." The blades disappeared beneath the Wolf's Breath and Josh returned to his meal.

The doorman stepped back cradling his hand and trying to conceal his pain. Speatsh jumped from his chair, leaping over Josh, the bar and all who sat at it. Mid-jump, he took up the sawed-off from the bartop and smashed the bartender's nose with the barrel. He tackled the doorman and hoisted him by the scruff of his t-shirt and skin.

"I am Speatsh Cheatham." He slammed the fat man down on his back. "I know you've heard my name. I've started more wars than you could ever count and I've made enough wolves to make a fat clump of dirt like you etch your own tombstone in your shorts."

"Enough," Josh ordered.

"Compared to me, you are still a baby. You are juvenile." Speatsh said and raised his leg to smash down on the man. How dare you touch those who protect you from the dangers of this world."

"Speatsh," Josh said. "I said that's enough."

Speatsh heard the order, and kicked the doorman's injured hand instead. He turned on the customers at the booth. "And I'm the nice one." He spit in one of their drinks before returning to his stool at the bar.

Speatsh nodded to Josh and he returned to his meal. Josh knew he hated

Speatsh.

Josh had nearly finished eating when Thug reentered the café. He was short and stout with a long, dusty, brown beard, which reached down his chest and ended in about a half a dozen mangled strands. He covered his head with a black bandana bearing a red skull breathing ice. He wiped black smudges from his hands and onto his yellow butcher's apron. He noticed the doorman fidgeting to tie a white towel around his hand.

"Where's Ty," Thug asked, also noticing that his bartender was missing.

The doorman looked up. "Bathroom cleaning a wound."

"Speatsh," Thug asked.

The doorman didn't want to reply and didn't want to be embarrassed any further. Thug looked over the customers in his bar. One of the men at the booth drank his beer in silence as two Dobermans watched them. Speatsh picked his teeth. Reggie was deep in conversation with Bricktain, occasionally looking at the doorman who was trying his best to show he could handle the pain that Speatsh and Josh had inflicted upon him. The new paladin was chewing his steak. Cadence's hand rested close to her Glock. Thug wiped his hands through his beard and broke out laughing.

"Criminy, Speatsh," Thug said. "If the devil walks on Earth, he stays clear of you. Do you have any idea how long it took me to find another staff after your last visit?"

"Where is she," Speatsh asked.

Thug's smile disappeared. "Elevator's this way."

Speatsh remained seated. Thug was waiting at one of the unmarked doors. Josh realized the others were staring at him. Thug turned his attention to Josh and Josh watched the stout man's face suddenly change, as he focused his gaze at the doorman and back to Josh. He nodded and Josh knew what everyone was waiting for. He stood. Speatsh stood. The others followed suit. Thug gestured to follow and led everyone down a narrow dismal hallway encased in cinderblocks. Josh could hear music coming from somewhere above his head.

"I wasn't sure if she would start," Thug said. "I try to start her every now and then, but it seems every now and then isn't often enough. Of course, we know the batteries are good."

"Did you put in the new equipment I asked for," Speatsh asked.

"Yeah," Thug replied. "Opened up some space too."

Thug stepped inside a large freight elevator and everyone followed. Once everyone was inside, Thug pulled at a nylon strap and the jaw-like elevator doors snapped shut.

"I knew your uncle, Josh," Thug said as the elevator began its drop. "I fought with him a time or two. He was a good man, earned my respect, enough to respect his wishes to stay far away from the family when he gave up the hunt. He wanted to keep you all safe."

"He was a good man," Josh said.

"I was his eyes and ears," Thug said trying not to make eye contact. His voice quivered enough that Josh noticed. "They belong to you now. If you ever need something, you come to me, understand?"

"I do," Josh said.

Thug turned with a smile. "I haven't seen you since the day you were born, my boy. You look good."

Josh didn't know what to say to the stranger.

"Criminy, Speatsh," Thug scowled. "Did you give him the 'you have to be mean to be a hunter' speech?"

First one snicker escaped, and another and soon Speatsh was laughing along with Thug.

Thug's eyes sparkled as he looked at Josh. "You do have to be mean," he said. "But your act is safe with me."

"Do you know I just stabbed a man's hand," Josh blurted.

Thug burst out laughing harder. "You remember that pub in Dublin, Speatsh? I'll bet I was a few years older than you, Josh. Speatsh and Richard convinced me I needed to mark my territory like a wolf, if you'll excuse the term, and I punched the biggest man I ever saw in my life when he tried to help himself to my soup. Turns out, Speatsh here sent the man my way to share in a Catholic meal. And I knocked him out cold because I thought I had to be mean. Next thing I know, I'm against the wall and fighting for my life."

"His buddies," Bricktain asked.

"His wife," Speatsh replied and started laughing with Thug again.

The elevator stopped and Thug opened the doors. "There she is."

The flickering lights weren't the best to see under, but Josh was still in awe. Its chrome trailer was at least forty feet long and reflected almost every detail of the room, including the people staring at it. Four wheels held up the back of the trailer and protective plates encased their sides. A wider sturdy roof, filled with oval holes, crowned the top. The tractor looked like a bullet train with a blade-shaped nose. It had a full cab with an extended roof filled with mirrored windows. Eight tires held up the back of the tractor and protective, chrome plates covered them too. The front wheels were three times the size of the other wheels and their tread ran deeper. A black accordion tunnel attached the back of the tractor to the front of the trailer.

247

"That's the silver bullet," Thug said. "Best mobile command post a hunter, or anyone for that fact, could want."

"She's mine," Speatsh said. "Make no mistake with this girl. She's powered with a nuclear reactor built in 1837."

"You're kidding, right?" Bricktain interrupted. "Nineteenth-century nuclear power? Impossible."

"Look who suddenly has a degree in nineteenth-century nuclear engineering theory," Speatsh said. "The reactor was originally designed for a stagecoach, but it was sorta difficult to hide a carriage that horses weren't pulling back then. Freaked out a few people. A few years back, your uncle suggested we try reviving the idea and we put our heads together and came up with this, a front wheel drive nuclear powered diesel that ain't no ordinary diesel." He grabbed Bricktain by the arm and led him to the back of the trailer. He pulled a handle beneath the floor of the trailer and two doors hissed and swung out. "Up, idiot," Speatsh said as he leaped into the trailer where he flipped a switch and flooded the insides with light. Bricktain climbed up.

Flat-screen monitors lined one of the walls of the trailer.

"There's sixty-seven screens here," Speatsh said. "Each one's connected to a camera at various points around this baby. There's fifty guns mounted throughout and around, above and below the trailer as well as some in the tractor."

"What kind of guns," Bricktain asked.

"Big guns," Speatsh returned. "The kind that go bang." Speatsh turned to a cabinet and withdrew two plastic video game guns. "These are the same as what you've been practicing with."

Bricktain fumbled with the guns as Speatsh shoved them into his hands.

"It's not a game anymore," Speatsh said. "With those cameras and your glasses, you can see three hundred and sixty degrees now in daylight and night vision. Don't shoot us."

"So, now what," Josh asked, looking up into the trailer.

"It would be a bad idea to stay here," Speatsh said. "And we better not go home 'til we know how they got in."

"What about my junkyard," Reggie said. "It was designed to be a fort against the dogs."

"You mean the junkyard up on the hill," Thug asked.

Reggie nodded.

"It's been condemned," Thug said. "The authorities found bodies up there and shut it down. Manipulated, if you ask me. Found a wrecked truck nearby, too. I believe they're looking for the owners."

"I'm sorry, Dad," Amber said, patting her father's shoulder as if to comfort him.

"Yeah," Reggie said. "Me too."

"We're hunters," Bricktain said. "Let's hunt."

Josh knew Bricktain was right. He didn't like the idea of hunting with his sister still being one of Jasper's servants. He still didn't take to the idea of coming across her in her animal form and possibly killing her. But he also knew Jasper used other people too, possibly more children, possibly as food, and he knew he was their chance to be freed.

"Would you know my sister if you saw her as a dog," Josh asked.

"No," Speatsh replied.

"Then I say we take this truck out to Jasper's and we destroy him in his human form," Josh said. "We managed to get here. We can get there. Maybe we're ready."

"That's a good idea," Cadence said.

Amber agreed.

"It doesn't work that way," Thug said.

"His control over his minions is absolute when he's in human form," Speatsh explained.

"All the more reason to save them sooner than later," Reggie said.

"If you kill a general in human form, the others will die from the mental shock. He can't be in their heads."

"Well, we can't stay in the city," Josh said. "They'll find us again."

"Why can't we stay here," Cadence asked. "Why not stay where the hunter numbers are greater. We have allies here."

"Not all hunters are after the wolves," Thug said. "Some are spies who belong to the wolves. The wolves know we're here. But they also know if they ever did anything to this place, it wouldn't take long for real hunters to know there's a clan nearby and start wiping it out. Because that's what hunters do. But for your group," Thug's eyes settled on Cadence. "I venture if they learned about you, they might just risk open war with the entire human race."

Josh felt a jolt strike deep into his heart. Thug knew about Cadence. If he knew, who else knew? If other hunters knew, would Josh have to fight them too. He thought he understood why he had to be the meanest hunter. He wondered about Cadence's importance. What was best for her? Keeping her out of battle and out of sight of the wolves? Leaving her to the shadows, just as Speatsh had been training her to do? Jasper broke into the bunker. Josh could improve the security, but how long until Jasper got in again? The city had too much light and too many human friends. They had to leave the city.

"What about Shallow woods," Josh asked. "Maybe it's just as dangerous for them as it is for people," Josh said.

"Oh," Thug said. "Wolves find it a little more than dangerous."

Speatsh clapped his hands and smiled. "Load up boys and girls."

Thug held out his hand to Josh. "Pleasure meeting you ,my boy. You should probably know that I'm your godfather. Surprise! Sorry about your parents. I believe they're watching over you, I truly mean that."

"We'll be back after the next full moon," Speatsh said."

Josh started into the trailer but stopped and turned to Thug. "Do you have any news?"

Thug smiled. "We had a hunter come through about a week ago, said a general he'd been tracking, a general named Travis, went silent."

"That means the general has been called to the ancient," Speatsh said. "Probably to punish him."

"I don't think so," Thug said. "Other taverns and other hunters report at least three other cases of generals going silent. He's up to something. Do you think he knows?"

"Impossible," Speatsh snapped back.

"I hope you're right," Thug said.

"Was there anything else," Speatsh asked.

"Yeah," Thug said. "Dracula's in town."

22 ~ Acotactac

Hickerbilly followed close behind the silver bullet. Speatsh hadn't said much, loaded everyone in the diesel and started it up. The truck was surprisingly silent. Bricktain commented that Speatsh had said silver doesn't kill a werewolf, but Speatsh pointed out that if a wolf got in the way of this bullet, it would.

Josh tried to keep up with the nuclear-powered diesel. He sat behind the wheel of Hickerbilly feeling his stiff knuckles turn white beneath the fang gloves. Where the chrome rig slid around corners, as if Speatsh were trying to outrun police, Josh feared the Silverado might topple. When he came out of one corner, the bullet was already a fair distance ahead of him, sometimes as its trailer was already drifting around the next turn behind the tractor. At one point, he could see the rear wheels twist sideways, allowing the trailer to drift, and straighten again. The machine submitted to Speatsh's driving as if it were a race car and not a diesel at all. Speatsh was clearly fleeing the city.

Amber and Cadence rode with Josh in the cab while the twins took their positions in the bed. Josh watched them slide around as if they were surfing some tremendous ocean wave. Normally, the twins looked so focused and in control, not that Josh knew much about reading a dog's facial expressions, but his friends actually seemed scared sliding around in the truck. They shrank at every little movement and tried their best to hold each other up as well. He wondered how much of the human side of Dustin was still alive. Did Dustin know who Josh was, let alone himself? What about Nick?

Dustin and Nick both seemed normal during the full moon when they became the friends Josh remembered. They barely spoke, because Speatsh kept them separated from the others. Speatsh made everyone train twice as hard during full moons while he disappeared into another section of the bunker with Dustin and Nick, claiming the shock of the environment would be bad for them.

Cadence had a hard time when she saw Nick during his first full moon since his return to the bunker as a Doberman. He didn't have his thick wavy auburn hair. She never told him that she secretly always wished she could run her fingers just once through that hair. When she saw Nick, she cried. Cadence and Nick didn't get to speak, but she could hear his screams when the full moon came and again when it left.

251

"We have fog," Cadence said.

"We have dogs, too," Josh said and motioned to numbers of dogs in mirrors and around the truck.

Josh tightened his grip around the wheel. He hadn't dismissed what dangers fog held. No one really said anything to him about how to fight in fog. The dogs were hard enough to fight in the open and he really didn't look forward to racing into the back of the silver bullet all because he couldn't see it.

A deep horn blast screeched and the fog withdrew.

"Apparently, you can fight the fog," Cadence said.

"They ain't nothing," Speatsh's voice crackled over the CB radio mounted on Hickerbilly's dashboard. "And now for all you cool cats, wild birds and stupid rookie dogs."

The diesel horn blasted again and again.

"Heeeere puppy-puppy-puppy-puppy-puppy," Speatsh called.

Blast! Blast!

Amber grabbed up the microphone from the radio console.

"I think they have some sort of noise ordinance here," Amber said.

BLAAAAAAST!

"Until we get earplugs for Nick and Dustin, knock it off," Cadence screamed at the microphone.

Josh couldn't help but notice the two dogs trying to bury their heads into each other with each burst of the horn.

"Fine," Speatsh replied.

Josh felt a little better with the fog disappearing, but he was also falling behind in his chase of Speatsh and the silver bullet.

Few accounts told about the center of the Shallow Woods. Dense trees made it difficult to photograph the ground from above and many dangers such as Shale Canyon made it impossible for most people to explore. People looking for outdoor adventures generally stayed in the outer flatlands of the woods where the trees were sparser. A few campgrounds set here and still people disappeared.

Hickerbilly fought even harder to follow the silver bullet off-road and into the outer rims of the Shallow Woods.

"You wanna go about forty in here," Speatsh's voice instructed. "Anything less and you might never get out of the ruts and vines."

The taillights of the silver bullet bounced around over the uneven ground. Hickerbilly threw its passengers into the roof and doors. The twins rolled around in the bed.

Amber's thoughts went to her dad who rode in the silver bullet. All this jumping around would surely do damage to him and his chair, and it wasn't likely they would find an electric wheelchair shop anywhere within these woods. She was scared. She grabbed Josh's leg.

The system's various pieces rattled around on the floor of the cab. It seems with as well engineered as the contraption was, its one drawback was that it made it impossible to ride in a car. Cadence made sure to complain about the contraption every chance she got. She hated the thing. She was tired of its bulk, but Speatsh swore up and down it was the most technologically advanced personal artillery unit and tried to make her feel a little stupid on the subject.

"Well, this could get annoying," Cadence said after the third time of her head hitting the back window.

The silver bullet stopped and Hickerbilly almost had to swerve to miss it.

*　　*　　*

Bricktain sat in front of the monitors, asleep. Speatsh had assured him that he would know if any dogs came near the vehicles, but Bricktain wanted to know it for himself so he tried to stay awake and watch. No one else could use the glasses like he could. No one else could wear the lenses and no one else understood the new shapes the glasses gave everything. He had spent so much time staring at the monitors in the apartment and playing video games that he had grown sick of it. Now, he was the fort watchman. He didn't know what the fort could do yet, but he realized that while the others would be outside fighting, he would be inside aiming toy guns at monitors that would tell a real gun where to fire. He didn't want to be responsible for shooting one of his own allies all because he read one of the slender figures wrong. For the first time, Bricktain had purpose. He watched the monitors with their green and white hues and thought he saw eyes from time to time, but concluded what he saw was really nothing.

The corridor of the trailer was much narrower with the four bunks on the opposite wall folded down where the others now rested. Speatsh slept on the floor and Bricktain volunteered to use a sleeping bag when enough fold-down bunks weren't available for everyone. A thick curtain separated the bunks from the glow of the flat-screen monitors. Speatsh snored loudly in the television glow.

Near the trailer doors stood the chariot, tied down. Often Bricktain's thoughts and eyes would turn from the monitors to its gold and inlaid design.

A year ago, it was just him. There was no death and no mockery and he was setting into his new job just fine.

He remembered being attacked and remembered watching the chief dissolve in front of him. Worst of all, he remembered how he felt when the body of the child was discovered in his own patrol car. When his superiors questioned him, he remembered that he wasn't sure what orders the chief had given him. Maybe the chief gave bad orders, but the fact that Bricktain couldn't remember made him realize he didn't know whether he had killed two people that night or not. Speatsh was right earlier; maybe all of this was his fault. He didn't want that responsibility. A little more than nine months ago, he saw a monster and no one believed him. Or maybe they did, and the right people worked to get him off the streets. Were the dogs really in positions to manipulate humans, to frighten them into doing Jasper's dirty work? He thought about the police dog that attacked Josh and Amber.

Today, Bricktain fought alongside a human razor blade, a former werewolf, a girl who walked on air, a human tank, two dogs, and now a ghost driven chariot. All these allies were dangerous. Of all, Josh frightened him the most. He was young, and the incident at the bar showed him how unpredictable the boy could be. Bricktain didn't trust him. Compared to the others, Bricktain felt he was nothing. He wanted nothing more than to prove to at least one of his allies that he wasn't the bumbling fool. He fought sleep, but drifted off anyway.

Reggie woke him. The sunlight filled the trailer from the back doors. Everyone had already been awake and the beds and curtain had all been folded back against the wall.

"He says you need to wake up," Reggie said.

"Are we driving again," Bricktain asked.

"No," Reggie replied. "We've been driving. You slept through it."

Bricktain stretched. He was sore. It seemed he found new sore areas every day. He didn't want to be old. He admitted that it was time to start thinking about that stuff. Maybe he was glad he was behind the cameras to fight, after all. He wondered how sore he would have been if he had taken the beating Josh took last night. After a few morning groans and more stretches, he started for the trailer's ramp.

The first thing he noticed was the smell. It hit him even before he got out of the trailer. The air was that of clean outdoors, not like the stifled stench of recycled oxygen he'd been breathing in Josh's dungeon. As he stepped outside, he saw all the half-naked people.

"Welcome to the twilight zone," Josh said, walking past the ex-cop.

254

"Again."

"What are they," Bricktain asked.

"Who are they?" Speatsh corrected. He stood about a hundred feet away talking with three of the men over an open fire where an animal of some sort turned pink on a spit. A large lady sat on a tall stool next to it and mixed something in a wooden bowl. A small group of women laughed with her. Others roamed nearby, either watching their new visitors or tending to chores. One boy skinned a rabbit with a sharp stone, while an older man kept amending his work. A circle of women pointed at Josh and his group and younger ladies nodded their heads. Curious children watched the group, but stayed close to their parents. Bricktain couldn't see everyone because of the large trees sprouting around. But he noticed more faces peering at the group from what appeared to be windows within those trees. He stared up the long Redwood stalks.

"Redwoods," Bricktain asked. "These aren't supposed to be here."

"Neither are you," Speatsh replied. "Impress us with your botany knowledge where we can't hear you."

Men walked around wearing strange shorts and vests out of what appeared to be vines, leaves and animal skin. Women wore long pants-like dresses, which covered their fronts and left the backs bare, and were adorned with more color. Their hair was long and filled with wooden beads, and strange decoration. It took a while, but Bricktain could see that the clothing material ran down their fronts to the strange wiry pants tied to patches of pelts.

"They are the Taichomée," Speatsh said. "They live here."

"They're Indians," Reggie added.

"You're so P.C., Dad," Amber said. She blended in with a group of women closest to him and Bricktain almost didn't recognize her. Other women adorned her with their decorations and some washed her face and tied her long blond hair.

"How is this possible," Bricktain asked.

"They're good at hiding," Speatsh said.

"They carve their homes in the trees," Josh said. "Look."

Bricktain followed Josh's finger up the side of a tree and noticed hand and footholds carved into it. All along the way, he saw more round windows and noticed more faces peering out at the strangers.

"Everything they need has always been in this forest," Speatsh said. "So far, no one's found them. And they know to keep to themselves."

"This is amazing," Bricktain said.

The man speaking to Speatsh said something to make Speatsh laugh.

"What did he say," Bricktain asked.

"He said you're an idiot," Speatsh blurted. "Go back to sleep if you can't shut up."

"They've hollowed the trees," Josh said. "There's hundreds of them here. And they're friendly."

"Surely the wolves could have found them," Bricktain said.

"It's because they used to be wolves," Speatsh said. "They've managed to stay hidden, since the queen died. Now they wait for their deaths in peace and hope their general doesn't return to the ways of the wolf. The wolves fear them because they know how to fight back. That's what sets the generals apart from the ancients. Because when the ancient passes on a part of himself, he continues to live within the generals even after he dies, but when a general dies, it's absolute freedom for those he turns. The general only passes on the mutation. Hence, the reason we can't just kill Jasper. Unfortunately, their general's not dead so they're afraid to start new lives for fear that their master might call them back to him and ruin what lives they've affected. Their power's dormant, but don't worry, these woods are filled with traps. No wolf could survive out here. Wolves tend to disappear too."

"But they could have followed us here," Bricktain said.

"They're too scared of this place," Speatsh answered. "We have nothing to worry about here."

The man speaking to Speatsh spoke again.

"The chief would like some water," Speatsh said.

"Come on," Josh said and he led Bricktain farther into the village.

The two walked past more trees. Josh had already made the trip three times and he knew right where the wooden bowls were to carry the water in. He guided Bricktain to a small pile of the bowls next to a log. He gestured for Bricktain to get one.

"Water's over here," Josh said.

In what could have been the center of the village, rested a long slab of wood with a braided vine threaded through a hole in its middle and tied on top. Josh knelt over and moved the slab out of the way. He grunted as he pushed the wood to the side. A hole about two feet wide appeared. Josh took his bowl and pressed the vine through two holes at the top of it. He lowered the bowl into the ground until the rope slackened, and he waited. Slowly the rope became taut and he started pulling the vine back out of the hole. The bowl reappeared filled with water. Josh set the container down and untied the vine. He handed the vine to Bricktain.

"It may not be much," Josh said. "But it's home."

"You mean we're staying here," Bricktain blurted. He noticed some of the faces turn to him.

"At least until the next full moon," Josh said. He drank from the bowl and poured the rest of the water back into the hole. "We're here for three weeks. You might wanna learn how to whittle or something." He handed the bowl to Bricktain. "Get the chief some water, will ya."

Josh left Bricktain, and Bricktain hated that boy even more. He shoved the vine through the holes in the basin and tied as good a knot as he knew how. He lowered it into the hole and waited for the bend created by slack, but it didn't come. He lowered the vine until only the bit tied to the plank was above ground. When he pulled the vine back out. It was empty, not just because the strange dish didn't hold any water, but the vine no longer held the bowl. Bricktain cursed under his breath and stood up, stormed to the pile of vessels and snatched up another one. He returned to the vine and again tied a knot but before he could lower it into the hole in the earth, it slid off the vine. He fumbled with it, but it fell into the hole. Again, Bricktain swore and he noticed small groups of Taichomée pointing and laughing in his direction. Some pointed fingers at him while others nodded and even frowned. He fetched another bowl, sat down and tried to tie another knot.

"Hey genius," Speatsh cried from afar off. "Lose that one and that's three you'll have to make to replace the ones you lost."

Bricktain pretended to ignore Speatsh. He tied and pulled on the rope, but the vine gave way. How stupid did a person have to be not to be able to tie a simple knot? And why was this vine so slick? He tied and pulled and again the line came loose. He slammed the basin against the ground and stared at as if it would explain what he was doing wrong. He was tired of people laughing at him.

But she gently took the item from Bricktain.

At first, all he noticed was her hand. It appeared smooth, but the insides were callused and scarred. She wore wooden gauntlets painted and adorned with polished rock. A hollow tube attached to the backside of each gauntlet. Her feet were bare and the tops resembled the backs of her hands. The exception was that her right foot had a round star-shaped scar about the size of the tip of one of her fingers. She knelt next to him. Her dress was different from what the other women wore. It was fuller, covering her back. She wore a full shirt made from the vines and leather. Her shorts were a little fuller too and less see through, as well.

Now that Bricktain thought of it, her skin was darker than the other Taichomée also. She didn't smile at him. She pulled back her brown hair,

257

which almost matched her darker skin. She took the vine from Bricktain's hand and gently pushed it through the holes in the bowl. She began to tie the knot. He watched her more than he watched the knot in her fingers take form. When she finished, she untied the knot and handed the vine and the bowl back to Bricktain. He was angry with himself again when he realized he hadn't been paying as much attention to the knot as he thought he had. The girl yanked back the vine and the bowl. She demonstrated the knot again and Bricktain tried once more.

"I did it," he said, pulling the vine without it pulling away from the water dish.

The girl smiled and patted his head.

Bricktain lowered the basin into the hole and this time the slack appeared and slowly grew tight. He pulled up the bowl and it held water.

"Thank you," Bricktain said.

She smiled.

"I'm Bricktain," he said. "Bricktain." He pointed to himself.

She stared at his finger and stood up. Bricktain scrambled to his feet, splashing himself with water, but the girl was already returning to a group of five other young women who were eager to giggle with her when she rejoined them. He untied the knot and waited for her to turn around so he could see her again, but she didn't turn. He waited and hoped she would, but she wouldn't. Bricktain returned to the chief, Speatsh and the other Taichomée men in that group.

The chief smiled and held his hands out. Bricktain thought the man was thin to the bone. He envisioned handing the wooden container of water to the bare-chested, old man and having to catch him before the weight of it pulled him over. Bricktain wanted to laugh. He set the bowl in the chief's hands.

The chief stared at Bricktain. Bricktain smiled and nodded, but the chief stopped smiling. Speatsh smacked the back of Bricktain's head.

"He wants you to wash his hands, stupid," Speatsh said and yanked the bowl from the chief. "Go back, cover the hole and stop insulting our hosts."

Bricktain trudged back to the slab, hating every step along the way, but when he noticed the girl and her friends watching him, he wasn't angry anymore. He hefted the slab and smiled at the young girl as he reset it over the chasm. The end of the slab toppled into the hole and before Bricktain knew what was happening, the entire plank and its vine sucked into the earth. A moment later, a splashing sound came from the dark opening. In the distance, he could see the young woman looking back at him. She wasn't smiling.

From across the village, Speatsh's voice rang, "Did you just drop the village's only access to water down the hole? You are just too much brains for any one man, you know that."

*   *   *

Cadence saw Josh smiling and playing and she stopped walking. Half-naked children chased after Josh with their skirts and beads flapping around their hyperactive bodies. He turned this way and that, but the children weren't fooled. They knew how to play this game. Half of the playing children wore leather shirts and the other half didn't. Josh turned and handed a large pinecone to a small child on his team of leather shirt children. The bare-chested children slapped at Josh's hands and all the boys started yelling, laughing and screaming. The child Josh had handed the pinecone to ran with it. Josh ran too and broke away from the depths of the little bodies. His white undershirt was stained with sweat and he laughed as much as the children. The boy with the pinecone handed it to a smaller boy who screamed when he got it and threw it straight up in the air. A Doberman caught it and at once Cadence knew it was Dustin because Nick had been walking with her and Amber. The children laughed some more and chased after Dustin.

The leather-shirted team ran after the dog and he leapt over their heads. The children chased him after he landed. They tried to reach Dustin, but he was a little harder to catch. Dustin broke away from the group and charged straight for the basket. Children cheered and groaned and cheered and groaned louder as Josh leapt out of nowhere and tackled Dustin. Dustin growled and Josh taunted him with the pinecone, now in his possession, before running toward the same basket. The children clamored around Josh once more. He handed the pinecone to another teammate. The teammate handed to a bigger teammate. The bigger teammate handed to the smallest teammate. The smallest teammate screamed again and ran. He held the pinecone as far in front of his body as he could and ran as fast as his little legs allowed. Villagers laughed at the spectacle. The bare-chested children gained on the smallest teammate and Dustin was right along with them. The little boy stopped in front of the basket and dropped the pinecone. It fell straight for the basket, but Dustin quickly reached in and snatched it up before it could hit the bottom.

The little boy smacked Dustin's nose and Dustin dropped the pinecone into the basket. "Dobu lami."

"Yeah," Josh said, picking up the pinecone. "Bad dog." He gave the pinecone back to the smallest teammate. Again, cheers and groans erupted.

259

"That's one for us, buddy."

Dustin growled.

The little boy took the pinecone, spun around four times and launched it high into the air. The pinecone sailed over everyone's heads before toppling back to the ground where it plopped into the basket. Again, cheers and groans followed.

Josh cheered along and turned to his Doberman companion. "Two! Two! Thanks, dobu lami."

Dustin leapt at Josh and both fell over. The children joined in.

"Those kids love him," Amber said. She couldn't stop watching him.

"They do," Cadence said and continued again to walk with her basket of berries. She had come to enjoy gathering berries. It gave her time to think and to relax, to get things right in her head. She appreciated the outdoors after spending so long underground. She felt her spirits rise since being in the fresh air. It was good to have the Taichomée as friends. They were courteous. She didn't completely understand the language, a few words here and there became revealed, but Speatsh had been pretty good at translating. Josh seemed to be picking up the language OK too. He understood some simple statements and sometimes even held small conversations. It was good to see him enjoying himself. She really almost forgot he was capable of smiling. She felt happy for him.

"Did you find anything," Bricktain asked, approaching Amber.

"Will any of these work," Amber held out her basket of berries. Five chunks of wood rested on top.

Bricktain pulled one at a time out of the basket and scrutinized their appearance. One after another, he frowned, but he tucked them away in his pocket anyway. He turned to walk away and saw the Taichomée girl he had grown to admire. She glanced his way and looked away before disappearing through an oval doorway into one of the tree apartments.

"What are you doing with the wood, Bricktain," Cadence asked.

Bricktain nodded. "It's nothing, really."

"She's half your age," Cadence said.

"Yeah," Bricktain replied. "Doesn't matter. She hasn't spoken to me yet."

"Who hasn't spoken to you yet," Josh asked running up to the group, out of breath. He reached into the basket and took a handful of berries.

"No one," Bricktain said.

"The one he's crushing over," Amber replied.

"I'm not crushing," Bricktain said.

"Oh, that one," Josh said before his face turned sour. He spit a berry out onto the ground and wiped his tongue on his shirt.

"That's why you soak them in sap first," Cadence said.

"Even I knew that," Bricktain said.

"Well, at least I can talk to women," Josh responded as he dropped the sour berries back into the basket.

"Yeah, I'll remember that," Bricktain said and sauntered away.

Amber kicked Josh and he realized his mistake

"Bricktain," Josh said. "It's nothing to be ashamed of."

"Maybe not for you," Bricktain said and continued to walk away.

"She can't talk," Josh said.

"What do you mean," Bricktain asked.

"She's not Taichomée," Josh revealed. "Speatsh said she wandered into the village about seventeen years ago when she was small and barely alive. She has no tongue."

Bricktain glanced at the oval doorway the girl disappeared into and couldn't take his eyes off it.

"They call her Acotactac," Josh said. "It means wind that is still, or silent wind, quiet wind, something like that."

Dustin started tugging at Josh's shirt. The children encouraged him.

"Guess I'm needed," Josh said stepping back with each of Dustin's pulls. "Anyone wanna play?"

"Can I," Amber asked.

"I'll take the berries for you," Bricktain said.

Amber followed Josh and Dustin back into the game of Pinecone.

*   *   *

Bricktain took a break from whittling. All he did around here was whittle, whittle bowls. And it took him fifteen tries just to make one bowl so far. Now he held what appeared to be a small archery bow. It was hard to pull the string. It wasn't really a string. It was, well, Bricktain didn't know what it was exactly. It had strands of hair, pieces of ivy, and the veins that run through leaves mixed into the string. The bow was hard, smooth and oily except around the handgrip, where a hard strip of leather and white fur wrapped it.

"Ah," said Speatsh as he approached Bricktain. He popped a walnut shell into his mouth and crunched it between his teeth. "I see you found the vine spinner."

"The what," Bricktain asked.

Speatsh spit a few pieces of walnut shell at the ground. "You tie small pieces of vine to it and you braid stuff like leaves, fur and sometimes manure into it and it makes rope. That girl you like to stalk uses it, that's her job around here, to make ropes."

"Like, the rope I lost in the hole," Bricktain inquired. "She has to make a new one now?"

"Funny you should ask," Speatsh said. He spit out more pieces of walnut shell and started to walk away. "It's time to train."

Before Bricktain could ask what Speatsh meant, Acotactac was standing before him and snatched the small bow from his hands. She led Bricktain to a tree where large baskets held leaves, broken ivy, manure and other odds and ends of nature. An animal pelt of some sort hung on a small branch above them. And long poles about twenty feet long rested against the side of the tree. From one of the baskets, she took a ball of thinly wrapped vine and tied an end to the curve of the bow-shaped vine spinning instrument. She led Bricktain to an open area and threw the ball over a branch high in the air. The ball of vine unraveled and Acotactac bagan to pull the vine spinner up to the branch. She placed a large stone on the ivy running from the ground, over the branch and tied to the vine spinner, to hold it in place. She turned to the dumbfounded Bricktain. He couldn't tell if she was angry with him still or not. She led him back to the tree with the long poles and set them on the ground. She lifted an end of one of the wooden poles and motioned for Bricktain to join her.

The end of the pole was flat and plier-like pincers protruded from its tip. A string ran from the pincers down the side of the pole to a small wooden ring. Acotactac pulled back and forth on this string and the pincers opened and closed. She pulled out another ball of vine and broke off a length about twelve inches long. She tied a loop in its end and stuffed it into the pincers on the end of the pole. She made two more pieces just like it and stuffed them into the plier-like fingers as well.

She led Bricktain to the opposite ends of the slender poles and demonstrated to Bricktain how they'd been tapered on the end. She slid her gauntlet with the tube on its backside over the tapered end of the pole. She attached the second pole to her other gauntlet. She hefted both poles straight into the air as if she were curling weights and walked back beneath the vine spinner. She attached the three looped pieces of vine to the string on the vine spinner. She smacked an end of the vine spinner and it began twisting. Acotactac tied the three short vines into one piece. Bricktain watched as the vine spinner began to move faster and Acotactac moved even faster pulling at the string along the side of the pole to move the pincers at the tops to braid the vines together. Suddenly, Bricktain found himself ducking out of the way as one of the poles came crashing towards him. Acotactac made a sound that could have been a chuckle or could have been a hmph.

The pole fell to the basked with leaves and the pincers grabbed a small wad of them and raised them into the air back to the vine spinner. She weaved fast and the spinner kept moving as the two poles continued to create a new rope. The poles fell fast and rose fast to the baskets. They grabbed more leaves and more vine as well as tore hair from the animal pelt attached to the tree. Bricktain could see a thin rope begin to grow longer. As the rope drew closer to the ground, Acotactac, began to loop the rope around the bow in a way that it didn't fly off in all the spinning, and yet a single strand continued to dangle so Acotactac could braid more leaves and fur into it.

She made about twenty feet of rope before she suddenly stopped and turned to Bricktain. She held an arm out to him with its twenty-foot pole pointing straight in the air.

"I don't understand," he said.

"Take the pole," Speatsh said as he tossed another walnut into his mouth.

Bricktain reached for the pole.

"Put your glasses on," Speatsh ordered.

Bricktain thought about arguing but realized he'd only lose. He slid on the glasses and looked for the pole. It looked like a sliver, but Bricktain eventually saw it enough to grab it and slid it up and out of the wooden gauntlet. It was heavy. For a moment, he thought he would drop it, and almost did, but Acotactac helped him control it. She pointed to the baskets.

"You've got to be kidding me," Bricktain said.

"She might like you more if you'd stop complaining," Speatsh said through his mouthful of shells. She helped him lower the pole to the fur pelt. Bricktain pulled at the pelt a few times until he was sure he had gripped hair in the pincers and he pulled back with every bit of strength he had. The animal pelt jumped a little. The pole swung hard toward the small bow and teetered over Bricktain's head. Bricktain stumbled, lost control of the long pole and smacked his head against the ground.

When he opened his eyes, Speatsh stood above him inspecting Bricktain's glasses.

"Congratulations," Speatsh said. "Now she knows you're an idiot, too."

23 – Gravity

"No," Cadence scowled and threw the mask at the ground. She stomped off toward the silver bullet and left Josh holding the yellow apple and the white blindfold.

The wind had picked up a little more today. It fluttered through the leaves and shook the branches. A set of wooden sticks hanging by ropes clacked together as Cadence fell headfirst into a large pile of leaves.

"Do it again," Speatsh yelled. "Get up there and fall."

Amber sat up cradling her arm. "No," She yelled back. "I'm done."

"Until you can catch yourself in a fall," Speatsh said. "I say when you are done."

"We are done now," Cadence replied reeling herself around with the system fully loaded on her body.

"Do it again," Speatsh yelled.

"We are tired," Cadence returned.

"And hurt," Amber added standing up and curling her wrist into her chest.

"Tired," Speatsh asked. "And hurt?" He cursed some more and looked to Josh. "What do you think about that, boss? You tired and hurt too?"

"They have been at it for four hours," Josh said. "Let 'em rest."

In a flash, Speatsh tore the brown bear pelt from his shoulders and hurled it at Amber. The bear pelt came to life with a roar. It reached for Amber with its long black claws. It bit into her hurt wrist and wrapped its flat body around her face, suffocating her. Amber grasped at the living animal pelt and pulled at its fur. The bear screamed and bit at her some more. Amber fell into the pile of leaves. An orbit flew straight up into the air. The whip kept unfurling until the disk stretched as far as it could before it careened back to the ground. The bear unwrapped from around Amber's head, coiled itself like some sort of fuzzy scroll and rolled out of the pile of leaves. Amber avoided her own falling orbit. She stood and the bear snarled at her.

Both orbits flew. First, one struck for the bear and Amber screamed. Josh had never imagined she could be capable of such visible hatred as he saw possessing her narrow sharp brow now. The orbit whizzed past the bear as its thin pelt body simply bent and contoured out of the orbit's. The second orbit flew for the pelt, but the bear dodged the attack, it dodged the rebound of the first orbit and the rebound of the second.

The pelt scrolled back up and scampered for Amber, dodging the orbits by coiling and twisting around and through the steel whips and rings. It bit into her leg and pulled her foot from beneath her. Amber crashed back into the leaves. The bear unrolled, leapt backwards and floated gently to the ground where it twisted in midair and landed on the tips of its thick black claws.

"I hate your games," Amber yelled and was back to her feet. She climbed the air on an invisible staircase and circled the bear like a vulture eyeing its prey. She snapped orbit after orbit at the pelt. She cocked a foot and twisted in the air. Both orbits rotated around her body and when she stopped, both sprang for the pelt. Metallic deafening pangs cracked from each of the steel whips. The bear jumped sideways and narrowly slid between the attacks of both rings. He grabbed one of the steel cables and as Amber pulled it back, the pelt opened itself like a parachute and the orbit's return slowed making the drawback clumsy and uncontrollable. Amber flipped her uninhibited orbit back at the bear pelt to knock it off her weapon, the attack missed.

The bear wrapped itself around the whip it held.

"Tell him to get off," she yelled at Speatsh.

The bear climbed hand over hand, halfway up the steel whip and started throwing the razor ring back at Amber, even though she still held it.

"Control your weapon," Speatsh demanded.

Suddenly, Amber was dodging her own orbit. Speatsh's shoulder garment swung the orbit fiercer than Amber was capable, but Amber snapped the attacks away with the orbit she still had full control over. She twisted and pulled at the bear-coiled whip, trying anything to throw the bear off, but still the bear kept swinging at her, once grazing her ear.

Amber managed to free her hand from the wrist strap and she dropped the orbit controlled by the bear. The bear leapt from the falling whip to the one still in her control and coiled around it just as he had done the first time. Again, it climbed halfway along the whip and started throwing attacks at her. The other orbit flew up in front of her, and this time Speatsh controlled it. Cadence dodged both her whips now, one of which she still held, but Speatsh's dead clothing controlled.

She dropped the second orbit and climbed into the air out of reach of Speatsh's attacks. She had to watch the high branches. Speatsh warned her that they could be more dangerous than the actual fighting. If she wasn't paying attention to where branches were, she could knock herself out and she'd surely fall, And if she fell on a branch, she could break her back and everything would be over before she hit the ground. To her left, she watched the bear scamper along one of the boughs and leap for her. It caught her hand

and jumped to her chest, wrapping its arms and legs around her shoulders and her waist. Its hands and limbs grappled and squeezed Amber until she couldn't breathe. The bear roared in her face and, as if only to annoy her, licked her nose.

As she fell over backwards, she realized she had climbed higher than she had before done. The trees still towered above her, but she was too high up. No branches stuck out below her, but she was still falling and the pile of leaves wasn't beneath her.

Cadence screamed something at Josh as he ran as if he thought he could catch Amber.

"Do it," Speatsh yelled.

Amber kicked her feet searching for that constant pressure beneath her. She suddenly found that pressure and her back jerked violently. She felt every muscle in her body fighting to keep her knees from slamming into her chest. She felt for the stream of pressure against her other foot. Her body jerked and she stumbled forward, but caught another stream of wind under her other foot. Again, her body jerked from the sudden halt in momentum, rattling her teeth in her head, but she found another breeze under her other foot again. Each step she found to brace against her fall to the ground, strained and shook every muscle and bone in her body. Finally, she caught herself. She stopped herself from falling. The bear's grip loosened and Amber could breathe. She leaned into her knees and stared at the dirt not more than a foot below her feet. She stepped from the air to the dirt and rolled onto her back.

The bear licked her ear before it peeled away from her front. It scampered up Speatsh and flopped itself around his shoulders once again.

"Wolves don't care if you're tired or hurt," Speatsh said glaring down on her. "Now, do it again."

24 – Target Practice

"Are you out of your mind," Cadence asked, returning to the village center.

"I'm tired of this game," Speatsh said. He left Amber to her training, tired and beaten, and returned to Cadence. "Put on the mask or I'll nail it to your face."

"I'm not doing it," Cadence replied. "I'll fight without it."

"You can't see or shoot straight enough without it."

"I'll take my chances."

"No you won't. We leave in less than two weeks," Speatsh snapped as he stormed toward the mask lying in the dirt. He suddenly stopped. "Josh, stop. Get back against the tree and put the apple back on your head, now."

"Neither of us are comfortable with this, Speatsh," Josh replied.

The former werewolf snatched up the mask and crumpled it in his fingers. "Oh, cry. Are you comfortable enough to fight Jasper?"

"I'd rather have my friend fighting with me than the demon that controls her," Josh replied.

"Your friend?"

"The person I trust, not the mask," Josh said.

"After all this time and you still don't get it," Speatsh yelled flapping the mask in Josh's face. "She controls the mask. She breathes life into the mask. It knows what she wants and it obeys her."

"I trust Cadence," Josh said.

"You're full of it," Speatsh replied. "You can't handle knowing that your friend becomes a monster when she thinks about you."

"That's a lie."

"She hates you."

"That's not true," Cadence screamed. "I would never hurt Josh."

"You already have," Speatsh said. "Just like he would have hurt you, but you haven't hurt him enough have you?"

"That's unfair," Josh said.

"The mask is too strong for me," Cadence said.

Speatsh hiked back to Cadence and bent down until his nose met hers. "You don't know what strength is." The bear pelt flailed through the air again and before Josh knew it, he was stumbling backwards. The bear's head peered around Josh's waist and its little legs ran Josh's back into the tree. The bear strapped itself against Josh's chest and drove its claws into the tree bark, holding Josh to the trunk.

Speatsh surprised Cadence and grabbed at one of the slim guns retracted at the side of her arm. He dropped the ammo clip into his hand and emptied his bronze shells from it. He reached under his white fur coat and brandished a clear diamond bullet.

"Let's try your theory." He shoved the diamond bullet into the clip. "Stop pulling away." He forced the clip back into the gun.

"What are you doing," Cadence asked, but she already knew the answer.

"Asking the wizard to give you a brain," Speatsh said and pulled the leather mask over Cadence's head.

"Hackmanyatoya," Cadence yelled and hatred sculpted her eyes. The gun lunged forward into her hand.

"Stop," Josh cried.

"Aren't you going to shoot," Speatsh asked. "He's right there."

Cadence was a statue, staring only at Josh.

"Antu makka addako, Speatsh," she hissed through the mouth of the mask.

"Oh yes," Speatsh said. He rushed back to Josh and pulled up the yellow apple from the ground. "Almost forgot." He placed the apple on Josh's head. "Just think of it as an upgraded version of William Tell."

"Don't let her shoot me," Josh said.

"Have you noticed she hasn't shot," Speatsh said. "Look at her. She does hate you. You can see it in her eyes."

"Exactly why you need to stop her."

"Here's proof of the instability of the human mind," Speatsh said.

Suddenly, Cadence reached over her shoulder and tore a Glock from the system with her other hand. The system ratcheted and Cadence pointed the Glock in the air and fired off a shot towards Amber.

Amber stood frozen, as the Glock took aim on her, the orbits hung at her sides. Amber was now afraid to launch the attack she had planned, which could have cut the mask off Cadence's face.

"It wants to decide," Speatsh continued. "The mind wants to be independent, figuring things out on its own. It doesn't want to learn, yet it yearns to solve puzzles."

"This isn't a puzzle," Josh replied.

"Isn't it?" Speatsh replied. "Cadence doesn't know what she wants. If she didn't want to shoot you, the gun wouldn't even be in her hands, but if she wanted to shoot you then why hasn't she fired? Look at her. A moment ago,

268

she didn't want the mask on and yet she's pulled a gun on the one person running to help you both. Such a precise mind, and so confused. But she has to learn before she can do what she wants, solve her own puzzle."

"And if she kills me," Josh yelled. "What will she learn from that?"

"That she's weak."

Josh's face twisted at the loud pop. It wasn't deep like the cry that the powder of a normal bullet lets out. It was more like a loud chirp, and it was powerful enough to shake the leafy canopy. The air fell silent.

"You see," Speatsh said. "She knew what she was doing."

He held the side of his head and fell to the ground.

The slim gun snapped back against the side of Cadence's arm and she tore the mask from her head. "Nick, Dustin, Speatsh is shot," she screamed as she ran to Josh, ignoring that Speatsh lay bleeding from his head onto the dirt.

25 – The Moon and the Stars

Dustin knew secrets, the same secrets Nick knew, but he couldn't tell Josh any of them. He wished he could speak to Josh, tell him about the things he'd seen and heard in his mind since he turned to the way of the wolf, but Speatsh wouldn't permit it.

"You're not all there in the head," Speatsh said each month. "You might think you're only thinking, but might tell someone something you shouldn't."

For now, Dustin stared into the dark night alongside Nick. They kept watch just as Jasper had ordered them to do. It was a boring job and Dustin could feel himself growing lazy in this peaceful place. The only person who there was to watch at this time of night was Bricktain, and here he came, just like clockwork.

Bricktain tried to be silent, creeping through the village. He nodded to the twins as he roamed, unable to sleep. His time was short among the Taichomée and he didn't want to leave. What he wanted was to see Acotactac. She held his mind. He was an idiot to his companions. The chief avoided him and the children liked to stare. One poked him with a stick while he sat whittling under a tree earlier in the day. He didn't know why the child did it, but the other children thought it was neat. But, only Acotactac ever did anything to help him. The watering hole memory would never leave him. He found himself standing at that same spot often. He always came during the night where he remembered her and made sure the new slab he made to cover the hole hadn't fallen in again. Flickering flames livened up the trees through the many windows up their walls. Large pieces of bark plugged up some of them. When the windows were sealed, no one could tell people lived inside the large misplaced redwoods.

He also thought about the vine spinner. He still hadn't done well with the long sticks, but he managed to weave about five feet of vine. Of course, his work was nothing compared to Acotactac's. She finished the new rope for Bricktain's water hole slab. She was patient with him and never said a word, not that she could, but she never even looked on him as if he were stupid—not as the others had.

From his pocket, he withdrew the chunks of wood he had collected over the last couple of weeks. They were smooth now and had shape. Most were stars, but the one he focused on tonight was in the shape of a slivered moon.

270

He also held a small gray stone and rubbed it over the moon piece to smooth the wood. He gradually became aware of someone watching him.

He didn't hear her sneak up. She was no more than five feet away from him. Her shadowed face barely held form under the burning windows and a nearby torch. She stepped closer.

"Acotactac," Bricktain said.

She stopped and began to leave.

"Wait," Bricktain called. He had never mentioned her name before. He wanted to. It had become precious, yet he had no need to speak it.

Acotactac disappeared into the dark.

Bricktain settled on a log and went back to his work with the wooden moon, but all he could see was her, her face, her shadows, her silhouette, her eyes and he had to stop his work. Her eyes were dark tonight, but they looked at him. The moon slipped through his fingers and fell in the dirt. It sat there, dull in the dirt and hardly visible against its black backdrop. The moon used to be pretty to him, now it was desecrated, food for worms. What he would give to see the moon in its full luster and glory, but now it was no use. It had fallen.

Her hand appeared in front of him again. It picked up the woodcarving and her slender fingers felt over its rough and smooth surfaces. She held it to Bricktain. She looked puzzled.

"It's a moon," Bricktain said.

She mimicked the motion of Bricktain's lips.

"The moon," Bricktain said pointing to the sky. "You know? The moon." He stopped and stared at the black roof provided by the trees. "Maybe you don't know." How did he explain the moon? Everyone should see the moon. Everyone should see the sky, the stars and all the beauty only they provide. And the moon was so simple, yet he couldn't describe it. It was a beautiful black filled with lights and a moon. How could he explain it? He took her hand and directed her down to the log where he sat. He stood and ran to the torch in the center of the village and quickly returned holding it. He stood next to Acotactac and pointed up. He shook the torch and orange and red embers speckled the obsidian background of the canopy and fizzled to the ground. He shook the torch again and more embers flew in all directions showering spots of fire over their heads. He sat back next to Acotactac and stabbed the torch into the earth.

"It's like that," Bricktain said waving his finger all through the black and pointing out the falling, burning ash. "Stars, everywhere." He took the moon from Acotactac's beautiful hand. Now she watched him and this time she

271

smiled at him. She watched him hold the moon against the black high above their heads and watched him look up at it. When Bricktain looked back, Acotactac was also looking up. She smiled at him and they watched the moon for at least another hour, each taking turns holding it high.

*   *   *

Josh helped Cadence with the system and made the final adjustments. "There, it's done," Cadence said. "Now, get it off me."

"You know I can't," Josh said. "You have to be ready."

Cadence turned and kicked the truck.

"I hate this," she yelled and repeated as she kept kicking the truck. Josh reached for Cadence.

"Don't touch me," Cadence snapped. "Don't you ever touch me."

"What's wrong," Josh asked.

"This is wrong," Cadence replied. "Me having to wear this thing, you having to be the backbone of this group, the wolves, this place." She kicked the tire again and climbed into the bed of the Silverado. "Let's just get out of here. I hate this place." She leaned against the cab and cried.

Josh wanted to say something, but didn't know what. One of the Dobermans nuzzled her. She ran her fingers over his head.

"You're not right either, Nick," Cadence said.

Josh joined Speatsh with the chief and did his best to thank him for the hospitality.

Speatsh walked Josh back to Hickerbilly.

"Are you ready," Speatsh asked.

"Does it matter," Josh asked back.

"Fight like a banshee, Josh," Speatsh said. "You find whatever drive you have and you let it loose. Don't watch us. Make us afraid to be near you, make yourself the target, and we'll keep him off you."

Aggon sat in the front seat and pounded the steering wheel.

"Vy doesn't da tooter vork," he yelled. "Let's go already."

"You're not supposed to be driving," Reggie said.

"Get out of my seat, Aggon," Speatsh yelled. He climbed the ramp into the the trailer and stopped before closing the doors. "Where's the idiot?"

Bricktain heard him and jumped at the sound of Speatsh's voice. He didn't want this moment to be here. If they didn't come back, he'd have something to say about it. He didn't want to let go of Acotactac's hand. He placed a necklace decorated with the woodcarvings into her hand. Eight stars with

272

three sharp edges each filled a short string he made on the vine spinner and in their center was the sliver of the moon.

She placed her hand on Bricktain's face.

"I'll be back," Bricktain said. He returned the smile and leaned forward to kiss her. He believed he'd wanted to since that day at the water hole. He thought Acotactac leaned forward to kiss him back

"Let's go, idiot," Speatsh cried.

"You couldn't wait just a few seconds," Bricktain asked.

"Hello," Speatsh erupted. "Full moon, not kissing season."

Acotactac wasn't smiling anymore. She threw a rock at Speatsh.

"What's her problem," Speatsh asked.

"I'll be back," Bricktain said.

"In a body bag," Speatsh replied. "Let's move."

Bricktain reluctantly marched to the silver bullet, turning his back on Acotactac. Tonight, he fought for her.

26 – Bricktain the Valiant

Langley found the house crude, old and rotten. How anyone could stand living in such a place was incomprehensible to him. Of course, he wasn't sure he had the right house, but he went where the parcels took him and he had a big smelly parcel addressed for this decrepit address. He made his way to the door, past the two big piles of broken wood lining a path that screamed tetanus. He knocked on the door expecting it to fall away into the house, rang the doorbell, snapped his gum and knocked again. He heard noises inside, so he knew someone was home and he rang the doorbell once more.

"Fast Parcel," he cried out.

The door swung open.

"What is it," Jasper asked, leaning close to Langley.

"I have a delivery for this address," Langley said.

"I didn't order anything," Jasper said. "You have it."

"I can't do that, sir," Langley replied before Jasper could close the door on him.

Jasper's gaze made Langley uncomfortable. He grit his teeth and rattled his fingers on the door jam.

"You could refuse it and it will return to its sender," Langley said. "But it's a pretty large package."

Jasper stepped down from his front door and charged past Langley, knocking him into one of the piles of debris. "No harm in opening it up first," he said.

Langley stood from the pile and hoped nothing stuck him.

The two men walked down to the delivery truck and Langley rolled up the back door.

"Could you help me get it down," Langley asked.

"No," Jasper replied. He looked up and down the narrow road. If it weren't for the fact that parcel services had good tracking systems, Jasper would bite this punk right here just to shut him up. The kid was no hunter, Jasper knew that much. He could see it in the boy's stupid face.

A large cardboard box sat on an orange plastic pallet.

"You want me to open it," Langley asked.

"No, I want you to paint it for me and install a car alarm," Jasper said.

The box burst with laughter from within it.

Langley stared at the box and Jasper held up his cane as if to strike something. The box flaps burst open and chunks of cardboard hit the walls of the truck. A man stood up from the debris. He placed his hand on Langley's shoulder and used it as a crutch to step down from the truck. He was a slender Asian man with a knot tied onto the back of his black head. He wore a black suit with a black shirt and white square on his collar.

"Greetings, Father Travis," Jasper said.

"Umm," Langley said. "You're not supposed to do that. That's like illegal to mail people."

"My son," said the Asian priest. "You are correct. I promise to confess my sin at once."

"Sign here to signify you got your human being," Langley instructed.

Jasper signed the clipboard and Langley returned to the driver's seat and drove off without closing the door to the back of the truck or removing the rest of the box.

"So he's reduced himself to sending mail has he," Jasper said. "Explains why I don't hear him anymore."

"Yes, it seems it's faster to travel that way sometimes," Travis hugged Jasper. "You've been cut off." Father Travis ran his hands over his black jacket to smooth it. "You let an outsider touch him. What is that smell?"

"So you're here to punish me, then," Jasper said.

"Oh, yes," Travis said starting for the house. "You actually breathe this air? Where's the pollution? Where's the death?"

Jasper said nothing. He watched for any sign of attack. He gripped his cane and untwisted the small sword inside in case he needed to pull it.

"Your little city is too important to leave in a bungler's hands," Travis said. "In case something should happen to you, your entire clan and all your work will be destroyed and we'll have to start all over. He'll have no influence over humans in this area again for some time, unless he brings some major attention to himself. And he doesn't want that."

"I see," Jasper said.

"Either you work with me and show him that you're still in control of the situation, or I've been instructed to destroy you."

"It seems I have no choice," Jasper said.

"My son, you could die," Travis said. "Either I came or his inquisitor came and I know how you two feel about each other. I volunteered."

"He was going to send the inquisitor," Jasper asked. "You underestimate me."

"The master underestimates no one," Travis replied suddenly without emotion. "You're no match for me." Travis started toward the house. "Now, if you don't mind, I'm hungry, feed me."

"Well it won't be long now," Jasper replied. "You can feast very shortly."

"I want milk," Travis said.

Jasper locked his cane, followed Father Travis into the house and served him warm milk and old prunes.

"How's the congregation business," Jasper asked.

"Win some, eat some," Travis replied.

They spoke this way for several hours. At one point they ventured into Jasper's backyard where Jasper called in his guardians and scouts and locked them in their cellar. The two men returned to Jasper's kitchen where they resumed their conversation until the pain of the full moon struck both men.

The two generals fell to the floor and heard each others' screams as their bones crackled and their innards forced their organs high under their ribs. Jasper recovered more quickly and smelled the other wolf in his territory. His claws readied to kill and the moment he saw Travis stand and bark at him, the house crashed down around them both. He might have sensed it, had the assassin's presence not been occupying his mind.

The truck smashed through the front door, tore through the living room and drove right through the bedroom and kitchen. The blade nose of the tractor made it easy for the vehicle to slice through the walls while the gigantic front tires pulled its truck and the trailer through the old structure. Jasper wanted to chase Travis, as his visitor leapt through the kitchen window, but the silver rig was now more important. Now, he and Travis would fight together. The house crashed down around the silver bullet as it drove through the back wall of the house. It stopped in the backyard, swinging its trailer around to face the house. Jasper leapt from the rubble and rushed the trailer. The headlights of Hickerbilly gave little warning before its front end bashed Jasper into the air.

Josh leapt out of the truck and both sets of blades erupted from under the baggy sleeves of Wolf's Breath. He rushed Jasper and flipped in the air towards him. Jasper swatted the flying ball of Josh and screamed when the braided ropes sliced his arm open. Josh tumbled on the ground and before he could stand Jasper was on top of him. He grabbed Josh and Josh stuck his gut with the set of blades on his right hand. Jasper pulled at the blades and broke one off inside his stomach. Josh withdrew the remaining blade on his right arm.

Jasper smashed his paw into Josh's face and then stomped his chest. At once, the pressure on Josh's chest told him he should be dead. Jasper suddenly arched his back and grabbed his ears, screaming in pain. The whistles of the silver orbits rang out and Jasper's body contorted strangely as one of Amber's discs whizzed past him. It bounced off his shoulder. Another one whistled and shot down the front of Jasper's face, but it left no mark. Amber whipped the orbits out and around again. The metallic crack broke the air a moment before one of the orbits whistled again. This time, Jasper caught the whip, avoiding the razor sharp disc at its end and pulled on it.

Amber's body fell from above and Jasper punched her out before she hit the ground. She laid still on the cold grass, tangled within her own whips. Jasper turned his wrath on his new attacker, swiping at her with his sharp claws. Blasts of nitroglycerin filled the air. Jasper stumbled, landed next to Josh and immediately grabbed him.

Josh snapped a corner of Wolf's Breath and it was enough to break Jasper's hold on him. He climbed to his feet and did the first thing that came to his mind—he kicked Jasper. Jasper stood and kicked Josh into the side of the silver bullet. Cadence fired off more nitro bullets at the monster Jasper, and he charged her.

"Let's go, old man," said Nick suddenly, entering the fight. He wore strange black pajamas, which almost made him appear invisible against the black night. He kicked Jasper in the back.

Dustin, just as invisible, kicked Jasper's face.

Jasper shoved them both into Cadence. Cadence fell under their weight.

Speatsh helped Cadence to her feet.

"I told you idiots to stay in the trailer," Speatsh ordered.

Jasper howled at the sight of Speatsh, and such a howl it was, beyond anything nature had ever offered. He growled and hissed several times as he poised himself and flew after Speatsh. Speatsh fled with Cadence around the back of the trailer of the silver bullet and swung one of the trailer doors into Jasper.

Speatsh and Jasper swiped at each other. Both moved fast and fiercely. Josh ran to help Speatsh with Jasper when a loud gunshot erupted from the roof of the silver bullet trailer.

"There's two of 'em," Bricktain's voice announced into the small earpieces in everyone's ears. Another blast burst from the crown of the trailer, followed by yet another. Josh saw the ground light up from the other side of the trailer.

"Get Cadence out of here," Speatsh ordered just as Jasper quickly ran off.

"I got him," Bricktain's voice yelled out. Another large orange blast exploded from the crown of the trailer and another followed. A barrage of gunfire burst from around the trailer. "There's definitely two."

Jasper disappeared over the nose of the tractor with Speatsh trailing him.

"Get Jasper," Speatsh yelled into his mouthpiece.

"Which one's Jasper," Bricktain asked.

"I don't know. Get the one I'm not going after," Speatsh ordered.

Speatsh disappeared into the darkness and more gunfire broke out, this time from Cadence's rifle as she cursed in her strange tongue from beneath her mask.

"Let's go," Reggie cried and just like that, six white horses and the gold chariot sped out from the back of the silver bullet. Dirt and grass showered high in the air as Aggon pulled the reigns and the chariot skidded around.

"Ve is comin, volf," Aggon cried and the chariot raced for Jasper.

Reggie sat in the back holding the blade-less pommel as the gold chariot chased after Speatsh and Jasper.

Josh ran to Amber. She was alive, breathing.

"Get up, Amber," Josh said. He grabbed her shoulders but Wolf's Breath fell against her neck and nicked it. He cursed himself for knowing better than to allow this to happen. More than anything, right now, he wanted to take the cloak off, but knew of the dangers that would leave him and the others in.

"Is she all right," Cadence asked, rushing to help Josh untangle Amber from her whips.

"Get out of sight, Cadence," Josh ordered.

"This fight's not over," Cadence yelled back.

The silver bullet continued to blast off shots and suddenly they were faster on Josh's side of the silver bullet.

Father Travis suddenly appeared and towered over Amber and Josh.

"You won't take this one," Josh said, leaping to his feet and twisting his body around with blades drawn. Before he could connect, the silver bullet fired and Travis flipped sideways.

Travis didn't stand. His body began to turn human.

"You're not Jasper," Josh said.

Travis screamed as his bones began to shift. Josh knew this creature was finished.

"Are you kidding me," Josh asked. "You got him, Brickface. He's dying."

Brickface cheered into the earpieces and gun shots, loud as cannons, burst from various places around the silver bullet.

Speatsh cried out, but from where, Josh couldn't tell.

"Amber, you have to get up," Josh said upon returning to her.

He untied Wolf's Breath and let it fall to the ground, now that only one wolf remained and Speatsh was dealing with him. He carried Amber, still wrapped in her own whips, to the side of the trailer. He held her against him.

"Don't you leave me," he said.

Cadence knelt down. "I'm sure she's okay."

Dustin limped to Josh. "You want me to lick her," he asked.

"No one's licking me," Amber replied.

"Guys," Bricktain said. "Speatsh needs help."

"Speatsh, where are you," Josh asked his headset. "Speatsh? Why won't he answer?"

"Maybe he lost his headset," Cadence said.

"Go find him," Amber said. "Cut him once for me."

Josh climbed up from behind Amber and started looking for where he dropped Wolf's Breath. He found it and drew it around his shoulders once again. The trailer fired another shot and Jasper was back. He pounced near Travis's almost human form and sniffed him.

"The lucky punk got me, old friend," said Father Travis and coughed a laugh.

Jasper growled and his teeth flashed. He bit at the air and without warning raced towards Amber, perhaps because she appeared to be the weakest member of the group. He was so fast. Josh ran after Jasper and quickly found himself punched to the ground.

Amber screamed as Jasper hoisted her above his head.

"Wolf," Cadence screamed from behind her mask. She fired off two shots, pointblank, into Jasper's chest, forcing him to free Amber. She shot again and Josh hit him with Wolf's Breath.

Jasper screeched and Josh's head ached from the horrific sound. Jasper slashed at Josh, but Josh managed to dodge the blow. Without warning, Speatsh was at Josh's side once more. His face bled into his animal pelts and he no longer wore his headset. Speatsh and Jasper grabbed at each other, squirreling in and around each other in graceful, yet dangerous positions. They pretzeled around each other's limbs and bodies until Speatsh finally groaned and Jasper's claws glistened with Speatsh's blood. Jasper swiped again, but Speatsh broke away from the monster.

The bear pelt howled as Speatsh slapped it into the werewolf general's face. The pelt bit anywhere and everywhere. Its paws became small blurs, striking one after the other and fast against the sides of Jasper's head. Jasper stabbed his claws through the bear's skin as if to tear it asunder, but the bear strapped itself around the his paw and started striking at his face again. He bit into Jasper's neck.

Speatsh waited no longer and kicked Jasper's leg from beneath him. He kicked again and the knee cracked. The general cried and the bear pelt climbed back around Speatsh's neck. Speatsh threw his body into the wounded general and would have rammed him into the side of the trailer, but the general climbed over Speatsh, launched himself into the air and landed near Travis. Jasper gripped his leg and forced his knee back into place. He stomped on the foot as if to make sure it still worked and he screamed at the sky. Speatsh blew his bugle and silenced the general.

At that moment, the chariot rushed past. Reggie swung the sword pommel. The silver flash of blade speared from the hilt for Jasper, but missed him. The chariot looped around for another attack and as it passed again, the general kicked it on its side. The chariot, horses, Aggon and Reggie tumbled through the air. Reggie fell out. The chariot hit the ground and rolled past Speatsh and Josh, until it pinned Cadence, just as she was taking aim on Jasper, against the trailer, forcing her to drop her Glocks.

Speatsh ran to her.

"Drive, horsies," Aggon cried popping his ghostly whip over the six steeds' heads.

Jasper slashed through Aggon's empty body as the horses ran off, bringing the chariot's cart back upright.

"It vants to kill me," Aggon screamed and kept screaming as the chariot drove away.

The flat silver guns leapt into Cadence's hands.

"Wolf," she yelled again as she fired. At the same time, Josh wiped Wolf's Breath across Jasper's back.

The general screamed.

Amber sprang to her feet and ran for her father. The general caught her and shoved her into both Speatsh and Josh.

Jasper laced his long bony fingers through the heavy wires over the front of the system and slammed her body, system and all, against the side of the trailer. He pounded her into it again and once more after that. Each time he smashed her into the trailer wall, the system broke and crumpled around Cadence.

Cadence gasped for breath. When Jasper bashed her again, some of the wires broke and on the next hammer, wires dug into her abdomen. She cried out and the general drew her back to strike again. Cadence knew one more pounding could be the end of her. Wires stabbed throughout her chest. One more slam would drive them into her heart and organs. Speatsh jumped between Cadence and the trailer and grabbed the back of Cadence's system. He wrestled with Jasper over the deadly prison and eventually tore the back of the cage away from her body. Jasper still held the front of the system and after he slammed Cadence into Jasper and the trailer, she stopped screaming.

"You'll not have her," Speatsh yelled and he tore Cadence's body away from the system. She fell to the ground on top of Speatsh.

Jasper threw what remained of the mess of broken wire and cables into Reggie and Amber. He stomped at Cadence, but struck Josh's back instead. Josh didn't know how he made it, but he dived between Cadence and Jasper and took the attack himself—he fell flat on his chest. Jasper stomped again just as Aggon rushed past with the chariot.

"Leave dem alone, you," Aggon cried. The horses ran straight for and through Jasper before the gold chariot hit him to the ground and rolled over him. "Ha ha, I am ghost. You can no kill me."

Jasper climbed to his feet, howled at the chariot and screamed at Speatsh. Speatsh yelled for Josh to get off him and Cadence. Jasper stomped at Josh again and reached for him. Josh threw Wolf's Breath, trying to hit the general anyway he could. The cloak struck nothing.

A shotgun blast fired and Jasper fumbled to keep his balance again.

"Get off of them," Bricktain yelled.

"What are you doing," Speatsh yelled.

"There's a blind spot," Bricktain yelled as he fired off another shot into Jasper's face and poked the barrel hard into Jasper's gut. "You're a coward."

Jasper tore the shotgun from Bricktain's hands and stabbed the butt back at the ex-cop. Bricktain ducked away and the butt splintered against the wall of the trailer. Bricktain threw all his energy and strength into his fist and clocked the side of Jasper's head. But, Jasper struck Bricktain with the shotgun barrel and the cop fell into the trailer door. Bricktain drove his elbow into the gun, ending the creature's grip on it. He uppercut Jasper's jaw with one fist and hammered it again with his other. He jumped into the creature, driving elbow after elbow and fist after fist into Jasper's neck face and stomach.

"Get up," Bricktain ordered as he continued to unleash a barrage of punches, elbows and kicks.

Josh was to his feet and helping slide Cadence off Speatsh when he saw Jasper bite for Bricktain, but Bricktain threw both fists into Jasper's neck.

"Get her in the cab," Bricktain said. "I've got him."

Finally, Jasper leapt away a step and roared at Bricktain just as the ex-cop ran at him, this time with Josh close at his heels.

And at once Bricktain's attack stopped. Jasper held Bricktain up and broke his right arm from his shoulder. He dropped Bricktain, huffed at the sight of his demise and disappeared into the darkness.

281

"I did it again," Bricktain said as he slid into Josh's arms and both knelt to the ground. He stared up at the stars and the moon and knew he wasn't returning to Taichomée or his beloved Acotactac.

Speatsh flew. Before anyone realized what was happening, Speatsh draped Bricktain over his back. The bear pelt hugged itself around Bricktain's blood-spurting shoulder and the three disappeared into the black of the night.

"You," cried the weak voice of the fallen priest general. "I found you." He started laughing. "I found you."

"What's he talking about," Amber asked.

"I don't know," Josh said.

"What about Bricktain and Speatsh?"

"I don't know," Josh yelled back. He stood up. "Get everyone inside and keep anything from getting in. Don't you come out for anything."

"What are you doing," Amber asked.

"What I'm supposed to do." Josh ran to Hickerbilly. "I'm going hunting."

"Not alone," Amber said. "I'm coming."

"No, protect Cadence," Josh said climbing behind the wheel. "I'll take Dustin and Nick."

"We stay with Cadence," Nick replied

"Then I'll be back," Josh said.

"We couldn't beat him together," Amber yelled. "You're stupid if you think you can beat him alone."

Hickerbilly sped off before the high beams and roof lights burst on, revealing Jasper's from fleeing towards the Shallow Woods.

27 – The New Paladin

Hickerbilly chased Jasper for nearly three miles before following him into the grove of birch trees. It didn't drive much farther when Jasper darted from out of nowhere, swiped at the front of the truck, breaking a headlight, and disappeared again. The glass of the headlight filled the night like glimmering rain. The truck halted and Josh jumped from it.

"No more, old man," Josh yelled.

He reached into the truck and turned the engine off. He pulled his headset off, tossed it on the front seat of Hickerbilly and listened to his surroundings. He didn't know what else he could do, but he couldn't keep chasing Jasper blindly through the tall birches anymore or he'd end up crashing. The general was out here hiding somewhere among the trees and Josh hoped the maniac would show himself once more. He flashed on a spotlight on the driver's door and dragged its heavy beam through the tops of the trees. The single working headlight and the roof lights flooded the ground floor, but left the treetops barren. The leaves rattled in the cool breeze. Stupid leaves! Stupid city! Too bad this wasn't winter, there might be snow then, even though it never snowed here anyway. With snow, Josh could track Jasper. He could follow any trails of blood, and he knew Jasper was bleeding. In the snow, Josh could hear the monster's footsteps crunch.

"You are a coward," Josh yelled.

The spotlight lit up the head of a balding tree. The spindly branches tangled around the full, fat, yellow moon and long fingers filled with sharp leaves drooped to the earth.

"Only a coward steals a child," Josh cried.

The wings of angry bats fled from the next birch tree that the spotlight fell upon.

"Why won't you fight me," Josh cried.

The next tree had angry eyes peering back, but they belonged to an annoyed owl. Another tree held nothing. The tree standing next to that one had nothing, just harmless whispering leaves.

"Run, you coward," Josh cried. "I'll hunt you down, and I will find you."

Firefly bellies lit up one of the branches of the next tree.

Josh shut off the truck lights. They weren't doing him any good right now anyway. Instead, he listened, closed his eyes and listened. The leaves chattered. Josh's breath roared through his head as the air gently rushed into his lungs. The bats returned to their overhead solace. The fireflies' wings buzzed. The fabric of Wolf's Breath made no sound. Jasper was nowhere.

Josh looked again, but the trees were black. He gazed up to the moon one more time and watched it sway inside the fingers of the dying tree. But, something in it flickered. The fireflies? No. Jasper's gold eyes. Why hadn't Josh seen it before?

"I see you, coward," Josh said to himself and drew the fangs. One of the thicker branches broke from the tree and scaled to the tops of the smallest branches. "The moon betrays you."

The werewolf's black figure leapt from the balding tree down to a younger one. Josh ran after the shadow.

"I'll bring you to me." He threw his arm sideways and twisted his body into almost a kneeling position. The cloak flew open and Josh heard Jasper's feet scamper through the branches as the birch he hid in timbered to the ground like a mallet. Josh fired off two darts. Jasper kept moving and Josh watched his silhouette leap into yet another clump of branches of another tree. Josh twisted again and Wolf's Breath sliced through this tree trunk as well. It began to fall. Jasper and Josh both escaped the dangers of yet another falling birch.

Wolf's Breath snapped upward at Jasper's shadow, which sat perched on another bough. The monster stood barely out of reach of Wolf's Breath.

"You'll come down if I have to tear it all down," Josh said.

Jasper leapt again and Wolf's Breath cut through this timber too. Jasper leapt again into a higher tree. Josh cut into this one and the cloak stopped.

Josh pulled at his cloak, but the thick trunk pinched Wolf's Breath halfway through it. Josh couldn't retrieve it. The leaves over his head clamored and Jasper flew down at Josh. Josh fired the remaining dart from one of the fangs and missed. Jasper clamped onto the branch above Josh's head and smelled in the hunter's breath. He drew close to Josh and tasted the air with his tongue.

"I thought that might bring you to me," Josh said and swiped the other edge of Wolf's Breath through the trunk of the thick tree. Josh pulled Wolf's Breath free. Jasper leapt over Josh's head and they both rolled out of the way of yet another falling threat. The tree smashed into the ground and branches and leaves littered the air. Josh continued his chase after Jasper, through the mess of falling limbs and trunks. "I'm going to mount your head in my trophy room."

The wolf seemed to run a little slower. He coddled one of his hands as he fled Josh, but Josh wouldn't let him get away this time. He would be faster than the old man. He followed Jasper, leaping over the fallen trees and cutting down the ones Jasper tried to hide in. The wolf disappeared and Josh stopped. The swords telescoped from his arms, two from his left and one from his right and again he listened.

The trees were thinner here, their leaves more silent. He listened to the leaves rattle, but it was the sound hiding in the leaves that he heard, the sound of something trying to pretend it had control of its heavy breath. Josh chased the noise and found Jasper once more. He tore down two more trees with Wolf's Breath and stopped when he lost sight of the monster yet again. Before Josh realized it, the trees were gone, left in the small grove behind him. Now, he stood in a wide field, black as the sea. Only the moon and the twinkling of the city gave off any light. Blades of long grass and barley crashed into each other. Nothing else made a sound. Jasper was gone.

"Fight me," Josh begged.

Even the wind fell silent.

"Then, I'll return to those you made and destroy them all," Josh yelled and he turned back for the grove where Hickerbilly sat buried.

The shadow sneaked up behind the new paladin. His eyes pierced Josh. Jasper swung and raked Josh's head. Josh fell and thought for sure he was dead, but knew he wasn't when Jasper pounced on him and punched a new definition of pain into his gut. Jasper punched again. Each strike sent a new sensation of anguish through Josh's belly.

Jasper stood and kicked Josh into the air, caught Josh by his foot in mid-flight and slammed his body against the ground. Josh felt the werewolf's foot stomp his back. Another kick sent the new paladin rolling. Josh hit the ground and Jasper went on a kicking frenzy. Before Josh knew it, he was back among the trees. He stood, or tried to stand and stumbled. He cowered behind a nearby tree and dropped to the ground just as Jasper's claws swung and barely missed him.

Josh slashed back with his swords and cried out under the surge of pain of his newly broken arm and the impact of the swords against Jasper's wrists. Jasper screamed and stomped down where Josh cowered, but Josh had crawled backwards, rolled, ran and managed to get out of the grove again.

The night seemed even darker. Josh's head pounded and he felt stickiness stream down his head. His sides hurt. He couldn't breathe in without crying. His broken left arm was limp at his side. He was alone. When he died here, would his friends find him or just his bones?

Jasper emerged from the dark hollow of birches and walked tenderly toward Josh. He still held one of his arms close to his body and as he took small steps, he dragged one of his feet. Josh's single sword telescoped from his right arm and he eyed the broken blade still protruding from Jasper's body. The general pulled Josh from his feet and held him by the throat. He appeared to smile.

"You win," Josh said and watched Jasper's jaws open. Jasper snapped at Josh, but bit into the blade. Josh yanked the sword from Jasper's mouth and Jasper dropped his opponent. The monster thrashed his head, screaming and huffing at the night. It dropped at Josh and bit for him again. Josh rolled and rolled again as Jasper tried and tried to sink his teeth into Josh's flesh.

Josh knew it was only a matter of time now. Jasper had turned his sister and now he wanted Josh. Why shouldn't he? Josh taunted him for this fight. Maybe Josh had proven himself worthy to Jasper to become one of his servants. Maybe Jasper wanted to turn Josh so he could control and torture him. Or maybe the old man wanted to eat.

Jasper bit.

Josh slashed the attack away.

If only Josh had brought just one friend with him.

Jasper bit at his face.

Josh stabbed.

Why didn't Josh let Amber come? Why? Because he loved her. He thought he lost her tonight, lost her the same as he lost Natalie. He let her go just like he let Natalie go. Now Amber would feel as he felt. She'd torture herself, wishing she had forced herself to come with Josh. If only his strength wasn't failing him now. If only he hadn't left Amber.

Jasper turned Josh onto his stomach and shoved his adversary's face into the dewy grass.

Josh's good right arm pinned beneath his body as Jasper climbed onto his back. He knew that Jasper's attack would connect this time. Josh had used the last of his fight.

Josh wished for the whistle of the orbits or pangs of bullets, but none came. If only he were stronger. He was so stupid to run out after Jasper alone. Did he think he was as strong as the general? Did he think he had the power the werewolf had? Did he think he was Speatsh, holding some sort of mythical strengths? If Josh had been a wolf, he would have beaten Jasper. He would have ended this entire mess when Cracey was taken. If he were a wolf, he wouldn't be face down in the ground waiting for Jasper's teeth to sink into his flesh. If he were doing what he promised Speatsh he'd do, he wouldn't have left Cadence's side. But why shouldn't he have left her to chase Jasper? Speatsh left her, but Speatsh left her knowing Josh was still at her side.

Speatsh left her in Josh's hands. Josh couldn't violate his promise to protect her. He couldn't let Jasper take out his friends once he was finished here with Josh. His friends were in worse condition than he had been when he started this chase.

Josh flexed his broken arm and the set of blades snapped forward. Josh screamed and he threw his arm blindly over and behind his shoulder. The surge he felt before pulsated down his arm. He had to hold the fist though. He felt Jasper stand, also screaming, lifting Josh with him. Josh sailed into the air. As Jasper flipped Josh into the air, Josh saw his blades sunk halfway into Jasper's collar. Josh opened his fist and the blades retracted. Josh continued to tumble through the air before he finally came down hard on his knees. Jasper's screams were loud and terrifying, but were nothing compared to those of Josh's, which were agonizing.

Josh forced himself to his feet. "I won't be yours," he yelled, which somehow helped him find the power inside to stand even against the torment of his knees.

Jasper's ears suddenly perked.

Josh heard the cracks and the whistles too.

Two flashes of silver raced past Jasper, one sliced open his bicep and the other cut his face before returning to Amber.

"Don't touch him," Amber cried. She stood above Jasper and Josh and threw the other orbit.

Jasper grappled the whip as he had before and pulled Amber. Amber fell again. Jasper timed his strike and swiped for the falling Amber, but she caught herself in midair and held herself just above his reach.

"Not this time." Amber snapped the orbit again and it wrapped around Jasper's head until the silver cut into his face.

Amber yanked and Jasper's body twisted around uncontrollably. He gained his balance and turned on Josh. Dark blood ran down Jasper's face from an empty eye socket and a large gash on the side of his head.

"Let's end this," Amber said.

Josh mustered his strength and lunged for Jasper, but Jasper kicked Josh back to the ground. The orbits stopped Jasper from launching into Josh again. Jasper growled turned to Amber and spit.

Amber might have dodged if she could have seen it, but she felt it spray her cheek. It burned and she fell.

Jasper grabbed his throat just as Josh charged at him, snapping two corners of his cloak at him. Before Jasper could recoil, Josh drove the single sword into Jasper's arm and drew an empty fang. Jasper couldn't scream. He swatted at Josh, but the new paladin slammed the steel grip of the fang against the broken blade still stuck in Jasper's belly. Jasper fell back and, as Josh prepared to strike again, Jasper mustered a leap that took him several feet out of Josh's reach. Both adversaries were horribly wounded, filled with cuts and broken bones.

Josh gave a slow chase after the slower general. Josh's knees hurt. Jasper limped but still put up a good run. Josh would too, and he started loading one of the fangs as he continued his pursuit. But he distinctly heard Amber whimpering his name.

"Amber," Josh asked and returned to her side without taking his eyes off Jasper. Jasper, too, stopped running and watched Josh from the darkness. Josh wanted to chase Jasper first. He knew he could kill him now, but which was more important, vengeance, or Amber, who suffered a small dose of Jasper's venom? Josh screamed his frustration. "We beat you." He aimed his reloaded fang on Jasper. The t-shaped wrench was still stuck in the star-shaped impression on the side. All three cylinders shot from the small crossbow. Jasper keeled backwards. Josh watched for movement in the grass. Slowly, the shadow stood and Jasper's werewolf form stumbled into the birch trees.

It was now or never. Josh started after the old werewolf again.

"Josh," Amber cried.

Tears streamed from Amber's eyes. Josh knew his fight with Jasper was over. It shouldn't have been, but it was over. If Jasper returned to his friends in his condition now, he'd die for certain. Now, it was a different fight for Amber.

"It hurts," She said. "Make it stop."

"I don't know how," Josh replied. He withdrew his good arm from Wolf's Breath and let the cloak drape only one side of his body. He tied the orbits to the fangs and helped Amber to her feet.

"It hurts," Amber cried grabbing her face. She screamed even louder when she realized her jawbone had become exposed beneath her melting skin. She knew she needed to tell Josh before it was too late, despite the pain it caused her to open her mouth. She had to tell him before her head melted away. "I'm sorry I didn't listen."

"You saved me," Josh replied.

"I'm so sorry," Amber said.

"Why?"

"It's my fault," Amber said.

"Don't say that."

"I saw the whole thing," Amber said. "I watched your uncle die, but I didn't do anything because I was scared for my family."

"What do you mean?"

"It's my fault your sister's gone."

Josh reached under his sleeve and withdrew the retractable sword and its small cage from around his forearm. He removed the other sword and had Amber hold them so she'd stop pawing at her face.

"Hold on to me," Josh said and he wrapped his good arm around Amber.

"You're hurt."

Josh drove his broken arm under her knees and lifted her. They both cried as Josh rose to his feet. "I'm sorry if the cloak cuts you."

Josh started back toward the grove of trees. Each step felt like his legs were shattering. The steps surged up his spine and he wanted to scream. He was already crying. Amber's weight on his chest hurt, but it was the only way. He couldn't leave her.

"I'm dying," Amber whispered.

"I won't let you die," Josh said.

Amber held Josh, afraid this would be her last time. She felt his arm trembling beneath her knees. With every step, she felt something cracking from within Josh. She knew he was broken. Her face was hot and numb now. More of her flesh burned away, revealing more of her jaw, but she only felt Josh's pain. Even he grew dark. Her head grew heavy and she laid it on his shoulder.

Wolf's Breath slowly gnawed through Amber's trench coat. Josh would have dropped it, but he feared what would happen if he were unarmed should Jasper return. He clearly couldn't reach for the fangs with the orbits at his side.

Josh carried Amber into the trees.

"We didn't beat him," Amber said.

"Oh yes we did," Josh replied. "And we're not finished yet."

*   *   *

Josh hobbled down the ramp of the silver bullet. "I don't know what to do," he said. "Maybe Bogi will know how to help her, but who knows if the bunker's safe. Anyone who goes back to find out could be in danger. And who knows how to drive this thing?"

"We have to do something," Cadence said.

"You think I don't know that?"

"I'm sorry Cracey's not here."

"Who would have taken her?"

"I don't know," Cadence said.

"Did you find Banks," Josh asked.

"Yeah," Cadence agreed. "And the bodies of everyone else who helped her escape."

"Dead," Josh asked.

"I'm afraid so," Cadence said. "Everyone else is afraid to say anything else."

Josh didn't know what to think anymore. The vampire had his sister. All he could wonder was where Speatsh had disappeared to and how to help Amber, whose face was now covered in gauze.

"The moon will be gone soon," Cadence said knowing it was up to her to help Josh understand their situation and decide what the group should do before Jasper's slaves changed form and brought another fight our from the cellar.

"Yeah," Josh said, not believing it.

"You did good, Josh," she said before disappearing into the trailer.

Josh scanned the area, his arm now taped to his chest. He had already swallowed four different types of painkillers, which he found in a flimsy first aid kit along with the gauze, but he still hurt. He looked over the dark orchard.

Where was Jasper now.

"He's coming," someone called from the dark.

Josh searched.

"Over here, hunter," the voice called again, grinding against the air like pebbles in a vacuum.

Josh found him buried beneath a brown robe.

"He's coming," Father Travis said.

"Nice try," Josh said.

Travis grabbed Josh's arm and Josh nearly took his head off for it.

"The descendant of the youngest ancient travels with you," Travis said. "And he is sworn to protect the rightful queen, and I found her." He took a long, wet breath and smiled. "He protected her. You did too. Isn't that interesting?"

"Not really," Josh said.

"You revealed her, who else would you fight with Speatsh Cheatham to protect," Travis asked. "And now he knows who she is."

"Who? The rogue? Tell him where she is and I'll make your death slow," Josh said. He flexed his arms for his swords, and remembered they were lying in the trailer.

Travis started laughing but ended up coughing blood. "Thank you," Travis finally said.

"What are you talking about?"

"You just confirmed it," Travis said. "I wasn't sure if it was her or if it was you. All this time, and she's sitting in that trailer."

"You leave her alone," Josh said.

"Leave her alone," Travis asked. "Could I stand, I'd tear your body and claim her reward from my master."

Josh threw his knee into Travis's throat.

"No one's claiming her," Josh said driving his knee against Travis's throat.

"Wrong," Travis forced out. "He's coming."

"He," Josh asked and let up on the pressure. "The rogue's coming here?"

"Oh, they're all coming."

A Word on Allies

The cat hunkered in the dark, damp hole of the alley. The small group of dogs thought they picked up her scent, but ran off bickering about which way she had run. Once they passed, she emerged from her hiding and fled down the alley. Here, she climbed a tree, skittered along one of its branches and leapt to the roof of a building. She climbed through an open window.

"Hey, Shana," the short portly man dressed in white said as the cat trotted onto the kitchen floor.

His smile was always welcome to the cat, but not as much as the meat that he would give her. She swallowed down the red and listened to the sounds of dogs barking from the other side of the door leading from the kitchen to the alley. How stupid were they?.

"After you again, huh," the chef said. He pet the cat and she appreciated him with a hard push of her head before bouncing out of the kitchen into the dark room with small round tables. She found a familiar leg and pressed against it.

"Hello, Chloe," the customer said as he picked her up and let her sit in his lap, just as he'd done for the past two weeks of his visit. He stroked her fur. The golden Labrador at his side paid no mind to the feline.

"You're sure about your information," a large man asked from across the table. His face concealed itself well beneath a deep brown and black beard.

"I'm sure, Quill," the customer replied. "Find Thug and he'll lead you to him."

"And he'll know how to end this?"

"He needs every ally he can get."

The customer took a long swig of tea and set his cracked mug with its broken handle on the sticky table.

"What do you say," the customer asked.

"Sounds like a trap," Quill replied. "I'll think on it." He finished his beer. "It sounds fishy, Mr. Revlon." Quill walked away and exited the establishment through a heavy wooden door.

The golden Labrador reached up and gently pet the cat.

"Well, Eric," Stan said. "That's another one who didn't believe us." Stan opened a notebook and studied a list and a map within it. "Looks like we try Dallas next."

www.ingramcontent.com/pod-product-compliance
Lightning Source LLC
Chambersburg PA
CBHW070216030726

47505CB00006B/1704